W9-AWD-306

Soldier Girl

Soldier Girl

Margaret Gilkes

THE LEISURE CIRCLE

Copyright © Margaret Gilkes 1986

All rights reserved

This edition specially produced for
The Leisure Circle Limited
by Century Hutchinson Limited
Brookmount House, 62–65 Chandos Place,
Covent Garden, London WC2N 4NW

Printed in Great Britain

To my dear father and mother, Thomas and
   Annie Sadler, and Helen Sadler
To Colonel Mary Dover OBE and all the
   soldier girls who served in the CWAC,
   especially my close comrades Cubby,
   Marjorie, Sherry, Nelly and Frenchy
And to Peggy

Chapter 1

I'm lost. Marjorie Hatfield gripped the steering wheel tighter in her small hands. She glanced right and left trying to pick out a landmark. Suddenly the air raid siren started its banshee wailing, rising and falling ominously. Any minute now they would come like killer bees rumbling their message of death through the heavy skies above London. The drizzle of rain had made the street like glass beneath the tyres of the staff car. She skidded and almost sideswiped a London taxi-cab.

The driver rolled down his window and gobbled at her, 'Watch it, Mitey. Do you Canadians want the 'ole street to drive on?'

She rolled down her own window and returned his verbal barrage. 'When are you Limeys going to learn to drive on your own streets?'

He grinned and suddenly the rising panic in her dropped. 'How do I get to Moon's Garage on Baker Street?' she called.

'You're 'eadin' the wrong way, Canada. Just turn left down there at the end of the street. Go on for a couple of blocks and you'll see a pub called the George and 'Orses. Turn right there and keep on going and you'll find yourself in Oxford St. Just keep going then you can't miss it.' He waved his hand, gave her another friendly grin and forged ahead in the deserted street.

As she lost him in the gloom panic returned. And then she heard the unmistakable rumbling of a buzz bomb flying low in the inky sky, the sinister sound growing louder and louder, until she felt it was chasing her like a hare down the darkening street. She reached the corner and spun around it, skidding almost out of control. Wrenching the wheel over she pulled out of it, looking desperately for any sign of a pub. Suddenly she saw it on her right – the George and Horses. Abruptly the sinister

1

rumbling above her stopped. She sucked in her breath. *Is this it?* she thought, a cold sinking in the pit of her stomach. She pictured the silver robot plane with a ton of TNT in its pointed nose dropping silently towards her.

'Not yet,' she prayed desperately. 'Please, not yet. I haven't even really lived yet. I'm only twenty-four years old. I don't want to die a virgin.' She hoped God was not angry with her for such a carnal prayer as she pulled the car into the kerb, snatched the keys from the ignition and dived for the sheltering doorway of the pub.

Somone pulled her to the ground and flung his body on top of hers as the world around her shook and thundered. She felt herself fading out in the roar of falling rubble and bricks and the sucking blast tearing the air from her lungs. She heard her own lips murmuring, 'A virgin. I don't want to die a virgin.'

Gradually the mist lifted. She swam back to consciousness, hearing her own voice still murmuring, 'A virgin. I don't want to die a virgin.' Her head was against someone's chest and she was looking up into a pair of amused yet sympathetic brown eyes. A drawly English voice said, 'You've plenty of time to change all that, you know. All you have is a bit of a scratch on your forehead and a very dirty face.'

She could feel the grime mixing with the wetness of her tears running down her cheeks and warm, sticky blood trickling down her forehead. Coming back fully to consciousness, she saw that she was in the arms of a young British airman, sitting in the doorway of the pub in a street filled with rubble.

Looking into his twinkling eyes she realized suddenly what her lips had been muttering. She felt her face grow hot beneath the grime. She struggled to sit erect.

'Steady there,' he said soothingly and, pulling her back into the circle of his arms, he took a handkerchief from his pocket and gently started to mop the blood from her forehead. 'It's the blast that gets you, you know — blows your stomach out. If I hadn't pulled you down just then I'm afraid it would have been all up, don't you know. But the only thing that got it was your car. I'm afraid it was rather squashed when the front of that building toppled on to it.'

She followed the direction of his eyes. The flattened remains of the big staff car peeped out from under a heap of bricks and rubble. 'Oh,' she said, distressed. 'This was my first real assignment since I started driving for CMHQ. I was evacuating the brigadier's car from our garage in Chelsea to Moon's Garage at Baker Street.'

'Well, I'm rather afraid it's evacuated for you,' he drawled.

The air raid wardens had arrived and were cordoning off the street as a crowd of people, shadowy in the gloom, appeared from nowhere. Marjorie realized she was shaking as she continued to stare at the flattened mess of what had been the big shiny Buick.

The airman said, 'We'd better move out of this doorway, you know. It's not really comfortable. Thank heaven they didn't get the George and Horses. What you need is a good stiff brandy. Can you stand up?'

'Of course.' Marjorie felt suddenly ashamed of her performance in front of this cool young airman. I'm a soldier, she thought, and I've been acting like a schoolgirl.

Out of the gloom an air raid warden flashed the pencil of his torch on them. 'You two all right?'

'Absolutely, old man. Just going down for a pint,' the airman answered. 'Rather a close one, what?'

'Yes. Lucky it fell out in the middle of the bloomin' street. 'Asn't 'alf made a mess of that big, posh Canadian car. 'Ave to see about getting the driver and others out. Fraid it's ta-ta for them, though.'

'Not this time, old man,' the airman answered. 'This lady is the driver, and the brigadier wasn't in it.'

'Well, thank 'eaven for that. Must be your lucky day, miss. Seeing as you're looking after 'er, sir, I'll 'urry along and see who else needs 'elp.' With a cheerful smile at them, he went about his business.

The airman helped Marjorie to her feet and together they went down the short flight of steps into the warmth of the crowded pub.

Over in a corner someone was playing the piano and a group of service people were gathered around him singing. In another corner two old men were playing darts below a picture of George III. Except for a few old men and women, everyone was in uniform. Sprinkled in the crowd, hanging around the bar were women with bright orange and black hair, their sleazy

3

dresses and hawk eyes proclaiming them to be Piccadilly Commandos.

Marjorie had heard of these prostitutes who hung about London, particularly Piccadilly Circus, but since she had never encountered anyone like that in the farming community she had been raised in near Calgary Alberta, she did not recognize them.

The airman brushed the dust from her khaki CWAC uniform and seated her at a small table in the corner. Then, after performing a similar service to his own uniform, he seated himself opposite her, removing his peaked officer's cap to reveal a shock of heavy, wavy brown hair. He had wings on his tunic and a row of ribbons on his chest. Marjorie saw the two bands around his cuff and recognized him for a flight lieutenant in the RAF. He smiled into her face.

'I – I shouldn't be here with you, you know. I – I'm an Other Rank,' she said.

He laughed. 'If that buzz bomb had been a little closer we'd both be the same rank, wouldn't we? How long have you been here in London?'

'Just over a week,' she answered. 'I arrived the next day after D-day. Today was the first time I've been out on my own. Before this they sent me out with another driver so I could learn the city and not get lost.' She laughed ruefully. 'But I guess I didn't learn very well. I got mixed up somewhere around Piccadilly Circus. Everything just became a maze and I think I lost my directions. I simply couldn't find where I was going.'

'Of course you couldn't,' he laughed. 'No one can in London unless he's very tipsy. You know what they say, the streets were laid out by a group who had been drinking all night. That's the only explanation that makes sense.'

Gradually, as he spoke, the shaking went out of her limbs. 'I must look a sight,' she said.

'There's a bit of blood on your forehead, and your face is just a bit smudgy, but you are by far the best-looking sight I've seen since I reached London on my forty-eight hour pass today. Can you bring us some water, miss?' he asked the barmaid who came up to take their orders. 'The young lady had a bit of a brush with a buzz bomb.'

'Of course, sir. 'Orrid things. We aint 'alf going to cop it one of these nights if old Winnie don't do something to get rid of

4

them flying things. What'll it be next, I wonder?'

'Old Winnie will look after it, never you worry,' he answered, smiling up at her, and her face lightened.

'What will you and the pretty soldier girl 'ave, sir?' she asked.

'What would you like to drink?' he asked Marjorie.

'I – I don't drink.'

'You don't drink,' he said. 'I never met a soldier who didn't drink. Well, in that case you'd better just have a little medicinal brandy. And I'll have a gin and bitters,' he told the barmaid.

'We never had liquor in our house,' Marjorie protested half-heartedly. 'Mother said she signed the Good Templars pledge when she was seven.'

'But you didn't sign it, did you?'

'No, but, you see, I was always told that ladies don't drink. Mother said women do the most appalling things when they drink. She said men aren't much better,' Marjorie added and laughed shakily. 'Only it doesn't matter what they do.'

'I was brought up just the opposite way,' the airman said. 'There was always plenty of drink in our house, but we were always taught that a gentleman does not get drunk, especially if there are ladies present, and if he should happen to get drunk he still behaves like a gentleman. And, speaking of being a gentleman, you know we English don't speak unless we're introduced. My name is Colin Enderby.'

'I am Marjorie Hatfield,' she said solemnly, reaching her hand across the table to shake his. 'Thank you for saving my life.'

He held her hand, looking deeply into her eyes with a mischievous twinkle in his own. 'You know what the Chinese believe about that,' he said. 'I saved your life so now it belongs to me.'

'That's wrong. It's just the opposite. You saved my life so now you have to take care of me for the rest of my days.'

He laughed merrily as he took his hand away. 'I say, you know too much,' he said. Just then the barmaid came with their drinks and a small jar of water. He came around to her, damped his handkerchief and gently wiped her face. 'You see I've already started,' he said. 'Now you'll feel better and I can see what you look like.' He continued looking down into her face. 'By Jove, I think I've made a jolly fine bargain,' he said, his brown eyes twinkling warmly.

To her dismay, Marjorie felt herself blushing furiously. She dropped her eyes from his.

'Now, do drink some of that brandy.'

Obediently, Marjorie picked up the glass and took a swallow. She coughed and spluttered and almost choked.

'I say, you really have never had a drink before,' he marvelled.

'Did you think I was lying to you?'

He shook his head. 'Not with those great, honest blue eyes. Though girls who look like fair-headed blue-eyed angels have been known to lie to men before, you know. But somehow you're not the lying type. Now, try another sip, and I do mean a sip. It really will do you good.'

Marjorie sipped slowly, and after the first burning sensation left her throat, she felt a warm light-headed glow seep through her body. As she drained the glass she heard the long, steady blast of the All Clear. 'The raid's over,' she said gratefully.

She realized with a start that she had completely forgotten the raid and the brigadier's car lying a mass of scrap iron out on the street. Here she sat in some pub called the George and Horses, drinking brandy with an airman she did not know, and she was feeling very, very happy.

She had no idea where she was, or how she would reach Moon's Garage. They would be wondering by now why she had not checked in. And there was the brigadier's car . . .

'Why the sudden distressed look?' Colin said, watching her face closely.

'It's the brigadier's car – it was brand new. They just shipped it over from Canada, and now it's a heap of junk. We're responsible for the vehicles we take out. There'll be a court of inquiry.'

Colin smiled at her. 'I really don't think cars are like ships, you know. I shouldn't think you'd be expected to go down with your flag still flying from the masthead and drums beating.'

His whimsical humour made her laugh. He was so different from any other man she had met, with his drawly, cultured English voice and air of unconcern, and yet there was an underlying thoughtfulness in his face, a depth of feeling under the flippancy. She looked again at the row of ribbons on his tunic and saw the ribbon of the Distinguished Flying Cross. Her eyes widened. Next to the Victoria Cross it was the highest decoration awarded an airman for valour.

Studying his face, she noticed the tiny scar just below his hairline on his left temple. He caught her eyes on it and said with a smile, 'No, not enemy action. I got that wound when we were children at home. My brother and I and Ashley from next door were playing Beau Geste and they were giving me a Viking's funeral out on the pond and the punt capsized. I scraped my face on a nail, or something, as I went overboard.'

She asked him, 'How long have you been a pilot?'

'I got my wings back in 1939,' he replied.

'You're one of "the few",' she said in an awed voice.

He laughed lightly. 'Old Winnie was really wound up when he made that speech. Too much brandy, I expect.'

' "Never have so many owed so much to so few",' she quoted softly. 'We heard him in Canada and we prayed for all you brave airmen over here.'

He reached across the table and took her hand. 'That was jolly good of you. Probably the only reason I got through it.' But there was a serious light behind the twinkle in his eyes and he squeezed her hand. 'You must have been a child in 1939.'

'I was nineteen. They hadn't yet formed the Canadian Women's Army Corps. But as soon as they did, in 1941, I joined up, but I couldn't get overseas until now.'

'I was nineteen in 1939 too,' he said. 'What were you doing before you joined the army? I understand all Canadian girls have careers.'

'I'm afraid I didn't. After I finished high school my father wasn't well, so I stayed on the farm to help out. Father and Mother still live there in the old home, and my brother – he's ten years older than I – farms it for them because Dad is a semi-invalid. My brother has been married since he was twenty. They have a darling little boy and girl. They call me the Little Corporal.' She laughed. 'I had my corporal's stripes until I remustered to a private to come overseas. I was stationed in Calgary the whole time until now. Oh dear, that reminds me, I shouldn't be fraternizing with you. And I must get back to the garage somehow and report what happened to the brigadier's car.'

'I think you should have one more brandy before we go,' he

said. 'And then I'll see that you get back to your garage and to your barracks. I find the fraternizing perfectly delightful.'

'Are you still flying?' she asked as the barmaid brought them each a second drink and she sipped the now pleasantly warm, amber liquid.

He nodded. 'Yes. Spitfires. But my flying days are almost over, I'm afraid. When I finish this tour of ops they're going to tie me to a desk in charge of operations on a squadron, and then I'll be sending other chaps up to get the job done.'

An unreasonable joy shot through her at his words. He would be out of danger. She wondered at herself. Something strange was happening to her. She felt she was being caught up into another world. She sensed that Colin felt it, too – as if they were isolated in a small, intimate magic circle all their own. She did not want to break the spell.

'I never met anyone named Colin before. In fact, the only time I ever heard the name was in a book I read when I was a child. It was about a little girl who came from India to live with her uncle in England.'

'*The Secret Garden*,' he said. 'I hope I'm nothing like that Colin. As I remember the book, he was beastly spoiled. You certainly are nothing like Mary Lennox. She was rather a disagreeable little girl if I recall rightly.'

To Marjorie's delight, she found he was familiar with many of the books which had been a joy to her as a child – books which relatives had sent them from England. '*Chums*,' she said. 'I adored it – all those dashing young English heroes. We were sent the *Chums* book every Christmas. It was the biggest part of Christmas – watching for that big red book to come at the post office. Mother used to read it out loud to us, sitting around a coal-oil lamp in front of an old coal heater when it was about forty below outside. I think I liked the pirate stories best. Didn't you love the pirates?'

'Oh, rather,' he said enthusiastically. 'As a matter of fact, I once attempted to dash away for the Spanish Main. I think I got as far as the local village station before someone came and fetched me home.'

They both laughed. Marjorie felt light-headed and happy. She had even stopped worrying about the brigadier's car. However, Colin brought her back to reality. As she finished the last drop of her brandy he said, 'Now, I really must set about seeing you home, little Marjorie.'

Her spirits drooped. 'Oh. Yes. Of course.' She wondered if he was going to meet someone and a strange little twinge ran through her. Who was Ashley, she wondered. It could be a man, of course. But it could be a woman. Was that who he was going to meet? She thought, if only everything could just mark time for a little while and I could stay here in this safe warm place talking to him and watching his face. For the first time since I arrived in London I don't feel lost.

She had been feeling so strange since she came here, with the blackout and the mysterious, winding streets and the ancient buildings that seemed to belong to ages past – and the V-bombs, sailing like ships of death through the skies. Night and day they rumbled above her barracks at Sussex Square, shaking the building with their vibration. In the darkness of the night, when the motor cut, she and the others waited in breathless silence until they heard the crunch of it landing, sometimes so close that their building shook. Then the same words came from all their lips as they let their breath go: 'There she goes.' Marjorie wondered guiltily at the ruthless spirit of survival that gladdened her while she knew full well when she heard the crunch that it meant death to someone else. But she was safe.

They came over by day, too. Breakfast time was the worst. It was the silence – the silence and the waiting that got to you. They had to remember they were soldiers – go on eating, get on with the job. Not always when the motor cut did it plunge earthwards. Sometimes a vagrant breeze caught the bomb and it sailed on for miles, skimming the rooftops, until it took its sudden fatal plunge.

Only her roommate, Jessy Cole, seemed to have no fear of the things. She slept beside the window and often at night she would pull back the blackout curtains and they would see the long silver bullet shape outlined by the plume of fire shooting from its tail as it droned over like some evil dragon.

Marjorie did not join the other girls from barracks drinking in Molly's pub, just around the corner from the block of flats that was their barracks. She had been brought up very strictly by her straight-living religious family and she had a fear of having her body found in a pub if it should be hit. Anyway she did not drink. But she did feel she would like to be with the others, even if she was only drinking tea. She would hear them, coming home after the pubs closed, laughing and teasing with servicemen outside her window on the street below and singing 'Roll Me Over in the Clover' and other racy ditties.

Except for Helen Huntley, she saw little of her roommates. Jessy had already found a boyfriend. Bonny spent all her free time on the baseball diamond in Hyde Park, and at Molly's after dark. Helen had been bitterly disappointed to find her husband, Carl, gone to Normandy with the invading Canadian forces. She wrote to him every night. Elsie – she had to smile when she thought of Elsie, who spent her time eating and being scared. She was such a toad.

Until now, in this pub, Marjorie had been feeling lonely. She had confined her activities, outside of duty, to strolling by the Serpentine, or walking the half mile down to Marble Arch to listen to the soap box men at Speaker's Corner. She was looking forward to going to the theatre, but she had not yet learned to find her way around London.

Tonight, though, she was happy, sitting across the table from this airman, thinking: He's the best-looking man I've ever seen, with his fine features and his head set so gracefully on his shoulders – like a knight of old in one of my story books. But it's his mouth I like the best – a humorous, gentle mouth. She wondered suddenly what it would be like to have his mouth on hers, and blushed.

He reached across the table and took her hand in his. 'You know I haven't felt so jolly in ages,' he said wistfully. 'Quite like the war hadn't come and things were like they used to be.'

'Were they good for you?'

'Rather,' he answered enthusiastically. 'But you know, I don't think anything has ever been quite as good as this moment.'

Before she could answer, a man in the livery of a taxi-cab driver came up to their table and greeted Colin effusively. 'Blimey, it's you, Lord Enderby,' he said.

10

Chapter 2

Colin stood up and took the man's hand. 'Why, it's Blaine,' he said delightedly. 'I didn't know this was your district. How are you liking it?'

'Oh, proper fine, my Lord. Not of course like driving for the Enderbys, but still, times change.' He turned his head and saw Marjorie. It was the cab driver who had pulled up beside her earlier and told her the way to the George and Horses. His face cracked into a smile of delight as he recognized her. 'Why, blimey, it's the little Canadian what wants the 'ole street to drive on. I'm glad to see you sitting 'ere safe, miss. When I saw that big, posh car lying out there under them bricks I thought that poor little Canadian girl 'as copped it for sure.'

'You two know each other?' Colin said.

Marjorie smiled. 'I tried to push him off the street when I was looking around trying to find my way. He told me how to get to the George and Horses.'

'Marjorie, this is Michael Blaine,' Colin said.

Marjorie held out her hand to him. 'I used to drive for 'is Lordship before 'Itler started 'is show and things changed,' Blaine said regretfully.

'Well, Jove, it's a bit of luck, you coming here, Blaine,' Colin said. 'If your cab isn't engaged, I should like to hire it to take the young lady home.'

'I brought that Yank with me who's getting drunk over there at the bar. I'm supposed to wait for 'im, but, blimey, 'e can find 'imself another cab. I'll tell 'im I've 'ad an urgent call from the War Office. Just 'old still, your Lordship.' With a grin he shuffled off to the bar to speak to the Yankee airman who was standing rather unsteadily with a Piccadilly Commando hanging on to either side of him.

11

'Your Lordship?' Marjorie said, looking wonderingly at him. 'Are you really a real English lord?'

Colin smiled into her eyes. 'I'm afraid so, you know. Father is a belted earl. I do hope you don't mind?'

'No, only, I've never met a real English lord before, but my father said one of his ancestors was a French marquis.'

'I knew it,' he said. 'I could tell as soon as I started mopping the blood from your forehead. Absolutely laced with blue.'

They both laughed. Just then Blaine came back. 'It's all right, my Lord,' he said. 'The Yank doesn't want to leave now any'ow. 'E'll be lucky if 'e 'as enough money left to pay for a cab when those two get through with 'im.'

'Oh, Yanks always have plenty of money, Blaine. You know, I think they brought the mint with them when they came over here.' He turned to Marjorie. 'Now, if you will allow me, Marjorie, I'll see you safely back to Moon's Garage and you can tell them about the awful fate of the brigadier's car; and then I'll escort you back to your barracks.'

A sinking feeling came over her. She wondered again if he was going to meet someone – Ashley perhaps? I've had my shining hour, she thought. Now, I suppose I shall never see him again. Don't be a little fool, she told herself scornfully. Less than an hour ago you had never even seen this man. How can it possibly matter to you whether you see him again or not? But it did. It mattered terribly.

Colin was smiling into her face. 'Don't look so woebegone. I'm sure they won't really court martial you, you know.'

She managed to smile back. 'We're supposed to pay for any damage to the car assigned to us if we're careless. They take it out of our pay, and I only make a dollar twenty-five a day.'

'I'm glad the RAF don't do that sort of thing with aeroplanes.'

The three of them left the pub together and went out into the dark street to Blaine's cab.

Helen Huntley chewed the end of her pen and stared into space. What to tell him? Her thoughts seemed to lump in her throat. She kept seeing him locked in the hell of battle. After she told him she loved him her pen went dry. The little, everyday things seemed like a mockery to tell him over there in Normandy. At this moment, he might be lying wounded – or even dead. She

12

clutched for her beads and said a quick prayer. It was bad luck even to think such things. She had to keep believing he would come through it somehow and return to her. But every day the news came back of the Canadians advancing in the face of savage defence by the enemy.

She could see Carl's merry blue eyes and his wide grin.

Could she say that she had just been assigned to drive for a major? Certainly, she was not going to mention the buzz bombs that were uppermost in all their minds here in London.

Across the room, on the far bed against the wall, Elsie Love leaned over and pulled her barrack box from under her bed. She extracted a neat little parcel and put it beside her on her bed, her full lips pouting in anticipation.

Lying on her bed beneath the wide window with her head propped up on her pillow and her hands behind her head, Jessy Cole watched her two roommates. She observed with warm sympathy Helen's worried look. It quickly changed to amused contempt as her eyes swept across to Elsie Love who had taken an immaculate white linen napkin from the box beside her and was carefully spreading it out on her bed. Methodically, she proceeded to lay on it an assortment of goodies – little pots of meat, fancy cheeses, biscuits, small tins of fruit and jam and a box of chocolates.

Completely ignoring her roommates, she spread a biscuit with meat and cheese and very slowly, with great relish, lifted it to her full-lipped mouth and began chewing with obvious pleasure.

She was a plump girl with pale hair, and eyes that were not quite any colour. She had even white teeth and a smooth complexion.

Jessy thought, she looks like some kind of a pretty pig – no, not a pig. More like a little, fat silver fox. The arrival of a parcel from home was always the signal for a party among the lucky roommates of the recipient. Everyone shared the precious parcels that came from home – everyone, that is, but Elsie Love. Elsie not only did not share so much as a crumb, she blatantly enjoyed her treats under their noses. Her rich parents in Toronto sent her more parcels than anyone else. She usually spun them out for several days, eating only a small portion at a time, and finishing off with a chocolate or two. Then she carefully wrapped up the rest, returned it to her barrack box and locked the box.

Bonny Brennan, who occupied the bed between Helen and Elsie when she was in, had remarked, 'I'd like to get into that pig's barrack box some time when she's out and fill all those damn chocolates of hers with poison.'

Marjorie, as was her custom with everyone, had tried to defend the absent Elsie. 'Oh, I don't think she's really such a bad sort.'

'Bad sort,' Bonny had snorted. 'I never saw such a pill. And did you ever see anyone with such a yellow streak? She's so damn scared every time one of those flying boxcars comes over, she just about shits her pants.'

'I can't say I like them much, either,' Marjorie said.

'Yeah, but you're not like her. I came into the room the other day when the raid was on and where do you think I found her? Skulking under the bed.'

'Maybe she was just having a snack,' Jessy had drawled and they all laughed.

Fortunately for Bonny's state of mind she was not in to see Elsie's performance tonight.

Jessy turned back to see Helen still nibbling on the end of her pen and gazing helplessly at the ceiling. 'What's wrong, Helen old girl?' Jessy asked gently. 'Can't you think of anything to write? I'll give you a little story I heard today about a CWAC who went out on a hospitality weekend to this big posh Limey place in the country. When her host said good night, he told her, "Have a good sleep now, my dear. I'll knock you up early in the morning." '

Helen's worried look gave way to a laugh. 'I guess Carl could use a good story, wherever he is. What's the rest of it?'

Before Jessy could answer they heard the wail of the air raid siren and, a moment later, the rumbling approach of a V-bomb.

Elsie Love turned pasty white and a gasp came from her lips. Helen drew a quick breath and quietly put down her writing pad. The rumbling grew louder, with an ominous hesitation. The building seemed to shiver from the vibration as it skimmed over the rooftop, then they heard the rumble fading as it went on its way.

As they heard the rumble of another one coming Jessy said,

'Hey, douse the lights Helen, and let's get a look at old Hitler's flying boxcar.' She cast a sly sideways glance at Elsie Love. 'They sure look pretty coming through at night with all that fire behind them.'

'Oh, for God's sake,' Elsie said, 'leave the lights on.'

Helen reached across and plunged the room into darkness. Jessy pulled back the curtain on the wide window beside her bed. 'Would you look at *that*!'

A slight shiver running through her, Helen came and perched on the bed beside Jessy at the window.

'You know, I think those Heinies are trying to kill someone with those things,' Jessy said.

'Oooh.' A moan of terror came from Elsie's bunk.

Abruptly the motor stopped and the fire flickered out, leaving a momentary, weird glow in the blackness.

In the abrupt silence, Elsie whimpered piteously. 'Ohh, oohh! It's coming down on top of us. We'll all be killed.'

'Well, at least you'll go on a full stomach,' Jessy retorted.

Helen's hand bit into her arm as they waited, but no crunch came and they started to breathe again. Jessy pulled the curtains back across the window and Helen turned on the light. 'It must have glided on for miles.'

They looked across at Elsie's bunk, but there was no sign of her. On her bed was a fancy homespun quilt, sent to her from home. It touched the floor. Suddenly Elsie peeked out from under it, white-faced and goggle-eyed.

'Having another little snack?' Jessy asked pleasantly.

'You – you . . .' Elsie muttered. 'You're supposed to keep the blackout curtains closed, Jessy. Why do you open them all the time?'

'It doesn't matter as long as the light's out. There are no pilots in those planes, anyway.'

'But you aren't supposed to pull the blackout curtains,' Elsie insisted, pursing her lips. Cautiously she pulled herself out from under her bed and collapsed on the edge of it. She sat staring at the wall and shaking.

'Cheer up, Elsie,' Jessy said. 'It can't get you unless it's got your number on it.'

'But how do I know it hasn't?' Elsie wailed.

'What was the end of that story you were telling me about the

CWAC who went out to visit the people in the big country house, Jessy?' Helen asked.

Jessy laughed and finished the story and Helen wrote it in her letter with a smile on her wide pleasant mouth. 'That will give him a chuckle, I hope,' she said wistfully.

The All Clear sounded and Elsie exclaimed with relief.

'Whatever made you volunteer to come over here anyway, Elsie?' Jessy asked curiously. 'Didn't you know England is in the war theatre?'

'They said the raids were all over. Then, on the ship I heard about the robot planes.'

Elsie's real reason for volunteering for overseas duty was her own secret. She looked at the two girls without any expression, but feeling a venomous dislike, particularly for the pleasant-faced Helen. *If it wasn't for you*, she thought viciously, *I would be Mrs Carl Huntley.*

She had been posted to Calgary from Toronto, and at Currie Barracks, at a dance, she had met the big burly infantryman, Carl Huntley, and had immediately conjured up a picture of herself marrying him. Sometimes he had coffee with her in the Sally Ann hut, after she had manoeuvred to bump into him in the evening there. And once or twice she had contrived to sit with him at the movie they showed for the service people. She felt sure he was starting to love her and she built up wild daydreams about the nights they would spend together after they were married.

She was sitting with him and a group of soldiers having coffee when a party of new girls who had just arrived at Currie Barracks from Red Deer came breezing into the Sally Ann.

She writhed inwardly, remembering the look on Carl Huntley's face when freckle-faced, blue-eyed, red-haired Helen with her merry crooked grin and her jolly laugh came up to the table where they sat.

From then on it was all over. Within a month he and Helen Carter were married by the Catholic padre in the little Catholic chapel on the army compound.

Elsie had told no one how she felt and none of the girls had ever thought of Carl as her boyfriend, but she had built the thing up in her mind until she believed that the other girl had stolen him away from her. When the chance came for her to come to

England, she had volunteered, thinking: He'll still be in England – and Helen will be in Canada . . . And anything can happen.

To her dismay she found herself on the same draft for overseas as Marjorie Hatfield, Jessy Cole and Helen Huntley. The closeness of the three friends had always irritated her, although she did not feel too antagonistic towards Marjorie. She disliked Jessy almost as venomously as she did Helen. Elsie had been posted to Ottawa not long after Helen and Carl were married, and had not seen any of the other girls until she met them on the troop ship at Halifax Nova Scotia.

She had been dreadfully seasick all through the voyage and had almost collapsed from fright when the rumour went around the ship that an enemy sub was trailing them. Then came the dreadful night when the ship alarm started its awful hooting and they rushed into their clothes and went to their boat stations. She had particularly hated Jessy that night. 'Never mind, Elsie,' she had said as the frightful hoot, hoot, hoot went on and on and Elsie cowered, moaning with terror. 'If we're cast adrift in a lifeboat, you'll be the one we eat to save ourselves, since you're the plumpest.' Jessy was never afraid of anything and she bounced about the deck all through the voyage as if she had been born on the sea.

As she looked at Elsie now Jessy was thinking: Poor old scaredy-cat Elsie. I wonder if she's still mooning over Helen's husband? Poor Carl if he'd got her. She'd probably just cook enough dinner for herself and then eat it in front of him. But it's time for me to get on down to Molly's pub and meet that big Yankee major, Bob Anders.

It was a long time since she had seen a man who made her feel the way he did. Too bad he would soon be on his way back to France. He had picked up a small wound to his hand, but his Blighty jaunt to London was about over. Oh well, men were like railway trains – always another one coming. 'I wonder where Marjorie is?' she said to the others. 'She should have been in by now.'

Elsie Love said with a curl to her lips, 'Oh, she's probably lost again.'

Helen said, 'Poor Marjorie, she always has the worst time trying to find her way around. She always did get her directions mixed. Remember when she got lost all night out at Sarcee and we had to send out a posse for her?'

'Yes. You and I went out,' Jessy said. 'We found her out at Twin Bridges. I don't know how she got away out there.'

Helen laughed.

'If you ask me,' Elsie said severely, 'she shouldn't be driving at all, especially here in London. She'll never find her way around.'

'How do you manage when you're driving around, Elsie? Do you stop your car and crawl underneath every time a raid comes?' Jessy asked.

Elsie put her nose in the air and disdained to answer. Her trips about the city were a nightmare to her. As a matter of fact, she was thinking of going to Captain Burns and asking to be transferred to one of the country postings, pleading that the London climate did not agree with her. But she did not want to get away from Helen. She knew Helen must eventually hear from Carl, if he was alive. And if he came back and if she saw him again . . . Somehow – somehow she would make him realize she was the one he loved, not that man-thief Helen.

Before anyone could speak again, Marjorie walked in. 'Where have you been?' Jessy asked. 'You left the garage just ahead of me to evacuate the brigadier's car.'

'You look pale,' Helen said. 'And there's a cut on your face. What happened? Did you have an accident?'

'You might say so,' Marjorie said with a little smile. 'I almost got blown up by a doodle bug.'

'What!' Her two friends jumped to their feet and came across to her. 'Are you all right?'

'Yes, but I – I just got a little cut on my forehead – and it took my breath away and knocked me out for a bit when it landed. And they took me down into a pub called the George and Horses until I felt better.'

'The George and Horses,' Jessy said. 'You mean the one on Shaftesbury Avenue? How did you get way over there?'

Marjorie gave a sheepish little laugh. 'Well, I got lost. I found myself at Piccadilly Circus – I guess I took a wrong turn somewhere – then I just got . . . Everything seemed to get all mixed up.'

Jessy said, 'Lucky thing you didn't have the Brig with you. You'd have scared the pants off him. They wouldn't be too

18

pleased with you down at the garage if they knew what you'd done.'

'I don't think they're going to be pleased with me, anyhow, when they find out what happened to the brigadier's car.'

'You've wrecked the brigadier's car?' Elsie asked.

'It's wrecked, all right,' Marjorie answered. 'The whole top of a building fell on it.' She told them the whole story, but for some reason she left out the part about the airman who had rescued her and said only that bystanders had taken her down into the George and Horses until she felt better.

'Now that you've finally been in a pub,' Jessy said, 'how about coming down to Molly's with me? You can meet my nice Yank and have a meat pie, or something. The mess hall's closed by now. Of course, some people do have food around here.'

Elsie ignored the remark and lay down on her bed.

'No thank you, Jess,' Marjorie said. 'I'm not really hungry. I think I'll just go to bed. I need to have a bath and wash my hair, if there's any water. I got sort of dusty.'

'OK, Marj,' Jessy said, giving her friend a keen glance from under her thick, black lashes. 'Well, I'll see you around eleven then – after they close – if the major and I don't decide to go somewhere else.' She put on her tunic and cap and went to the bathroom to check herself over before leaving.

Looking in the mirror, she took a bright orange lipstick from her shoulder bag and applied it to the curve of her lips. The mirror showed a lithe, provocatively curved young body even the khaki tunic couldn't conceal, black, crisp curly hair peeping from under her peaked cap, enhancing the rich warm colouring of her skin. Tip-tilted, sensual brown eyes smiled naughtily back at her. She stood for a moment with her hands resting lightly on her hips, then she left, hips swaying gracefully. She thought as she went out on to the black street with only the tiny pencil of light from her torch pointed down at the pavement to guide her: There's something strange about Marjorie. She looks different to when she went out – sort of a dreamy look. Well, maybe it's just the shock, or maybe I'm imagining it. She looks like a girl in love.

Molly's pub, the favourite hang-out for the girls of 43 Company, was just around the corner and across the street from Sussex Square. As usual, it was stuffed with service people. Jessy was greeted enthusiastically by the group of CWACs, already seated at tables drinking with airmen on leave in London.

The Yankee major was waiting for her. His eyes lit up when she came in. He took her to a table and ordered her favourite gin drink for her. He was tall and fair, with a gleam in his eye and a reckless laugh.

As he looked at Jessy, the gleam brightened to a flame. 'I'd love to see you in a low-cut evening dress,' he told her. 'Wouldn't I like to take you to the Grantview Club with me! You'd make all those other girls look like left-over tanks.'

'The Grantview Club in New York? I've been there.'

'You have?'

'Yes. But I was only ten. My mother and father used to dance there – on the stage.'

'Your mother and father are professional dancers?'

'Yes. They call themselves Pierre and Anna La Flamme.'

'Oh, I've heard my father speak of them. They were a big hit. My father said she was the most beautiful woman he ever saw. Now I see where you get it from.'

Jessy looked across at his clean, hard, good looks and thought to herself: What a guy. I haven't felt like this over a man in a long while – maybe I've never felt like this.

They finished their drinks and he bought another round for the table. Jessy felt warmth flowing through her. They were joined at their table by a tall, thin-faced, serious young RAF flying officer. The jokes started to fly around; then the talk turned to love and they all gave their different versions of what they believed love to be. The thin-faced airman listened quietly, then he said, 'You don't know what love is, any of you. It's not any of that. It' just – well – I'll tell you. I was married, you see. When I came back to London after a mission, I found our place bombed. My wife was killed.'

A hush fell on the table. The airman said, 'Love is just – well – you just like to have them around.' He got up and wandered off. They were all still for a moment and then the laughter and the talk broke out, a little more boisterously than before.

In a while the alert sounded, but they pointedly ignored it. A buzz bomb rumbled overhead, but they went on talking and drinking as if no one had heard it. When closing time came, Bob tucked Jessy's hand under his arm and they went out into the blackness.

A few paces down the street he drew back against a building and pulled her into his arms. His lips sought her mouth and his hands wandered down her back to her buttocks and pulled her body close to his.

Jessy felt a warm, wild pleasure course through her as she returned his kiss. 'Let's go out on to Sussex Square,' he whispered huskily into her ear.

The 43 Company building fronted on the lush green park. In the morning when she walked across it with the other girls on their way to work it was always littered with French letters, left by the young service people who made love there in the concealing darkness of the blackout. With her head on his shoulder and his arm around her waist, she let him lead her around the corner and out into the blackness of Sussex Square. The grass felt soft beneath her feet.

They almost tripped over two people and a girl giggled. All around them they could hear the rustling and shaking of bodies. They managed to find a quiet spot. He spread his trench coat on the grass and they sank down on to it.

The intimate darkness wrapped itself around them. His lips found her mouth and his hand slid up her leg, sending a tingling ache into her thighs. She twined her arm up around his neck as he undid her tunic and shirt and fastened his lips on her thrusting nipples, sucking them avidly in turn; while his other hand took her pants away and found the sensitive spot between her spread legs. His breath was coming in heaving sighs and she was panting breathlessly.

Then he was on top of her, thrusting between her legs, and she was heaving up to meet him, thrill after thrill shooting through her.

'Jess, oh Jess, you really are something. You really are something,' he said when at last he rolled off her and lay spent with his arms cradling her.

She was still for a moment, then she gave a throaty little laugh. He started and she felt him tense. 'You Yanks really were telling the truth,' she said softly.

'Eh?'

'Everything you have really is the biggest and best,' she said caressingly.

He laughed and kissed her. 'If only there was no war and we had time,' he said huskily. 'If only we were at home and you were my girl and I could take you places and show you things. But tomorrow I have to go back over there.'

She let her hands caress him. 'I know, but we're here tonight and tonight is all any of us have right now.'

He rubbed his cheek against hers. 'Thank you, Jess,' he said quietly. 'When I'm up there on that flamethrower I'll be thinking of tonight and you. Will you think of me?'

Jessy pulled his lips down to hers again. He put his hand up into the back of her hair and held her lips for a long time. All around them Jessy could hear the sounds of other couples making love, but the night was so black that if they had been touching her she could not have seen them.

She wondered if any of them were virgins and were taking their love out here in the darkness for the first time. This was not her case. She had discovered the joys of lovemaking when she was fourteen, and a young actor, a friend of her mother's, had found her alone in the dressing room. She remembered how handsome she had thought him and then suddenly he was kissing her and his hand had wandered under her skirt. They had ended up behind the row of dresses. She remembered, after the first pain of penetration, the joyful thrill that had shot through her.

Her mother had come in and discovered them, sent the young actor packing and had a heart to heart talk with her daughter. The first thing she had asked her was if the man had used a French letter, and when Jessy told her that he had, her mother was not nearly so concerned and the heart to heart talk had consisted of the facts of life and the need to protect herself in a sexual encounter. Her mother was a woman of the world.

'What did you do before the war?' Bob asked.

'Oh, I was on the stage in Montreal, like Mother, only she was a dancer and I was a singer and an actress. At first I waited on tables in a little old hash joint to keep myself going. I've written one or two things. I sold a play once for a hundred dollars. I was on my way up, singing in the Glen Club, then one day I quit and joined up. What did you do?'

22

'Well, I went to college. I was studying to be a lawyer when this show came on. And I was a pretty good football player. I was torn between the law and becoming a professional player. My parents wanted me to be a lawyer. Football players don't make much money and they get injured.'

'But they learn to tackle,' she said with a mischievous chuckle.

He kissed her again and she lay back in his arms. The blackness was warm around them as they lay entwined. 'What a pair of legs you've got,' he said, running his hands up towards her thighs. 'You have the most beautiful body I've ever seen.'

'But you haven't seen it,' she said with a throaty laugh. 'In these long khaki skirts and tunics we might as well be wearing a tent. You should have seen me in my black silk evening dress with the slits up the side when I was singing at the Glen Club.'

'I'd like to see you in nothing,' he said.

For a while they lay quietly, whispering and teasing and running their hands over each other. Then, once more, they made love, more tenderly this time, but still with an ecstasy of passion. It had never been like this for Jessy before. The thought of him leaving for Normandy tomorrow gave her passion an urgency that was like a flaming pain. I know now what they're blabbing about when they say war is hell, she thought, with a twisted smile in the darkness, as once more they lay still and spent in each other's arms.

Their warm intimate world was shattered by the intruding wail of the air raid siren and in a moment they heard the rumbling approach of the V-bomb. They saw the ghostly, pale silhouette of the robot plane, lit by its red wake of flame, then abruptly the motor cut and only the weird glow was left.

In the blackness Jessy could feel the tensely held breath of the young men and women lying out there on the square with them. She squeezed Bob's hand and said with a light laugh, 'I think those Fritzies are trying to spoil our fun.'

As the words left her mouth a thud and a roar filled their ears and they saw flames lick towards the sky as the earth shook under them. 'That one was close, about a quarter of a mile away, I'd say, down by Marble Arch somewhere,' Jessy said.

'And they sent me for a nice safe leave in London,' Bob said with a laugh. 'At least, at the front I got to shoot back.'

23

'But isn't the blackout lovely,' she said, squeezing him naughtily with her hand.

'I don't think you're scared of anything, Jess.'

'Well, I just don't believe they're going to get me and I don't believe in being scared. Being scared is like paying for something you haven't bought, all the time.'

All around them they could hear the other couples getting up and leaving but still they lingered on, holding each other close. 'When we get Herman back in his place,' Bob said huskily, 'I'll take you to that Grantview Club. All the fellows will be green with envy when I walk in with you on my arm.'

'And the girls will be weeping with jealousy,' Jessy said, stroking his body.

Very gently then, with the last little bit of passion left in his body, he took her.

Finally, he lifted her to her feet and she pulled her clothing straight. With his arms around her, he took her to the door of her barracks and very gently kissed her face and eyes and her lips. 'Goodbye, Jess,' he said with a break in his voice. 'Don't forget we've got a date for after the war in the Grantview Club. I'll write you if I can.' He pulled himself away from her and then he was gone into the night.

Jessy went back up to her room.

At the top of the stairs she met Bonny Brennan wearing her tin hat. 'Jeepers. Did you get a look at that doodle bug?' she said. 'I was on fire watch on the roof and it was coming straight at me. I was sure it was going to shave the top of the building off and me with it. It landed over by Marble Arch. What a thud. I almost fell off the roof.' Her eyes swept over Jessy. 'You look a mess. Where have you been?'

'In paradise.'

'You've been out on Sussex Square with that Yankee major. Your skirt's all crooked. Here, let me straighten you out.' Bonny brushed her friend down and pulled her skirt straight.

The lights were out in the room and Jessy crept into bed in the dark just as the All Clear sounded. She could feel the warmth of Bob Anders in every part of her body as she pulled the covers under her chin and drifted off into a sleep not even the air raid siren could rouse her from.

*

24

Marjorie heard Jessy come in, but she lay still and pretended to sleep. She was plunged deep in her own thoughts and she did not want to surface.

Strange emotions had been chasing through her mind ever since Colin dropped her at the door of 43 Company that night. She kept seeing his face, smiling down at her as she lay in the crook of his arm, and heard his drawly voice saying, 'You're a funny little soldier girl.' She blushed in the darkness and her temples throbbed. What was the matter with her?

She could see his warm, humorous brown eyes and his firm sensitive mouth. She had had such an urge in the pub to reach over and push back the shock of wavy brown hair from his fine forehead.

She went over their conversation and lived again the warm intimacy they had shared as they sat and discussed books they had both enjoyed.

I wonder why he never said anything about seeing me again, Marjorie thought. I'm sure he liked me. No doubt he has a girlfriend in his own set. Ashley? He could even be married.

After all, she really knew nothing about him. And yet she felt she did know him. She was usually a shy person, but with him her reticence had dropped away. Sitting beside him, chatting in the taxi, it was as if she had known him all her life. She was sure he felt the same closeness to her.

Yet when he dropped her off at her door he had merely wished her good night pleasantly. If he had been a Canadian, or an American, she knew he would have tried to kiss her. But although they had sat so close in Blaine's taxi that their sleeves were brushing he made no attempt to even put his arm around her shoulders. Perhaps, after all, he only found her a dull little country girl from Canada, someone he was being kind to. And that's just what I am, I guess, she thought ruefully as she tossed in the darkness.

She could not see him in the blackout when he took her to the door of 43 Company but his voice had been gentle as he took her hand and pressed it and said comfortingly, 'Now, don't worry about that court of inquiry. I'm sure they won't send you to the Tower, or wherever they send Canadian girls. After all, you couldn't really be expected to do much about a V-bomb, you know.'

25

'But I shouldn't have been way over there in that part of town at all. If I hadn't been lost, I would have been safely back in Moon's Garage.'

'You're expected to get lost in London,' he said. 'Goodnight, little Marjorie. Go to bed and get to sleep before that brandy wears off.'

She was glad it was too dark for him to see her face. After all, it was just a chance encounter. There was no reason in the world for her to have this forlorn, empty feeling as she said good night to him and found her way inside.

Finally, as he had predicted, the brandy did its work and she drifted off to sleep. Her sleep was filled with dreams of dashing across the pasture on her pony, who mysteriously changed into a great white charger, and she was being carried on his back in the arms of the airman, flying over the green grass, leaping coulees and badger holes, being rescued from something – she did not know what.

Chapter 3

'Where to now, your Lordship?' Blaine asked after Colin returned to the cab from seeing Marjorie to her door.

'Take me to Baker Street station, please Blaine, if you're free.'

'If I wasn't free I'd always make myself free for your Lordship,' Blaine answered.

Dear old Blaine, Colin thought with a glow of pleasure. How lucky I was to bump into you. He remembered affectionately how happy it had always made him on coming home for school holidays to see Blaine's cheerful red face at the station at Wendover when he came to pick him up in the Rolls-Royce. Colin always plied him with questions as they drove the three miles to the ancestral home of the Enderbys in the country.

He couldn't remember a time without Blaine. Blaine had been the Enderbys' chauffeur since before Colin was born, and his wife had been their housekeeper; but most of the big house was shut up and the servants gone to do war work. The staff had dwindled to only his nanny, Mrs Anderson; Giles, the butler; the elderly Mrs Meadows, who kept house for them; an old gardener; and an old groom.

The Rolls-Royce had hardly been out of the garage since the war had come. The little driving they did on their petrol ration was in the Baby Austin. The earl insisted on riding his horse into Wendover whenever he found it necessary to go there.

They would never have let Blaine go. But he could see that his services as a chauffeur were no longer required. He wanted to join up, but an old shrapnel wound in his leg from the first war kept him out of active service, and there was a shortage of taxi-cab drivers in London. When he told the earl what he

27

wanted to do, the earl had insisted on setting him up with his own cab.

'When this bloody show is over, I 'ope 'is Lordship will take me on again,' Blaine said as they drove towards Baker Street station. 'This 'ere London is all right but it isn't Enderby, not by a long shot.'

'I'm sure that he will,' Colin said. But he thought to himself: When this war is over can anyone say they'll go back to where they were before it started? He thought wistfully of the long, happy years, flowing in a smooth, broad stream – the carefree days of country parties and boating on the pond, riding fat happy ponies down country lanes, and trips abroad to the continent with his parents.

No one had thought of anything but life going on in the same easy, carefree way. Then a man with a funny little Charlie Chaplin moustache had changed all that and death was swarming over Britain, in the form of Dorniers and Heinkels dropping their loads of venom on peaceful towns and cities. And the sky was full of Messerschmitt 109s and Focke Wolf fighting planes. And he was up there in his Spitfire, whirling and twirling above the earth, with his gun spitting death at another boy spitting death back at him. And neither of them had ever seen the other, nor had any reason to hate him.

But keeping these desecrating invaders away from the green earth of Britain was all that mattered now. Life was one day, or one hour. Each dawn was the world. He marvelled that he had come through those days when they had gone up day after day with their pitiful few to meet the locust hordes of enemy planes. So many of those smiling boys he had idled away his time with, playing cricket and riding the country lanes, laughing together at parties, were gone – shot from the skies they were keeping free. But he had survived. He wondered how. Well – he laughed to himself – maybe it was because *she* was praying for me.

'Give my respects to 'is Lordship and 'er Ladyship,' Blaine said as he let Colin out at Baker Street station, 'and bless you, my Lord.'

'Bless you, too, Blaine,' Colin said, shaking the older man's hand. 'And please give my regards to Mrs Blaine.'

The compartment was empty. As he settled down to wait for the train to pull out from the station, he was seized with an overwhelming desire to open the door and leap back on to the platform. All at once, he did not want to leave London. But he remained seated and in a few moments the train pulled out.

Tonight was Ashley's twenty-fourth birthday party and he would slip the big ruby and diamond ring that had been in the Enderby family for generations on to her finger and announce their engagement to the few old friends and relatives who could be there.

What jolly times he remembered at Ashley's birthday parties. As children, he and Raif had been breathless with excitement as they raced the short distance up the hill to the big house of Lord and Lady Medhurst. The Medhurst's only child, Ashley, was their constant companion. Although she was closer to his age than to his older brother, it was Raif she followed around as the three of them played about the two estates.

As they grew up he had taken it for granted that one day she would be his sister-in-law and Viscountess Enderby, future Countess of Rivermere. But Dunkirk had finished all that and now he, the younger son, was Viscount Enderby, heir to Rivermere – the last heir, unless he left a son behind when he died.

He knew his parents and hers hoped wistfully that he and Ashley would unite the families of these two old friends on adjoining estates. His people had a tremendous affection for Lady Ashley – and so did he.

She had spent the night at Enderby Hall and was with them the morning the fatal telegram came. He was home on a rare few hours' leave. Only a few days before, they had said goodbye to Raif, splendid in his naval lieutenant's uniform. He had kissed Ashley before boarding the train at Wendover and then clasped his brother's hand in a fond grip. Colin could see him still, handsome, tall and smiling as he turned to wave to them before entering the compartment.

They were not really surprised when the news came. A hushed silence, broken by sudden bursts of casual talk, was on them at breakfast. They were sitting in the library having eleven o'clock tea when the telegram was delivered. The earl had picked raspberries and the countess had made jelly and they were using the last of their week's butter ration on their hot biscuits.

29

The countess sat rigid in her chair, her face quite expression-less, as the earl, with fingers willed to steadiness, opened the telegram. His face turned grey and he was silent for a moment. Then very quietly he read it to them. During the evacuation of Dunkirk Raif Enderby's small craft had suffered a direct hit and blown up, killing all aboard.

Ashley's warm, healthy complexion turned to marble. She sat like a woman of stone. Then she drew a deep breath, stood up and crossed to the countess and touched her lightly on the arm. 'May I pour you another cup of tea, Aunt Honora?' she said.

The countess turned her head and looked up into her face. 'No thank you, my dear. I will continue to pour for all of us.'

Within a few hours, Colin was back to deadly duels in the sky. There was no time to think, or to mourn. When he came home for brief hours of leave, he and Ashley had grown closer to each other. She was one of the few women not in uniform. Most of the servants from the estate of Lord Medhurst had gone into war services, and Ashley and her parents turned to the business of producing food for the war effort.

Now that the Battle of Britain had been won and the war was being carried into enemy territory, he had more time to think and his thoughts turned to Ashley. He was aware of the wistful look in his mother's eyes as she watched them putting their horses over the jumps out in the paddock, or strolling down to the pond where they had played as children.

It was down by the pond, on his last leave, that he had come to propose to Ashley. They had been sitting side by side in a little nook close to the boathouse, with the sheltering rho-dodendrons which lined the shore hiding them from sight of the house. It had always been the favourite retreat of Raif, Ashley and himself.

Ashley said with a laugh, 'Remember the time we almost drowned you giving you a Viking's funeral? How you loved to play you were Beau Geste.'

Colin laughed. 'You had set the tin of twigs on fire and it was sending up billows of smoke and I was lying rigid, looking up at the sky. Everything was going nicely, and then Raif decided he wanted to be Beau Geste and tried to board my craft.'

Ashley laughed with a catch in her throat. Then suddenly, for the first time, they started to talk of Raif. The overwhelming loneliness in them drew them closer together, until he took her in his arms and kissed her, and then he found himself saying, 'Will you marry me, Ashley?'

She answered simply, 'Yes, Colin.'

They sat looking at each other, not quite knowing what to say next. Then he said, 'I shall have a forty-eight the week after next, on your birthday. Remember the jolly birthday parties we always had at Medhurst Hall? What do you say we make it an engagement party? We'll announce our engagement when we cut the cake. Mother and Father will be delighted.'

'So will my parents. I think they've been praying that this would happen.'

Colin had never had a serious girlfriend. There had been one or two light flirtations when he was a lad before the war, and since he had been flying, a few episodes with women he met on leave. Once he had spent a rather jolly time with a little barmaid. But these had only been to satisfy his male craving for a woman when he came away from his encounters with death in the sky. He was quietly happy that was over now.

Lately strange feelings had been disturbing him. When he died he wanted to leave something behind. He wanted there to be a fifteenth Earl of Rivermere. For centuries, above the lake they called the Pond, the great old house had been the home of the Earls of Rivermere and for centuries the Medhursts had lived in the big house on the hill above it and shared their lives, in peace and in war.

He had been quietly happy – until now. Now suddenly, unreasonably, he wished with all his heart that he was free.

Floating before his eyes he kept seeing a smudgy fair face and a pair of wide, sincere blue eyes and a head of bright, golden-blonde hair. And he heard a wistful, frightened voice saying, 'I don't want to die a virgin – I don't want to die a virgin.'

He laughed softly to himself. How she had blushed when she realized what she was saying as she lay in his arms. She had looked like a tiny, frightened angel with her tremulous expression. She had been so concerned about the brigadier's car, and about breaking army rules and being with him when she was only an Other Rank and he was an officer. 'I don't drink.' How simply she had said it. She had a sweet quality of almost childlike honesty that had intrigued him. He had never met a girl like her before.

Sitting across from her in the pub talking, he had experienced something he had never before felt for anyone – a closeness and a yearning. And in Blaine's taxi taking her home it was all he could do to keep from putting his arm around her tiny shoulders and pulling her to him. But he was engaged to Ashley.

Dear Ashley. Nothing in the world would ever make him let her down. Least of all a strange girl he had just met who did not even belong to his people. Perhaps he had been experiencing battle fatigue . . . He thought he had detected disappointment in her when he had said goodbye and had not asked to see her again. He knew she had liked him.

Yes, no doubt it was battle fatigue. After all, he had been living on borrowed time for years now. Most of the friends he had started out with were gone, shot down in combat, or captured or they had been put at a desk in charge of a squadron. Well, he would soon be in that position himself – if he made it. Then he and Ashley would be married. This little soldier girl from Canada whose life he had saved would only be a tiny memory.

He was being schoolboyish. No doubt he had imagined her disappointment. In all probability she had someone. She was the type of woman that men love. Yes, she must have a man, either at the front, or in England, or even back at home in Canada. It was certainly unlikely that she had no attachment and yet . . . Her words when she woke in his arms – it was as if she was waiting for the right man.

But that man was not him. In less than two weeks he would be married to Ashley Medhurst – beautiful, talented Ashley Medhurst who, if he survived this war, could share his thoughts and his way of life as no one else could.

Why could he not replace the face of Marjorie Hatfield with that of dear Ashley? And why suddenly did he wish desperately that he was not going to Wendover tonight to place the family ring on her finger?

If he was free tonight he would have asked Marjorie to go dancing at the Officers' Club. Would she have accepted? He smiled, imagining her saying, wide-eyed, 'I can't go there with you, I'm an Other Rank.' He shook his head and tried to think of how happy they would be at Enderby when he and Ashley announced their engagement.

The journey from Baker Street station took just over an hour. It was late when he left the train at Wendover. Since he had missed the earlier train he was supposed to have arrived on, he did not expect there would be anyone at the station to meet him.

As he stepped on to the platform a shadowy figure moved to meet him and Ashley's warm, rich voice welcomed him. 'Colin, darling, you're here.'

He stooped and kissed her lightly. 'Yes, and I'm sorry I'm late. Your party will be well under way by now. How good of you to come for me. You'll be missing your own cake.'

'No. When you didn't arrive on the eight o'clock, we simply held everything up to wait for you.' She ran her finger down his arm. 'I wondered, a bit, what had gone wrong. I know those nasty buzz bomb things are all over London.' She tucked her hand under his arm. 'I suppose I'm just becoming jittery. But they really are rather horrid.'

'As a matter of fact, I was rather held up by one, but never mind that now. I'll tell you all about it some time. Now, we mustn't keep that cake waiting. I expect you've used up a whole month's rations to produce it.'

'Yes. And we have champagne, too.'

Chapter 4

Marjorie woke in the morning to the sound of the air raid alert, and Elsie whimpering in her bed.

'Ah, for Christ's sake, shut up, Love. You're the worst scaredy-cat I've ever seen. You'd be scared of your own shadow if it barked at you,' Bonny snarled disgustedly.

'So would I be, come to think of it,' Helen said, and everybody laughed.

Jessy pulled the curtains back. 'Look, the sun's shining. It's going to be a gorgeous weekend. You don't have to worry about the doodle bugs. When it's bright like this the gunners will pick them off at the coast before they ever reach London.'

'But how can you be sure of that?' Elsie wailed.

'Things quit being sure the day you joined the army,' Jessy said.

'Yeah,' Bonny said. 'Only one thing is sure about the army, if there's any way of fouling it all up they'll find it.'

'Who's working today?' Helen said.

'I am,' Jessy said. 'I have to head down to the garage right after breakfast.'

'What about you, Marj?' Helen asked.

'No, I'm off,' Marjorie answered. Then, with a wry little smile, she added, 'Unless they decide to court martial me for the brigadier's car. How about you, Bonny?'

'Oh, I don't have to drive today. I'm playing ball in Hyde Park. We're practising up for the big one. We're going to take this London area championship. We knocked the shit out of that Limey team last week.'

'That must have been a pretty sight,' Jessy said, and they all laughed, except Elsie who stared at Bonny with a bewildered expression.

34

'I don't see how you can play ball out there in the park when the raids are on,' she said.

'Why not?' Bonny said. 'It's just as safe as anywhere else, maybe safer. There aren't any buildings to fall on you.'

'Don't –' Elsie cried. 'Don't talk about that. Don't talk about buildings falling on you.' She looked fearfully around.

'Don't worry,' Jessy laughed. 'If a building falls on you, Lovey, we'll pry open your barrack box and bring some of your goodies to you.'

Elsie pursed her lips and turned her head away. 'I'm going to get up and go to breakfast. I have to go to work, too.'

When Jessy arrived at CMHQ garage in Chelsea, the dispatcher handed her a special detail. 'They've just brought in a whole lot of wounded to the hospital in Horsham, and they're running short of blood,' she said. 'I'm giving you the detail because you know the way out there and you can take that station wagon through traffic faster than anyone here. Pull out the stops. They need that blood.'

After picking up the precious bottles of blood, Jessy snaked through the London traffic, weaving between the lumbering London buses, lorries and taxis filling the narrow streets, so close there was only a knife blade between her station wagon and them. Then, when she was out on the open highway, she really opened up. She thought gleefully as she pushed her foot down on the accelerator: If those provosts catch me in a speed trap, this is one time they won't haul me up.

Her thoughts travelled almost as swiftly as her vehicle as she drove through villages and past cottages and long stone walls covered with ivy and flowers. Gentle English sunlight, soft as if filtered through gossamer, bathed everything in its light – so different from the bright, sharp sun of Canada.

She lowered the windows and let the soft moist air, warm with the scent of green things and flowers, blow across her face. It was hard to believe on such a day that, in another world just across twenty miles of water, men were dying in a hell of hate and noise and sheets of flame and groans and blood and cursing – and praying.

She wondered where Bob Anders was. The morning news on

the wireless had told of heavy fighting in the American section of the advance.

She topped a hill and the illusion of peace evaporated. Ahead of her, rumbling towards the coast, was a long convoy of loaded tank carriers. Bob's words came back to her: 'I'll think of you when I'm up there on that flamethrower.'

She had only known him for three days, but they had been three days like no others in her life. She had been sitting in Molly's pub with a bunch of drivers and servicemen, when he came in and their eyes found each other's across the room.

He came straight across to her table, walking with that cocky, Yankee self-assurance. As he stopped and stood looking down at her, Jessy thought: This one has really got something. Time had suddenly started to race and it seemed it was time to leave almost as soon as she got there.

He walked her home after the pub closed, and she responded lightly to his good night kiss, knowing she would be seeing him again the next night. There had been one more night with him at Molly's and then the next night they had gone out on to Sussex Square.

Her body still glowed with the memory. She could not understand her feelings. She had never been one to brood over things, or to look back. She treated each day as a fresh adventure. Why did she keep reliving the moments spent with Bob and the final ecstasy with him out on the square?

Episodes with other men had been a quickly forgotten thrill of pleasure shooting through her body and the light pleasure of their company. With him it was as if all of her fused with him as she accepted his body, so that she was no longer a separate person.

She kept hearing him say in his soft Yankee drawl, 'If only there was no war and we had time. If only we were at home and you were my girl and I could take you places and show you things. But tomorrow I have to go back over there.'

She thought: If there was no war and we were in New York I would probably be looking forward to a night in the Grantview Club with him. She smiled, hearing him say, 'When we get Herman back in his place, I'll take you to that Grantview Club. All the fellows will be green with envy when I walk in with you on my arm.'

36

If there was no war, they would be dancing and watching the entertainment and drinking cocktails and enjoying themselves with other young people like themselves. But since this war had started 'hello' meant 'goodbye' in almost the same breath, especially here in London in the war theatre. So different from what it had been in peacetime.

The hardship of the great depression, which had seen men hurled from it into war, had not affected her young life to any extent. The famous La Flammes had danced their way through it. She had spent her life moving about, living in hotels or apartments, enjoying herself with the carefree, lively set of the entertainment world.

She had loved the excitement, the different people and, most of all, the stage. She had started singing and acting in small parts when she was not yet ten years old. When she was seventeen she had developed a throaty, sultry contralto voice that held the audiences spellbound in the small clubs where she performed in Montreal.

She was intoxicated by the thrill of looking out over the audience and feeling the electric current vibrating between her and them.

When the Canadian Women's Army Corps was formed in September of 1941, and the call had gone out for women, she had been singing in the Glen Club in Montreal and she had known that she was on the verge of making it into the big time. She woke up one morning, after a particularly successful performance, got dressed and went down to the recruiting office and applied to join the CWAC. Within two weeks she was in uniform and off to basic training.

Her parents were in the United States entertaining at service clubs. When they returned to find her a private in the CWAC, her mother said, 'But darling, why on earth did you have to get into that dreadful uniform? It makes you absolutely shapeless. With your voice and figure the troops would absolutely adore you. Don't you know soldiers like to see women dressed like women? They're sick of uniforms. You could do so much more for the war effort entertaining the boys as a singer.'

Her father had looked her over and said, 'Oh, it's not really as bad as that, Anna. Even in that outfit she looks pretty good, I'd say.'

Her parents had never interfered with anything she really wanted to do. She was an only child and they adored her in a carefree sort of way. They believed in complete freedom of expression. Jessy knew that she could have contributed to the war effort as an entertainer, but since she had been a child she had always wanted to try new things and she had hated to be left out of anything that was going on around her. Now that the world was plunged in this gigantic conflict, she wanted a real part in it. There were girl soldiers in Canada for the first time in history and she wanted to be one of them.

At the end of her basic training she was posted to Currie Barracks in Calgary Alberta, and along with Marjorie Hatfield and Elsie Love, had taken the motor transport course. A little later Helen Carter had been sent to Currie as a driver and had met and married Carl Huntley, who was taking his infantry training at the centre.

She and Helen had each been driving a truck in the convoy that night when Carl left for overseas, and Marjorie was the corporal in charge, driving the lead truck, when they lined up on the square and the men in battledress climbed aboard to go down to the railway station.

Sharp in her mind was the picture of Helen clinging to Carl at the station, not letting herself cry, forcing herself to smile at him as the train pulled out. Then they had all returned to the empty trucks and driven them back to Currie barracks.

That had been two years ago. How excited Helen had been when they were on draft, waiting at Kitchener Ontario for the order to go to Halifax and embark for England. She would be seeing Carl again. He was over there as a reinforcement in the Calgary Highlanders.

Just before they arrived the news came of the invasion of Europe. The Highlanders had already gone to France and were now in the thick of the fighting. Helen had had no word of Carl since before she left Canada.

This morning Jessy knew how Helen felt. She herself was thinking of a tall, fair Yank taking his crew into battle on a flamethrower. She shook herself. What's the matter with me, she thought. 'Could it be that there isn't always another one coming?' she wondered out loud, with the trace of a smile on her lips.

After unloading her precious bottles of blood in the dispensary at the hospital, Jessy went to the ward where the wounded who had just been returned from France were being treated. Before entering she carefully hitched up her khaki skirt and folded the waistband over under her tunic so that the hemline just touched the top of her knee – a manoeuvre strictly forbidden by the army. She looked down at her long, slim, beautiful legs with a crooked little smile. 'I'll give those boys something to look at,' she said, removing her cap.

With her black hair shining and her hips undulating Jessy walked through the ward among the wounded and bandaged young Canadian soldiers. Whistles and calls greeted her as the less seriously wounded devoured her with their eyes. 'Hello Canada. Come and comfort a wounded soldier.' 'There's lots of room in my bed.'

She paused to talk and joke with them as she went slowly through the ward, and young eyes that a short time ago had looked at horror and death smiled mischievously up at her.

In one of the beds a young soldier with a face almost as white as the bandage around his head called to her and she went over to speak to him. 'Hallo, Canada,' he said in little more than a whisper. 'How long have you been over here?'

She told him not quite two weeks, and he asked her where she came from. When she told him Montreal his face lit up. 'I knew I'd seen you before. You used to sing in the Glen Club.' He caught her hand and squeezed it.

She chatted with him for a few moments and then his head drooped on the pillow and she went on her way, weaving between the beds. She was almost clear of the ward when she heard a voice call her name from one of the beds and she went over to the wounded man. His lips moved and he said in a husky whisper, 'Jessy . . . Jessy.'

She looked down at the white, pain-filled face with a shock of recognition. 'My God – Carl!' Following the moment of shock, joy flooded her. It was Helen's husband and he was here, safe. But his face was ghastly – drawn and parchment-white, with bloodless lips and eyes sunken and clouded with suffering.

A pang of fear knifed through her as she looked into his face, but she hid her feelings behind a smile as she took his hand and stooped down over the bed to speak to him.

39

'Helen,' he whispered. 'How is Helen?'

'Good, Carl. Good. She's with me in London. We're both driving for CMHQ. But she'll be a lot better when I go back and tell her you're here.'

'Helen is here in England?' he whispered, a light coming into his eyes. But it died quickly and he gave a moan, and again Jessy was afraid, seeing the anguish in his eyes. He turned his face away on the pillow and she saw a tear run down his cheek, and her stomach felt as if it were being gripped in a cold giant hand. Surely he must have a mortal wound. What could she say to him?

'How bad is it, Carl? Are you in a lot of pain?' she asked, putting her hand on his forehead.

His tormented eyes met hers. 'Pull back the covers and look,' he whispered.

Jessy pulled back the covers. Where his right leg had been was a bandaged stump.

In her carefree life Jessy had never seen wounded and suffering men before, but she had been an actress. Nothing of her first shock showed on her face. She looked coolly down at Carl with a little smile on her face, as if she was seeing nothing more serious than a broken toe. 'Is that it?' she said.

His eyes never left hers. 'My leg – it's gone.'

'Well, it looks like you've had this war, Carl. It'll be Canada for you.'

'Helen,' he whispered. 'Helen – Jess, do you – think – she – will – still – love me?'

So that was it. She let her smile widen. 'Why not? Everything else is working all right, isn't it?'

He caught her meaning and a faint blush tinged his white cheeks. 'Yes – of course,' he stammered.

'Well then, what's a leg? Your legs aren't really all that pretty, anyhow, Carl. Not like mine. I'm sure they aren't what made Helen fall in love with you.'

A faint smile touched his mouth. 'Oh, Jess, you're as bad as ever.' Then clutching her hand he said anxiously, 'Jess, do you really think Helen will still love me when she sees me with only one leg?'

Jessy pulled the covers back over him and leaned over so her face was close to his. 'Carl,' she said, looking earnestly into his eyes, 'Helen will love you more than ever now. Stop worrying and just get better. I've got the best news in the world to tell her when I get back to barracks. You're alive and you're in England and you're out of the fighting for good. Now just get well, and remember Helen loves you and she'll always love you – more than anything else in the world.'

She saw the anguish leave his face at her words and he relaxed on the pillow with a smile. Just then the nursing sister came to give him a shot. Jessy leaned over and kissed him on the cheek. 'You'll be seeing Helen soon,' she said.

The nursing sister caught up with her as she was leaving the ward. 'I don't know what you said to him, but he's a different man now. We were worried about him. He didn't seem to come out of the shock.'

Jessy flashed her quick bright smile. 'I just told him his legs aren't all that pretty, anyhow.'

The nursing sister started and looked at her.

Jessy laughed. 'His wife's a friend of mine. I told him she'll still love him with one leg.'

She met Elsie Love coming into the hospital as she was leaving. 'What did they send you out here for, Lovey?'

Elsie said with a superior lift to her head, 'Major Ellis wanted to come out, so, of course, *I* had to bring him.' Elsie was very proud of being the personal driver of Major Ellis. She looked at Jessy and pursed her lips disapprovingly. 'You've got your skirts hitched up again, I see. You know it's against regulations.'

Jessy laughed. 'That rule is just to protect the girls with fat legs,' she said significantly.

Elsie Love sniffed and went on into the hospital, and Jessy went to her station wagon and drove back to London.

Chapter 5

Seething with rage, Elsie sought out the hospital dining room, carefully avoiding going anywhere near the wards where the wounded lay. She detested hospitals, as she detested anything unpleasant. The thought of seeing men all bandaged and wounded, even dying, sent shivers up and down her spine.

How she hated Jessy and Helen, with their resolute laughter in the face of danger and the sly way Jessy mocked at her fears. She wished with all her heart that she could get even with them, especially Helen – Helen who had stolen away her boyfriend.

The way Jessy kept opening the blackout curtains and terrifying her with the sight of those terrible buzz bombs – and her taunting remarks about fat legs . . . She writhed with resentment. How she hated London and that horrible little room where they were all herded together and she hated all her roommates – except perhaps Marjorie. It was pretty hard to hate Marjorie; yet Elsie did resent her beauty and the fact that everyone seemed to love her.

In her life she had become so adept at hiding her feelings that nothing of her seething emotions showed in her face. She simpered pleasantly at the dining-room staff who gave her a cup of coffee and one of those hard little currant buns she hated.

People came and went in the dining room and two hours passed and still Major Ellis had not sent word that he was ready for her to drive him back to London. She ate her lunch by herself in a corner of the dining room, her thoughts seething. Her mind went back over her life as she brooded. She recalled every unpleasant incident that she could ever remember happening to her and her resentment grew like a repressed fire breaking suddenly loose.

It was true that she was the child of very wealthy parents. Her mother was a daughter of one of the most prominent families in Toronto and had been a leading socialite and a great beauty. She made a brilliant marriage to someone as socially prominent and successful as her own people. She and her husband entertained lavishly and travelled abroad and enjoyed the good life.

Then, after they had been married for ten years she found she was pregnant. From the start she made it clear to everyone that she had no intention of letting the advent of a child in any way interfere with her social life. Elsie was provided with a highly competent nursemaid, a lavishly furnished nursery and all the toys any child could possibly want.

Her mother saw as little of her as possible. At a very early age Elsie, who had developed the habit of eavesdropping, over-heard her mother tell a friend, 'What a mistake. I loathe children. I was simply furious when I found I was pregnant and now I've got that fat, stupid little thing, whatever am I to do with her?'

Elsie went back to her nursery, bit her nanny on the leg, took a big bag of cookies and hid under the bed eating them and refusing to come out. All the efforts of the servants to coax her out met with defeat and when her parents came home late at night from the party they had been attending she was still under the bed.

Elsie peeped from under the edge of her satin bedspread at her mother, beautiful in a flowered evening dress, but with an expression of exasperation on her pretty face. 'Wretched little thing,' she heard her mother say. 'Whatever am I to do with her? As soon as she's big enough, I'll certainly pack her off to boarding school. Oh well, just let her sleep under there. It won't hurt her, it's lovely and warm. After all, the carpet must be a foot thick.'

'Yes, and tomorrow morning I'll bring her a new rocking horse – one of those expensive ones that look like a real horse, with a little red saddle and a real mane and tail,' her father said, yawning.

When they were all gone and she was alone in the room, Elsie crept out from under the bed, climbed under the covers and went to sleep. And in the morning a beautiful rocking horse that looked like a real horse, with a red saddle and bridle, was sitting in the nursery. She gave it a vicious kick.

When she was ten years old she was sent away to her first

boarding school, a very exclusive school for girls with ultra-rich parents.

She did not join in the usual sports and activities with the other children. But, contrary to what her mother had said, she was not stupid. In fact she was very clever at learning from books, and as she grew older much of her baby fat dropped away and her face became quite pretty. But she was plump and she felt cumbersome beside the willowy girls. She hated them bitterly.

But she hid her feelings and, except for the small cutting remarks she was in the habit of making to deflate anyone who was feeling particularly happy, she managed to get along with the other girls; yet she was never popular. She still could not explain to herself what had made her join the army.

She was twenty-one and taking a university course as a dietician when she heard about the newly formed Canadian Women's Army Corps. She was uptown in Toronto, after one of her brief visits to her parents. On the street ahead of her she saw a group of CWACs walking in step and laughing together. Something inexplicable compelled her to the recruiting office. She signed the application form and within a week was called up and sent away to take her basic training.

She knew that secretly she had hoped to be accepted into a group of laughing girls, together, like those she had seen on the street. But it did not work out that way. She whined her way all through basic training, complaining about sore feet, the attitude of the NCOs and the officers, the food and the living quarters and anything else she could think of that did not meet with her approval; until to the girls she became 'Poor old Elsie'; even though she was actually only twenty-one.

One day, looking through her documents and discovering her standard of education and who her parents were, her superiors sent her for officer training. But she flunked out of OTC and never knew why. It was another source of bitterness to her. Then they sent her to Currie Barracks at Calgary to take the motor transport course. At last, she felt, her life was bursting into bloom as she had always dreamed it would.

She met Carl Huntley. Bathing in the kindly good-natured smile of this burly infantryman, she was sure he returned her love. Then *Helen* came into the picture.

44

Helen! She stabbed viciously at the watery boiled potato on her plate. What rotten food they had over here. How rotten everything was. Whatever had she been thinking of when she joined the army? But if it hadn't been for Helen everything would have worked out wonderfully. *She* would be Mrs Carl Huntley now, safe at home in Canada waiting for him. Suddenly her feelings overwhelmed her. She pushed back her plate, jumped up from the table and rushed from the dining room. She would go outside and walk around the grounds until Major Ellis was ready to go back to London.

As she was going out the door she met a young nursing sister and stepped aside to let her pass into the mess hall.

The sister paused, observed her distressed face and jumped to the conclusion that she must be Carl Huntley's wife, rushing to his side, after learning from her friend that he was a casualty here at Horsham.

She put her hand out to stop Elsie. 'Are you Mrs Huntley?' she said.

Elsie was stunned. Her face turned white. Before she could say a word the sister, convinced that she was right in her assumption, reached out and patted her arm with a reassuring smile. 'Don't worry, Mrs Huntley. You will be the medicine he needs. I'm sure he'll soon recover now that you're here.' She called to an orderly who was passing, 'Take Mrs Huntley to her husband – Bed 3, Ward C. I have to hurry and have my lunch, we're so short-staffed in there, I hate to be away from the ward. But at least I'll be sure one patient is getting the attention he needs.'

Bewildered and stunned, not knowing what was happening, Elsie followed the orderly. Through the fog in her brain the sister's words had generated, one thing was suddenly clear. Carl was here. Even her fear of going in among the wounded men could not keep her from going to see Carl.

Closing her mind to the sights and sounds and smells of the ward of wounded men, keeping her face averted from them all, she followed the orderly in a daze, ignoring their 'Hello Canada' greetings, until she found herself looking down into the white face of Carl Huntley.

He opened his eyes just as she stopped beside his bed. They lit up as he recognized her. Weakly he held up his hand to her and opened his mouth to speak. Looking into his eyes – blue eyes she had been seeing in her dreams for more than two years – trembling, she took his hand and leaned over the bed to hear his faint words.

'Helen,' he whispered. 'Have you seen Helen? Are you in London with Helen, too?'

The venom she had kept locked deep inside her came bubbling up in her brain. His first word to her had to be *Helen*. He couldn't even say *Elsie* first. He couldn't even say, 'I'm glad to see you, Elsie' – just '*Helen*'. And she had been so overjoyed to see his face again and know that he was alive. She drew a deep shuddering breath, looking into his eyes with a carefully concerned expression. She did not answer him.

'Helen,' he repeated anxiously. 'Have you seen Helen, Elsie?'

She answered very carefully and slowly, turning her head away as if distressed and reluctant to let the words come out. 'Yes, Carl, I'm in London with Helen. We share a room.'

Fear leapt up in his eyes at her evasive manner. 'She's all right isn't she, Elsie?' he said, clutching her hand. 'Helen is all right, isn't she?'

'Oh, yes – there's nothing *wrong* with Helen.' Elsie spoke in a low reluctant voice, keeping her head turned away, as if the words were being dragged from her against her will.

His grip tightened on her hand. 'Do you know I have a leg off?' he whispered fearfully.

Elsie felt horror rush through her. Her face blanched and she thought she was going to vomit. She wanted to bolt from the room.

Carl's feverish eyes saw her reaction. 'Helen,' he whispered in an anguished voice. 'Oh, Elsie, do you think Helen will still love me when she knows my leg is gone?'

Elsie hesitated for a moment, then she turned her eyes deliberately away from his tormented face. He tugged at her hand, his feverish eyes beseeching her answer.

At last she turned and looked down at him. Forcing her eyes to fill with tears, she spoke as if with a great effort. 'Oh, Carl, she should have told you.'

'She should have told me what, Elsie? What should Helen have told me?'

The terror in his voice almost unnerved her, but she forced

herself to go on, speaking in a low distressed tone. 'Oh, Carl, I told her it wasn't fair – but she was afraid. You know how kind Helen is – she – she couldn't help herself. You were married for such a little while before you left – and you were gone such a long time, Carl and – and he was her boyfriend before she ever knew you. When he came back and started to take her to the Sally Ann for coffee with him, I know she was just lonely. And then she – she couldn't help herself, Carl.'

'You mean,' he panted, looking at her like somone from a torture rack, 'you mean that Helen – is – in – love – with – someone – else?'

She forced the tears to spill from her eyes, down her cheeks. 'Oh, Carl, I knew I shouldn't tell you.' She turned her head aside.

'But she's been writing to me every day. How can she be in love with someone else?' he asked in a choked, bewildered voice.

Elsie let a little sob escape her. 'Oh Carl, what have I done?' she wailed, squeezing his hand in both of hers. 'But I thought you should know. I told her – but she wouldn't write and tell you. She was afraid. You were in the fighting and if you were killed she didn't want it on her conscience. She said if you came back and the war was over and you were safely out of it, then she would face telling you. I told her she should tell you the truth.'

For a moment he stared up at her in dumb horror, then he closed his eyes and his head fell sideways on the pillow.

One of the nursing sisters came up at that moment to tell Elsie that Major Ellis wanted her to take him back to London now. She took one look at Carl's white face on the pillow and concern leapt into her eyes. She seized his wrist and felt for the pulse. 'He's taken a bad turn,' she said. 'He's unconscious.' She turned to the orderly at the next bed. 'Quick, get the doctor over here,' she ordered.

Elsie turned and fled from the ward, terrified all at once by what she had done. *What if she had killed Carl!* If only he had spoken her name first. The plan had come to her so suddenly as she looked at him lying there. *If I can make him believe that Helen doesn't love him any more, he'll turn to me*, she had thought. *He's my boyfriend*. It was she who stole him from me. *Now I'll get him back again*.

But now that she saw the result of what she had done, she felt like a child who has set fire to a house, not realizing the power of

47

the leaping flames until she sees them consuming everything.

Her guilty thoughts followed her like hounds all the way back to London. But after she had garaged her car and was on her way back to barracks, they took another turn. She thought back on her own loveless life and how much she had wanted Carl and how the other girl had come between them and she had been pushed aside, as always; and of the way the other girls laughed at her fears, and suddenly she thought viciously: *If he dies, at least Helen won't have him.*

The dreadful thought sent fresh fear coursing through her. Everything was so terrifying these days. Thank heaven, for once the air raid siren had not sounded; but she knew night time would bring the dreaded buzz bombs back again and she shivered, picturing what would happen if one landed on their barracks and the bricks and rubble came tumbling down on her.

Chapter 6

Ashley had the car hood back. The night was clear and soft and the gentle breeze lifted her brown hair as she drove expertly along the winding, tree-lined country road towards Medhurst Hall. Colin was quiet beside her, drinking in the familiar road, the twists and turns and the intoxicating warm country smell. How peaceful the sky looked, with its host of friendly stars winking benignly down at them.

She spoke at last. 'Are you tired, Colin dear?'

Guiltily he pulled himself out of his silence. 'Oh, no. I was just rather enjoying the night, really. Would you please stop at Enderby for a few minutes before we go on to your house?'

'Oh yes, of course. Did you want to pick up something, Colin?'

He laughed gently. 'The Enderby ring. Have you forgotten tonight is the night I put it on your finger? I don't carry it with me, you know.'

She did not answer as she negotiated a difficult curve. Soon they turned in at the lodge gates and drove up the long winding drive to the massive entrance doors of Enderby Hall.

'It's so late. It's a shame to disturb poor Nanny. She'll be up in her sitting room having her cup of tea,' Colin said.

'Let's not disturb her, then. Let's use the secret passage, like we did when we were children.'

'What a jolly idea. It's ages since I've been in there.'

Holding hands and laughing like excited children, they went around to the north side of the big house to where a small rose garden, surrounded by a high stone wall joined a wing of the house. Breathing in the sweet scent, they walked up the path among the rose bushes to the well-remembered small door concealed behind trailing ivy on the wall. Using his torch, Colin

49

found the loose brick behind which the key was always hidden and opened the ancient oak door, and they stepped into the concealed passage that led to the library.

Colin thought, as they walked the short distance along the musty stone tunnel: I wonder what Marjorie would look like if she was with me? He remembered with an inward smile how her eyes had widened when she heard Blaine call him 'Lord Enderby'. A secret passage would certainly set her romancing about knights in armour. *But she would not be seeing the secret passage, nor any of the other treasures and sights of Enderby*: he would not be seeing Marjorie again.

They came to the end of the passage and he pressed the remembered spot on the wall. A section of the heavy bookcase slid open and they entered the library. Colin went to the small wall safe concealed in a bookcase and opened it. From among the family jewels glittering inside, he selected the ruby and diamond ring that, traditionally, the eldest son and heir placed on the finger of his future bride. The huge ruby gleamed blood-red in his hand and the two great, flanking diamonds flashed white in the broad band of heavy gold. It was a ring made by a master craftsman.

Ashley started. It was the ring Raif would have been slipping on her finger, if it were not for Dunkirk!

As Colin turned to place it on her finger, suddenly the thought intruded: *I wonder how it would look on Marjorie's finger?*

Ashley was watching his face closely. 'What's the matter, Colin?' she asked softly.

Colin forced a smile to his lips. 'Nothing. Really. Nothing at all, dear.'

She continued her long searching look into his face. 'There *is* something Colin. I've known that face too long not to know when there's something wrong. I've sensed it since I met you at the station. There's something on your mind that was not there the last time we were together.'

Colin met the questioning look in her deep hazel eyes and felt suddenly transparent. Things were not going as they should. This was where he was supposed to kiss her and slip the ring on her finger, not be standing here gawking at her like a schoolboy caught out in some prank. Suddenly words deserted him. He stood holding the ring in his hand and looking down into her face.

She laughed gently and put her hand on his arm. 'Dear old Beau. You never were any good at hiding your feelings, you know. Raif and I always knew what you were up to. Now sit down on the chair there and tell me what this is all about.'

Obediently he sank down on to the heavy leather chair and she perched on the arm.

'You've met a girl, haven't you?' she said. She placed her fingers lightly on his lips as he started to speak. 'Don't look so distressed. No need for you to go to the block for the honour of the Enderbys, Beau Geste. You see I – I . . .' She walked across to the fireplace, turned and stood for a moment with her back to it, looking at him, before returning to stand with her hand resting affectionately on his shoulder.

She went on, speaking softly, 'I've been thinking about us too, Colin. And it won't do, you know. Remember we were all in here having tea the morning they brought the news about Raif? But we knew, didn't we? We knew when we woke up that morning, because we had both seen the same thing in the night, hadn't we?'

'*Athelstane!*' he whispered.

'No children were ever closer than you and I and Raif. That day down by the Pond when you and I were drawn together, it was really Raif we were both wanting. I knew it as soon as you'd gone, and I've wanted to tell you since but I – I'd given you my pledge and I wasn't quite sure what you really felt for me.'

'You didn't want to hurt me.'

She smiled and nodded, 'Just as you don't want to hurt me. You see we do love each other Colin, but it's not *that* kind of love, and wherever we went, Raif would always be there with us, and we just can't sleep three in a bed.'

'No. Beastly uncomfortable.'

'And now, if you were thinking of another girl that would make four.'

'We *would* be rather packed.'

Suddenly they both laughed and hugged each other and everything was very right between them as it always had been; and Colin had the strange feeling that somewhere, not too far away, Raif was laughing with them.

51

'Put the ring back in the safe Colin, and let's go, and you can tell me about your new girlfriend on the way to my birthday party.'

'There really isn't that much to tell,' he said as he locked the ring back in the safe. As they drove up the hill to Medhurst Hall, he told her about his encounter with the Canadian army girl.

Ashley said earnestly as they were about to leave the car to join his family and hers, waiting expectantly at her party, 'I have a feeling, Colin, that this girl will be the special one for you. Go back to London and see her again and don't waste any time about it.'

'My parents are going to be beastly disappointed, you know. I'm sure they've been secretly hoping we would announce our engagement tonight.'

'Mine too. You didn't say anything to yours, did you?'

'No, did you?'

'No, but they have a way of sensing things. I've noticed them watching me since the day we came back from the Pond after you proposed.'

'Mine, too. Like hawks.'

'Parent hawks, guarding the fluffy little hawklings in the nest.'

He caught her hand in his. 'Come on then, little hawkling. Let's go and dip our beaks in that champagne.'

Laughing like children, they went in to join the others.

Jessy arrived back at the garage in Chelsea to find another out-of-town detail waiting for her. It was after eight o'clock before she finally reached 43 Company at Sussex Square. All day she had hardly been able to contain her impatience to tell Helen the good news. But to her great disappointment there was no one in the room but Elsie, huddled in her bed with her face turned to the wall, apparently asleep.

Jessy went over and shook her. 'Hey Elsie, wake up.'

Elsie stirred and turned a flushed face up to her.

'Where is Helen?' Jessy asked.

'I don't know,' Elsie answered sullenly. 'I haven't seen her all day.' She shook off Jessy's hand and turned her face back to the wall again.

Jessy looked at her curiously. 'What's the matter with you,

Lovey? You look as if you'd seen a whole covey of ghosts doing a tapdance around your bed.'

Elsie hunched down further under the covers. 'Go away, Jessy,' she muttered. 'Leave me alone. I've got a terrible headache and I don't want to talk to anyone. I think I'm catching the flu, or something.'

Jessy put her hand on the other girl's forehead. 'Whew, you do feel a bit hot. Do you want me to see if I can spear you a cup of tea, or something, from the mess hall?'

'No. Just leave me alone,' Elsie said angrily.

She's probably just worked herself up because she's so scared of the raids, Jessy thought as she sat on her own bed. She would not tell anyone about seeing Carl until she had first told Helen. It did not occur to her that Elsie knew already that Carl was at Horsham. She knew Elsie, and she knew nothing in the world would induce her to go into a ward full of wounded men.

After a short interval she heard footsteps on the stairs. She looked up eagerly but it was Bonny, dressed in her baseball uniform, her cheeks flushed and her eyes sparkling. 'Boy, did we ever beat the shit out of them today, Jess. You should have seen us. I pitched a shut-out. Our gang were knocking themselves out hollering, but you never saw anything like those Limeys! All they ever say is "hurrah", or "well played", when their team does something. It's no wonder they can't play baseball. Moose Morrison was umpiring. Some of his calls were lousy. But those Limeys just muttered "bad show", or something like that.'

Jessy laughed and Bonny went on excitedly, 'Our gang nearly bust the umpire's head open when he called Polly out at home base when they figured she was safe—and she *wasn't!* They were all hollering, "Kill the umpire", and Moose was standing there just grinning at everybody and not giving a shit. That Moose is really something.'

'Oh, oh,' Jessy said. 'Who is Moose?'

'He's the brigadier's new driver. He's a sergeant, and he was with the Loyal Edmonton Regiment in Italy, but he was wounded and he's got a category now and he can't get back in the fighting; so they sent him here to CMHQ to drive the brigadier. He's really cheesed off about it. He says all these officers at CMHQ are a bunch of old women with shit in their veins. He says, if anyone ever fired off a gun near them, they'd drown in their own pee.'

Jessy laughed. 'Moose sounds like a poet. You didn't tell him he isn't going to have anything to drive the brigadier in, did you?'

'Naw. I was too busy fighting with him over some of his decisions. We had a real rhubarb out there.'

'Have you seen Helen?' Jessy asked, changing the subject.

'She had a call to go to work just before I left for the ball game, darn it. She was going to come and watch me play. None of you was there to watch us play, except Marjorie for a little while.'

At that moment, Helen walked into the room. She took off her cap and ran her fingers through her bright red curls. Her face looked white and tired. 'Whew, what a day,' she said, sinking down on the edge of her bed. 'The wounded are pouring in from the coast and the hospitals are running short of blood. They didn't have enough drivers on duty so they called me in to take blood out to Twenty-three General.' She wiped the perspiration from her brow with the back of her hand. 'I – I went all through the wards. Those poor boys. I thought – maybe – Carl . . .' Her words trailed off.

Jessy crossed over to her and put her hand on her shoulder, and Helen looked up into her face inquiringly. Jessy flashed her best smile down at her. 'You went to the wrong hospital,' she said. 'I've got some good news for you, Helen.'

Helen's blue eyes flew open. 'You – you mean – Carl?' she whispered.

Jessy nodded. 'I saw him. I drove blood out to Horsham,' she said. 'He's wounded. But he's all right, Helen. He's *all right!*'

Helen's florid face turned ash white. The freckles stood out across her nose. She clutched Jessy's arm. 'Oh, Jess! How – how – bad – is he?'

Jessy continued to look at her with her wide reassuring smile. 'Well, if he was in the habit of swinging the lead, I'd say he wouldn't need to this time. He's really picked up one to keep him out for the duration.'

'Tell me, Jess.' Helen's grip tightened on Jessy's arm. 'How bad is it?'

Jessy sat beside her friend and put her arm around her

trembling shoulders. 'His right leg is amputated, Helen,' she said gently.

'Oh, God!' Helen panted. 'Jesus! And He died to save me,' she added quickly, making the sign of the cross. 'Poor Carl!' She drew quick shuddering breaths while Jessy held her shoulders tightly. Then she straightened up. 'At least he's out of it now,' she said. 'Jess, is that all? Are you sure there's no other wound?'

'That's all, except worrying himself sick for fear you might not like the looks of him with one leg,' Jessy drawled.

'As if I cared about that. Oh Jess, he must be suffering terribly.'

'Carl's a pretty tough guy. He can handle it,' Jessy said coolly. 'It will take more than losing a leg to keep him down.'

Helen jumped up and grabbed her cap. 'I must go to him. I must go and see Captain Burns.' Colour was rushing back into her face.

'Don't go barging in on old Hot Burns without someone announcing you,' Jessy said with a grin. 'She wouldn't like you to catch her cuddled up playing toesies with Major Farrow.'

It was common gossip around 43 Company that their officer commanding was having a steamy love affair with a married major from CMHQ.

'Don't worry,' Helen said as she shot out of the room.

Bonny had not known any of her roommates until she met them on the ship coming over. She had been raised in a small lumber town in British Columbia and she had been posted as a driver in Edmonton Alberta. But although she had never met Carl, she had shared Jessy's concern for Helen's husband, fighting with the Calgary Highlanders in Normandy; and she listened with delight as Jessy told Helen her husband was safely back in England.

'Carl's back in England!' she said, thumping Jessy on the back so hard she almost knocked the wind out of her. 'Great news, Jess. I'm glad those Nazi Shit Pots didn't get Helen's husband. Hey, won't Marjorie be glad to hear about Carl?'

'Where *is* Marjorie?' Jessy asked, getting her breath back. 'She didn't have a call back to work, did she?'

Bonny grew excited. 'Oh, I was going to tell you. No, she didn't go to work. She went to my ball game and she was on the sidelines cheering to beat the band, and then when I was waiting to go up to bat I saw this Limey air force officer with ribbons all over his chest come up to her. Was he ever handsome! He looked like Tyrone Power and Charles Boyer all rolled into one. He was the best-looking Limey I ever saw. Marjorie's face lit up like a bucket of cream when she saw him. I never saw her look like that before. I got called up to bat right then – that was when I hit the two-baser and got into the fight with Moose – and when I got back, I saw Marjorie walking off arm in arm with that Limey airman towards the Serpentine.'

'Ah ha!' Jessy said. 'I knew our little Marj had something on her mind when she came in last night. I bet she met him in that pub when the Brig's car got blown up.' Suddenly she remembered Elsie and looked quickly across at the other girl's bed. *I wonder how she feels about Carl being back?* she thought. But Elsie was, apparently, fast asleep. 'Elsie isn't feeling too good,' she told Bonny.

'Aw,' Bonny said contemptuously. 'The little creep is just scared out of her pants by those old doodle-bugs, most likely.'

'Haven't been any over today, have there?' Jessy said.

'No. The siren went a couple of times but nothing came over. They get 'em at the coast when the weather is clear like this. Hey, I got to get changed back into my monkey suit. I'm going out.'

'Where to?'

'Moose is taking me pub-crawling.'

Chapter 7

Watching the other girls all hurrying off in the morning, Marjorie almost wished she was going to work with them. But it was her turn to have Saturday and Sunday off. She had nothing planned for the weekend, other than loafing around barracks reading her book and writing a letter home or, perhaps, listening to the wireless.

Perhaps she would stroll down by the Serpentine in Hyde Park. She loved watching the graceful white swans floating on its smooth surface.

She had hoped she might go to see some of the sights of London, if she could have interested any of her roommates in such an expedition. She had not yet been to the Tower, or Westminster Abbey, or seen Number 10 Downing Street. She was intrigued with Buckingham Palace when she drove past it each day on her way to Moon's Garage from Chelsea, or going to Canadian Military Headquarters at Trafalgar Square, but she wanted to see the changing of the guard. The soapbox men holding forth at Speaker's Corner at Marble Arch fascinated her with their dry English humour and ready answers for the hecklers who hung about listening to them.

Somehow this morning she could not get interested in anything. The unusual mood of the previous night still held her in its grip. A strange lonely yearning she could not comprehend had descended on her usually happy spirits. Her mind kept returning to Colin: the curve of his mouth, the twinkle in his brown eyes, his drawly, teasing English voice. She kept going over the things they had said to each other and remembering the warm happiness of sitting with him in the pub.

Stop this nonsense, Marjorie Hatfield, she told herself sternly. You're twenty-four years old and a soldier and you're acting like a sixteen-year-old with her first crush.

Maybe I'm slow starting, she thought. She had never had a real crush on anyone in her life. Most of the girls she grew up with were already married and had children. They simply moved from one farm to another and continued leading much the same lives as before. They were all accustomed already to cooking and sewing and doing other household chores, as well as milking cows and tending chickens and pigs.

Marjorie had been much sought after by the local boys; but although she enjoyed dancing with them at the schoolhouse dances, playing ball and skating with them, she had never wanted to marry any of them and they had gradually drifted to other girls who were more susceptible to their charms.

She had finished high school in the small prairie town of Sandridge, some forty miles east of Calgary. Then her father became ill and she had stayed to help run the farm and care for him. She had helped her brother to plant the crops, she had stooked the grain and milked the cows and hauled grain to the elevator in Sandridge in a big horse-drawn wagon.

Her father had come with his parents to a farm near Kamloops in British Columbia after his high-born English family lost their money and estates in bad financial dealings. He had homesteaded in the Kamloops district and it was here that he had met soft-spoken beautiful Helga Sorenson, a schoolteacher from the Sandridge district in Alberta, vacationing at her uncle's homestead. Her beautiful blonde Nordic looks and laughing manner captivated the stern Jonathan Hatfield and she was intrigued with his patrician manner.

After they were married he went with her to Alberta and took up a farm next to her parents'. It was here that Marjorie and her brother Eric were born.

Marjorie grew up loving the broad expanse of prairie that was her home, with the great ridge of the Rocky Mountains rimming the sky to the west, a hundred miles away. The Hatfields were not rich, but there was always plenty of food and she always had a good horse to ride. Best of all, there were always good books to read.

It had been cold riding the four miles to school in the winter, but Cochise, her little Indian pony, was sure-footed and fast and she loved him.

She had enjoyed the snowball fights and playing fox and geese, and the wonderful Christmas concerts. On weekends there had been the fun of skating on the sloughs and making bonfires with her friends.

When she was a little older there had been parties on Friday night at friends' houses in the district, and the schoolhouse dances.

And there was the school fair, held in Sandridge each autumn. She had enjoyed the simple country life and her friends, but always at the bottom of her heart she knew that this was not the life she wanted for the rest of her days. She felt a restlessness and a desire to see other places and other people.

During the carefree days when she was growing up, although the depression had suddenly hit and money had virtually disappeared, everything had been peaceful. The thought of war had been the farthest thing from all their young minds. War was something that happened a long time ago in history books, when Germany had a kaiser and there was no League of Nations.

And then had come ominous rumblings from far away across the sea in Europe. First had come Mussolini, and then the German with the moustache, until Europe was full of goose-stepping soldiers and a dark cloud was rolling over the horizon, coming closer and closer to her world until it burst one day in 1939 and the unthinkable happened – Britain and then Canada were at war again with Germany. It wasn't history now. But it couldn't be real – the grain was too golden in the fields and the chinook wind too scented with the smell of the harvest, and the big, romantic harvest moon too peaceful in the sky. Everything was as it always had been in September.

Then boys she knew suddenly appeared in air force blue, or navy – it was funny how many prairie boys joined the navy. Perhaps the ocean and the prairie were alike. And there was the khaki of the army. Mothers sat and knitted scarves for boys who were far away in England or out on the North Atlantic. There was a shortage of farm help. And there was a sober silence in farm homes where there had been laughter.

When the Canadian Women's Army Corps was formed, Marjorie knew she had to join.

She had been nurtured on tales of British traditions of valour and honour and she knew she must go with the others to do her bit for the empire and for the cause of freedom. Apart from her feelings of patriotism, she was thrilled at being a part of something big and heroic. This was her youth. This war was happening to her. She wanted to march with the others of her generation.

Her parents understood when she joined the army – almost. If it had been their son they would have understood completely, but he would not be accepted into the armed forces. He was a farmer and needed to grow food and, anyway, an old injury sustained when he had been in a runaway on a mower had left him with a limp.

It was hard for them to accept the idea of their daughter becoming a soldier. That was not something that ladies did. Ladies knitted, or rolled bandages, or made quilts, or sent parcels to soldiers, or married them. But ladies did not become soldiers themselves.

However, they were forced to accept the idea when Marjorie quietly informed them one day that she was accepted into the CWAC and would leave for basic training in the armouries at Calgary that week.

She remembered, with a guilty twinge, their faces when she told them she was on draft for overseas. When the actual day came for her to say goodbye, her unemotional mother clung to her with choking sobs wracking her body and her stern father held her against him and stroked her fair hair with his frail hand, as if she were a child. He tried three times to speak before words would come.

'Marjorie, my dear child,' he said at last, 'take care of yourself away over there so far from our protection. Remember the things we've taught you. Say your prayers every night – and don't let anyone persuade you that in war time it's right to do things you would not do in times of peace. Your mother and I will always be thinking of you and praying for you.'

Marjorie read the meaning of his words. He was telling her, delicately, that she must remain a virgin – that any relationship with a man outside of marriage was a sin.

Well, certainly, she did not want any other relationship for herself. Since she had been old enough to dream the dreams of young girls she had cherished the picture of herself floating

60

white and virginal to her waiting Prince Charming at the altar. Then, after a suitable length of time, they would have beautiful children and live happily ever after.

It was a dream shared by most of her girlfriends and for many of them it had partially come true, except for the white wedding part. No one in depression times could afford a big white wedding. They had slipped away to Calgary secretly and come home to announce to their friends that they were married. Then the fun started. The whole neighbourhood got together and gave them a shower and dance in the country school, and there was also the excitement of the chivaree. All the other girls envied the blushing bride, standing beside her self-conscious groom, after they had, supposedly, been surprised and roused from their bed by the beating of pots and pans and the blowing of car horns.

But that had been before the war started. When the goodbyes had been said and it was time for her to leave, her brother and her little niece and nephew drove her to the railway station to catch the train back to her barracks in Calgary.

There were two others beside herself in uniform – young district boys home on leave – waiting to catch the train.

Her brother, self-conscious in his worn work clothes, beside her uniform, kissed her goodbye and said, 'It's not right, little sister. It should be me going over there and you staying here.'

She knew how deeply it hurt him to see her in the army when he had to stay on the farm. 'I wouldn't be any good at looking after Dad and Mother,' she said, hugging him. 'And I couldn't grow that grain they need so badly to win this war, and I couldn't fix the binder or haul feed for the livestock when it's forty below. It's you that has the tough job. I'm just having all the fun.'

Her little nephew said, 'I'm going to be a soldier when I grow up. Will I be grown up before the war is over, Aunty Marjorie?'

'Well, I certainly hope not,' she said, kissing him.

Her niece said solemnly, 'Are they going to shoot you, Little Corporal?'

'Hush,' her brother said.

Marjorie laughed. 'No, it's really quite safe where I'm going. They don't let soldier girls go where there's any shooting.'

This morning, sitting on the edge of her bed, watching Bonny

61

making ready to go to play ball, she thought: *They don't have any rules about buzz bombs, though*, and a wry smile touched her lips.

'What are you smiling at, Marj?' Bonny asked.

'I was thinking about something my little niece said when I said goodbye to her to come over here.'

'You're always thinking,' Bonny said. 'What are you going to do today?'

'Oh, I don't know. I thought I might take a little stroll down by the Serpentine and look at the swans.'

'Aw, why don't you come and watch us play ball? None of you have ever been to any of my ball games. Come on, Marj.'

Although she was more in the mood for solitude, Bonny looked so eager that Marjorie could not refuse.

'What were you doing before you joined up?' she asked Bonny, who was bouncing along beside her as they walked through Hyde Park towards the baseball diamond at Marble Arch.

'I only joined up two years ago when I turned nineteen. Before that I just went to school. My dad is a lumberjack and Mom cooks in the lumber camp – you should taste her food, not like that shit they give us over here. There isn't anyone in the world can cook like Mom. After I left school, I sort of bummed around for a year and played ball – we just missed winning the BC softball championship – and I stayed home and helped look after my little brothers and sisters. There's eight of us in the family and I was Mom's bull cook. Then, when they lowered the age to nineteen for the CWACs I just joined up and left my sister, who's a year younger than me, to be Mom's bull cook.'

How I envy you, Marjorie thought, watching the other girl's glowing face. She was sure no troublesome thoughts writhed and twisted and fought each other inside Bonny's head. Clear-eyed and cheerful, she looked out at life, eager for whatever it might bring and never doubting it would be good, as the present was.

Marjorie wished life to her was as simple and uncomplicated. Conflicting thoughts were always welling up to do battle inside her. Guilt tugged at her because she enjoyed the companionship and the fun and the jokes of the CWAC. She was stimulated by the excitement of being in something big together with the other

62

girls, with driving the army vehicles – doing things Canadian women had never done before. And the people she met . . . They were like no people she had ever met at home on the farm.

Sometimes she had almost forgotten there was a war on – until they lined up the trucks on the square at Currie Barracks and the boys in battledress piled in on their way to the railway station, on draft for overseas. Then the young men she had sat and laughed and joked with at the Sally Ann canteen, just outside the barracks gate, were not there any more. Like that awful day Helen's husband left . . .

Here in England you couldn't forget there was a war on. You felt its black shadow hanging over the crumbled buildings, and you heard its message of death in the whining sirens and the earth-shaking explosions. And rumours were flying of another deadly weapon to be hurled against Britain – the V-2. No one knew what it would be, but it would come any day now, descending like the black angel of death from the sky.

And all the while you knew that, just across a short few miles of water, men were dying in blood and noise and agony, and the wounded were pouring in a relentless stream into the military hospitals here in the south of England.

It was all so mad. As if a lot of irresponsible children, with deadly toys, were thoughtlessly destroying each other. She had watched with pity the strain on Helen's face as news of the casualties in Normandy came to them on the wireless. Marjorie thought guiltily that she was glad she had no one of her own in the fighting. She was glad her brother was exempt from military service. She was glad he did not have to go to war and kill people. But she felt she was not making any sacrifice.

The face of Colin Enderby flashed into her mind. His short forty-eight-hour pass would soon be ended and then he would be back over Germany, escorting bombers in his Spitfire. She was glad that he was not a bomber pilot. The hell the Germans had unleashed on London and Coventry and other British cities was being paid back to them now. She knew they had brought the terrible retribution on themselves, but she could not bear to think of Colin dropping bombs on helpless babies and old frightened people. Colin who had such kind, laughing eyes.

'Hey, Marj, wake up. You're thinking again,' Bonny said. 'You're awful dreamy since last night. If I didn't know you haven't been anywhere to meet anyone, I'd say you were in love.'

Marjorie laughed, but to her consternation she felt her cheeks growing red. But Bonny didn't notice. They were arriving at the ball diamond, where a crowd was gathering already.

'See ya in a little while,' she told Marjorie as she dashed off to join her team.

Marjorie found herself a spot to stand, along the base line between home plate and first base, where she could get a good view of Bonny pitching against the opposing ATS team.

In spite of her sombre mood, Marjorie found herself drawn into the game. It was impossible to be anything else watching Bonny. Her enthusiasm and determination to win inspired the whole team. Marjorie laughed heartily at some of her antics. She protested violently when the huge man umpiring called one of the Canadian side out, and she cheered loudly when he called out one of the ATS.

Marjorie wondered what Colin would think of Canadian softball. The watching Canadians were as violently enthusiastic as Bonny – shouting and cheering for their own team and jeering at the other team. They threatened to kill the umpire every time he made a decision they disliked.

The English bystanders looked on with a sort of amused tolerance, giving the occasional gentle cheer. Marjorie knew cricket was really their game, and good sportsmanship did not include threatening to murder the umpire. During the last half of the third inning, Bonny stood beside her chatting.

'We've got those Limeys going,' she said. 'They haven't had a base hit yet. You watch me, Marj. I'm going to pitch a shut-out game. Hey, they're calling me. I gotta go bat.'

She dashed off to home plate just as the air raid warning started its banshee wailing. A voice at Marjorie's elbow said, 'I'm so glad they haven't hauled you off to the Tower, little soldier girl.'

Her heart gave a leap and she felt the blood rush hotly to her cheeks. Her legs felt as if they were going to give way under her. Shaking, she turned to look up into Colin's smiling eyes.

For a moment she looked at him with unrestrained joy, then realizing what she was doing, she babbled to cover her confusion, 'My friend is just going in to bat.'

Ignoring the warning notes of the alert, Bonny gave a little wave towards Marjorie as she stepped up to the plate and the ATS pitcher threw the ball. Bonny drove it into left field, rushed to first base and rounded it, heading for second at full speed. The outfielder sent the ball sizzling in and the second-base girl caught it as Bonny slid in, and tagged her. The umpire jerked his thumb, calling her out.

The roar from the watching Canadians almost drowned out the wail of the siren as they swarmed out on to the diamond, shouting and waving their arms.

Colin laughed delightedly.

'I say, I think war has broken out between Britain and Canada,' he said. 'If you don't feel that you really have to get into this mêlée, Marjorie, will you come for a little walk with me?' Taking her hand in his, he tucked it firmly under his arm, smiling down into her eyes.

With the sound of the rhubarb fading behind them, he led her off towards the Serpentine.

Chapter 8

Marjorie was in such a happy fog as she walked away from the ball game with Colin, she forgot to listen for the threatening buzzing in the sky, and the peaceful blue was undisturbed. If any of Hitler's toys penetrated the coastal defences, they fell somewhere else than Hyde Park.

'Please, let's go and look at Peter Pan's statue,' Marjorie said. 'I love Peter Pan – the little boy who never grew up.'

Colin smiled down at her. 'When I look into your eyes shining like that, Marjorie, I think perhaps that you're the little girl who never grew up.'

She flushed and turned her face away. 'I'm sorry if I seem childish to you,' she said stiffly.

Colin laughed and drew her hand closer into the shelter of his arm. 'You know, you're awfully pretty when you blush like that. You're a funny little soldier girl, Marjorie. You don't drink and you blush.'

She tried to pull her hand away, but Colin held tightly to her fingers.

'Don't be angry,' he said. 'I'm only teasing you. We all have a bit of Peter Pan in us. To be able to keep the wonder and delight of life through all this is a rare and wonderful gift, you know. Come, let's go and see Peter Pan, and the swans. Don't you love the swans? When we were children and we drove up to London, one of our treats for the day was to come to the Serpentine and watch them.'

The happy glow in his face transmitted itself to her and she smiled back at him. But in a moment she was blushing again.

A soldier and his girlfriend were lying under a big oak tree. He had her skirt pulled up and was on top of her openly copulating, without the slightest concern about several other couples sprawling about with arms and legs entwined in various stages of lovemaking, or people strolling by.

Marjorie kept her face turned rigidly away as Colin and she skirted them.

The sight was common in Hyde Park since the war, but Marjorie could not get used to it. She had been amazed when she first went for a walk in the park, to see a London bobby standing by with stolid indifference while such flagrant immorality went on all around him.

She had spoken about it to Jessy.

Jessy squeezed her arm and said soothingly, 'It's the only place they have. And they might not be here to do it tomorrow.'

'He looks so happy and free,' Marjorie said, as she and Colin gazed up at the statue of Peter Pan.

'But a bit as if he could cause a spot of trouble too, don't you think?'

'Oh, yes, especially if that nasty Captain Hook came along.'

'Yes, he definitely has a firm cut to his chin. Reminds me of young Attwater, who used to batter me about at Eton if I tried to get him to knuckle under.'

'Oh, did you go to Eton?' Marjorie cried delightedly. 'I drove out that way with one of the girls on a detail the other day and we saw some of the Eton boys in the village. It was in the morning and they were all dressed in long-tailed cut-away coats and black silk top hats. Did you dress like that too?'

'Rather,' he answered. 'It was our school uniform, don't you know.'

Marjorie tittered. 'When I went to school I wore a pair of boy's blue denim pants and red felt boots, in the winter and a mackinaw coat and a red woollen toque my mother knitted for me, with a matching scarf. The school was over four miles from our house and I rode there on Cochise – my horse. He was an Indian pony. The schoolhouse was just one room, with a cloakroom for the boys on one end and a cloakroom for the girls on the other. At lunch time we sat at our desks and ate frozen sandwiches when the weather was really cold.'

'Oh, dear, you're making me feel dreadfully guilty about all my privileges. While you were roughing it like that, with the wolves snapping at your heels, I was playing cricket and going in for boat races on the Thames.'

She looked up into his face and saw that his brown eyes were twinkling mischievously at her, and she laughed. 'Oh, don't think we had a bad time on the farm. We had lots of fun. After we'd eaten our lunch at noon, we went outside and played fox and geese and made snow forts and had snowball fights. Then, after school, mostly on weekends, we used to clear the snow off the ice on the sloughs and skate. We made big bonfires to keep us warm while we were putting on our skates and taking them off.'

'And what did you do in the summer?' Colin asked, watching her glowing face.

'In summer we played baseball every noon hour, and then on some Fridays the richer farmers picked us up in their trucks and drove us to a neighbouring school to play against them, and some Fridays they came to our school to play us.'

'And what about when you became a young lady?'

'Well, in our teens we went to card parties and dances at the schoolhouses, and sometimes in the little towns.' She wrinkled up her nose. 'Only usually our parents wouldn't let us go to the town dances because sometimes city boys would come to them from Calgary and they didn't want us to mix with them because they might be too fast. We used to drive for miles in our old Ford cars to go to dances on Friday night. No one had much money. They charged the boys twenty-five cents to get in, and the girls supplied cake or sandwiches, and some of the boys played music.'

'And I suppose you had lots of young men dancing attendance on you?'

Marjorie dimpled up at him. 'Well, they weren't exactly dancing attendance, but there were lots of young men to dance with and in the winter time lots of young people used to come to our house and play cards and have tea and sandwiches and cake. And then in summer they would come round on Sunday on their horses, and sometimes on other evenings when I was milking the cows they'd turn up and help me – or help feed the pigs. We kept pigs, you know. I nearly always fed them when the seeding time, or harvest time was there and the men were busy in the fields. My mother's afraid of cows and pigs.'

'Really, what an amazing girl you are,' Colin said admiringly. 'You have a sort of Dresden china look about you – as if you had never done anything more strenuous than pour tea in some elegant drawing room. And here I find you in London driving in the middle of the raids. And you've ridden horses and – and fed pigs and milked cows and all that sort of thing. But, tell me, little Marjorie, how is it that you never married one of those young men who used to squire you around the country?'

Marjorie turned this over soberly for a moment and then she looked up into his face and said honestly, 'I wasn't in love with any of them.'

He squeezed her hand and looking deeply down into her wide blue eyes asked, 'And what kind of a man *would* you love, Marjorie?'

She dropped her eyes from his, suddenly unsure of herself, feeling colour rise to her face. Then she said, laughing lightly, 'Well, I always loved Ivanhoe and the Young Lochinvar, so I suppose he would have to be a knight in shining armour.'

'Oh, jolly good choice,' Colin said. 'One who had saved you from some dreadful fiery dragon, of course.'

Marjorie thought in a flash of the fiery dragon that had almost fallen on her the night before, and of the words she had been murmuring when she came to in his arms in the entrance to the George and Horses, and once more confusion brought the bright red to her cheeks.

Before she could find words, she saw approaching from behind him the officer commanding 43 Company, Captain Ellen Burns.

But this was a different Captain Burns from the brisk efficient CWAC officer they knew at 43 Company. This Captain Burns was completely oblivious to everything around her as she gazed up into the face of Major Farrow, walking with her hand in his and hanging on every word that fell from his lips.

Marjorie pulled her hand loose from Colin's arm. 'Oh, dear,' she said. 'Here comes our OC. She'll see us in a minute now and I – you – I'm an Other Rank. We aren't supposed to fraternize, you know. At least, it wasn't allowed in Canada.'

'I don't think you'll find it matters here,' he said. 'Anyway, no one dares interfere with the liege lady of a lord. One unkind word to you and I shall order her to the block.'

Captain Burns turned her head and saw Marjorie and her own cheeks went pink. She dropped Major Farrow's hand and pulled herself upright and her military face dropped on like a mask.

Marjorie saluted the two officers. They returned the salute and the three officers all greeted each other.

'Oh, Hatfield,' Captain Burns said. 'I have a message from CMHQ transport office for you. You're to attend a court of inquiry there at ten on Monday morning. Something to do with the brigadier's car.' She looked at Marjorie severely.

'Thank you, ma'am,' Marjorie said respectfully.

'What happened to the brigadier's car, Hatfield?' Captain Burns asked.

'It was crushed when a V-bomb fell on it last night when I was evacuating it from our garage in Chelsea to Moon's Garage on Baker Street,' Marjorie said.

'*Good God Hatfield!*' Captain Burns said, 'Where were you?'

'I was lying in the doorway of a pub across the street, ma'am,' Marjorie said.

'Well, thank heaven you weren't in it,' Captain Burns said. 'I don't see how you can be held responsible in any way. It must be a mere formality.'

After the other two had gone on their way, Marjorie said, 'Oh dear, I knew there would be a court of inquiry. I bet the brigadier is just furious over his new car being smashed up. He's been waiting for months to get it.'

Colin smiled comfortingly down into her distressed face. 'Don't look so worried, little Marjorie, I'm sure it's just a formality, as the captain said. After all, you can't really be responsible for what a V-bomb does, now can you?'

'If only I hadn't been lost. We're not supposed to get lost. You don't know how sticky they can be. They might take away my driver's standing orders and transfer me somewhere.'

'No bally chance,' Colin said. 'Now you're not to worry about it any more. Remember I saved your life and it belongs to me, and that's an order.' He was rewarded by seeing the smile return to her face. 'Now let's hurry. I want to take you somewhere very special for lunch.'

'I'm not allowed in the Officer's Club,' she said hastily.

He tucked her hand once more into the shelter of his arm and strolled off with her in the direction of the gate leading out of

Hyde Park on to Bayswater Road, near 43 Company.

'Did you know,' he told her, 'that at Christmas time they always did Peter Pan at the pantomimes? We all used to come up to London for them when I was a child.' He laughed softly. 'What a bellow we all set up when Tinker Bell's little light was fading out and the man came to the front of the stage and asked us if we believed in fairies, and what a relief it was after we all shouted, "Yes," and it started growing brighter and brighter again.'

'Oh,' Marjorie said excitedly, 'do they still have the pantomimes in wartime? I'd love to see it.'

'Oh yes, rather. I – I 'll take you.'

Marjorie noticed his slight hesitation as he made the promise and guessed the reason. A cold thing bit at her stomach. She had for a short time forgotten the war in the pleasure of his company and she thought, perhaps, he had too. But he had remembered. Fliers did not make long-range plans. And this was only June.

He saw her face whiten and immediately launched into an amusing tale of his boyhood. They emerged on to Bayswater Road. 'Oh, look,' Marjorie said excitedly, noticing the heavy, luxurious car, equipped to be chauffeur-driven, standing at the kerb. 'It's a Rolls-Royce. That's the first one I've seen. Isn't it beautiful?'

'Oh, rather,' Colin said, looking at her with a twinkle in his eyes. 'Let's go over and have a look at it, shall we?'

They stopped beside it and Marjorie stared at the regal-looking car in awe. Colin leaned over and tried the door.

'Oh, I don't think we should touch it,' Marjorie said anxiously. 'It must belong to someone terribly important and you know how English people are about you touching their things.'

'No. How are they?' he asked, smiling.

'They don't like it,' she said. 'They don't even like you to walk on their grass.'

'That's probably because they're a stuffy lot. Or maybe there are too many of them for the little bit of grass they have. Well, anyway, I have some keys here. I'm jolly well going to see if one of them will open the door so we can have a look inside.'

'Oh no, don't,' Marjorie said in alarm.

Ignoring her protest, Colin took the key from his pocket and opened the door. 'Well, there you are, you see. It opens it quite nicely. Now if my liege lady would care to step inside . . . '

'I – we – no. We can't do that,' she stammered. Then suddenly realization came to her. 'Oh, it can't be . . . Is it – is it yours?'

'Well, not exactly,' Colin said with a laugh. 'It really belongs to my father, but he does allow his son to drive it. I managed to scrimp up enough petrol coupons to come and take you back to Enderby with me for lunch. I'm afraid we don't have a chauffeur to drive us, though. Would you mind terribly sitting beside me while I drive?'

Marjorie laughed excitedly. 'I've never ridden in a Rolls-Royce before. What fun. But are you really sure your parents won't mind? You bringing me to lunch, I mean. After all, they've never met me.'

'Oh, you needn't bother about that. One weekend I turned up with a Gurkha. I'm sure they won't object to a nice little Canadian soldier girl.'

He helped her in and then sat behind the wheel. The faint, delicate scent of her fair hair came to his nostrils. Suddenly he said impulsively, 'Marjorie, I don't have to report back until tomorrow night. It's only an hour's drive to Enderby. I'd love to show you my home. Would you be our guest for the weekend? Then I can show you the Pond and all the things I've been telling you about. And we have a horse or two about.'

Almost two whole days with Colin. Joy surged up in Marjorie, but apprehension came on its heels. What would his parents think when he turned up with her? 'I – I don't know,' she said.

'Well, that's settled, then,' he said. 'I'll drive you back to your digs to pick up your toothbrush or whatever, and it's off to Enderby Hall.'

Marjorie had already fallen in love with the English countryside. After the bare prairies it seemed like one great garden. Today, riding beside Colin in the Rolls-Royce, it was an enchanted land of green fields and thatched cottages with roses hugging them. The winding road climbed gentle hills and dipped down to cross little rustic bridges above sparkling streams. She saw cattle and horses and sheep grazing peacefully under giant, centuries-old elm trees; and the intoxicating, warm sweet scent of growing things was carried to her nostrils on the sun-warmed breeze which caressed her face.

72

She sat very quietly, studying Colin's dark, finely chiselled face under the peak of his air force cap. He turned his head and smiled into her eyes, a happy boyish smile.

Suddenly she thought of him in the cockpit of his Spitfire. How impossible to believe that those kindly, smiling eyes had looked with cold intent through his gunsight to send another young man crashing to his death in blood and flame and agony. And yet she knew by the row of ribbons on his chest that he had done this many times, and had been decorated for these deeds.

All at once she wondered if, when they were not dealing out death and destruction, young German pilots smiled tenderly at German girls. What about the enemy who launched the buzz bombs? Did they leave their deadly work to go home, and lift up babies in their arms and smile at girls? It was hard to imagine them as human beings, and she knew that if it was in her power, to keep them from sending their fearful weapons of destruction where she lived she would unhesitatingly order them all annihilated.

She wished with a sudden desperate longing that there was no war and that she and Colin were just a young man and a woman meeting each other, with plenty of time to get acquainted, and not an airman and a soldier on a forty-eight-hour pass, living one moment at a time. But she pushed the sombre thoughts away and smiled back at him.

Colin knew that Marjorie had never completely abandoned her small-girl enchantment with castles and knights in armour and all the romantic things she had listened to her mother read about from the books that came each year from England. He was eager to see her face when she had her first look at Enderby Hall, and anxious to show her the world she had dreamed of and to see the little-girl excitement bubble up in her sweet face.

He watched her closely from the corner of his eye as he turned in at the lodge gates, wishing suddenly that it was peacetime and the lodge-keeper was there to welcome them in style and the grounds and the house were full of servants bustling about. Everything was so empty and quiet now, with so much of the big house shut up and nearly all the servants gone. If this was before the war Enderby Hall would be bursting with eager guests, young friends full of pranks and laughter, playing tennis and punting on the Pond, with the more sedate friends of the earl and the countess pursuing their leisurely diversions and enjoying tea on the clipped lawns.

He was rewarded by her expression. Marjorie's eyes opened wide and she gasped as they came out of the winding, tree-lined drive and Enderby Hall burst into view with its ivy-covered wings and turrets and wide steps leading up to its massive oak reception doors. It stood stately and magnificent on a slight rise, overlooking a broad expanse of lawn which was dotted with great trees.

Colin noted that the lawn was freshly clipped. He guessed that his father had been helping the old gardener to cut and trim it himself.

'Oh,' Marjorie exclaimed. 'Oh, it's a castle.'

'Not quite,' Colin said, delighted, 'but it has been in the Enderby family for centuries. My father is the fourteenth Earl of Rivermere.'

'What on earth do I call him?' Marjorie said. 'Your Grace?'

'No, that's a duke,' Colin said with a smile. 'Actually his friends call him Teddy, or Rivermere; but you might feel a little strange doing that, on first acquaintance. You may feel more happy calling him Lord Rivermere, and my mother is a countess. People who do not address her by her first name usually call her Lady Rivermere.'

'Oh dear,' Marjorie said, suddenly nervous. 'Do you think we should have come? Did you tell them you were bringing me here for the weekend?'

Colin shook his head, smiling at her frightened face. 'We've always been free to bring any of our friends home for the weekend. You should have seen the old place in the days before the war. It absolutely swarmed with people.'

For a moment a wistful look clouded his face. Then his smile came back. 'Don't worry,' he said with a twinkle. 'You're much prettier than the Gurkha and they made *him* welcome.'

Before she could protest further, he pulled up to the broad steps, helped her out and led her up to the heavy oak doors.

She drew a quick breath of delight as they entered the great, oak-panelled hall, with a huge stone fireplace, and a massive carved stairway leading up to the upper part of the house.

Marjorie glanced around quickly. There were oil paintings on the walls and suits of armour on the broad staircase. A scattering of deep, richly coloured persian rugs enlivened the darkly-gleaming oak floor and there were great vases of cut flowers standing on small tables, and big tubs of flowers on the floor. Two heavy leather chairs and a settee were in front of the fireplace, above which were crossed swords and a coat of arms.

Six dogs of various shapes and sizes rose from the rug in front of the fireplace and came bounding delightedly across the hall to spring up at Colin, each one trying to monopolize him. He laughed and patted them in turn.

Marjorie loved dogs. Quick to sense her feelings, they came to her, lifting their heads to be petted. Marjorie felt a rush of pleasure. This was the first time since she came overseas that she had been in a home where there were animals. She spoke softly to them and patted them in turn.

Then Colin spoke to them and they calmed down to a more sedate behaviour although they still clung to his heels.

'Come on,' he said. 'Let's go and find my mother and see what's on the go for lunch. It's almost noon.'

Marjorie watched nervously as he crossed the hall to one of the doors, poked his head in and called, 'Mother.'

She heard a feminine voice from inside the room and then Colin said, 'I've brought someone home for the weekend, Mother.'

She did not hear the answer. Colin returned to her side and in a moment the Countess of Rivermere appeared in the doorway. Marjorie was reminded of a portrait she had seen of Queen Mary.

Chapter 9

The tall white-haired woman approached her, with stately grace, across the softly gleaming floor.

Standing very tall, with his hat in his hand, Colin said, 'Mother, may I present Miss Marjorie Hatfield. Marjorie, this is my mother, Countess of Rivermere.'

Marjorie looked into the dignified, aloof face of the countess and didn't know whether to shake hands, bow, or curtsey – so she saluted.

The countess inclined her head and a slight smile touched her lips. 'Welcome to Enderby Hall,' she said in a quiet, cultured voice. 'I trust you will forgive us for not being as well prepared for guests as in other days. Since the war, we've been rather short of help. I'm afraid you may find you have to rough it, a little.'

'Oh, Marjorie won't mind,' Colin said innocently. 'She's used to eating frozen sandwiches and being chased by wolves.' His eyes twinkled mischievously.

The countess raised her eyebrows. 'Indeed?'

Marjorie found her voice. 'He's teasing me, Lady Rivermere, because I'm from Canada and I told him I used to ride four miles to school on a horse and in the winter time we had to eat frozen sandwiches.'

The countess smiled graciously. 'How interesting. You must tell me all about it at lunch. In the meantime, perhaps you would like to come upstairs and freshen up. I'm afraid the only maid we have left is busy in the kitchen at the moment, preparing lunch. So I'll show you to your room myself.'

Marjorie thought: She's very polite and gracious, but somehow I have the feeling she was happier to see the Gurkha.

The countess took her up the broad stairway, past suits of ancient armour standing like sentinels guarding the home of the

Enderbys from intruders. She showed her guest to a bedroom at the end of a long corridor off the gallery that looked down on to the main entrance hall. The room had dark green panelling and a heavy fourposter bed. A tiny slit of a window peered out on a clump of trees against a steep hill that blotted out any further view.

Marjorie reckoned that this was not the most luxurious bedroom at Enderby Hall.

'I'm afraid, my dear,' the countess said, 'that you will have to do your own unpacking. We do not have any personal maids with us any more.'

Suddenly, in spite of herself, Marjorie tittered. Her luggage consisted of her khaki haversack.

'Oh, I think I can manage,' she said, with her blue eyes twinkling up into the countess's.

The faintest of smiles touched her lips, and Marjorie turned her face away, feeling her cheeks grow scarlet.

The countess said politely, 'The bathroom is just down the hall on your left. Lunch will be ready very soon. Can you find your way down to the hall again when you're ready?'

'Yes. Thank you,' Marjorie said faintly, putting her haversack down on the chair beside the bed. From the corner of her eye she was aware of the countess's deep grey eyes studying her intently for a moment before she left the room.

Marjorie did not bother to unpack her haversack since all she had brought with her was some khaki army-issue bloomers, a pair of army-issue flannelette pyjamas, a toothbrush, toothpaste and a clean khaki shirt. In her canvas shoulder purse she carried her make-up and comb, her army pay book and driver's standing orders, her wallet and other personal things.

She took off her hat and dropped it on the chair beside her haversack and ran her comb through her wavy blonde hair. Then she went to the bathroom. After she had freshened up she descended the great staircase.

Colin stood waiting for her. A light came into his eyes as he watched her blonde hair shining and the eager, half-timid look on her face. He thought admiringly what a naturally graceful carriage she had, and how even her uniform could not hide the exquisite curves of her figure. She really does look like a liege lady, he thought. Dress her in an elegant flowing dress, with a coronet on her hair, and here would be a lady whose favour any knight would be proud to carry on his lance.

He bowed low as she came down the last step and carried her fingers to his lips. 'My homage, Lady Marjorie,' he said with affected courtliness. 'May this humble knight escort you to the luncheon table?'

She smiled and blushed, a thrill running up her arm from the place where his lips had touched her fingers.

Colin tucked her hand under his arm and turned towards one of the doors leading off the hall.

Oh, Marjorie thought in panic. *I still have to meet the earl!* She felt overcome suddenly by the vastness and ancient dignity of the place, as if generations of Enderbys were watching her from the shadowed corners.

'I – I haven't met your father yet,' she said, hanging back.

'Frightful old ogre,' Colin said. 'Gallops about the place evicting tenants and bashing serfs about with his riding crop.'

At that moment the great outer door opened and the earl strode into the hall, dressed in riding clothes and carrying a heavy, gold-headed riding crop. He stopped when he saw Colin and Marjorie and for a moment looked surprised, then he crossed the hall to them.

Marjorie saw where Colin's looks came from. The earl was an inch or two taller than Colin, but with the same chiselled features and fine brown eyes with the hint of a twinkle lurking in their depths.

Colin introduced them and, without pausing to think whether it was English etiquette Marjorie held out her hand. The earl took it in his in a firm clasp, bowing slightly at the same time, with a smile of welcome lighting his face.

'How delightful,' he said when Colin told him that Marjorie was to be their guest for the weekend. 'Colin, you must allow me to escort Miss Hatfield in to lunch.' He offered her his arm.

Colin fell in on her other side and they went into the small breakfast room off the hall, where the luncheon table was set.

Lady Enderby rose from where she was sitting at the French window on to the garden, and came to welcome them.

Marjorie thought again of Queen Mary. Dressed simply though she was, in a soft green and rust tweed suit, her only ornaments the jewelled rings on her fingers, tiny gold earrings and a heart-shaped gold locket on a gold chain, the Countess of Rivermere still looked regal.

Colin took his mother's arm and escorted her to the table. The earl seated Marjorie on his right, Colin sat across from her and the countess presided at the other end of the table. It was set with gleaming silver, delicate china and crystal.

The countess said, 'You must forgive us. Since the war, we lunch informally in this little room.'

Marjorie gathered that they ate their evening meal elsewhere and she wondered why.

In a moment a round-faced, elderly woman with grey hair came in and served a simple meal of fish and vegetables, with heavy dark bread and margarine.

Marjorie realized that, like everyone else in Britain, the earl and the countess were on strict wartime rations. All through the meal they treated her with flawless courtesy and graciousness, but Marjorie sensed an undercurrent almost of bewilderment beneath their polite manner, as if they had expected something quite different today. Perhaps they thought he would bring another Gurkha home, she thought wryly.

Even Colin appeared to be under a slight strain. She wondered what was troubling them. Of course there was the knowledge always in their minds, as it was in hers, that tomorrow night he would be again over enemy territory. Perhaps they had hoped to have him to themselves for these brief hours of leave. But somehow she did not think that was it.

After lunch the earl said to Marjorie, 'Since you're fond of horses, perhaps you'd like to come for a ride? I have to ride over to the Browns' cottage. You and Colin could come with me and then he can take you around the estate and show it to you, if you would care to see it. I'd enjoy a spot of company.'

Marjorie could hardly keep her feet from skipping over the cobblestones as she walked with the earl and Colin to the sprawling stone stables. *A horse! She was going to be on a horse again!*

The old groom brought out three magnificent-looking animals, clean-limbed hunters with proudly held heads and slender strong legs. The mounts for the earl and Colin were tall brown geldings. Marjorie was given a smaller white-faced bay mare, with delicate, pricked-up ears and wide-set intelligent eyes. She saw with consternation the flat English saddle. She had never before ridden on anything but a big western saddle. But she quickly recovered her good spirits. I've ridden so much bareback, I shouldn't have any trouble handling the flat saddle, she thought.

The earl held her horse while she mounted and once she was in the saddle and felt the rippling of the mare's muscles under her, her pulses quickened with elation.

They set off at a fast pace across the grassy slopes. Coming to a small stream, the earl jumped his horse across. Colin, who was riding on her other side, did likewise, and her mare lifted over it like a bird. Marjorie laughed aloud, joyously.

She found no difficulty staying in the flat saddle, and although she was not accustomed to riding with four reins and a snaffle bit, the mare felt the firm hand and the fearless ease of her rider and responded confidently to her lightest touch. Marjorie found, though, that she had to get used to posting in the stirrups when they slowed to a trot.

The countess had unearthed some old riding boots and breeches and a tweed jacket – all about three sizes too large. I must look a sight, she thought, but somehow she didn't care. The breeze was blowing through her hair and the smell of the grass, the trees and the flowers was intoxicating, as was the warm, teasing sunshine. London and war and V-bombs were an unreal dream.

Colin watched her happy face with a strange tender yearning. She looked so sweet and young and vulnerable.

The earl pulled up his horse at the top of a knoll looking down at a swift little stream with a high hedge on its far bank. He pointed beyond it to a distant cottage. 'The tenant I'm going to see lives over there,' he told Marjorie.

'I do hope you're not going to evict them,' Marjorie said innocently, with a sideways glance at Colin.

'Eh? What's that?' the earl said, looking at her blankly.

Colin laughed. 'She's punishing me, Father, because I told her you were an ogre who gallops about the estate evicting tenants and bashing serfs with your riding crop.'

'Impertinent young devil,' the earl said. 'For that I shall race you across Beecher's Brook. I'll teach you a bit of respect for your elders.' He turned to Marjorie, his brown eyes twinkling.

'I'm just going to teach this young jackanapes that he can't keep up with his father.' He pointed his riding crop. 'There's a break in the hedge there and the stream is shallow. You can ride Minnette through it and meet us on the other side. Ready?' he said to Colin.

Colin's eyes were dancing. 'Watch me show Father the young fox can outrun the old,' he said. 'Come on, Father!'

They charged down the slope and she saw the two horses lift up as one and sail over stream and hedge, disappearing on the other side.

Minnette pranced and snorted and tugged at the reins. For a moment Marjorie held in the prancing mare. The blood was pounding in her veins. *Why should I ride around?* she thought. I was practically born on a horse. If the two Englishmen can jump that hedge so can this Canadian girl. 'Come on Minnette!' She tightened her knees and turned the mare to the slope. She sprang away joyously and raced down. The wind tore through Marjorie's hair. As hedge and stream rushed up to meet them, she realized what a tremendous leap it was. She felt the mare gather herself under the saddle and then it seemed they were flying. Up! Up! And then they were over. But as the mare landed Marjorie missed the rhythm of the jump, lost a stirrup, tumbled sideways out of the saddle and landed beside the bewildered mare.

Colin and his father were off their horses and by her side in an instant, but she was already on her feet, crestfallen but laughing. The earl caught the mare and brought it back to her. 'By Jove,' he said delightedly, 'what a nerve! You must let me give you a few lessons in riding in the English style. Once you get the knack of it you'll be fit to enter the Grand National. You're a born horsewoman.'

Colin's face glowed with pride as he listened.

Marjorie said to the earl, 'I'd love to have you teach me how to jump a horse. I never tried it before and your English saddle is so different from a western one. I seemed to be doing just fine and then, all of a sudden, I simply fell off.'

Marjorie spent the rest of the afternoon, after they had said goodbye to the earl, in a kind of enchanted dream. She had enjoyed the earl's company but finally she was glad to be alone with Colin. It seemed the precious time was fleeting by too fast.

Enderby was exactly as she had imagined a lordly English

81

estate to be, with its beautiful deep woods, streams and hills and carpets of gloriously scented flowers brightening its meadows. Colin and she rode through it knee to knee at a leisurely pace and he told her tales of the countryside and legends of the Enderby family and neighbouring great families. They did not talk about the war.

Eventually they came back to the stables and the groom took the horses from them.

'Now,' Colin said, 'would you like to see the grounds and the Pond where I received this ghastly wound, or would you prefer to go indoors and see the rest of the ancestral mansion? It has all sorts of winding passages and strange little rooms, exactly like the house that little beast, Colin Craven, lived in, in *The Secret Garden*. And there's the gallery with all the family portraits leering at you. The place dates back to the time of the Tudors, you know.'

Marjorie said, 'I should like to see the outdoors first, please, although I do want to see all of Enderby. I've never been in a great old English mansion before, and I've read so many stories about them.'

'Right. It's too nice a day to spend inside a musty old house. Most of it has been shut up since the beginning of the war. Actually, it's icy cold in there. I'm sure it must be full of spiders and things. None of the fireplaces have been lit in those rooms and we don't have central heating like you do in Canada. Of course it was different before the war, with maids rushing around dusting everything, keeping things in shape for guests. Come, we'll go through the gardens and along by the fish ponds, down to the big Pond. I'll see if I can find the old punt and take you out in it. We used to have such fun with it when we were children.'

Marjorie was enchanted as she walked beside Colin along the footpath through the gardens, leading one into the other, sheltering behind stone walls covered with tiny, clinging flowers and ivy. Gentle terraces led down to fish ponds connected by a shallow, bubbling stream. Bright fish darted about in the clear water.

But she was eager to see the Pond where Colin had delighted in make-believe games.

She gave an exclamation of delight as they came out of the

thick foliage and she saw it shimmering in the sunlight, reflecting the clouds and the blossom-laden shrubs dipping their branches towards it, their sweet scent filling the warm air.

The boat-house was in front of them – and there was the punt.

Colin found the pole and helped her in.

'*Away, me hearties!* We're off to the Spanish Main,' he cried, as he climbed aboard and pushed off, his eyes shining.

He poled vigorously and soon they rounded a bend and entered a tiny, secluded cove, hidden from view by tall shrubs dipping across from three sides and entwining their branches above, so that the sunlight filtering through them made a dancing pattern on the water.

Colin pulled into shore and tied the punt to a branch. Then he held out his hand to Marjorie, standing smiling at her.

She thought how handsome he looked. He had changed his uniform into old riding clothes. His shirt was open at the neck and his heavy brown hair was ruffled in the breeze.

'My most secret place,' he said. 'Welcome to Smugglers' Cove!'

With her heart suddenly starting to beat wildly, she let him lead her back to where a flat, moss-covered rock, almost hidden in the warm sand, reposed against the high bank. The tiny ripples from the lake lapped almost up to it.

Colin pulled her gently down beside him on this natural seat.

Chapter 10

Leaves rustled softly together and the warm, earthy smell of growing things was strong.

Colin's shoulder was pressed against hers and she felt a tremble run through his body. There was a huskiness in his voice when he spoke.

'This is where I used to come when I was a boy to hide out from everyone. I used to pretend I was Captain Kidd, and Drake, and Raleigh, and Frobisher. I was a great hero in this cove, all by myself. It was especially gratifying if I'd done something to offend Nanny and was not in good standing around the house. There's a secret path from the garden down to here. I hacked it out in places where the bushes were too thick to worm through. I may show it to you some day, if you're a good girl.'

'It's a beautiful spot,' Marjorie said, feeling a quiver in her own voice. 'When I was a little girl on the farm and I wanted to get away from everyone, I used to make a tunnel through the grain field and trample down a small circle at the end of it, and play all sorts of games. Sometimes I was Betty Zane running with the bag of powder on my back to save the fort, with the Indians shooting their arrows at me. Sometimes I was Laura Secord struggling through the woods to warn the fort that the Americans were coming. And sometimes I was Queen Boadicea, fighting against the Romans.'

'Strange, isn't it,' he said thoughtfully, 'how we were always playing war?'

'Yes. And now we're really in one.'

'And it's so different. In your dreams you could always win and even if you went down with your ship and were killed, or died in battle, you could always revive yourself the next day and

84

play the same game over again.'

Marjorie felt a strange shudder run through her at his words. She turned her face up to his to find him looking at her with all the laughter gone out of his eyes, replaced by a serious, sober look of longing.

She knew that, like her, he was wishing that there was no war.

In dreams none of the horror came through. The Lorelei voices promised uniforms and medals and the sound of boots marching all together and the thrill of the bugles and the bands playing. Not until the voices had lured them on to the rocks did men see the cruel destruction of youth and beauty and love.

Without thinking she reached up and touched his cheek.

He drew her close in the circle of his arms and kissed her mouth. Such a thrill of joy went through her, she felt as if her breath would stop. He moved his lips to her eyes and her hair and kissed the dimples in her cheeks. Then found her lips again and clung to them like a parched man drinking clear cold water, as if he could never get enough. 'Marjorie,' he whispered huskily. 'My little Marjorie.'

Marjorie felt herself quivering as her lips clung to his, and his body shaking against hers.

At last he drew away and looked down into her wide soft eyes. They were both breathless.

'We'd better go,' Marjorie whispered.

With her cradled against his chest, he looked down at her for a long moment. Then he let his breath out in almost a sigh and said huskily, 'You're right, little Marjorie. We'd better go.' His arm loosened around her and he bent his head and kissed her lightly on the tip of her nose. Then he pulled her, trembling, to her feet and led her back to the punt.

They were silent as he pushed away from the shore. Marjorie's heart was rioting and her mind was in a turmoil. It was not the first time a man had kissed her, but it was the first time she had felt like this. She was so overwhelmed by her emotions, she wanted to run madly away from him, and at the same time, she felt that she never wanted to leave his side for even a moment.

She thought: I must be in love. *This must be what it feels like to be in love!*

Don't be a little fool! she told herself. He's an airman on leave and you were alone together in an enticing spot and he kissed you because – well – because you're nice to kiss. But you mustn't think it means anything to him. You're just a friendly Canadian girl he brought home for the weekend.

She looked up to see Colin watching her face with a tenderly amused smile in his eyes, and she blushed deeply.

He said, 'How would you like to see the spot where I fell out of the punt and was wounded during the Viking's funeral?'

Marjorie nodded without speaking and he turned the punt around and pushed off to a spot near the boat-house.

'It was right here. Ashley had started a fire of twigs in a tin can in the prow of the punt and the two of them were standing on the shore watching.'

Marjorie felt a start run through her at the mention of Ashley's name.

But he did not notice and went on, 'It was smoking nicely and I was lying with my face turned up to the sun, completely still, and everything was going splendidly, until Raif decided *he* wanted the Viking's funeral and came and climbed into the punt. Of course, we had a terrible row and I tried to push him out, but he was older than I and he pushed me out and I scraped my forehead on a little bit of a snag on the ship.' His eyes were laughing at the memory. 'We had on our Sunday clothes and Beau Geste got into a dreadful row with Nanny when we went back home.'

For some reason Marjorie found the story oppressive. She asked, 'Who is Ashley?'

Colin pointed across the lake to the great house standing on the hill looking down at Enderby. 'She lives up there in that house on the hill. Her father is Lord Medhurst and she is Lady Ashley, if you give her her title. The Medhursts and the Enderbys have lived side by side for generations. We children all played together. She's an only child, so I think she particularly enjoyed the companionship she found here with us.'

Marjorie wondered about Lady Ashley Medhurst as she returned to the house with Colin. She had noticed a note of fondness in his voice when he spoke of her and the tender look that had come into his brown eyes. She felt a sudden drooping of her spirits.

I am not of his world, she thought. Today is just a brief

interlude in his life. I'm only a girl he met in an air raid and he has brought me down here to let me see a little of English country life. No doubt he finds me amusing. He told me I'm a funny little soldier girl. Well, I won't let him see how I feel.

She put on a bright smile and said, 'Will you show me the house now? It will be something to tell the girls about.'

He looked at her keenly, noticing the almost imperceptible change in her manner – as if she had withdrawn herself from him. Have I done something to offend her? he wondered. Perhaps I should have waited a little longer before I kissed her, but I've been longing so for the feel of her lips since we first met – but no, I'm sure she wasn't displeased with me. She's so different from any girl I've ever met – so completely unsophisticated, almost like a child. And yet I have the feeling of a great depth of character in her. She's beautiful and unspoiled.

He took her hand and tucked it into the shelter of his arm. 'I say, you made quite a hit with Father, you know, when you jumped Beecher's Brook. It certainly was a nervy thing to do, and a bit rash, I might say. How did you know the mare could jump?'

Marjorie laughed. 'I didn't,' she said, feeling suddenly warm and close to him again. 'I just took a chance. I considered that possibility for a moment. But then I thought, well, if she hasn't jumped before, she'll stop and not try to take it. But when she started gathering steam going down the hill, I knew she was going for it and I knew she must have done it before. But it was humiliating to fall off. I've ridden bucking horses, you know – in a western saddle.'

'Well, Father will teach you to jump as he promised, and then you won't fall off. But I think you should practise on something a little less difficult than Beecher's Brook. Now come on, I'll show you the ancestral mansion.'

Their tour began with the gallery that ran around the top of the great hall.

'When we were children,' Colin said, 'we used to hide up here when they were having a big party and watch the guests arriving.'

The entire gallery was hung with portraits of stately men and women, looking down on the great hall from their heavy frames.

'Ancestors,' Colin said, 'keeping an eye on us, don't you know. Would you like me to tell you about them?'

'Oh yes, please,' Marjorie said, her eyes roving along the gallery, feasting on the robes and uniforms of the men and the elaborate dresses of the ladies.

'Very well, you're in for it then. That gentleman looking down on us so keenly is the first Earl of Rivermere – whom I'm named after – Colin Dudley Percival Enderby. He was knighted by Queen Elizabeth.'

Marjorie looked with awe at the swashbuckling, dark-faced young man, whose dress reminded her of pictures of Sir Walter Raleigh. His handsome chiselled face bore such a resemblance to Colin's it almost took her breath away.

Colin went on, 'I think he was a pirate, actually. He was killed in a sea battle against the Spaniards, but not before he'd been knighted, married, and fathered a son.'

As they walked slowly along the gallery and Colin regaled her with the exploits of his ancestors, so many of whom had died in the service of their sovereign, Marjorie had the uncanny feeling that their spirits hovered about her, looking at the Canadian soldier girl walking beside their descendant.

She could almost hear the clank of armour and the rattle of sabres, and feel the eyes of the high-born Enderby women in their satins and brocades looking down their noses at this intruder into their sacred halls.

She clung tightly to Colin's arm.

He smiled. 'Formidable-looking lot, aren't they? You mustn't let them intimidate you, you know.'

He stopped in front of a portrait hanging apart, with no accompanying lady beside it. 'Our black sheep.'

The gentleman was dressed very plainly compared to all the others, in hunting clothes and carrying a riding crop. His hat was tilted rakishly and his lips were twisted in a disdainful smile. His black reckless eyes looked down on the hall of the Enderbys with amused contempt.

Marjorie felt herself drawn to him in fascination.

Colin smiled at her. 'My great – great – great – uncle, Daniel Enderby,' he said. 'Gambled and drank and killed a man in a duel over a wench. He went to Canada and became a squaw man and was killed in a drunken brawl. Bad lot. Only reason his picture hangs here, his mother adored him and she insisted.'

'I can understand that. A mother would always adore her son, no matter what he'd done.'

Colin squeezed her hand as he took her to the last portrait in the gallery and stopped, gazing up at it with wistful longing. 'You're right,' he said softly. 'And the love we have for the people of our own blood can never be killed.'

Marjorie saw a fine-looking young man with the high forehead and deep grey eyes of the Countess of Rivermere. He was dressed in the uniform of an officer in the Royal Navy. His lips were smiling and his eyes seemed to be looking down at her and Colin with a warm approving twinkle.

'My older brother, Raif, true heir to Rivermere – but he was killed at Dunkirk, and the heritage now falls to me.'

Marjorie felt the colour draining from her face. 'Oh, I'm sorry.'

Colin gazed pensively at the portrait of his brother. 'Yes,' he said wistfully, 'we had some jolly times together, Raif and I.'

And Ashley! Marjorie thought.

Colin pulled his eyes away from the face in the portratit. 'Come. Let's see the rest of the house.'

The size of the house almost overwhelmed her as they wandered down long corridors and into bedrooms and little sitting rooms with tiny balconies overlooking gardens and tree-covered hills. She thought that if Colin was not with her, she would never find her way back to the great hall again.

She felt the power of antiquity in this massive mansion and the notion persisted of Enderby ancestors walking the silent halls and looking on the empty rooms, draped in white dust covers.

'You must have a family ghost,' she said.

'Yes, rather. Athelstane.'

'Who is Athelstane?'

They were in the room where Queen Elizabeth had once stayed, long ago. The bay window looked out at a green hillside studded with huge oaks. Colin took her to the window and stood with his arm loosely draped across her shoulders.

His touch made her quiver and she wished he would kiss her, but he continued speaking. 'There used to be a forest beyond that hill at the time when Queen Elizabeth stayed here. The first earl was a great huntsman. The woods were full of deer and among them was a huge black stag with great white antlers. He was so clever and elusive that none of the huntsmen could ever get close enough to shoot him. The great queen had heard of him and she wanted his head for a trophy. Colin Dudley Percival Enderby vowed to bring it to her, and he did, the very next morning.

'He killed the great stag just out there on that hill and brought it down and laid it at the feet of his queen. Elizabeth was delighted. It was the most gigantic stag that had ever been seen in all of England. Its huge antlers glowed with an unearthly white in the sunlight as it lay at the queen's feet. Some of her attendants said uneasily that this was no true stag at all, but some ancient Druid who had taken a stag's form.

'Not long after that Queen Elizabeth made Colin Dudley Enderby the first Earl of Rivermere. He was given command of a ship and before long went on an expedition to the new world. He encountered a Spanish man-of-war and, although his ship was able to repel and sink the Spaniard, he was killed in the affray.

'That night his wife, who had recently borne him a son, was sleeping here in this room. She awoke with a start and something drew her to the window. She pulled back the heavy curtains. There was a full moon and she saw outlined on the hill a great black stag, with huge antlers glowing white.

'She became filled with fear; and within a month news was brought to her that her husband, the first Earl of Rivermere, had died in battle against the Spaniards. Legend now has it that whenever an Enderby is killed in battle for his sovereign, if the moon is bright, the black stag is seen stalking the grounds of Enderby, with his antlers gleaming white in the moonlight.'

Marjorie shivered. She looked up into Colin's face. It was very sober. 'Do you believe this?' she whispered.

Colin shrugged. 'The tale has come down from generation to generation. I only know that one night during the evacuation of Dunkirk I woke up suddenly from my sleep and, going to the window, I saw on the hill a big black stag, whose antlers were glowing white in the moonlight. Ashley was spending the night. She saw it, too, she told me the next morning, after we heard that Raif had been blown up with his ship.'

Marjorie shuddered. His arm tightened around her and she

90

thought he was going to kiss her, but he only looked tenderly into her face and said soothingly, 'It was probably only an ordinary deer.' He laughed lightly. 'You know we English love our ghost stories.'

But Marjorie did not think he believed that.

'Come on,' he said. 'We must get back to our rooms and tidy up for tea. Mustn't be late for tea, you know. We English do all sorts of magnificent things for tea. Absolutely bad form to be late. Mother will be pouring very shortly now.'

Marjorie was glad to leave the room and they hurried down corridors until they reached the door of her room.

'Is this where Mother put you?' he said with just the suggestion of displeasure in his voice.

With unfamiliar emotions churning inside of her she left him and went inside to tidy up. She could not shake off the weird feeling that she was an interloper in this ancient dwelling; and she wondered why Colin had not attempted again to kiss her as they toured through it.

He was waiting at the foot of the stairs when she descended and escorted her to the drawing room.

Lady Rivermere was seated on an embroidered-backed chair, presiding behind a silver tea service on a low table, on which was a delicate, china plate of thinly sliced bread and butter and another of tiny cakes, and a small dish of red jam.

She had changed into a soft green dress but still wore the gold locket. She smiled graciously at Marjorie and her eyes lit up with warmth as she greeted Colin.

'I trust you had a pleasant ride?' she said to Marjorie in her polite, modulated voice as they seated themselves and she began to pour the tea into exquisite china cups.

'She's an absolute Valkyrie, Mother,' Colin said enthusiastically. 'She jumped Minnette over Beecher's Brook.'

The countess lifted her eyebrows. 'How marvellous. I didn't know you were familiar with our style of riding. I thought you only chased cattle and rode in blizzards and things.'

Colin gave his mother a quick look from under his eyelashes.

The countess appeared flawlessly polite and interested – and yet Marjorie had the feeling that she had been picked up and placed firmly outside the circle of their lives at Enderby.

'I'm so pleased,' Lady Rivermere went on pleasantly, 'that you're enjoying seeing a bit of our country life out here. It's

91

always so interesting to see how other people live in their natural habitat, as it were, don't you think?'

Before Marjorie could think of a suitable reply she went on: 'I remember, when we used to go abroad before the war, how much I enjoyed learning about the strange customs and foods and that sort of thing in foreign countries . . . Do try a bit of that raspberry jam, my dear. The earl gathered the berries himself, out in the Monks' Garden. He was frightfully stung by a wasp, poor dear. They seem to think they own the raspberry bushes . . . Oh, by the way, we're having rather a nice dinner tonight. The butcher let me have something a little extra. Frightfully wicked of me, I'm afraid. But after all, having a visitor from Canada is a bit of an occasion. And I've invited Lady Ashley Medhurst to dinner as well. She is our dearest friend and neighbour; in fact, I look on her as a daughter. She'll be absolutely charmed to meet you, Miss Hatfield, I know, and hear about life in Canada – riding to school in blizzards and eating frozen sandwiches and all that sort of thing.'

Chapter 11

Marjorie, from her position on the right of the earl at the head of the table, looked down the vast expanse of white tablecloth to the countess, flanked by Lady Ashley on her right and Colin on her left, and strained to hear the conversation.

The table at either end was set with gleaming silver and crystal and heavy, gold-rimmed china. There were flowers, and candles glowing in their silver holders. And everyone had dressed for dinner – the countess and Lady Ashley in long dresses and the earl in a dinner jacket. Marjorie was thankful that a uniform in England today was considered adequate for any social occasion. She and Colin wore theirs.

The countess had replaced the tiny earrings she wore that morning with emerald pendants set in heavy gold. But she still wore the heart-shaped gold locket.

She had been guiding the conversation throughout dinner and encouraging Colin and Ashley to reminisce about past experiences at Enderby and they, wishing to share the fun with Marjorie, had launched innocently into accounts of various escapades and adventures.

Marjorie was growing more and more bewildered. She had observed the warm affectionate glances Colin and Ashley directed at each other and the twinkle in their eyes as if they shared some delightful secret.

Seated as they were, with the length of the table designed to seat thirty guests between herself and the earl at one end and the countess, Colin and Lady Ashley at the other, she was given the feeling that she was in a different world from the others, and that the countess was making it clear that she was graciously willing to show this girl from Canada this alien world, as long as she did not attempt to enter it through any relationship with her son.

The countess raised her voice above her normally modulated tones. 'Miss Hatfield is interested in our life here on a country estate,' she said to Ashley. 'Perhaps if you're not otherwise engaged tomorrow, you and Colin might show her something of Medhurst Hall – Would you enjoy that, Miss Hatfield? Medhurst Hall dates back to an even earlier period than our place, and the Medhursts have lived there longer than the Enderbys have lived here.'

Across the flickering candles Marjorie's eyes met the aloof gaze of the Countess of Rivermere. Before she could answer, the earl spoke.

'My dear Honora,' he said, 'I think our table is just a little too large for the size of our dinner party; therefore, I shall relinquish my place at the head of the table and join you at the other end, so that we may speak to one another without shouting as though we were at a fox hunt.'

He motioned to the elderly butler who was hovering attentively over them. 'Giles, would you mind moving Miss Hatfield's place and mine to the other end. Please put her plate beside Lord Colin's and mine on the other side of hers.'

He stood up as he spoke and assisted Marjorie from her chair.

'There,' he said when they were seated again, 'now, that is better. We can all see each other.'

He turned towards his wife. 'My dear Honora, we must not impose on Ashley. Perhaps Colin and Miss Hatfield have made other plans for tomorrow, and if her entire day is not taken up, I should like very much to show her the proper seat for jumping – on the small jumps down in the meadow, of course.'

He smiled at Ashley. 'We have a magnificent rider here, Ashley. Did Colin tell you about her jumping Minnette over Beecher's Brook? And she has never jumped before, or ridden in an English saddle. She'll show us all up, when I've given her a few lessons.'

Marjorie smiled across at Ashley. 'He forgot to tell you that I fell off.'

'Even if you are an expert, it's no disgrace to fall off at Beecher's Brook,' Ashley answered warmly. 'I've had many a tumble there. That's why we call it Beecher's Brook, it's unseated so many of us. I remember when we were children we were not allowed to try it. We used to love to sit on our ponies and watch the guests tumble off.'

'Yes,' Colin said, 'and then when we were old enough to try it ourselves every one of us fell off at one time or another.'

'Everyone but Raif,' Ashley said softly. 'Raif could always get over Beecher's Brook.'

Colin said, 'Yes, but then Raif could always show us the way in everything.'

Marjorie saw the momentary shadows that passed across their faces before they went on to talk of other things.

She found she had little to say herself, although Ashley was very careful always to see that she was brought into the conversation. In spite of her doubts as to the relationship between Ashley and Colin, Marjorie found herself drawn to the other young woman. She had such frank, friendly hazel eyes and such a warm manner, and she seemed to return Marjorie's friendly feeling. And yet it was clear from the countess's manner that she regarded Ashley as Colin's girl.

Marjorie found the situation incomprehensible. If Ashley was indeed Colin's girlfriend, then why was she so friendly towards this strange girl he had brought here? Unless, like the countess, she looked on her as just a guest from Canada, whom they were favouring with a glimpse of upper-class country life.

She remembered the tender, understanding looks she had seen pass between Colin and Ashley. They must have some kind of an understanding, but then why had he brought her here?

Her spirits drooped. But she felt sure there had been something more than just a casual touching of lips when he had kissed her so hungrily down there in Smugglers' Cove. What did it all mean? And what was happening to her? Why was she so intensely nervous, as if her whole world depended on these tormenting questions? I'm more scared than I am when the doodle bugs are coming over, she thought.

Lady Ashley said, 'You're driving in London for the Canadian Army, Colin tells me. How very decent of you to come over here to help us out. I understand you had a rather nasty brush with a V-bomb the other night.'

'You did?' the earl said. 'I say, you didn't tell me anything about that.'

'There's nothing much to tell,' Marjorie said. 'I was

95

evacuating the brigadier's car and it got smashed to bits, but I was in the doorway of a pub called the George and Horses, and Colin saved my life. He pulled me down and sheltered me from the blast.'

'Well, you know what that means,' Lady Ashley said, smiling, 'he saved your life, now he has to take care of you for all the rest of your life, or so the Chinese believe.'

Marjorie's dimples flashed. 'That's what I told him. But he thinks it's the other way around. My real problem, though, is the brigadier's car.'

'Yes,' Colin broke in, 'apparently, in Canada cars are looked upon the same as ships. Marjorie would be expected to go down with her colours nailed to the mast.'

· The earl said, 'You don't mean to tell me there will be a row over the car in those circumstances?'

'Well, there is going to be a court of inquiry,' Marjorie said. 'You see, I was lost and we're not supposed to get lost.'

'Everyone gets lost in London,' Ashley said. 'I'm sure you'll be exonerated.'

'Is that Brigadier Raham?' the earl asked.

'Yes.'

'I met him when he came out to Major Middleton's, not long ago. Middleton lives just a few miles away. He's the British liaison officer with the Canadians.'

Colin said, 'I was telling Marjorie how we all used to go up to London at Christmas time to see the pantomimes and how we loved Peter Pan.'

A smile lit the countess's face. 'Dear Peter Pan.'

The conversation turned to theatre and books.

After dinner they withdrew to a small sitting room for coffee and liqueurs. Marjorie politely refused the liqueur, but sipped the coffee, which was not particularly good, since in wartime coffee was not really coffee at all and the English system of brewing even the best coffee left much to be desired.

The rest of the evening passed quite pleasantly. The countess joined little in the conversation, but the earl got on to his favourite topic—horses. He brought out pictures of the winners of the Grand National back as far as you could go. Marjorie shared his love of horses and bent over the albums with him, completely fascinated.

The countess sat with a piece of needlework.

Ashley had walked the short distance down from Medhurst Hall to Enderby. When she announced that she must be going the countess said, 'Colin will drive you, Ashley dear.'

'Yes, and Marjorie will come with me,' Colin said, 'if Father can let me have her for a short time.'

'When you come back,' the earl told Marjorie, 'I'll show you some jolly fine pictures of the Derby winners. There's an absolutely marvellous one with Gordon Richards up. We had a horse entered too, but Gordon beat them all out.'

The evening was soft, and gentle moonlight silvered everything with a mystical beauty.

Ashley said as they stepped outside, 'It's such a beautiful night. Don't take the car, please, just walk me home. Do you mind walking, Marjorie?'

'I'd love it. It's such a long time since I've walked in the country and your countryside is so beautiful here. It's like being in one big garden.'

They cut through the field at the end of the Pond, went across a stile over a low hedge and up the hill to Medhurst Hall.

At the big door to her home, Ashley took Marjorie's hand and held it warmly in her own. 'I'm so glad to have met you,' she said. Then she turned to Colin and put her hand lightly on his arm and looked up at his face with a little nod and they smiled at each other. It was as if they shared some wonderful secret, Marjorie thought, and wondered.

'Bring Marjorie to tea tomorrow afternoon, will you Colin? I should like her to meet Father and Mother. Do you think you can stand another one of our English teas, Marjorie?'

'Oh, yes, I'd love to come,' Marjorie said politely, but she felt some slight misgivings. She wondered if Lord and Lady Medhurst would really welcome her.

After they had said goodbye to Ashley, Colin took her hand and they went back down the hill.

On the other side of the stile, beside the hedge, he pulled her down beside him on a little rustic seat. The moonlight sparkled on the Pond and put lights into her blonde hair.

Her heart was pounding as she looked up into Colin's face, and she felt a quiver run through his body, pressed close to her side. He turned and folded her in his arms and found her lips with his. Unknown sensations raced through her body. She was quivering and throbbing in every part. She wanted his warm tender lips never to leave hers, and yet she felt she was smothering under them.

At last he lifted his head and kissed her closed eyelids and her hair and the dimples beside her mouth. Then his lips sought hers again. They were trembling in each other's arms.

'Marjorie, my dear Marjorie,' he whispered with his lips against her ear. He lifted her chin gently with his hand. 'Open your eyes and look at me.'

She did so and felt that she was drowning in the depth of longing and passion that she met in his eyes. She whispered, 'Colin.'

With a kind of ecstasy and agony, he gazed into her great, innocent blue eyes, swimming with emotion – love and fear and bewilderment chasing themselves in their soft depths. He drew in his breath sharply. The blood was pounding in his temples. He pulled her head against his shoulder and stroked her hair as if she were a child, then he lifted her face again to his and kissed her very gently.

'I rather think I'm falling in love with you, soldier girl,' he said with a quaver in his voice. 'Do you mind terribly?'

Marjorie could not answer him. Her heart was pounding and her breasts were heaving and she was suddenly frightened by the wildness of her own emotions. She moved from the circle of his arms and was quickly on her feet.

'Colin,' she whispered, touching his shoulder with her fingertips, 'can we go back to the house now, please?'

He stood up instantly. 'Of course. Father will be waiting to show you his pictures of Derby winners. I can't expect to compete with all those horses.'

He smiled into her face as he took her hand and tucked it under his arm.

'I think your father is very nice,' Marjorie said.

'But you don't like my mother.'

'Oh, I didn't mean that. It's just that – I – I don't think your mother likes me very much.'

'You mustn't mind if Mother seems a bit stiff. She'll unbend when she comes to know you. You have no idea how really warm and jolly she can be once she takes you in.'

He noted her doubtful look and went on, 'It isn't that she dislikes you. It's just that – well, you see, since we lost Raif she doesn't like anything that she thinks might threaten our old way of life. She'd like things to stay as they've always been for us here.'

His voice became wistful. 'She doesn't realize the old way of life is gone for ever. When this war is over Britain will never be the same again. The days of landed gentry living lives of leisure will be over. Britain will have lost her power and be almost bankrupt. The days of the Raj are finished. Aristocrats from the old houses will have to go to work, or into trades. They'll never be able to keep up places like Enderby Hall and Medhurst Hall. I expect it's a good thing, really, but one does cling to the ways one has been brought up in.'

The note of boyish wistfulness in his voice sent a surge of sympathy through her. She knew that for her, too, when the war was finally ended life could never be the same. There had been too many marching feet. The world was in a state of upheaval, and yet she was full of the hope expressed in the words of the song: 'There'll be love and laughter and peace ever after, tomorrow. Just you wait and see . . . '

When they arrived at the house, looming huge and mysterious, with the moonlight shining on its ancient stone turrets and walls and myriads of windows, Colin said, 'You like secret gardens, Marjorie; we have a secret garden, you know. At least, we have a garden with a secret.'

'You do?' She was intrigued.

'Yes, do you want to see it?'

'Oh, yes, please.'

'Well then, come on.' Holding her hand he led her through the garden to the secret doorway concealed beneath the ivy.

He was delighted by her expression as she watched him take the key from its hiding place and open the ancient door.

'Oh – it's a secret passage!' she exclaimed.

They stepped inside and Colin closed the door behind them, flashing his torch down the long stone passageway. Then he flicked off the torch and they were in blackness. Marjorie gave a little squeal.

Hungrily he drew her close against his body and his lips sought and found hers. His long sweet kiss set her trembling.

Timidly, she slipped her arms up around his neck and clung to him. In the inky darkness with his body moulding with hers and his breath warm against hers, she felt that not only their bodies but their inner selves were like one person, and she was dizzy with joy.

At last he lifted his lips from hers and she could feel him struggling with himself.

'Sweet, sweet Marjorie,' he whispered huskily.

He loosened his arms from around her and she dropped hers.

After a moment he said lightly, but with a tremor in his voice, 'Come on, I'll show you the secret escape passage of the Enderbys. At the time of Oliver Cromwell, many a bold cavalier slipped down this passage when the Roundheads were after him.'

She clung to his arm, joyous emotions spinning through her as they proceeded along the passageway. I'm sure now – I felt it when we were kissing there in the dark – I'm not just an amusing little Canadian girl, Marjorie thought. *He does love me!*

They reached the wall of the library and Colin was searching for the secret spot to press so the section of the bookcase would swing in to admit them, when the voice of the Earl of Rivermere, raised slightly above normal tones, came clearly to them from the other side: 'Honora, you are not being kind to Colin's friend. You have been playing the grand lady ever since she arrived.'

The countess's voice answered him: 'Being Countess of Rivermere does qualify one to be a fine lady, wouldn't you say?'

'Humbug,' the earl answered. 'There's no need to push it down someone's throat, especially a visitor from Canada where they don't have titles and don't understand that kind of thing.'

The countess's voice came back, 'I suppose you think I should have clapped her on the back and asked her to call me by my first name. Don't you see what's happening, Teddy? I was so sure that Colin and Ashley were going to announce their engagement at her birthday party last night and I'm sure it would have happened, had he not met that little creature.'

'She looks like a jolly fine young woman to me – splendid rider.'

'I'm not saying there is anything wrong with her,' the countess replied. 'She may be perfectly splendid, but not for Colin. She's practically a little savage compared to the Enderbys. She might even have native blood in her. We know absolutely nothing about her.'

'We know she volunteered to come over here and risk her life to help save England. Jolly plucky, I'd say – driving about in London in those V-bomb raids – and she didn't even have to be over here.'

'Oh, I have nothing against the child.' Lady Rivermere's voice sounded weary. 'But Ashley is of our own kind. Her ancestry can be traced back to the Plantagenets.'

Marjorie didn't hear the earl's reply. She had been standing like a stunned person, unable to move, but she regained control of herself now and turned and fled down the passageway, with Colin hastening behind her.

When they were once more outside in the garden, Colin saw her face, drained of all colour, looking at him out of eyes huge and full of pain.

'Is it true?' she whispered. 'Were you going to announce your engagement to Ashley last night at her birthday party?'

Colin took both her hands in his and looked into her eyes, his own face white with strain. 'Marjorie, let me explain,' he pleaded.

Too numb to protest, she let him lead her to a seat on a little rustic bench, and he told her the whole story.

'It was always Raif she loved, not me. It was Raif we were both thinking of when we became engaged. We were feeling like lonely lost children, and in those moments our longing for Raif drew us together and we made a commitment that suited neither of us.'

Marjorie was silent and he sat watching and waiting for her to speak. She stared across the garden and he could feel a great gulf opening between them. Then she said, 'But you did ask her to marry you, and if you hadn't met me you would have announced your engagement last night. You must have some love for her.'

'Yes, I do love Ashley, but not the way I love you. She's the dear companion of my childhood and almost my sister-in-law. She'd already realized it wouldn't work. She has no more desire to marry me than I have to marry her. We were both jolly glad to get out of it.'

He tried to put his arm around her, saying coaxingly, 'Come

101

on, little soldier girl, say that you understand, and kiss me. You haven't forgotten that I saved your life and now you belong to me, have you?'

But Marjorie pulled away from him and stood up, her face set. 'I do understand, Colin. But your mother was right. I don't belong in your world. I'm just a girl you met in an air raid in unusual circumstances, and perhaps you are a little taken with me, but it will blow over when I'm gone from your life and you'll realize that you belong with your own kind. No doubt you and Ashley will marry and be very happy with each other. Now I want to go in the house.'

Colin jumped up and tried to take her in his arms. 'No, Marjorie. No. It's not like that. You must believe me. I love you,' he pleaded.

But she pulled away from him. 'I want to go inside now, Colin,' she said resolutely, turning and walking rapidly away from him, without looking back. She could not bear to speak another word to him.

Never in her life had such misery gripped her. It was as if a steel band had been fastened about her by cruel hands and was being twisted and twisted, squeezing all the life out of her.

She could not bear to lose him, but she made a fierce resolution never to see him again.

Chapter 12

Jessy Cole lay on her bed with her hands behind her head, smiling faintly at Lord Haw Haw telling the allies, on the nightly German radio broadcast to them, to lay down their arms and save themselves from certain annihilation at the hands of the invincible forces of the Third Reich.

It was five o'clock on Sunday afternoon. She had not seen any of her roommates since that morning. Helen, who had finally managed to find transport to Horsham to see Carl, had said goodbye to Jessy at eight o'clock, feverish with anticipation, anxiety and love.

'Oh, Jessy, do you think he'll be all right?' she asked anxiously.

Jessy sat up, with her bright reassuring smile. 'Of course. Just don't try to jump into bed with him. I don't think he'll be up to anything like that yet.'

Helen blushed and laughed. 'Oh Jess, you're awful,' she said as she hurried out.

Jessy found herself in an unaccustomed mood. She spent the day poking around, laundered a few clothes and went for a stroll along the Serpentine by herself. She lunched alone in the mess hall. Then she spent the rest of the day reading and daydreaming and listening to the wireless.

Lord Haw Haw always amused her, but she did not find him so funny today. He was talking to the American boys in Normandy: 'You have wives and sweethearts waiting for you,' his cultured English voice intoned persuasively. 'George Washington fought to free you from English tyrants. Why should you leave your mangled bodies over here for them? Go home Yankees, to the women who love you. Go home to Uncle Sam and apple pie. England will soon be blown out of the water;

don't go down with her. Save yourselves.'

Jessy thought of a tall blond Yankee riding high on a flamethrower.

She had not been brought up in any orthodox faith, but she believed in God – a cheerful sort of belief, coupled with love and life and fun. She never pictured God as angry or punitive, or having any hand in the bad things of the world. If men wanted to kill one another, stupidly, certainly they could not blame God for their foolishness. Really, there was plenty of food for everyone, in fact, plenty of everything if only they wanted to share it.

She wanted to pray for Bob Anders – although she seldom asked God for anything – but she could not bring herself to do it. It seemed unfair for her to ask Him to intercede for the life of someone she loved when there were so many other boys dying over there. Bob would just have to take his chances, as she took hers. But she was grateful for that last night out there in Sussex Square.

For the first time since she had enlisted she wondered what she would be doing now if there was no war. If I had met him and there was no war, she thought, last night I would have been singing at the Glen Club and he would be there listening to me and we would go to a party afterwards. She smiled naughtily. Today Bob and I would, most likely, just be getting out of bed to go out.

Her happy daydream was broken into by the sound of footsteps coming slowly up the stairs, and in a moment Helen came dragging herself into the room and fell down on to her bed. She buried her face in her pillow, moaning and clutching the blanket.

Jessy leapt from her bed and rushed to her. 'Helen! Helen! What is it?'

Helen moaned hopelessly.

Jessy shook her. 'Helen, stop it! Speak to me.'

Helen let her friend turn her over and stared with tortured eyes in her white, twisted face. 'Carl,' she whispered. 'Carl.'

Fear shot through Jessy. She drew in her breath sharply. 'What is it, Helen? Carl isn't – isn't?'

Helen continued to stare up at her dumbly, shaking her head from side to side. At last words came in a cracked whisper. 'He wouldn't speak to me, Jessy. He wouldn't speak to me. I know he's dying.'

Jessy stared at her in bewilderment. Carl had certainly not been that bad when she saw him last. She put her arm around Helen and waited for her to continue.

The words tumbled out jerkily. 'I was so excited. The nurse took me to the ward. The curtains were pulled around his bed. I went in with him. His face was towards the wall and he looked so – so white and terrible. I thought he was dead. But I bent over him and he turned his head and opened his eyes and looked into mine. He stared at me with the most awful look. Then he turned from me and said, "Go away Helen. Go away."

'I got down on my knees beside his bed and begged him to look at me. I told him how much I loved him, but he just kept his face turned and said, "Go away. Go away." Then he went unconscious and the doctor and the nursing sister rushed in. They made me leave him. They said my being there upset him terribly.

'I stayed all day, before they would let me in to see him again. I thought he must have lost his mind from shock and as soon as he came to himself it would be all right. But as soon as he saw me again he became really angry and lost consciousness again. They wouldn't let me stay with him any longer. And then it was time for me to return to London because I have to go on duty tonight. They're short of drivers and I have to take the ambulance to the coast to bring our wounded boys back to Twenty-three General. I know Carl is dying. Why, oh why wouldn't he talk to me, Jess?'

'He must have gone bomb happy,' Jessy said. 'He was all right when I left him. His face was all lit up and smiling and he was looking forward to seeing you.'

Helen continued shaking her head from side to side in dumb, helpless misery.

Just then Elsie Love walked into the room. She took in the scene and her face went white. 'What's the matter?'

'It's Carl,' Jessy said briefly.

Elsie's face went the colour of old putty and her eyes started from her head in terror. 'He – he isn't – dead?' she whispered.

Jessy shook her head and told her briefly what had happened when Helen visited her husband.

'He – he isn't going to die, is he?' Elsie said fearfully.

105

Before Jessy could give her an answer, Marjorie came in. Her face was white and drained, but she managed to smile feebly as she said hello to the other girls. Then she saw their faces. 'What's the matter?'

'Carl,' Jessy said.

'Killed?'

'No, but he's in bad shape.' Jessy told Marjorie what had happened at Horsham hospital that morning.

Marjorie watched Helen's pathetic face as she sat and fingered the rosary that always hung around her neck, and her heart went out to her friend.

'Oh, I'm sure it must be a mistake. Of course Carl wants to see Helen. He must be in shock. Perhaps he thought the Nazis had him.'

Helen shook her head. 'He looked at me and turned his head away. He said, "Go away, Helen." He knew me.'

'But perhaps he thought he was speaking to someone else. Perhaps he thought it was the enemy and he said "go away", and then he said "Helen" because he was calling for you. Oh, I know it will be all right. The thing you two have between you is too big for anything to come between it.'

Helen shook her head. 'You didn't see him, Marjorie. I know him so well. Carl is dying and I can't do anything to save him except to pray. Will you, too?'

Marjorie put her arms around her. 'Of course,' she said. 'I always pray for Carl every night.'

Helen looked at Jessy. Jessy nodded. Since she had no personal stake in it, she had no scruples about praying for Carl. It was not like asking for a personal exemption.

'I have to go to the mess hall,' Elsie said and rushed from the room.

Terrifying voices were screaming in her brain: She had killed Carl. No one must ever know what she had done. What if the nursing sister had told someone that she had been in to see Carl? What if they put it all together? What if Jessy found out? Well, she would deny it. Tomorrow she would ask for a transfer. She would find some way to get away from here – back to Canada. She would have her mother cable to say that she was ill, then she could get home on compassionate grounds – but how would she get her mother to send the cable? Letters back to Canada from

106

the war zone were censored.

She had not really wanted to go to the mess hall for anything. It was the first thing that came to her mind to get her out of that room – away from the eyes of her roommates. She would go and find an officer and ask for a transfer. She would make up some story to get away from London, and England.

The officers' quarters were beside the mess hall. She was going up the stairs towards the second floor where Captain Burns had her office, when the awful wail of the air raid warning struck fresh terror into her. Stumbling with panic, she fled up the stairs and knocked frantically on Captain Burns's door. She must get out of England. There was no answer. Then she heard the blood-chilling chug-chugging in the sky. She knocked again, bruising her knuckles. The sound in the sky stopped abruptly and a deathly silence, like a smothering blanket, descended.

She screamed and ran wildly back down the stairs. She was at the door when her ears were deafened by a thunderous crash and she felt herself driven to the floor in the midst of falling bricks and mortar, while the world rocked crazily about her and all the breath was sucked from her body.

Chapter 13

'Better not get too close,' Jessy warned. 'The rest of that building looks like it's ready to go.'

The choking dust was still rising from the mass of rubble blocking the doorway of the remains of the CWAC officers' quarters. It had taken the three girls only moments to race across the street after the V-bomb landed.

'But what if there's someone inside?' Marjorie took a step forward.

Jessy caught her arm. 'No way we can get in there I'm afraid, Marj. Let's hope old Hot Burns was cuddling up with Major Farrow at his flat tonight.'

The three of them were turning away, when a sound made them halt abruptly. A faint cry came from under the debris in the doorway.

'*Help! Oh, help! Please, please, help me!*'

'Elsie!'

Ignoring the teetering slabs of plaster and brick, they rushed forward and peered down under the remains of the doorway arch.

Elsie's grimy and tear-stained face looked up at them.

'*Oh, God! She's trapped under there!*' Helen cried. 'Jesus – Mary.' Her hand flew to her rosary.

'Don't panic, Lovey,' Jessy said coolly. 'We'll get you out.'

'Helen,' Elsie whispered. 'I have to speak to Helen – Oh please.'

Marjorie said, 'I think she's caught in a little pocket. I don't think she's really injured. If we could only lift this slab a little, I think we could get her out.'

'No. No.' Elsie rasped. 'Helen. I must speak to Helen. I can hear it moving above me. It's coming down. I'm going to be killed. Get Helen – *please!*'

They heard the pile of debris creak above her.

'You aren't going to be killed Lovey,' Jessy said, looking the situation over carefully. 'You haven't had supper yet, and we can't let you go on an empty stomach.'

Helen knelt and put her face close to Elsie's. 'I'm here,' she said. 'We're going to get you out of here. Then you can tell me.'

'No. No, you can't get me out,' Elsie said frantically. 'I'm going to die. It's Carl – Helen – I – I lied to him. I saw him. I lied. I told him you didn't love him any more. I said you had another man. I said you were afraid to tell him.'

Helen gasped and started back. 'Why? Why? Elsie?'

'I thought he would love me. *Oh, I've killed Carl!*'

'What a prize little bitch,' Jessy said and started moving bricks.

'Oh, God,' Helen cried, then quickly crossed herself as she stooped to help.

Marjorie had her hands on the corner of the great slab of plaster that pinned down Elsie. 'If you can get enough bricks off, we can manage to raise this and pull her out, I think.'

Then they heard the ominous approach of another V-bomb and looked at each other, the same thought plain in each face. If this one fell anywhere in the vicinity, the rest of the building would come thundering down on them.

The angry, bumblebee rumbling was filling the air. In the sky above them, approaching fast, they saw the sinister silver bullet with its red wake of fire.

'Pretty,' Jessy remarked, and carefully removed another brick.

The earth vibrated as the bomb passed over their heads. The structure groaned.

'It's no good,' Elsie cried. 'You'll all be killed.'

'I can reach her now. Take my hands, Elsie,' Helen said through her teeth.

'Pull, Helen, pull,' Marjorie said. 'The slab is loose. I can hold it up – I think. Hurry.'

Jessy gingerly put a brick aside and grabbed Helen around the waist settling back on her heels. 'Come on, tug-o'-war!' she grunted, pulling back with all her strength.

Elsie's shoulders came out, scraped and bleeding, with her shirt shredded.

'*Move! It's going!*'

They dragged Elsie to safety and collapsed on top of her just as the rest of the building toppled, obliterating the doorway where she had been trapped.

'You saved my life,' Elsie whispered, her eyes fastened on Helen with awe and shame. 'You knew what I'd done and yet you risked your life for me.' She covered her face with her hands and great, wracking sobs shook her.

The street was beginning to fill with people.

Jessy leaned over and shook Elsie. 'Cut it out, Lovey,' she said lightly. 'You sound like a porpoise with asthma.' She turned her head to Helen and Marjorie. 'Let's get her upstairs.'

Between them they pulled Elsie to her feet. The All Clear went just as they deposited her on her bed and covered her with a blanket. She lay under it shivering, her eyes closed.

'I wonder – what about the officers?' Marjorie said with a note of dread.

Elsie opened her eyes. 'There was no one in,' she whispered. 'I was knocking on the door when the bomb came.'

'*Carl!*' Helen said frantically. 'I must get to Carl. Oh, Elsie, how could you? Why would you tell Carl such a dreadful thing?'

Elsie choked on a painful sob. 'I must have been mad,' she gasped. 'I hated you so for taking him away from me. He was the only person I ever loved. I thought I was going to be happy for the first time in my life. Then you came along. I thought, if he believed you didn't love him he would turn to me and I would get him back.'

Helen stared at her in bewilderment. 'But Elsie, Carl was never your boyfriend. You were just another friend he had coffee with sometimes. Honestly, he never even asked you for a date, or took you anywhere, now did he?'

Elsie covered her face with her fingers. 'I know, I know,' she sobbed. 'And you – you cared enough about me to pull me out of there.'

Jessy said, 'There's no more time to waste. We have to get down there to Carl, somehow, in a hurry, and explain this mess to him.'

'But will he believe me?' Helen said fearfully. 'And how will we get there and back? I have to be on duty at midnight.'

Elsie uncovered her face and sat up. 'I can get you there,' she said feverishly. 'If I can only get a hold of Major Ellis, he'll let me take the staff car, I know. He was an accountant for my father, and he'll want to go back to work for him after the war. I have his phone number.' She threw back the blanket and ran from the room.

'I'll take your detail,' Jessy told Helen.

'But have you ever driven the big ambulance before?'

Jessy laughed softly. 'If it's got a motor in it, I can drive it.'

'I wish I could help,' Marjorie said. 'I've driven the big vehicles too, you know.'

'You might end up at the wrong coast,' Jessy said, laughing affectionately.

Bonny came breezing in at that moment, dressed in her baseball uniform. She was scowling fiercely.

'How was your game?' Marjorie asked.

'Those damn Limeys beat us.'

'Was Moose the umpire?' Jessy asked mischievously.

Bonny's scowl deepened. 'Don't mention Moose.'

'Didn't you have a good time when you went pub-crawling with him the other night?'

'No. I told him off.'

'What were you quarrelling over – baseball?' Marjorie asked.

'No. He tried to get fresh,' Bonny said disgustedly. 'We were cutting across the square and he tried to drag me down on the grass, and when I told him I wasn't that kind of girl, he wouldn't believe me. He said he had been told all the CWACs were ground sheets for the officers. And that was when I slapped him good and hard across the face.'

'Goodness. What did he do then?' Marjorie asked.

'He grabbed my wrists and held them and said I was a nice little tid-bit and he would like to get into my pants. I kicked him good and hard on the shins and told him there wouldn't be room for him, because there's one asshole in there already.'

Jessy laughed delightedly and Marjorie was smiling. Even Helen smiled, in spite of her worry.

'Holy smoke!' Bonny said, looking out of the window. 'They've got the officers' quarters.' She had come in the back way and had not seen the shattered building until now.

'It's all right,' Marjorie hastened to explain. 'They were all

111

out. There was nobody over there except Elsie.'

'The poor little shit,' Bonny said, aghast, before Marjorie could finish her story.

Jessy cut in quickly, 'No. She didn't buy it. We got her out.'

By silent, mutual consent none of them mentioned what Elsie had done to Helen.

'Well, old Hot Burns doesn't need her quarters anyway. She spends most of her time with Major Farrow,' Bonny said. 'I hope those flying boxcars didn't knock out the mess hall. I'm so famished, even that gunk they give you will look good.'

Major Ellis was not sorry to have an excuse to get out of London. A V-bomb had fallen not far from his flat and he was as terrified by them as Elsie was; however his position, which he felt very strongly, forced him to put on a nonchalant front. But since his fair, rather colourless complexion took on a greenish shade every time the alert sounded, he was not very successful in fooling anyone.

He was small and pompous, with a light-coloured moustache and light blue eyes. He patterned his talk after the British officers and called everyone 'old chap', and said 'good show' and things like that. In fact, he was more British than the British themselves, although he had been in London only a few months.

Fortunately for his timid disposition, he was not fighting category. Jessy thought, as they drove towards Horsham: He's one of the kind Moose had in mind when he said they would drown in their own pee if a gun was fired off near them.

It was almost eight o'clock when they drew into the military hospital grounds at Horsham and hurried anxiously to Carl's ward. The nursing sister on duty at the desk started slightly when Helen told her who she was. Concern showed through her brisk professional manner.

'I'm afraid there's bad news about Sergeant Huntley,' she said with a pitying look at Helen.

Helen clutched her beads. 'No. Oh no! He can't be *dead?*'

The nurse looked away from her anguished face for a moment, then she said gently, 'Mrs Huntley, I'm sorry, your husband is dying. It seems the shock of losing his leg was too much for him. The doctor and the ward sister are with him now.'

Jessy had Elsie by the hand. She pushed forward into the ward, directly to Carl Huntley's bed, with Helen behind them, praying and fingering her rosary. The doctor and nurse who were working on him looked up sharply as they burst through the curtains.

Carl's eyes were closed and his face was completely without colour.

Jessy pushed the doctor and nurse aside and knelt beside his bed, her face against his. 'Carl! Carl!'

His blue eyes, shadowed by approaching death, flickered open and looked into hers.

'You silly bastard, Carl,' Jessy said. 'What are you trying to kick the bucket for? You ought to have your ass kicked. How could you believe those lies Elsie told you about Helen, just because she's all screwed up over you?'

A faint light came into his eyes and his lips tried to move.

'You shut up and listen,' Jessy said forcefully. She yanked Elsie over to the bed. '*Tell him!*' she ordered.

Elsie was sobbing uncontrollably. 'I lied – I lied,' she gulped. 'There is no other man – Helen loves you. I was jealous. I lied.'

'*Fight, Carl, fight*. You can't do *this* to Helen.' Jessy put her face close and her eyes locked with his, willing him to come back to life. Then Helen was beside her and she stepped back.

Helen knelt with her arm across his body and her face close to his, looking into his eyes and pleading, 'Carl, Carl, don't die – please, please, don't die. I love you. I love you. *Mary, Jesus, Joseph.*'

Her agonized prayer was answered. The shadow receded from his eyes and gradually the light strengthened in them. His hand moved feebly towards Helen's on the bed. She touched her lips to his. Almost imperceptibly his hand tightened on hers.

'My God!' the doctor whispered in awe. '*He's coming back.*'

Jessy looked up at the ceiling. 'Much obliged,' she whispered, then she grabbed the limp, sobbing Elsie by the hand. 'Come on. Let's get out of here.'

It was only when she heard Bonny mention her hunger that Marjorie realized she had eaten nothing since dinner the night before at Enderby. After the others had left for Horsham, she accompanied Bonny to the mess hall where, in spite of the close shave with the V-bomb, there was a hot supper.

Only half hearing, she listened to Bonny express her disgust with Moose. 'We'd have won the ball game today if it wasn't for that big ugly jerk calling my two-base hit a foul. I almost cracked him over the head with the bat . . . '

After supper Bonny prepared to go out.

'Are you going pub-crawling with Moose again?' Marjorie asked mischievously.

Bonny snorted. 'I wouldn't shit on the best part of him.'

Marjorie winced.

'I'm meeting some of the team over at Molly's. We're going to have a couple and then go to see Gary Cooper in *Sergeant York* at the Sally Ann hut. Hey, why don't you come along? You can have tea or something.'

Marjorie shook her head. 'I'm pretty tired, Bonny. I'm afraid they'd find me dull company.'

Bonny looked at her keenly. 'Ah, I know, you've probably got a date with that airman I saw you with. Hey, who was he anyway? Was he ever good-looking! And an officer too, with all those ribbons on his chest. He really looks like something, even if he is a Limey.'

Marjorie forced a smile. 'Oh, he was just someone I met very casually.'

'Humph. I think you're hiding something, Marj,' Bonny said suspiciously. 'But I've got to go now. You'll have to tell me all about it tomorrow.'

Marjorie thought when she was alone: How I envy her. Bonny would never sit around pining over a lost love. The misery that had been suppressed by the emergency of saving Elsie and their anxiety for Carl now came flooding back in an overwhelming tide. She buried her face in her pillow and moaned.

She wanted Colin so badly that her whole being ached with the pain of it. She saw the clean, strong line of his chin, the wavy brown hair and kindly, twinkling brown eyes. She remembered the taste of his lips and the smell of him, warm and clean and masculine.

Again she heard Lady Enderby's words cutting her dreams to shreds.

She wondered how she had managed to sit politely and listen while the earl told her about every Derby winner and showed the pictures in his big album. It had seemed an eternity before she could decently say good night and go up to her room. She

114

remembered how the earl remarked, with a sideways glance at his wife, 'I hope the next time you visit us, my dear, we'll be able to find you something a little more comfortable than the Nun's Cell.'

Marjorie thought as she crept shivering under the bedcovers in the icy room that the Nun's Cell was a name that suited it very well. She wondered if Lady Rivermere kept it made up especially for unwanted guests. She lay awake for hours, imagining long lines of Enderby ancestors moving down the ancient hallway and looking down their noses as they passed the room where the intruder from Canada was billeted.

She rose before the first rays of sunlight penetrated the darkness of her cell and wrote a note to Colin on the writing pad she carried in her purse, and another one to Lady Rivermere. She sealed them and left them on the reception table. With one last look around her, she stepped out into the rosy dawn and made her way on foot down the winding road, with the beauty of the country morning mocking her, to the station at Wendover.

It was not yet eight o'clock when she arrived at Baker Street station that morning. She could not bear to go back to her barracks just yet. She boarded a doubledecker bus and rode around London for a time, finally alighting at Kew Gardens, where she spent the rest of the day.

She wished suddenly, as she lifted her face from her pillow, that she drank. She remembered the pleasant feeling that had come over her after Colin had given her the brandy in the George and Horses. Maybe she should get dressed and go join Bonny at Molly's pub, instead of brooding here alone.

The wail of the air raid siren cut into her thoughts. She felt for the dog tags around her neck. No it would never do, if her body was found in a pub. Not when Mother and Dad hate liquor so much, she thought.

She heard the chug-chug of an approaching buzz bomb. It passed over and faded away, to be followed almost at once by another and then another, and another. Three times the motor cut and she heard the death-dealing thud of them landing. Once the building shuddered and the windows rattled and a roar filled the air.

It seemed Hitler had unleashed the full fury of his insane destructive hate against London.

She pulled back the curtains and sat in the darkness watching the spectacle as they sailed through the sky but she was insensible of the fear they usually inspired – detached, as if watching some weird kind of show that had nothing to do with her.

So black was the void within her, no other emotion could push through. I feel like a shell, she thought. No self-respecting doodle bug would expend its power on a shell.

She pulled the curtains back into place and went to bed.

The next morning at ten o'clock she reported to the Transportation Office. The sergeant marched her in to face the court of inquiry. She was told to sit down facing the three CMHQ officers conducting the inquiry and they began putting questions to her.

I do hope they don't take away my driver's standing orders, she thought as she observed their faces growing sterner as they probed as to what she had been doing so far off her route when the V-bomb fell.

She was becoming more and more flustered, when an orderly tapped at the door, entered and handed a note to the officer in charge.

He read it, gave a little whistle and looked curiously at Marjorie. 'This court of inquiry is cancelled by order of Brigadier Raham. Private Hatfield is assigned to Major Middleton, the British liaison officer at CMHQ, as his personal driver. You are dismissed, Hatfield. Pick up your orders at the dispatch office and report to Major Middleton at once.'

Chapter 14

Stunned and bewildered at the sudden turn of events, Marjorie left the room. Not until she reached the dispatch office did she recall where she had heard the name of Major Middleton, and her heart flopped over. The Earl of Rivermere had mentioned meeting Brigadier Raham at the home of Major Middleton.

Colin! Even though she would never see him again, he was still the knight in shining armour, riding on his white horse to save her. He must have asked his father to intercede for her. One last act of gallantry towards the Canadian girl he had saved from death, before he put her out of his life for ever.

Her mind was so full of Colin as she drove the Ford staff car towards Canadian Military Headquarters at Trafalgar Square that she almost lost herself again.

Major Middleton was a florid, middle-aged, cheerful-looking Englishman. He looked up from the papers on his desk with twinkly eyes as Marjorie stood before him and saluted.

'So, you are Private Hatfield,' he said, motioning her to a chair in front of his desk. 'Sit down. I'm told you have trouble finding your way around our London streets.' There was a humorous look on his face.

Marjorie flushed. 'I'm afraid, sir, I find it a bit – a bit confusing. But I expect I'll grow used to it soon. You see, it's the one-way streets. And nothing is laid out in blocks. I never saw a one-way street in Calgary, and when you went around a block you always came back to the same street. Over here in London, when I try to do that I end up in a different part of the city altogether.'

'Of course you do. However, you won't have to worry about finding your way around. I shall do the navigating for us, and I do believe I've managed to learn how to find my way about in London.'

His friendly informal manner put Marjorie at ease and she found herself liking him instantly.

'Today I'm taking you on a rather long trip. I have to visit a Canadian unit at Brighton. I suppose you know your way to Brighton?' he said, with the twinkle growing in his eyes.

Marjorie stammered, 'I'm – I'm afraid, sir, I've never been to Brighton. I do have a map,' she added hopefully.

Major Middleton smiled at her. 'Don't worry, you'll love it. In peacetime it's a seaside resort, and it's reputed to be a favourite rendezvous of Lord Nelson and Lady Hamilton; in fact, I'll take you to a little teahouse, on our way down there, where those two historical figures are said to have had clandestine meetings from time to time.'

He nodded his head.

'If you'd like to go back to the car now, I shall be down in a few minutes.'

Marjorie was an excellent driver. Her only difficulty was her inability to keep her directions straight and if she had someone with her who knew the way, as Major Middleton did today, she could thoroughly enjoy the drive. Good as his word, he took her to the famous teahouse. He also showed her the legendary tree where the village blacksmith had stood, according to the poem.

What a pleasure it was to be away from the wailing air raid sirens and the constant danger. Out here in the countryside, except for the military vehicles rumbling down the road, you could scarcely believe there was a war on.

'I hear you're a friend of the Earl and Countess of Rivermere,' the major said over tea.

Marjorie blushed. 'I wouldn't say that I'm really a friend. I did spend a weekend there.'

'Ah, you're more young Colin's friend, no doubt. Absolutely splendid man. Known him since he was born – he and Raif, and Ashley Medhurst. The three of them used to keep things lively around there in the old days before the war. Raif was such a dashing fellow. Poor Ashley – she and Raif absolutely doted on one another. Would have been married by now, if Dunkirk hadn't come along.'

He paused, gazing off into space, then changed the subject

118

abruptly. 'Rivermere tells me you're a splendid horsewoman. Jumped Minnette over Beecher's Brook, and you'd never been on an English saddle before.'

'The earl spoke to you about me?'

'Yes, rather. Told me all about the brigadier's car. Poor old Raham. He was looking forward no end to that car coming from Canada. Frightfully big posh job, wasn't it?'

'Oh yes,it was a Buick,' Marjorie said regretfully.

'Much too big for our London streets. He's better off without it.'

The merry twinkle in his eyes made Marjorie smile in spite of herself.

She was impressed by Brighton. While waiting for Major Middleton to complete his business at the Canadian unit, she drove the short distance down to the seashore, left the car and looked down the long strip of pebbled beach. Its beauty was marred by the endless rolls of heavy barbed wire.

She shuddered as she imagined the feelings of the men who had laid the wire, expecting the German hordes to come at them from the sea momentarily.

The sea was high today, the waves breaking hard against the shore. Standing alone, looking out over the Channel, she captured something of how the British felt about this island of theirs.

She understood that look in Colin's eyes and, behind the merry twinkle, in the eyes of Major Middleton. Their air of cool nonchalance covered a deathless determination and devotion beyond any other love. She knew that each of them was ready to shed his last drop of blood defending this wave-washed island of kings and conquerors.

In them moved the same spirit that had dwelt in Drake, Frobisher and Raleigh – and Sir Richard Grenfell, refusing to bow his head to the Spaniards and sailing his little *Revenge* into the midst of their great Armada.

She was proud to be kin to these people – glad that Canada had stuck by the motherland in her hour of need.

Colin's face came to her as she watched the vast waves roll in and break against the shore. The ache that engulfed her was crippling.

' "*Break, break, break, At the foot of thy crags, O Sea!*",' she whispered the remembered lines of Tennyson's poem. ' "*But the tender grace of a day that is dead Will never come back to me*".'

She turned towards her car with a dry sob.

What did he think when he read my note? she wondered, turning back for a last look out at the ocean.

It had been very short. She had thanked him for saving her life and for showing her his home. She had finished by telling him she did not intend ever to see him again and saying she hoped that he would find happiness with Ashley now that she was out of his life for ever.

In her note to Lady Rivermere she had apologised for leaving without saying goodbye, but explained that circumstances had arisen that made it impossible for her to stay any longer at Enderby. She included a message for the earl, telling him how much she regretted not being able to take advantage of his kind offer to teach her to ride in the English style.

No doubt Colin would feel a tender twinge when he first read her note, and then he would be relieved to be free of any obligation he feared he had led her to expect. She expected his declaration of love for her had been one of those swift surges of emotion that rushed up on you in wartime, like the surging waves out there – rushed up and then died quickly against the shore.

But her emotions were not dying. Her love and longing for Colin were rising within her, until she felt she was drowning.

She turned and fled back to the car.

It was dark before they arrived back in London. Near Aldershot they heard the steady drone of many planes overhead.

Major Middleton said with satisfaction, 'Those are our lads up there, going over to give 'em hell.'

Marjorie felt the blood drain from her face. British bombers on their way to destroy the enemy – *The escort!* – Maybe the Spitfires would be with them. *Colin could be up there. What if he never came back?* She would never know if Colin . . . If anything happened to him. Unless she heard it through Major Middleton.

The ghastly vision crossed her mind of his Spitfire tumbling through the air in flames. She shivered.

The major sensed her agitation. He said cheerfully, 'Don't worry about our chaps up there. Best flyers in the world. They'll knock spots off those blighters.'

It was past eleven when she arrived back in her room at Sussex Square. Apparently asleep in her bed, Elsie Love was the only one of her roommates at home. Suddenly exhausted, Marjorie undressed quickly and dropped into bed.

Her head had scarcely touched the pillow when the air raid siren sounded, followed quickly by the sound of an approaching buzz bomb. She heard the motor cut and then the crunch of it landing. Scarcely had she drawn a sigh of relief when another one came over. The explosion was louder this time.

Close on their heels came a third, growing louder and louder, until its droning threat filled the room. Then a ghastly silence fell abruptly and hung in the air for an eternity of breathless moments. The thunderous explosion seemed to rock the building. Even as she let her breath go in a sigh of relief, she said a quick prayer for the victims, whoever they were, who had not been as lucky as herself. That one must have landed very near by, she thought.

On the other side of the room, she heard Elsie sobbing and whimpering. Marjorie went to her, sat on the edge of the bed, and put her arm around the terrified girl. 'It's all right, Elsie,' she soothed. 'Don't cry so. Everything will be all right.'

In the darkness the other girl's voice came to her in a choking whisper, 'Oh, Marjorie, I'm so scared.'

Marjorie patted her shoulder gently. 'So am I. But don't give in to it. Remember we're soldiers.'

She heard Elsie struggling with her tears. Gradually, her body stopped heaving and she sat up. With her head against Marjorie's shoulder she said in jerking gulps, 'It's – it's not just the bombs. I feel so – so – Oh, I can't tell you how I feel. Even after you all knew what – what I'd done to Carl and Helen you – you all risked your lives to pull me out of there. You risked your lives *for me*. No one ever did anything like that for *me*, before.'

She started to sob again.

Marjorie patted her. 'You would have done the same if it had been one of us,' she said, wondering guiltily if she was telling a big lie.

'No, I wouldn't have. You know I wouldn't. I'm too much of

a coward. I would have been hiding under my bed.'

'Hush. Not a bad idea – hiding under the bed. I've a good mind to do it myself, if those darn things don't stop coming over. Let's put the light on for a bit.' She did. 'There now, isn't that better?' She patted her briskly on the shoulder and Elsie winced.

'Is your shoulder sore, Elsie?'

Elsie nodded pathetically.

'Of course, it was scraped when we pulled you out. Here, let me have a look at it.' Pulling up the pyjama top, she examined the ugly scrape on Elsie's shoulder. 'Has this had any attention?'

Elsie shook her head.

'You mean you haven't been to the MIR, or had anything put on it?'

'No – No. Oh, do you think I should have? Do you think it might get infected?'

She looked so alarmed that Marjorie laughed in spite of herself. 'What a worrier you are, Elsie. No, it isn't likely to become infected, but I have some antiseptic lotion in my first-aid kit that I'll put on it, and I'll give you a couple of aspirin. Then you can get a good night's sleep and stop worrying.'

When she had finished administering first aid, Elsie looked bewilderedly at her. 'You really *are* kind,' she said. 'You really *do* care if I hurt, or not.'

Marjorie stared at her in amazement. 'Of course. We're comrades.'

Before she could speak again, they heard a buzz bomb, so loud it seemed to be heading straight for their room. Then it went dead. Together they plunged off the bed on to the floor, with their hands over their ears, in a crouch.

The building shook and the windows rattled in the thunder of the explosion.

'That was close,' Marjorie said as they sat up on the floor. Then they looked at each other and laughed.

Elsie's mind flashed back to the army girls she had seen marching along the street in Toronto, laughing together. For the first time she felt she was a part of that group.

'Are you hungry, Marjorie?' she asked. 'I have plenty of food in my barrack box.'

'As a matter of fact, I'm starved,' Marjorie answered. 'The mess hall was closed when I got in and I only had a light snack out in the country. Somehow I never felt hungry till now.'

Marjorie met Jessy Cole coming up the stairs the next morning as she was going to work. Her face was white and tired, but she smiled brightly.

'How – how did Helen make out with Carl?' The question had been on her mind since the night before, but Marjorie had not liked to ask Elsie about what had happened at Horsham hospital.

Jessy put her two fingers up in the V for Victory sign. 'How's that little toad Elsie?'

Marjorie said, 'You know, I think she came a long way yesterday.' She told her friend about the night before in the raid.

'You mean she actually shared her food with you? She'll make a soldier yet.' Jessy went upstairs laughing.

She was bone weary. She had not slept in twenty-four hours, and her night, after she left Helen with Carl, had been filled with wounded, suffering men. As she was climbing into bed the air raid siren went. 'Heil Hitler,' she said, thumbing her nose in the direction of the sky. She was asleep almost at once.

Major Middleton had more Canadian camps to visit in the country. If it had not been for the gnawing anguish she concealed, Marjorie would have enjoyed the next day. They visited the huge country estates where the Canadians were billeted in Nissen huts, with the officers occupying unused wings of the immense old houses, surrounded by acres of gardens.

There were courtyards and great stone stables and once she saw deer feeding on a green hillside, their sleek sides shining in the sunlight. But she did not see any place as beautiful and imposing as Enderby Hall. Her mind returned like a homing pigeon to Smugglers' Cove and she felt again the sweet warmth of Colin's lips on hers and the strong protection of his arms pressing her to him. She writhed inwardly, picturing him with Ashley.

Jessy was sitting alone in their room at the end of the day when Marjorie returned, listening with a smile on her face to Lord Haw Haw. She looked keenly at Marjorie's drooping shoulders and tired white face, with her blue eyes looking enormous and shadowed by a secret distress, and snapped off the wireless.

123

'What's the matter, Marj?' she asked softly. 'You look like the last act of *Camille*.'

Marjorie forced a little smile. 'Just a bit tired, I guess.'

'Hmmm,' Jessy said. 'That's not tired. That's *love*. Do you want to tell me about that Limey airman?'

Marjorie shook her head and looked away. 'There's nothing to tell. He was just a fellow I met in an air raid.'

'You met him that night the Brig's car got blown up, didn't you?'

Marjorie nodded. 'He was the one who took me into the pub.'

'And he was the one who came to the ball diamond when you were watching Bonny play. What went wrong? Did he try to get fresh with you?'

'Oh, no.' Marjorie shook her head vigorously. 'He wasn't like that at all. He was – wonderful.'

A tear escaped and slid down her nose.

Before Jessy could say anything else, the girl on duty downstairs popped in and told Marjorie that she had a visitor down in the sitting room.

In spite of her firm resolution never to see Colin again, Marjorie went downstairs with a wild hope that it might be him. Her heart was pounding against her rib cage.

But her visitor was Lady Ashley Medhurst. Marjorie stood, stunned.

'Lady – *Ashley!*' she finally managed to stammer.

Ashley held out her hand. 'You must call me Ashley,' she said, smiling.

Marjorie felt confusion overwhelm her. 'Won't you sit down – Ashley,' she said uncertainly.

'No thank you,' Ashley looked at her with friendly warmth. 'If you can spare me a little of your time, I've come to take you out to dinner. I was very disappointed that you never came to tea with me.'

Marjorie flushed. She felt she had behaved rather badly, slipping away from Enderby without saying goodbye to anyone.

'I – I – you're very kind,' she stammered.

'Not at all.' Ashley continued smiling gently at her out of warm, friendly hazel eyes. 'I have a taxi waiting. I was lucky enough to find one at Baker Street station. If you're free, we can

124

go. I'm absolutely famished.'

The genuine friendliness of the other young woman left Marjorie defenceless against her persuasive invitation. 'Just give me a few minutes to tidy up.'

'To the Ritz,' Ashley told the driver when they were seated in the cab.

On the way Ashley chatted lightly about London and pointed out various historic streets and landmarks. Marjorie was relieved not to have the burden of conversation thrust on her.

Moments before they arrived at the famous hotel the air raid siren wailed, but Lady Ashley paid not the slightest attention to it, continuing her sentence without a break.

The doorman at the Ritz looked delighted when he saw Ashley. He let them out with a flourish. 'How nice to see you again, your Ladyship,' he said with a broad smile.

Ashley paused to chat a moment with him, asking after his family, before she took Marjorie into the hushed hotel lobby, and on to the quietly luxurious dining room.

The head waiter came hurrying up to them, his face wreathed in smiles. 'Lady Ashley. What a great pleasure. It's been so long since we've seen you.'

Ashley smiled at him. 'Good evening, Luigi. Do you think you could find us a quiet table somewhere?'

'For your Ladyship we have always the best,' he said and led them to a secluded table in the far corner of the dining room. He hovered about solicitously for a few moments before leaving them to the care of a waiter who hurried to their table at his summons.

Lady Ashley asked Marjorie her preference in wine.

When Marjorie told her that she did not drink, for a moment she had the same surprised look Marjorie had seen on Colin's face that first night. Then she smiled. 'How fortunate you are. The wines available these days are really rather awful.'

Marjorie was feeling more and more bewildered. Why should this young woman, so poised and obviously at home in these rich surroundings, have made a special trip to London to take her to dinner at the famous Ritz Hotel, risking her life in the V-bomb raids that made the city such a dangerous place to be?

She looked quickly about her. She had read about the Ritz,

but she had never expected to be dining there. She had seldom eaten in any hotel dining room.

Very occasionally her parents had taken her to eat in the little Chinese restaurant in her little home town, four miles from the farm. The greatest meals she could remember eating had been on the cook cars when the threshers came at harvest time – roast beef and delicious slabs of apple pie.

Now she was completely at a loss as to what she should order and she began to feel very shy.

Ashley, very unobtrusively, made suggestions and, in spite of wartime restrictions, the meal when it came was delicious.

I feel like Alice after she went through the looking glass, Marjorie thought wryly – visiting with lords and ladies and dining at the Ritz with bowing waiters hovering over me. If it were not for her unhappy state of mind and her uneasiness about the purpose of Ashley's visit, she would have thoroughly enjoyed her adventure.

Ashley was smiling at her across the table. 'Colin told me all about what happened at Enderby last Saturday night.'

Marjorie looked at her in consternation. Before she could say anything, Ashley went on.

'No one found your note until late in the morning. They thought you were sleeping in. Colin dashed off to London as soon as he found you were gone, but he couldn't find you and he had to come back to go on duty. He came to see me before he left. The poor old boy was in a frightful state. He knew I would help him. I've never seen him like this over a girl before.'

Marjorie listened, feeling the colour come and go in her cheeks. 'But he – you – aren't you going to marry him?' she stammered. 'You – he – you were engaged.'

Ashley replied, 'That was jolly silly.' She paused, looking off into the distance for a moment, then she went on softly, 'It was Raif we were both thinking of. It was always Raif with me since we were children. You know, we were to have married, except for – for Dunkirk.'

'But you were engaged to Colin,' Marjorie persisted. 'And if I hadn't come along you would have announced your engagement at your birthday party.'

Ashley said, 'You don't know how jolly glad I was to find out that Colin had a girl he liked. I think we both knew it wouldn't

126

work right after I said yes to him, but I had to be sure how he felt. I was certain in the back of my mind that he didn't really love me, but when the world is topsy-turvey like it is today the people you've known all your life are like an anchor in the wind. I couldn't cut him adrift if I thought he needed me, but dear old Beau never could hide anything from Raif and me. As soon as I saw him, I knew he had a girl on his mind. It was right in his eyes.' She paused for a moment, looking at Marjorie's flushed face. Then she put her hand across the table on to Marjorie's.

'You know Colin never really had a girl before. I've never seen him look so happy as he did with you at Enderby. I was absolutely delighted. I simply adore Colin as a brother, and every time we say goodbye to him when he returns to duty I – we – we never know if he's coming back to us. But I don't want to marry him.' She looked away and was silent. Marjorie saw a deep incurable sadness in her eyes when she looked back again.

'There will never be anyone for me but Raif.' She broke off. 'Please forgive me for intruding on you like this, but I felt I had to come to see you. It was that look on Colin's face when he came to me. It was the same sort of look he had the day we had the news about Raif.'

Marjorie felt her heart filling with a great tenderness for this young woman who had gone to such lengths for Colin and for herself. At the same time a dreadful fear welled up. The one sentence embedded itself in her mind: *We never know if he's coming back to us!* What if she never saw Colin again? What if he never came back? She had walked out of his life without even saying goodbye. They could have had a few more happy hours together at Enderby. Perhaps she had made his last visit home unhappy.

'Oh, you mustn't think you intruded,' she said. 'It was so kind of you to come. I – I've been so confused and – and . . . ' She couldn't finish.

They were both silent for a moment, then Ashley said brightly, 'Well, I'm sure it will all come right now. We mustn't make ourselves wretched now must we?'

Marjorie lay awake in her bed for a long time that night. Her mind was a turmoil of conflicting thoughts. She moved from elation to fierce doubts. Colin did love her. She hugged the thought. But even if what Ashley had said was true, perhaps if she was out of the picture they might find their common childhood would be a bond that would draw them together again. And how could she, just a Canadian farm girl, ever hope to achieve the depth of understanding these two from the same nation and class would have between them? Probably, even now, he was thankful to be free of what might have become an embarrasing entanglement. But he had looked at her as if he meant it when he said he loved her. She had seen that look in young men's eyes before.

Her mind see-sawed until she fell into a troubled sleep, to dream of Colin's eyes looking at her reproachfully through a screen of blood-red fire.

She made a stern resolution when she woke to control her confused feelings, and to some extent she succeeded; although Colin's face kept popping up before her.

She saw little of her roommates that week. Bonny was out every night and Elsie, who had previously stuck around at night whimpering in her bed, had suddenly developed the habit of going out immediately after supper and not coming back until long after lights out. Jessy Cole was on night duty, driving the ambulance to the coast to pick up wounded men returning from the war zone.

Although she was grateful to have such a pleasant assignment, Marjorie felt a twinge of guilt about her own jammy job chauffeuring Major Middleton around London. He treated her more like a friend than a CWAC driver. He did not ride in the back in state as most staff officers did, but climbed cheerfully into the front seat with her, spilling ashes from his eternal pipe over his slightly untidy uniform, and telling her droll stories of London high society in prewar days that set her laughing delightedly.

Gradually, under his guidance, the streets and lanes of the ancient city began to form a pattern and her first confusion left her. She was amazed, at first, at the cool way the Londoners went about their business despite the constant V-bomb attacks. They stood patiently in the long queues waiting for buses, or in front of the theatres, scarcely looking up when the alert sounded.

The street performers continued their acts, singing and

dancing and playing accordions and barrel organs to amuse the people in the queues.

Then, it came to her. These were people who had been under siege for years and had grown accustomed to constant danger.

And as the days passed she found herself sharing this almost fatalistic attitude, expressed by the girls who had been stationed in London for some time: 'If it's going to get you, it's going to get you, and it can't get you unless it's got your number on it.'

Once she thought a V-bomb did have her number on it. She was sitting in her staff car waiting for Major Middleton when the bomb's motor cut and she watched in horrified fascination as it came gliding towards her, dropping lower and lower as it drew nearer, silent and silver in the sunlight.

She realized she was praying the same prayer she had that night when she had had her other narrow squeak, when it lifted abruptly on a current of air and sailed on far past her.

She told Jessy afterwards, 'I saw W1311 . . . but the last letter was missing.'

Jessy asked curiously, 'What were you thinking?'

'I was praying,' Marjorie said, and blushed. She did not tell Jessy what she had been praying.

When Friday night arrived, in spite of her stern resolution she was hoping desperately that Colin might come to see her. But although she stayed in her room all night, he did not come.

The next morning she resolved sternly to put him out of her mind. She would not moon around after him any more. Major Middleton did not require his car and she was free for the weekend. After breakfast she walked the short distance to Hyde Park and her feet, of their own accord it seemed, found their way across to Peter Pan's statue.

She stood gazing up at the carefreee, boyish face. She and Colin had had such fun chatting here. Could it be only a short week ago?

She had not told Jessy the prayer that had sprung to her lips – the prayer she had prayed that night she met Colin – but this time there had been a name on her lips: 'Please God, don't let me die without having *Colin* make love to me.'

She felt her cheeks grow hot as she remembered.

A voice at her elbow said, 'Hello, soldier girl.'

Chapter 15

She turned her head, with a little cry.

Colin was looking down at her with a smile in his eyes.

'Colin,' she whispered, her face alight with joy.

'You must have been thinking something dreadfully naughty when I came up,' he said teasingly. 'You were blushing. Don't tell me you were thinking the same sort of thoughts you had that night outside the George and Horses when you woke up in my arms?'

Marjorie blushed again and dropped her eyes from his.

Colin laughed, took her hand and tucked it under his arm. 'Come on, I only have today off. I want to take you for tea at Windsor. Fortunately there's still a bit of petrol left in the Rolls.'

'Oh, I'd love that.'

She went with him to the car, parked on Bayswater Road, trembling with the joy of his closeness as he pressed her hand against his body in the protection of his arm.

'Oh, Colin, please may we stop and see the castle before we have tea, if there's time? It looks so romantic and exciting, even if we can only stand by the gate and look up at it,' Marjorie asked excitedly. 'It's the first royal castle I've ever seen.'

'Of course,' Colin said, smiling at her excitement.

They were passing close by Windsor Castle, after the drive from London during which they had sat close, speaking little.

He pulled the car over and they strolled slowly up to the great gates. Marjorie gazed raptly at the towers and walls and myriad gleaming windows.

'Look,' Colin said, 'the King and Queen are in residence. The royal flag is flying.'

'Do they ever come out and drive through the town?'

'Oh yes, rather. You'd see them in the town quite often in peacetime. No one ever stares at them or bothers them when they're being private down here – Look! There's something going on now.'

As he spoke the great gates were opened and an open car came out. A man and a woman sat behind the driver in the middle seat, with two men in plain suits in the seat behind them.

The woman was dressed all in blue, with a fluffy hat framing her face, and the fair man beside her wore plain tweedy-looking clothes and was bareheaded.

As the car approached the spot where Colin and Marjorie stood, he came rigidly to attention and saluted.

Marjorie gave a little gasp and followed suit. 'It's the King and Queen,' she breathed.

The Queen turned her head and saw them. She raised her hand and her face lit up with her exquisite, gracious smile. Then, suddenly, her face sparkled with recognition. She tugged at the King's sleeve and he turned his eyes towards them.

At once, he leaned forward and spoke to the driver and in a moment the car pulled up a short distance ahead of Colin and Marjorie. The Queen beckoned with her hand.

Stunned, Marjorie let Colin take her with him up to the royal car. Colin saluted again.

'Colin, my dear,' the Queen said, smiling fondly at him. 'How very nice to see you again. How is your dear mother?'

'Very well, your Majesty,' Colin answered, smiling back at her.

The King leaned forward, a pleased look on his serious face. 'Very good to see you, Colin. I trust your father is keeping well? It seems, since the war, we have had so little opportunity to enjoy his company. Please convey our regards to him.'

'I shall be honoured to, your Majesty,' Colin answered.

The King turned his gaze on Marjorie, standing silent and awed beside Colin. 'Will you present your friend to us, Colin?'

Colin bowed slightly. 'Your Majesties, may I have the honour of presenting Miss Marjorie Hatfield?' he said correctly.

Marjorie did not know what to do. She bowed and then

131

saluted. She remembered reading, somewhere, that you never speak to royalty unless they first speak to you. The Queen was so beautiful that she could not stop herself from gazing at her in awed admiration.

The King said in his quiet hesitant voice, 'I see you are in the Canadian Women's Army Corps. We are indeed grateful to the brave women of the armed services of our commonwealth who have left their homes and come here to share our dangers in our hour of need.'

Marjorie found her voice. 'Thank you, your Majesty. We Canadian women are honoured to be allowed to serve our King and our empire in this great cause.'

As she spoke, she couldn't help thinking with a twinge of guilty amusement, of Bonny's freely expressed opinions about '*Those Limeys!*' But her own sentiments were sincere, at least.

The King looked pleased at her answer and the Queen smiled her sweet smile and asked her where she was stationed.

Marjorie told her London.

The Queen said gently, 'I hope that, in spite of those V-bomb raids, you are managing to enjoy some of the sights of our city.'

When they had gone, Marjorie stood staring speechlessly at Colin. 'You – you know *them!*' she said, finding her voice at last.

'Of course,' he said, smiling at her look.

'Have they – have they visited at your home?' she asked in awe.

'Oh, rather. Since I was a child. Don't look so dumb-founded. Even kings and queens have friends, you know. And didn't I tell you that Queen Elizabeth slept at Enderby and created the first Earl of Rivermere? The Enderbys have been the friends of the monarchy for generations. Now, it's high time we went and had our tea.'

Marjorie began to understand how the countess felt about this Canadian farm girl. No wonder she looked on her as little better than a savage. After all what could Marjorie Hatfield possibly have in common with these Enderbys who were the friends of kings and queens?

She began to feel in awe even of Colin.

But as they sat over tea and chatted in the quaint little

teahouse, and he made her laugh with his droll humour, she once more felt at ease with him. Yet time was flying by and she knew he would soon have to return.

He saw the shadow cross her face. The tearoom was almost deserted. They were seated in a secluded, dimly lit corner, lingering over their tea. Colin leaned forward and took her hands in his.

'Marjorie,' he said, looking deeply into her blue eyes, 'I have something for you which I hope you will accept.'

She looked wonderingly at him.

He took a small velvet case from his pocket, opened it and held it across the table to her.

Marjorie gasped. Nestling like a great drop of liquid fire in the ancient green velvet, between two huge flashing diamonds, was the great ruby of the Enderbys.

Colin took the ring from its case and it gleamed in the palm of his hand, the three precious gems raised in a rare and intriguing setting in the heavy yellow gold.

He said, with a slight tremble in his voice, 'It last belonged to my grandmother. She left it to the eldest son and heir to the title, to be presented to his bride-to-be when they became engaged. Will you let me put it on your finger, Marjorie? Will you be my liege lady?'

Unable to utter a word, Marjorie stared from the ring to Colin's face.

His eyes shone with love. 'I know a little teashop at three in the afternoon is not a romantic place to propose,' he said. 'But I want you to know that here, in this ordinary teahouse, full of tea and funny hard little cakes, I'm very much in love with you, little soldier girl, and I want to marry you. Will you marry me, Marjorie?'

Marjorie felt wild elation leap up in her. At the same time she was terrified. 'I – I – I don't know.'

'You mean, you don't love me?'

'Oh no. Not that,' Marjorie cried in protest. 'I do. I do love you. It's just that I – you . . .'

'Now, you're not going to tell me it's because you're an Other Rank,' he said, smiling tenderly at her.

Before she could answer, he caught her hand and slipped the ring on to her finger. 'There, see, it fits as if it were made for your finger. Say yes, Marjorie dear. Say you'll marry me,' he whispered. 'I've loved you since the first moment you opened your eyes and looked up into mine in the entrance to the George and Horses. You're the only girl I have ever loved, you know.'

Marjorie looked from the ring glowing on her finger to his tender entreating eyes.

'I – I don't know what to say,' she whispered.

'Say *yes*,' Colin entreated. 'Just say *yes*.'

At last her lips moved. 'Yes,' she whispered.

He leaned swiftly across the table and kissed her and she felt her blood race at the touch of his lips.

'It's such a beautiful ring, Colin,' she said, looking wonderingly at her finger.

'It was given to my great-great-great-grandfather for his mem sahib by an Indian maharajah, when he was serving with the army in India. Tradition has it that it picks up the beauty of its wearer. On you it looks magnificent.'

'But Colin, I can't wear it,' she said, dismayed.

'Why not?'

'We aren't allowed to wear any jewellery at all, except a wedding ring.'

'Then we shall have to see to it that you get a ring you can wear, shan't we? Marjorie, at the end of next week, I shall have four days' leave before I take over as squadron leader and they tie me to a desk. Will you marry me then?'

'I – I have to ask permission. And what will your parents say? You heard your mother: she thinks I'm a savage.'

'Oh, Mother was just a bit carried away. She won't really oppose anything that will make me happy. And you've already won Father's heart. I know Mother will accept you when we're married and then you'll be amazed, once she takes you in, to find what a truly marvellous person she is.'

Marjorie looked doubtful.

'You know,' he went on, 'we British are a bit stuffy at first. After you left that night, I had a bit of a talk with Father and Mother and explained things to them. I told Father that if I were not' – he hesitated for a brief moment and then went on – 'if I were not flying combat missions I would ask you to marry me. Father said, "She's a soldier and jolly good stuff if I don't

134

miss my guess. Ask her anyway." '

Marjorie grasped the meaning behind his words. When she said goodbye to him tonight, it might be for the last time. She reached her hands across the table to him. 'I'm glad you did ask me,' she said softly. 'I'll wear your ring today until I return to barracks. I can hide my hand if we happen to meet any officers or military police. Then, tonight, I'll tie it around my neck with my dog tags.'

Colin said, 'Don't go back to London tonight, Marjorie. I don't have to rejoin my squadron until noon tomorrow. We could have a little more time together. Come with me to Enderby and we'll tell my parents we mean to be married at the end of next week.'

The prospect of facing the countess with the news sent shivers of apprehension through her, but Marjorie knew she must face up to it sooner or later, and the entreaty in Colin's eyes wiped out any objections that sprang to her mind.

She nodded slowly and they left the teahouse and drove off for Enderby.

Once they were on the country road with the traffic behind them, Colin pulled off to the side and eagerly gathered Marjorie into his arms.

'I can't wait another moment to kiss you,' he said huskily.

Marjorie felt herself float away into a rapturous world as his warm lips closed over hers.

He kissed her hair and eyes and the dimples beside her mouth, murmuring little words of endearment. Then his lips found hers again and clung to them.

She snuggled her head against his shoulder and twined her arms around his neck. At last he lifted his head. They were both trembling as they drew reluctantly apart and continued their journey to Enderby.

Chapter 16

The earl and countess were sitting in the library. They looked up in surprise when Colin entered unannounced, holding Marjorie by the hand. The earl stood up immediately.

'Father, Mother,' Colin said. 'I have some wonderful news to tell you.' He held up Marjorie's hand with the great ring of the Enderbys gleaming on her finger. 'Marjorie has done me the honour of consenting to be my wife. We plan to be married next weekend, when I have my four-day pass.'

The countess's face went white and she was speechless. The earl's eyes were twinkling at them. 'Lucky young bounder,' he said. 'It's high time we had some new blood around this place.'

He crossed over and kissed Marjorie on the cheek. 'Jolly decent of you to have him. Now, I hope we'll be able to find the time to teach you the proper way to jump in the English saddle.'

'Oh, I'm looking forward to it.' Marjorie turned her eyes anxiously on the countess, who had recovered her poise and inclined her head with a gracious, regal smile.

'I hope you will pardon me if I'm somewhat at a loss for words,' she said. 'Your news is rather unexpected. Since you are *his* choice, I hope that you and my son will find happiness together.'

Impulsively Marjorie crossed to her and placed a hand on the countess's rigid shoulder. 'Oh, Lady Rivermere, I'll do everything in my power to make your son happy.'

The countess looked up into Marjorie's wide, sincere blue eyes, filled with an entreaty to be friends. Something like a sigh escaped her lips.

'My child,' she said quietly, 'there is much more to life and marriage than you can know, and you have known each other such a short length of time.'

She straightened herself up even more rigidly in her chair. 'But, be that as it may, you are my son's choice so that is that. You will stay with us tonight, will you not?'

Colin crossed over and kissed his mother on the cheek, with one arm across her shoulders and the other around Marjorie. 'Of course she will, Mother, and don't give her the Nun's Cell.'

The countess brushed off his arm and stood up. 'I'll see to it and tell Giles we have an extra guest for dinner. Later in the evening we'll discuss the wedding plans.' She swept from the room.

That night Marjorie slept in a large beautifully furnished room, with a wide view outside its big window. The moon was streaming in. She lay awake going over in her mind the events of the evening.

She had had little time to be alone with Colin. They had managed a few moments together just before dinner when they went to look at the horses, and they had exchanged lingering kisses. But after dinner the countess insisted that they all go to the library to discuss the plans for the wedding.

Marjorie had thought that they would be quietly married by the army padre in London, but Lady Rivermere would not hear of it. Colin must be married in the church in Wendover, even if only a handful of his old friends could be present. The heir to the estate and future Earl of Rivermere could not sneak away to be married, war or no war. The tenants must be allowed to see his bride, their future lady.

Marjorie was too overawed to protest. After dinner the countess said, 'Will you please accompany me upstairs? I have something I want you to see.'

Wondering, Marjorie went with her to a room in one of the corridors leading off the main gallery. It was full of old trunks and collected family items dating back generations.

The countess opened one of the trunks and Marjorie exclaimed as she pulled out a white satin wedding dress with yards and yards of lacy white veil.

'It belonged to Colin's great-great-grandmother,' the countess said. 'She was tiny like you, but much taller. All the

137

Enderby men, until now, have married tall women. Fortunately I'm very handy with a needle. Slip into it and I'll see how much it has to be taken up.'

'Oh, I couldn't.'

'Don't you like it?' the countess said with a thin smile.

'It's absolutely beautiful,' Marjorie said, noticing the tiny seed pearls adorning the bodice. 'But I – I – It might get damaged.'

'Nonsense,' the countess said. 'Slip into it.'

With her heart beating rapidly, Marjorie obediently removed her khaki shirt, skirt and tie, and the countess helped her to slip the wedding gown over her head. It foamed around her feet, the satin folds caressing her body.

Grudging admiration came into the countess's eyes. 'I see Colin has kept up the Enderby tradition of picking beautiful women to become their brides,' she said stiffly. 'Except for the length it fits perfectly. I shall work on that tonight. Now, let us try on the veil.'

When she had pinned it in place, Marjorie looked at herself in the full-length mirror. She caught her breath in disbelief. The exquisite beauty of the dress, with its bodice all beaded with creamy pearls, the flowing folds of satin, the white lace veil cascading from her head, almost overwhelmed her. With her flawless, fair complexion and wide, heavy-lashed blue eyes and golden hair, she looked almost like an angel masquerading as a human girl.

That can't be me! she thought, gazing at her reflection.

Strange sensations began racing through her. This was what she had always dreamed of – walking down the aisle all pure in white to meet her dream man at the altar.

It was too much like a dream. She was frightened. When the countess said, 'Take it off now and I shall start work on it,' she was glad to be out of it and back once more in her familiar khaki uniform. It seemed almost like a suit of armour around her, protecting her from the slings of fate. She belonged again. She was one of the Canadian army girls.

Lying in her bed in the moonlight she wished she and Colin could just slip away somewhere and be married quietly. The end of the week that loomed ahead of her seemed an eternity away. And the thought of herself walking down the aisle in the church in Wendover dressed in that exquisite white gown and veil seemed an unreal vision.

She fell asleep at last. It was a restless sleep. The ancestors she had seen in the pictures filed slowly past her bed, with beautiful tall women floating on their arms in the white wedding dress. As they passed by the great oak fourposter bed, the women looked down at her with aloof disdain and the men all nodded their heads approvingly – all but one. He was the black sheep who had run off to become a squaw man. He was the last in the line and he stopped and looked down at her with a cynical, mocking smile.

She woke up shivering, and for the rest of the night sleep eluded her. Lying awake in this great bed in this great house, Marjorie began to feel very small and lonely. Her thoughts went back to the simple little farm home she had left behind in Canada. She pictured her father and mother pottering about the house, reading or talking, or having a cup of tea with homemade cookies.

I wonder if Cochise misses me? she thought, picturing him nibbling oats in his stall. The warm smell of the cows and fresh hay was so strong in her mind that she could smell it. A terrible lost homesick feeling seized her. She wanted to run away – away from England – away from the war – away from every-thing – back to the farm and the familiar things, her brother and his wife, her little niece and nephew. Back to her roots.

'Toldiers don't cry.' Tears smarted her eyes. She had walked into her brother's house one day, home on weekend leave, to find her little nephew sobbing over a bruised finger. 'Soldiers don't cry,' she told him. It had stemmed the flow of tears. She smiled, remembering him holding up his finger and saying bravely, 'Toldiers don't cry, Aunty Marjorie.'

'Are they going to shoot you, Aunty Marjorie?' Her little niece had looked so solemn, looking up at her as she asked the question.

'No, my dear, they aren't going to shoot me. I'm going to marry a lord, in a white wedding dress that is over a hundred years old, and live in an ancient castle filled with ancestors who died in battle and haunted by the spirit of a great black stag, stalking about in the full of the moon. The moon will be full next weekend.'

She sat up in sudden panic. What am I doing here? Life was so simple before she met Colin. Why couldn't she have fallen in love with a good old Canadian? Why did she have to love a lord who was the friend of kings and queens?

What did she really know about Colin? She had met him just over a week ago, and now she was going to marry him away over here in England, far from home with none of her old friends or relatives at the wedding. And where would they live if they both came through the war – here in a wing of this great house with the stern unbending countess watching her and wishing that she was Ashley?

She leapt from the bed, almost tumbling on the floor. How high they made beds in England. She must get away from here, back to the barracks – to Jessy and Helen and warm funny Bonny, even snivelling scaredy-cat Elsie. She started pulling on her clothes. It was three in the morning, she saw by the watch on her wrist. The motor transport company at Currie Barracks had all chipped in and bought it for her for a going-overseas present before she left.

She had on her brassiere and pants and slip, and was reaching for her shirt and tie, when Colin came into her mind. The tide of love pushed all other thoughts from her. She was flooded with the wild ecstasy of feeling his arms pressing her to him. She felt his lips on hers and saw his warm, kindly eyes smiling reassuringly at her, so that nothing mattered but being with him.

She stopped dressing and sat gazing off into space. Was Colin frightened, too, at the thought of marrying this strange Canadian girl his mother considered practically a savage? Somehow she could not imagine Colin being very frightened of anything.

His eyes had that quiet look of courage inherited from generations of resolute men who had always ruled others and served their king.

She undressed and went back to bed, and slept until the sun on her face woke her up. She slipped out of bed and crossed to the window. It was a breath-taking morning. The soft English sunlight bathed the tree-studded hillside and shone on the faces of the flowers winking from the carpet of verdant grass. A few soft white clouds floated airily across the blue of the sky.

A morning designed for lovers. With that thought in mind she went downstairs, hoping she might see Colin before the others were stirring.

But only the countess was in the little breakfast room when she entered. She told Marjorie that Colin had gone riding with his father on some business of the estate and they had already breakfasted. Marjorie tried not to let her disappointment show.

'They'll be back shortly,' the countess said. 'After you've finished your breakfast, my dear, we'll go to my sitting room. I have your dress ready for you to try on again.'

Marjorie barely managed to swallow a piece of toast and drink a cup of tea. She followed the countess wordlessly to her private domain.

The wedding dress was lying over the back of a gold-embroidered chair. Once more Marjorie slipped it over her head. It was exactly the right length now. The countess fastened on the veil.

Marjorie caught a glimpse of herself in a gilt-framed mirror and caught her breath sharply. She looked like one of those women who had floated past her bed last night.

The countess smiled thinly at her. 'You are indeed beautiful, my dear.'

Before Marjorie could say anything, the door opened and Colin burst into the room, calling, 'Mother!' in a cheery voice. He stopped short, staring at Marjorie with a quickly indrawn breath.

'Oh!' Marjorie cried, feeling her face drain of all colour. 'Oh! You're not supposed to see me in my wedding dress before I come up to you at the altar. *It's bad luck.*'

'Stuff and nonsense,' the countess said briskly, but her own face paled.

Colin laughed easily. 'Pagan superstition,' he said, but he left the room quickly.

Marjorie hastily changed back to her own clothes and followed him quickly from the room. He was standing with his back to the fireplace, whistling unconcernedly.

He looked at her white face with the enormous, frightened blue eyes meeting his from under dark lashes, and leaned forward and caught her by the hand.

'Come on, it's a wonderful day and I've a little time before I have to go back. I'll let you into my most closely guarded secret – *The hidden trail down to Smugglers' Cove.*'

He whisked her out of the door before she could say anything and hand in hand they slipped down the path through the gardens, past the fish ponds to where the thick bushes on the slope leading down to the Pond barred their way.

Hidden among the bushes, under Colin's guidance, she saw the little trail just wide enough for one.

Under the spell of his light-hearted cheerfulness her fear began to evaporate. He stopped to pass under the thick, clustering trees. She followed him, her hand held tightly in his, until they came to an old stone wall barring their path.

'Now,' he said dramatically, 'I am about to reveal for the first time the secret I have guarded with my life these many years.'

He pulled back a trailing section of the thick ivy covering the wall and quickly removed four large, loose stones, revealing a sort of tunnel under the wall.

'Follow me,' he said over his shoulder as he crawled through, 'and we shall share rich booty this day.' Laughing, she obeyed.

They came out under branches of rhododendrons forming an arch a few feet from the ground. Sunlight filtering through the fluttering leaves formed a dancing pattern. The scent of growing things was warm in the rich summer air.

Colin waited for her and she crept up beside him, giggling. He looked into her face, glowing with innocent childlike pleasure. Her blue eyes sparkled up into his and her dimples showed beside her mouth.

He caught her in his arms and tenderly kissed her face and then her lips. They were both laughing a little breathlessly, as if they had managed to put the clock back and were once more in some wonderful childhood world of adventure and secret passages, hidden coves and bold buccaneers.

She kissed him back and he tightened his arms around her as they lay cuddled close, the trees whispering above them.

His lips clung to hers and her heart beat against his chest and then they were suddenly children no longer.

Marjorie felt the thirst and longing in his lips and the mounting desire in her own. He folded her closer and closer against his body. At last he lifted his mouth from hers and she saw the agony of longing in his eyes. 'Oh Marjorie.' He put his face against hers and his voice was almost a moan as he whispered in her ear, 'Oh, Marjorie I don't want to stop.'

He buried his face between her heaving breasts. She twined her hands in his thick brown hair, drawing his head even closer to her thrusting breasts. His hand moved up on her back and he loosened her brassiere, then crept around to her front and undid her shirt until it fell open and he buried his face between her naked breasts with a long shuddering sigh.

'I love you so,' he whispered, his breath warm against the bare flesh of her breast. 'Oh, Marjorie, I love you so.'

'And I love you, Colin,' she whispered back, moving her nipple restlessly towards his lips.

She sighed as they found it and fastened on the pink eager thrusting point.

He raised his face after a moment and looked into her eyes, his own full of love and longing and a pleading question. Her eyes gave him back the answer he wanted and strongly and tenderly he took her virginity.

She felt a moment of pain and then waves of ecstasy surged up in her, rising and rising, filling her whole body and her spirit until she experienced a complete crescendo of union with him. Not even in her wildest imagining had she dreamed it could be like this. It was as if she had been lifted to some other plane and was floating in complete joy – one with Colin.

At last he withdrew and lay with her in the shelter of his arms, looking down into her face. Her lips were tremulous and her blue eyes, meeting his, were huge and glistening with tears.

Concern leapt into his face. 'Oh Marjorie,' he whispered contritely, 'you're not sorry? Please don't tell me I made you sorry.'

She shook her head. 'No. Oh no,' she whispered. 'It's just that I – I . . . Oh Colin, it was so wonderful. I – I feel like I'm another person now.'

He kissed her and smiled tenderly. 'But you're not, Marjorie. You're the same sweet little soldier girl.' He looked earnestly into her eyes. 'I know, Marjorie, how you feel about things. I know how much you wanted to be a virgin bride, walking up the aisle all in white to meet your future husband at the altar, and I'm sorry I spoiled your dream for you; but now you are really my wife. No matter what happens, remember that. *You are my wife.*'

An arrow of fear shivered through her at his words. She put her arms around his neck and drew his lips down to hers. 'Oh, Colin, I love you so,' she whispered. 'I love you so.'

'And I love you, my little wife,' he said huskily. They clung, almost desperately to each other. Then he said, 'Now we must go back to the house. I have to leave.'

I hope I've not done her a terrible wrong, Colin thought as they walked back to the house with her hand resting trustingly in his. He had not intended to take her like that, but in that hidden glen his love and passion had overwhelmed his good judgement. He had wanted her with an uncontrollable longing that had swept everything else from his mind.

He knew that in the back of his mind had been the fear that perhaps he would never hold her to him and make love to her, unless he did it now. But had it been fair to her? He had never before worried about coming back from a mission because he had never really expected to come through this war. But now, suddenly, desperately, he wanted this next week to be over, and to be alive and claiming his bride at the altar in the church in Wendover.

For the first time he was afraid. *If only there was no war.* This beautiful, trusting girl from Canada deserved better than a few quick moments of love snatched under the trees.

If it were only peacetime what pleasure he could have given her, showing her off to his friends, courting her. They would have gone dancing and horseback riding and punting on the lake with other happy, carefree young people. Then, with Raif beside him he would have stood at the altar as she floated up the aisle to him, white and virginal as she had dreamed, to the hours of joy that lay ahead.

There would have been a great party in the hall at Enderby, with friends and neighbours and tenants – *and the King and Queen* – gathered to wish them well.

Then they would, perhaps, have gone to Paris and Rome for their honeymoon. He could picture her almost childlike excitement as she entered into his world and he introduced her to the things she had woven dreams about in her girlhood.

So many things they could have done, but in a few short hours he would be escorting the bombers droning their way across the Channel to drop their loads of death on Germany. I wonder how many young German lovers will see their day of joy end when those bombs fall from the sky, he thought.

Marjorie was silent, clinging tightly to his hand. She, too, was thinking what it would be like if there was no war. She was not sorry for what she had done with Colin, but she was frightened.

She looked up into the blue sky and hoped desperately that God was not angry with her for not waiting until she and Colin were married. Please, she prayed silently, please understand. Please make everything be all right.

In the back of her mind, her father's words haunted her: '*Remember, that what is not acceptable in peacetime is not acceptable in wartime.*'

Would she have to pay for her action?

While they were still out of sight of the house, down by the fish ponds, Colin took her in his arms and kissed her tenderly again and again.

'Just one week – a few more days – and we'll be married,' he said. '*But remember you are really my wife now.* Of course you have really belonged to me since I saved your life.'

Marjorie smiled at him and her eyes lit up and her deep dimples showed. 'It's the other way around, remember?'

'Well, we'll settle all that after the ceremony,' Colin said. 'In the meantime, I'm sure my mother has many other little things to arrange. We'd better go inside and I'll leave you with her.'

Marjorie was alarmed at the thought of facing the countess. 'Oh, how do I look?' she asked anxiously, stopping to straighten her skirt and brush herself off.

Colin looked down at her wide-eyed, sweet face crowned by her sunny floating hair and smiled tenderly. 'Like the most beautiful liege lady ever a knight tilted lance for,' he said and kissed the end of her nose.

Marjorie hoped that she could go up to her room to tidy up and compose herself before she had to face the countess, but Lady Rivermere was in the hall when she and Colin entered.

145

She looked at Marjorie keenly from her deep, penetrating grey eyes and Marjorie felt her face flush deeply.

'I trust you had a pleasant walk,' the countess said. 'The flowers are beautiful at this time of the year.'

Marjorie murmured something, excused herself and went upstairs, her heart beating rapidly under her shirt.

Chapter 17

Sunday afternoon was the end of a long week for Jessy Cole. Her naturally courageous nature was fighting down the picture she carried in her mind of men with arms or legs gone – of bloody bandages – of men who would never walk again – of boys who looked up into her face and joked, with pain-filled frightened eyes.

She had worked long hours of overtime without a day off, driving her big ambulance down to the coast to pick up wounded men coming in from the battlefield. Helping to load them into her ambulance, she gave out with that natural come-hither talent that had made men stand and roar for more when she performed at the Glen Club.

When Jessy Cole looked down at a man with her sensuous, teasing brown eyes she got a responding smile from all but the most critically wounded men.

But tonight she felt drained of all energy. It was five o'clock in the afternoon. No one else was home yet. Tossing off her hat and battledress tunic and kicking off her shoes, she lay down on top of the bed in her battledress trousers – worn by the girls driving ambulances and trucks.

Before she came upstairs she had looked for the mail – as she did every day – half hoping there might be a letter from Bob Anders. But there was nothing. She was not really surprised. The news was full of stories of the Yankees in the thick of the fighting in France.

Well, perhaps one of these days he would find a chance to write to her, as he had promised? Her mind floated back to that last night with him out there in Sussex Square. She lived again the closeness of his body to hers in the black night. Day and night she carried the feel of him in her bones and her blood and her mind.

147

She hadn't been to Molly's pub since he left, which was strange since she had never missed a night there since she arrived in London, before he left for the front.

She loved the warmth and the drinking and the excitement and companionship of sitting chatting to servicemen and women, and listening to the tunes tinkled out on the piano by any musically inclined patrons. But now, somehow, she had lost her inclination to go there.

I must be in love, she thought as she drifted off to sleep.

She dreamed she was dancing in the Grantview Club with Bob. He was looking superbly handsome and happy in evening clothes – white tie and tails – and she was floating in a bright orange, low-cut evening dress that swirled around her feet. They were so happy they could feel the laughter and life in each other, as if they were inside each other's skin.

Bonny woke her. She was standing beside the bed shaking her shoulder. 'Hey wake up, Jess, you got a visitor downstairs.'

Jessy pulled herself slowly into wakefulness, reluctant to leave her dream behind, and sat up.

'Someone down in the sitting room wants to see you,' Bonny said. 'I gotta go. Old Hot Burns wants me to run an errand for her. You sure you're awake?'

Jessy shook the sleep from her head. 'Sure. Thanks, Bonny.'

Wondering who it was, she ran her pocket comb through her dark hair and applied a flash of her bright orange lipstick.

The little parlour where the CWACs entertained guests faced out onto Sussex Square. Her visitor was standing looking out of the window, with his back to the room. A wild thrill of joy shot through Jessy as she recognized the US army officer's uniform.

The tall broad-shouldered man turned to face her, and Jessy's heart plummeted. It was not Bob. It was a Yankee captain with his arm in a sling. She stopped on the threshold, a strange coldness creeping through her. He came quickly across the room.

'Are you Jessy Cole?' he asked in that familiar, heart-stopping Yankee drawl, looking uneasily into her face.

Jessy nodded. Her heart was up in her throat, choking her, and she could not open her mouth to say anything.

The eyes of the strange Yankee officer were very sober.

At last she found her voice and managed to smile at him.

'Yes. I'm Jessy Cole.'

He looked away from her for a moment, then his warning eyes found hers again. 'I – I've got a message for you. It – I've just come back from over there – Bob Anders was in the same outfit with me. We were buddies.'

Jessy caught the past tense. She stood motionless, watching his face, silently waiting.

He fumbled inside his tunic pocket and produced a crumpled, darkly stained envelope.

'It was a pretty hot engagement,' he said, speaking rapidly, almost mechanically. 'But we got Herman on the run, all right. We figured we'd cleaned 'em all out of there. Bob and I got out of our flamethrowers and walked over to talk to each other and then this sniper cut loose – ' He drew a quick breath. 'That sniper was some shot. He got away a couple before one of our boys knocked him out of his hiding place – His second shot got me in the arm and gave me this Blighty. Bob wasn't so lucky.' He paused and swallowed. 'His first shot got Bob in the chest. He was dying by the time I knelt down and lifted up his head. He just said a couple of things. "Jessy – Jessy Cole – letter in my pocket." Then he said, "Tell her to have one for me at the Grantview Club when this show is over" – *Hey, are you all right, kid?*'

Jessy looked into his anxious eyes, flashed her bright smile. 'I'm okay,' she said, and took the letter from his hand.

'You sure?'

Jessy knew there was no colour in her face, but she nodded and continued smiling. 'I'm okay, and thanks for coming around. Would you like to sit down?'

He shook his head. 'I've got to get over to Euston station and catch the train north. I've got a little English bride up there who doesn't know I'm back here. I just stopped to bring you the letter. Bob was my best buddy.'

She saw the loss in his eyes and put out her hand and shook his. 'Thanks for coming by.'

He nodded. 'I'm sorry about the letter,' he said. 'It – it was in his breast pocket when the sniper got him. I – I couldn't clean it up without wrecking it. So, I had to bring it to you like it was.'

She knew he meant with the bloodstains on the corner. She nodded. 'It's okay,' she whispered. 'It's okay.'

'Well, goodbye.' He gave her another distressed look as he

turned towards the door. He turned back again. 'I'm sorry,' he said awkwardly, and then walked quickly from the room, but not before she saw the glint of tears in his eyes.

She sank to the chesterfield by the window and sat looking at the letter in her hand, then very slowly, like someone in a daze, she carefully opened the envelope. The dark stain had seeped through on to the paper inside. It covered the corner where the greeting was, but she could still make out the words: 'Darling Jess'.

She stared at it. *That's Bob Anders' life blood*, she thought. She went on reading.

She could tell as she read that the letter had been written in bits and pieces. He had started it as soon as he had returned to the front. Then he had added to it whenever he could snatch a moment in the fierce advance of his unit.

Darling Jess,

You know what, honey, I'd a lot rather be back in Sussex Square with you than over here. As a matter of fact, I'd a lot rather be in Sussex Square with you than any other place. A few years back when I was a college kid, if anyone had told me I'd find heaven in a blackout in London on the grass in a square in a raid, I would have told them they were crazy. But last night that's where I was. I can't honestly say you're the first one I ever was with, Jessy, but you're the only one. The only one that ever counted. I never knew loving a woman could be like that.

No matter what happens out here in the days ahead, I know I've had the best life has to offer. I guess nothing could ever top those moments with you out there on the grass, Jess. It wasn't like it was just our bodies. It was like it was all of us. I'll dream of you tonight. Good night, Jess.

Well, I meant to write a little more to you yesterday, but it was kind of hot around here. We had a sort of busy day, but I kept thinking of you, just like you were riding along with me. Glad you weren't here really, though. Pretty quiet around here now. I haven't got much of a light to write by. You really have got beautiful legs, you know, even if I only did get to see them in those Khaki stockings. They sure felt beautiful. Can't figure out what I liked best about you, your legs or your eyes, or maybe it was that come-hither smile of

150

yours. Did you know, Jess, a guy would crawl over broken glass just to see that bright smile of yours? Of course there are *other things* I liked about you, too! I don't know when I can get this posted. There aren't too many post offices around here. In fact, the service is damn poor.

Remember the things we used to take for granted before the war? Like the iceman bringing the ice and the milkman delivering milk, and the bread man and the postman. Nice, easy homey things, weren't they? And the picnics and pretty girls and dances and playing football and cheering for your team. And now the only thing we're concerned with is killing people and keeping ourselves alive. You know, whoever thought up wars wasn't too bright. Now, if we were home, Jess, tonight it would be nice and warm in Southern California. And maybe you and I would be out in the roadster going to a party, with the hood down, driving along that ocean road near San Diego. And we'd dance and drink and have fun with our friends, and then when we came back from the party it would be late and you would be riding along with your head on my shoulder and maybe I'd drive the car down beside the beach and we'd find a little secluded cove. Then, well Jess, you know *what* would happen then. Goodnight, Jess.

It's been four days since I got a chance to write anything to you. One of these days I'll find a postman. Got to bump into one soon.

Anyhow, I'll finish this up tonight and get it to you some way. I promised I'd get a letter to you. I wish I could put myself in the envelope and get back to Sussex Square and you. Things have been a little hot and they aren't cooling off any yet. What was I saying to you the last time I wrote? I see, I was telling you about how we'd go down to the beach and the party we'd go to if there wasn't any war. You know, Jess, there's one thing I really would have liked. I sure wish I could have seen you singing in that club in a low-cut evening dress. I bet you were a knock-out. Some day, if I get through this, will you sing for me, Jess? Did I ever tell you your voice sends tingles up my spine when you're just talking? I bet your singing is really something to turn a guy inside out. I can just see you with your head back and that bright smile of yours and your eyes shining, belting out a tune, and all the guys drooling. Yes, I sure would like to hear you sing, Jessy. I'd like anything you do, Jessy. I wish I was at the Grantview Club with you. Got to sign off. I love you Jessy.

Bob Anders.

The dark stain had spread across the bottom of the paper. Jessy was looking at 'I love you Jessy. Bob Anders' through his life blood. She folded up the letter very carefully and slowly put it back in the wrinkled, bloodstained envelope and placed it in her tunic pocket.

Everything had suddenly gone very still, as if the whole world had been drained of life and she was completely alone in the universe. The only sound was her own heart beating. It had beat very fast that night out there in Sussex Square when her bosom was pressed tight against Bob Anders' warm chest. The night had been chilly but his chest had been so warm.

In her leaping imagination she could hear the thud of the bullet as it tore into that warm chest and see the spurt of blood, spreading and spreading. I'm glad that they shot the sniper, she thought, imagining the thud of the bullet striking him and seeing him spin and fall from wherever he was perched. But in the next breath, she wondered if somewhere in Germany someone had brought a German girl a letter like Bob's.

She got slowly to her feet and stood with her hand resting on the back of the chesterfield. The room felt icy cold.

Bonny came back into the room. 'My God, Jess, are you all right?' she cried, running to her. 'You look like you'd seen a ghost. What's wrong?'

Jessy smiled at her. 'Nothing's wrong, Bonny. Just haven't had enough sleep, I guess. I've been wheeling that ambulance steady for a week. I'd better get up to bed.'

She turned and walked quietly from the room. Bonny stared after her.

Jessy climbed the stairs and went into the bathroom across the hall from her room. Everything was spinning around her. Her stomach started to heave. She went to the toilet and threw up. She heaved and heaved until, finally, there was nothing left inside of her and she was retching dryly.

She felt as if she was choking and there was no air left in the world. She gasped and gasped.

At last she managed to catch her breath and pulled herself

erect. Thank God there's no one here, she thought. She staggered to the basin and splashed cold water on her face, just as she heard voices coming up the stairs, talking and laughing together. She recognized them as the voices of Helen and Marjorie. She heard them go into their room.

She straightened herself in front of the mirror with one hand on the edge of the basin. Gradually the room came into focus and stopped spinning around her. Resolutely she took her lipstick from her purse and applied a dash to her white lips.

Her great brown eyes stared back at her from her pale face. 'Jesus,' she whispered. 'I look as if I'd been into hell.' She blinked several times and pulled her lips into a smile. She put her head back, hummed a little tune under her breath and went to join her friends in the room across the hall.

Marjorie and Helen were sitting with their heads close together on Helen's bed. They were smiling. They both looked up at Jessy when she entered and Helen lifted up Marjorie's hand for her to inspect.

'Look,' she said excitedly. 'Look what Marjorie's got.'

Jessy saw the ring flashing on Marjorie's finger and gave a little whistle.

'She's engaged and she's going to be married next weekend – to an English lord,' Helen said breathlessly.

'Holy smoke,' Jessy said. 'You really have been up to something. Tell me about it.'

Marjorie's face was flushed and her eyes were bright. 'I met him that night when the Brig's car got it. He was the one who pulled me down in the entrance to the George and Horses and saved my life. He's a Spitfire pilot in the RAF.'

'And he's an English lord,' Helen broke in excitedly. 'Imagine, Marjorie will be Lady Enderby, and she's going to live in a huge house in the country – practically a castle – when this war is over. His father is an earl.'

'I have to get permission, of course,' Marjorie said. 'A week isn't nearly long enough to do that. I tried to tell Colin they won't give me permission that soon, but his father is going to speak to the brigadier, and he's sure it will come through all right.'

'Isn't it exciting, Jess?' Helen said. 'And that's not all the good news. Carl is coming along really well now and as soon as he's well enough to be sent home to Canada they're going to

.send me back with him and give me a discharge on compassionate grounds, so I can take care of him. Isn't that great?'

Jessy put her hands down and squeezed each one of her friends on the shoulder. 'Great news, girls. This war is looking up.'

All at once Marjorie noticed the pallor of Jessy's face. Her eyes filled with sudden concern. 'What's the matter, Jess? You look awful. Is something wrong?'

'Just tired, Marj,' Jessy reassured her, smiling brightly. 'I've been putting in some pretty long shifts this week – doing a lot of overtime. They're short-handed, you know. And then, I think they cooked the hoofs and the horns and the wool along with that mutton they fed us for supper. My stomach didn't like it.'

'Oh,' Marjorie said, jumping up at once. 'Why don't you lie down, Jess? Do you want me to get you an aspirin?'

Jessy shook her head. 'I've been leading too quiet a life,' she said, crossing over to her bed and sitting down. She took off her tunic and threw it on her bed and kicked off her shoes. 'I'm going to have a bath if there's any hot water, and then I'm going to go and see what's going on at Molly's. I've been neglecting them lately.'

'Oh, do you think you should, Jessy?' Marjorie said concernedly. 'You really don't look very well. I'm sure you haven't had enough sleep lately. Why don't you go to bed and I'll get you an aspirin and maybe scrounge up a cup of tea for you?'

Jessy shook her head. 'Thanks, Marj, no. It's Molly's for me.'

Thankful for the trickle of hot water, Jessy bathed quickly, deliberately keeping her mind a blank. In a few minutes she was dressed and ready to leave. Some of the colour had come back to her cheeks, but her eyes were unnaturally brilliant. 'See you later,' she said to Marjorie and Helen as she left the room.

They watched her leave with concern.

'She doesn't look well to me,' Marjorie said anxiously. 'She looks as if she had a terrible pain and she isn't letting on.'

'I hope she hasn't got an attack of appendicitis or something,' Helen said. 'I've never seen Jess look like that before. You know, she's never sick.'

'It's her eyes. They keep reminding me of something, but I can't remember quite what it is. It hovers in my mind and then eludes me.'

154

Chapter 18

Jessy stepped out into the damp thick blackness of the street. It was as if time and distance had ceased to be. All around her she could feel the ancient city breathing. She fancied that the ghosts of fallen warriors who had died for this little spot of earth walked with her in the night.

She welcomed the darkness wrapping itself around her like the heavy folds of an army blanket, keeping the searing tide of anguish locked deeply inside her being.

So, this is what it feels like, she thought. This devouring pain was an alien thing. She had danced through life, savouring it with lighthearted abandon, enjoying each magical moment as it came, without fear or regret. Like men, there was always another adventure coming. She walked slowly, each step echoing faintly on the damp pavement. She felt, as in a dream, that she was not moving.

The door of Molly's pub opening to her hand was a surprise. The swirl of light, laughing voices and music was a shock. She wanted to pull back into the night and go on walking in the dark, on and on.

She started to retreat out into the night again, pulling the door almost shut. She stopped, drew a deep breath and walked resolutely into the noisy crowded pub, the familiar smell of uniforms and beer and warm human bodies. With her head in the air, she walked across to her favourite table, the same table she had been sitting at the night she met Bob for the first time.

Some of the servicemen and women she had been with that night were here tonight. They welcomed her noisily: 'Hey where you been, Jess?' – 'We thought a doodle bug had got you.' – 'Did you take the pledge, or something?'

She eased herself into a vacant chair, smiling a greeting

around the table, and ordered a gin from the stout barmaid. The table was full of drinks. Over in the corner the Limey corporal who had music in his bones was hitting out tunes on the piano, the same tunes he had been thumping out the night Bob had walked in.

She had been in a darts tournament with four Canadian soldiers, playing for rounds of drinks and beating them all. 'Well, it looks like I'm not going to have to buy any of you boys a drink tonight,' she had boasted, laughing.

Then she saw this Yankee major come swaggering into the pub, with his hat set at a cocky angle, his face flushed and his blue eyes gleaming. His eyes riveted on her and he crossed the room and stood looking down at her. 'Did I hear you say you wanted to buy me a drink, honey?' he said, while the Canadian airmen glowered at him.

Jessy's heart did a quick flip inside of her as she met the challenge in his eyes. 'I warn you I haven't bought a drink in three nights,' she said, flashing him her brilliant smile as she handed him the darts.

'You haven't been playing with a Yank,' he said cockily and promptly tossed three darts into the bull's-eye.

The airmen were still giving this intruding Yankee dirty looks; but after he wrested the championship from Jessy and insisted on buying a round for the whole table, his open-hearted friendly manner won them over in spite of it being plain to see that he had beat them out at more than darts.

He slipped into the chair beside Jessy and remained there for the rest of the evening.

Jessy recalled the thrill that had shot through her when he rubbed his knee against hers under the table, with a naughty twinkle in his blue eyes. Those blue eyes will never twinkle at me again, she thought. They'll never twinkle at anyone ever again, unless it's Saint Peter at the Golden Gate.

She tossed off her drink and ordered another, imagining Bob marching on silent, ghostly feet, in a long string of GIs, past Saint Peter, through a huge golden gate, with blood still welling from the hole in his chest and his eyes smiling — smiling.

Jessy had been gone for less than an hour when Bonny came

bursting into the room looking for her. Helen and Marjorie were dozing on their beds in their khaki slips. 'Where's Jess?' Bonny asked anxiously, waking them up. 'She said she was going to bed. She looked awful after that Yankee came to see her.'

'Yankee?' Marjorie said. 'Was it Bob Anders?'

Bonny shook her head. 'He said he had a message for her. I thought maybe, he was bringing her a letter from Bob. She told me he promised he'd write her. I had to go run an errand for old Hot Burns. When I came back he was gone and Jessy was standing there looking like she was terribly sick. I never saw her look like that. She said she was tired and she was coming up to bed.'

'She went out to Molly's pub,' Marjorie said. 'She had a bath and changed into her good walking-out uniform.'

Bonny crossed over and sat down on Jessy's bed beside the tunic she had left lying there when she changed to go out. 'What is *that*?' she exclaimed. The others rushed over to look.

The bloodstained envelope containing Bob Anders' letter had slipped out of Jessy's tunic pocket and lay on the bed.

'It's a letter addressed to Jess,' Helen whispered.

'Those marks on it . . . They – they look like – like *bloodstains*,' Marjorie said.

The three girls looked at each other. They knew what message the strange Yankee had brought to their buddy – the message you don't think about – that's always on your mind – when you have someone over there.

Bonny carefully placed the letter back where she found it.

'I know now what that look in Jessy's eyes kept reminding me of,' Marjorie said slowly. 'We had a picture in one of our books when I was a kid, of the little Spartan boy who stood there smiling while the fox he had hidden under his cloak was devouring his vitals.'

'Poor Jess,' Helen said. 'I knew she really cared about that Yankee major, but I didn't know how much.'

'I did,' Bonny said. 'I saw her face that last night she was out with him. I asked her where she had been when she came in and she said she'd been in heaven.'

'Oh, darn, I have to go on duty,' Helen said. 'I've got to drive some guy to the radio station to make a pep talk.'

In Molly's pub, jokes were flying around the table and Jessy told the funniest, most daring stories of all, acting them out with a jaunty flippancy that kept the group of servicemen and women in gales of laughter, all except David Carlton, the airman who had told them about losing his wife in the bombing raid, and his definition of love. He sat quietly sipping his drink and watching the others with a half smile.

The gin Jessy drank failed to melt the coldness inside her, or wash away the picture of blood flowing from a gaping wound. The little Limey at the piano, on request, started beating out 'There'll be Blue Birds Over the White Cliffs of Dover'.

Words from Bob's letter leapt into her mind: 'I sure wish I could have seen you singing in that club in a low-cut evening dress . . . If I get through this, will you sing for me, Jess?'

She broke off in the middle of a story, while they all stared at her in surprise, unbuttoned her tunic and put it over the back of her chair, then she took off her tie and hung it over the tunic. Carefully she bent over and untied her brown oxfords and took them off and left them under her chair. Barefooted, she walked over to the bar and before anyone realized what she was doing, vaulted nimbly up on to it and hitched her khaki skirt high above her knees. She unbuttoned her khaki shirt far down the front and pulled it back almost off her shoulders, showing the V of her breasts.

The barman protested angrily. 'Oy, you Canadian, get off there. Come on now, or I'll send for the military police. What do you think yer doin' any'ow?'

Jessy ignored him. She called across to the man at the piano, who had stopped playing and was staring at her, along with the rest of the patrons. 'Pick up this tune, Blackie.' Then she turned and looked down at the faces raised to hers in the crowded pub. She put her head back and flashed her bright smile at them.

'Here you are, Bob. This is for you,' she whispered, and in that rich, throaty contralto that had held them spellbound at the Glen Club in Montreal she broke into 'There's a Star Spangled Banner Waving Somewhere'. The pianist picked up the tune and accompanied her softly in the background.

All eyes riveted on Jessy as she told them in her moving tones of the Yankee boy who wanted to be admitted into the

Valhalla of Yankee heroes. '. . . Only Uncle Sam's great heroes get to go there. In that heaven there should be a place for me . . .' They all stopped drinking and a hush fell on the noisy pub.

At the end of the song, she switched at once into 'Yankee Doodle Dandy', stepping along the top of the bar with a jaunty swagger, threading her way among the glasses, with a naughty gleam in her eyes as she sauntered to and fro with her hips swaying. Then she sang, 'Since the Yankees Come to Trinidad'.

The barman had stopped complaining, and joined the others gazing open-mouthed at her.

When at last she stopped singing, she stood looking down at them, smiling, and a great roar went up. They whistled and stamped their feet and clapped. 'More! More!' they shouted.

She waited, smiling provocatively at them; then, as the shouting died down, she lifted her arms in an embracing gesture and broke into the haunting notes of 'Lili Marlene' – the song stolen from the Germans – the soldier's song about the girl who waited underneath the lamp post for her soldier boy who could not meet her.

In Jessy's voice was the beat of marching feet and the heartbreak of 'all confined to barracks', the order that went out when the draft got their last orders to pull out for the front and there was no more chance to say goodbyes to loved ones.

As the last notes died away, silence engulfed the pub, tears glistened. Before they could find themselves again, Jessy called, 'Come on, sing with me. Roll out the barrel . . .'

Caught in the excitement and gaiety in her voice, they joined in, shouting out the popular ditty, while the piano player thumped it out loudly.

When she stopped they cheered and shouted and surged up to her. She looked down into the blur of faces and saw the face of Bob Anders smiling mistily at her. She reached her hand down and it was gripped in a firm handclasp. Bob's face faded from her and she was looking down into the understanding eyes of David Carlton.

He reached up and lifted her down from the top of the bar. His eyes met hers. 'Your Yankee is dead, isn't he?' he said quietly.

'That sniper was some shot,' she whispered.

With his arm around her he took her through the crowd back to her table and slipped her back into her tunic and tie again. Then he bent down and put her shoes back on her feet and tied up the laces.

The room had started to sway and she felt as if she had to hang on to her chair to keep it on the floor. Drunk, she thought. Time to get out of here, but how will I make it across the moving floor? She looked across at the door and saw Marjorie standing just inside.

She crossed to Jessy and put her hand on her friend's shoulder. 'I heard you sing, Jess. It was beautiful. Won't you come home, now? You've been working night and day and I don't believe you even had any supper.'

Jessy knew that Marjorie had somehow come to know what had happened. She put her hand up and closed it over the other girl's and smiled up into her concerned eyes. 'How can I, Marj,' she said impishly, 'when the floor's moving like that?'

'I'll hang on to you. You can put your arm around me,' Marjorie said.

'And I'll flank you on the other side,' David said.

When they went outside the air raid siren was going and as they reached the steps of 43 Company they heard the familiar chugging drone in the sky.

Jessy said to Marjorie, 'Go on in. I'm going to sit here for a while. I want to watch the show.' She sat down on the steps. 'Those dragons of Hitler's look like they came straight out of hell. They'll be something to tell my grandchildren about.'

Marjorie sank down beside her. 'I'll stay with you.'

David settled down on her other side. 'I've no place special to go.'

They linked their arms through hers. In a moment they saw the V-bomb streaking above, throbbing out its song of death.

Jessy said, 'You know, those things are the start of something big. Some day you'll hear that jet motor flying over in big planes filled with peaceable passengers. It's going to revolutionize flight. In twenty years' time when our kids are growing up, they'll think it was always like that and they won't be one bit interested in this part of our lives, because it happened in the "Olden Days".

'Oh, we'll get married and have kids, because we're that kind of people, or we wouldn't be over here. We'll go to their school dos like people have always done and they'll think we're quite dull.

'But way down inside of us, we'll be different from mothers before us – maybe from any women before us – because we left a piece of our lives over here that we can never explain to anyone.'

The sky went silent and black as she finished speaking. Jessy laughed softly. 'That is, if we get back,' she said and waited with the others until they heard the crunch of the V-bomb landing. 'There she goes. Let's go inside. After all, Marjorie, you aren't drunk, and they're a lot scarier when you're sober.'

She climbed to her feet, swaying slightly between them. 'Thanks for seeing me home,' she said to David.

'See you at Molly's,' he said as he vanished into the darkness.

Jessy threaded her arm through Marjorie's. She raised her face to the black sky. 'Goodbye, Bob Anders,' she whispered and let Marjorie take her up to bed.

As Marjorie pulled the covers up under her friend's chin, Jessy looked up into Marjorie's face and closed one of her brown eyes in a wink. 'Great war, isn't it, Marj?' she whispered with a crooked little smile.

Marjorie thought again of the little Spartan boy. Tears gathered in her eyes as she went to her own bed. Before she put out the light she took Colin's ring from her finger. She thought, as she held it in her hand, that the glowing ruby looked like a great drop of blood. She shivered. Then she quickly slipped it into the tiny chamois pouch she had already added to her dog tags around her neck, and put out the light.

The heavy, regular breathing coming from Jessy Cole's bed told her that Jessy was already asleep. But sleep did not come to her.

Conflicting thoughts tore at her like hounds. From remembered heights of ecstasy in Colin's arms and the anticipation of delights that lay ahead, she dropped down to a dungeon of guilt and fear. Had she done wrong?

Her father's parting words were loud inside of her. How shattered her parents would be if they knew what she had

161

done. Perhaps even her brother and her sister-in-law would wonder if she was a fit aunt for their children. She could think of no one in the strict Bible belt where she had been raised who would condone or understand her actions, war or no war.

But in spite of all of them and her own dream of being a virgin bride, she could not bring herself to regret the moments in Colin's arms.

Perhaps that's all Colin and I will ever have. The treacherous thought kept swimming to the surface. She forced it down. He must come back. He must survive this week stretching before her like an endless grey road. *Just five days.* Five short days and she would be standing with him at the altar.

'*Remember, you are my wife now.*' Were they ominous words? A premonition? She must fight off these beasts tearing at her. It was what had happened to Jessy's love that had shaken her.

How can I expect to be happy? she thought. *So many of them are not coming back.* Please, dear God, she prayed, keep him safe up there. Please, oh please, bring him home to me.

She covered his ring with her hand and pressed it against the warm flesh of her throat and at last drifted off to sleep.

Chapter 19

Captain Burns looked up from her desk at Marjorie, with a slight smile touching her lips. 'You realize, Hatfield, that your request for permission to marry this Saturday is most unusual. However, I will put it in for you at once and let you know, as soon as I hear from Headquarters, if it is granted.'

'Thank you, ma'am.'

Captain Burns walked across to the window and stood looking out on to the square. After a moment she turned back. Her face was no longer that of the reserved, stern company commander. Her eyes were large and swimming and there was a slight quiver to her mouth.

She came to Marjorie and impulsively held out her hand. 'Congratulations,' she said softly. 'You are indeed fortunate to be able to marry the man you love.'

Marjorie squeezed the hand in hers, feeling uncomfortably as if she were peeping for a moment through a window into a forbidden, secret room.

Captain Burns quickly withdrew her hand and, as if regretting her lapse, she said briskly, 'Very well, Hatfield. You are dismissed.'

Marjorie saluted and left, carrying with her the picture of the other young woman's eyes with the veil of reserve lifted from them, vulnerable and hurt. She remembered the way they had looked adoringly up into the face of Major Farrow. With a wave of sympathy for the other woman's hopeless love, she thought: This, too, is one of the casualties of war.

The next day she received word from Captain Burns that her permission to marry had come through.

Bonny was ecstatic. 'You little shit! Do we get to go to the wedding?'

'Of course. You're all invited. It's to be at eleven o'clock in the Anglican church in Wendover.'

Bonny and Elsie were the only ones of her roommates at home and they were both preparing to go out for the evening. Marjorie noticed that Elsie had a secretive, elated look about her and Bonny, too, looked as if something was pleasing her.

Their personal lives must be going very right, Marjorie thought.

Before Marjorie had left Enderby Hall, the Countess of Rivermere had told her, 'Feel free to invite any of your friends you wish to attend.'

Marjorie would have liked to ask Jessy to be her bridesmaid, but knowing how the Enderbys regarded Lady Ashley and the way Ashley had felt about Raif she thought it only right to ask her. Anyway, there was no certainty any of her roommates would be free from duty to come to her wedding.

Ashley had been touchingly pleased, and the countess smiled at Marjorie with more warmth than she had yet shown towards her son's future wife. At this moment, I think she likes me almost as well as the Gurkha, Marjorie thought with a wry smile.

'Lucky young blighter to be getting a girl like you,' Major Middleton had said. 'And you couldn't be getting a better chap. Always hoped he'd meet a fine girl like you one day.'

'But I'm not an aristocrat,' Marjorie protested. 'The countess thinks I'm practically a savage.'

Major Middleton laughed. 'You're a true lady if ever there was one. Didn't you jump Beecher's Brook? Poor Honora worshipped Raif and she desperately wanted Ashley in the family. Ashley's her goddaughter, you know. She's clinging to the old ways. She can't accept that they're gone for ever. Some new blood is just what the Enderbys need.'

Major Middleton's cheerful optimism infected her and kept her buoyed up all day. But when Elsie and Bonny had gone off for the night and she was alone in the room her fears came buzzing back. News of fierce fighting across the Channel came back to Britain as the Germans clawed to retain their position and the allies relentlessly pushed them back, blackening the sky above them with their bombers, and with that avenging

164

armada of the skies went the fighter escorts – *the Spitfires!*

Wednesday – Thursday – Friday . . . Three more days.

Marjorie had always been one to look forward tremendously to things. As a child she counted the days until the school picnic, dreaming of the ice cream, the races and athletics. She would wake up in the night desperately afraid that something would prevent her from getting there.

But nothing ever did. I always made it, she thought. *Except for the school concert.*

The disturbing thought leapt into her mind.

She had been eight years old, and she had the star part – Mary – in the Christmas play.

She thought of the dress her mother had made for her out of cheesecloth, dyed a deep midnight blue, the colour she was sure of the night sky above Bethlehem.

Marjorie felt uplifted in that dress. She pictured herself with her tinsel halo on her fair head, looking down at Polly Lindsey's fat-faced doll with the cracked head, lying in the manger. With the background of cardboard cows and donkeys, the shepherds and wise men, and Billy Grant as Joseph in an old horse blanket, she felt she really would be Mary gazing down at her baby.

There was almost a blizzard two nights before the big night. Her mother wrapped a heated sadiron in an old flannelette blanket and put it at her feet in bed to keep out the chill from the north wind.

She was drifting off to sleep, imagining the Snow Queen's palace on the frosted window pane, when a sudden catch in her throat made her cough.

That night she dreamed that Julia McKay was playing *her* part in the Christmas play, dressed in *her* pretty, midnight-blue dress.

In the morning she was icy cold and burning hot by turns and her chest felt tight.

She struggled out of bed and fought her way to the kitchen on shaky legs. She put her full willpower into trying to keep her condition from her mother. She had to get better. She couldn't miss the Christmas concert she had been dreaming about for months. She couldn't be sick now.

Her mother took one look at Marjorie's face, put her hand

on her hot forehead and sent her daughter back to bed, where she stayed for the next four days.

Julia McKay wore her dress in the Christmas play. Her friends told her all about it when she returned to school after the Christmas holidays.

The night of the concert Marjorie had lain in bed, wracked with the flu, and wondered if this was her punishment for having had that dreadful row with Ivy Hagen last week. She had said some very rude things to Ivy and had refused to loan her her crayons.

She smiled slightly, looking back on it all now, but there was still a little wrench in her heart that had never gone away . . . Perhaps her childish thoughts had been right. Perhaps there was something wrong with wanting something so desperately – desperately as she wanted to marry Colin. *And she had gone against all her teachings in giving herself to him before her love was sanctified by the Church.*

A superstitious dread crept into her heart.

Jessy Cole came into the room and found her sitting white-faced on the bed. 'What's the matter, Marjorie?' she said, looking at her with a kind light in her deep brown eyes. 'You look as if you'd been shooting it out with old Machine-Gun Cassidy.'

Marjorie laughed shakily. Machine-Gun Cassidy, as they had named her, had been their sergeant in basic training and all the recruits had gone in mortal terror of her.

'I was just wondering, Jess,' she said hesitantly, 'do you think – Is there something wrong with wanting something too much?'

Jessy shot her a keen glance. 'You mean like the beautiful Annabel Lee? The angels might get jealous?'

'Something like that, but not exactly. It's more like – like we know better than God and we want what we want so badly we forget to say, "Thy will be done".'

Jessy sat on Bonny's bed, facing Marjorie. 'You mean God deliberately snatches things away from us to show us He's Boss?'

Marjorie smiled in spite of her mood. 'It doesn't sound quite right when you put it like that.'

'You're all jammed up inside over your flyer. Things have

happened so suddenly, and when you found out about what happened to my lover that spooked you out. You don't suppose I think God snapped him out of here because I wanted him? What about all the ones that made it? Somebody wants them just as desperately as I wanted Bob Anders. It was just that that sniper was some shot.' She paused a moment, looking intently at Marjorie, then she went on, speaking softly.

'This is the first man who's ever meant anything to you, isn't he Marjorie?'

Marjorie clasped her hands, her eyes huge in her white face. 'Oh, and I want him to be the only man in my life ever.'

'Well, you have a pretty good chance. Our air force has the Luftwaffe on the run and your man's only a couple of days away from a desk job. And I wouldn't worry about your notion about wanting things too much. I don't suppose anyone ever wanted anything more than Helen wanted Carl to come back, and he's made it.'

'But Helen is such a good person,' Marjorie said. 'And they – they're married.' Marjorie blushed.

Jessy gave her another keen glance from under the shade of her eyelashes. 'And you're all equipped with hoofs and horns and a tail, I suppose. Good and bad are just in people's minds you know, Marjorie, except for the basic things like sharing the good things of life and not going out of your way to hurt anybody, or letting a friend down, and being kind to old ladies and animals. The rest of it all depends a lot on how you were brought up. Now, in Victorian times if a girl kissed a man she pretty near *had to* marry him; while the Eskimos think it's great form to loan a visitor their wives of a cold night. You don't suppose those Eskimos feel guilty, do you? Yet that stolen kiss would be enough to make a Victorian girl shuffle about in sacks all day with a great scarlet letter on her forehead.'

Marjorie laughed. Jessy's droll logic stilled the frenzied, unreasonable fears that had been surging out of control.

Jessy continued studying her friend's wan face, with her kindly, knowing smile. 'It's not wise to create dragons on the path ahead, you know. Most of the bogey men we're scared of turn out to be just stage props when we get up to them. Take Elsie, for instance, she was so scared of those old doodle bugs,

167

she spent nearly all her time skulking under her bed, afraid to step outside unless she absolutely had to. But since she got blown up and almost killed by one, she's been running around like a chorus girl and tossing that fancy food of hers around like it was sawdust. And you know what? I don't think she's ever had so much fun in her whole life. I guess, if there's one thing we're not supposed to do, it's be scared to live, and to quit living when something messes up our act. Take me, for instance, I loved Bob. Oh, he wasn't the first man in my life, but he was the first one I ever really loved.'

'Oh,' Marjorie said, 'but Jess, it hurts you.'

Jessy nodded slowly and all the laughter died out of her eyes, revealing for a moment a naked pain. 'It hurts like hell, Marjorie. I long for him in every aching part of me – and I do mean *every* part. I hear his laugh, and then I see him with blood all over his chest, staining the love letter he wrote me. But there's still a big wonderful world out there and I'm part of it and I mean to go on being part of it as long as I'm around. And one day it'll quit hurting and there'll be other men in my life, but the joy of being with Bob will never go away as long as I can think and feel; because whatever happens, I had those moments with him and they're in my life for ever. Nothing can take them away from me.'

'But oh Jess, how will you ever get over losing him?'

Jessy's face lit up. 'Just watch me,' she said impishly.

'Oh,' Marjorie said.

Jessy went on, speaking softly, 'I lived every minute of the good time. Now I've got to live every minute of the bad time and then I'll live the good times again and I guess life is like that.'

Marjorie said doubtfully, 'I – I don't think I could ever get over it if anything happened to – to Colin.' She put her hand up to her lips as her voice caught in her throat.

Jessy said seriously, 'You would, you know, Marjorie. The first law of nature is survival and survival means we get over the things that hurt us.'

'I don't,' Marjorie said ruefully. 'I never even got over the time I missed the Christmas concert.'

Jessy looked at her inquiringly and Marjorie told her the story. 'I still have the hurt feeling whenever I think of it,' she said.

'That's because you haven't let go of it, Marj. You were probably brought up to be so sincere you never let go of anything for fear of being disloyal. If you brood over the things that make you unhappy they sort of pile up, like layers of greasepaint. You have to take all of your make-up off at the end of each performance. That's one of the rules of the stage. You get a mighty bad skin if you let it build up and it'll spoil your next appearance.'

Marjorie was laughing when Jessy finished. 'Oh, Jess, it sounds just like you, but I'm afraid I don't have your brave spirit.'

'It's not a matter of being brave, Marj. It's just cutting your losses. Maybe that's what they mean by saying, "Thy will be done". But you don't say it before it happens, because things could turn out just the way you want them. If it doesn't, maybe there's a reason – maybe there isn't. But whether there is or isn't, you're a whole lot better to accept it and go on to the next thing than to spend your life brooding over the piece of cake someone else got.

'And you'll very likely get what you wish,' she added. 'Somebody loves little blonde women with wide blue eyes. It's been my experience that they nearly always get what they want.'

The sudden blast of the air raid siren finished her sentence. It was followed very soon by the sound of an approaching V-bomb, and then the abrupt, terrifying stillness. Jessy's hand tightened on Marjorie's shoulder.

The thud and thunder of the explosion set the building quivering. The window panes rattled convulsively. Jessy said softly, 'I hope it didn't get Molly's. I'm going to go take a look.'

'No,' Marjorie said. 'There'll be more of them coming. Better stay inside.'

But Jessy's eyes were dancing with a wild recklessness. She headed for the door. Marjorie grabbed her tin hat, jammed it on and followed her.

It could be me, not Colin, who gets it, she thought. But she couldn't let Jessy go out there alone.

Chapter 20

Colin and his father spoke little as the earl guided the small car down the winding, summer-scented road to Wendover. The companionship that had always existed between them needed few words. They did not mention the war, nor the week that lay ahead.

As always, Colin would allow no one but the earl to come to the station with him when he returned to his squadron.

He told Marjorie, 'I want to say goodbye to you here among the flowers in the garden where I can kiss you without strange eyes on us. Besides, Mother will want you to herself to make more of those plans for Saturday.' He smiled down into her troubled eyes.

Actually, his last goodbye to her had been said in his mother's little sitting room. He had kissed them both gently and gone out to the car to his waiting father, moisture stinging his eyes.

Sitting quietly on the drive to the station, he felt that his whole body and soul were filled with the wonder of her. The glorious love she had given back to him as he so gently took away her virginity and brought her up to his own ecstasy had brought him as close to heaven as any man could go on this earth. The sweet, womanly scent of her as she lay in his arms, looking up into his eyes, lingered in his nostrils.

He smiled tenderly, thinking of her joyful yet tremulous look and how he had kissed away the female fears that chased across her face, and brought back the dimples beside her sweet mouth.

She's like an innocent child, he thought, seeing her expressive face with all her love showing in her enormous eyes and the quiver of her lips. Other women might have tried to hide their feelings.

He knew that lovemaking before they were married had been an enormous step for her, something she had planned never to do. Misgivings took hold of him again. In his overwhelming passion and love for her, he had been like a man stumbling, thirst-driven, through the desert and suddenly coming upon a green oasis with a sparkling pool of clear, cool water. And he had drunk helplessly from the sweetness of her lips.

If only there was no war. Up to now he had given little thought to what he might do after the war. He knew the odds were against him surviving it and he had not questioned what he must do. He was an Enderby and Enderbys had always served their king and country. He had left his studies and the peaceful fields of his ancestors and gone with the other young men to defend the skies sheltering Britain from the dark hosts of the evil little man with the moustache.

Now suddenly, desperately, he wanted to survive this war, and he was afraid, not for himself, but for Marjorie. He wanted to return, to go to that church on Saturday and make her his wife. He wanted to make everything up to her – to give her his name and his life.

These were not lucky thoughts to go into combat with. His life had long been pledged. Probably the reason he had survived so far was because he had gone into each operation expecting no more than to do his job, whatever the outcome might be, living minute by minute. To care as he now cared about coming back was tempting Fate to turn her face away.

The earl glanced sideways at the handsome, sensitive face of his son. There had always been a deep understanding between them. For the countess that closeness between parent and child had been with Raif, but for the earl it had always been Colin.

He sensed now that something had happened between Colin and the sweet girl from Canada. He wished that he could do something to ease the turmoil he could see in his beloved son, as he had helped him over the rough spots when he was a little boy.

Unlike the reckless carefree Raif, Colin had always been a sensitive, feeling child, easily moved by the plight of others and touched by the pain of any living creature. He had never done the harsh, thoughtless things other boys did. The earl

171

remembered the day when Raif had brought home a frog he had captured down by the pond and had put the little creature in a box so that he could watch its habits, and had proudly brought his friends and family around to see *his* frog. Colin, who was only five, had looked with tears in his eyes at the frog sitting forlornly in the box, ignoring the food Raif had given it. Then when they had all gone off to play he had slipped back quietly, carried the frog back to the pond and let it go.

Raif had let out a bellow when he found his frog gone. The countess had found the two boys tumbling and fighting on the rug in the hall.

'Why did you take your brother's frog?' she had asked Colin severely. 'You know you do not touch each other's things without permission.'

'But, Mother, it's not Raif's frog,' Colin answered, looking up into his mother's face with his wide dark eyes. 'The frog belongs to God and it was lonely there in the box. It was homesick for its brothers and sisters in the pond, like I would be if I was away from you and Father and Raif. I just took it home and let it go. It was happy. It hopped away. I could see it laughing.'

The countess's mouth twitched, but she said severely, 'But you had no right to take it without your brother's permission.'

The earl stepped in and took Colin's hand in his. 'I want Colin to come and help me feed the horses,' he said quietly. As he left he said casually, over his shoulder, 'There will be no more taking the wild creatures from their homes.'

He could understand Colin's feelings because he had a gentle respect for the wild creatures himself. In fact, his main pleasure in life was seeing everyone and every thing around him enjoying life. So he understood later, when Colin was a young man and he flatly refused to go in for the foxhunt, as did all the neighbourhood boys.

'It just seems so beastly unfair, Father,' he said. 'All those hounds and horses and people running after one poor little fox. I keep imagining what I would feel like if I were the fox.'

Nor would he hunt, nor go near the pheasant shoot.

Raif had laughed at his younger brother, but it was a warm kindly laugh. Although in him was a harsher strain, he understood the kindness of Colin's nature and loved him the more

172

for it. Between the two brothers, but two years apart in age, was a great bond.

The earl thought it a strange quirk of fate that this son of his, who had been too kindly to hunt animals and birds, had become a hunter of men, rallying to the hunt with the cry 'Tally Ho!' And he had been decorated by his king for shooting those other boys from the sky.

He wished wistfully that he could put his arms around his son and carry him back to Enderby – to safety – to the beautiful woman he loved. He wanted to turn the car around. He did not want to take Colin to the train at Wendover.

They were passing a huge stone house, peeping through the trees at the far end of a long drive. The earl cleared his throat, nodding towards the mansion. 'Old Tea Kettle thinks his horse is going to win the National this year,' he said with a smile. 'But my money is on the Queen's horse. He wants me to ride over this afternoon and have a look at the animal over the jumps.'

Old Tea Kettle was Sir Thomas Kettle, a lifelong friend and school chum of the earl. Colin smiled. 'Well, Father, if anyone can judge his chances, you can. But don't be too hard on the old boy. You know how he loves his pipe dreams.'

All at once Colin noticed how the age lines had deepened in his father's face, lines that had not been there before Dunkirk. Affection welled up in him for this man who had done so much to make his life happy. He knew the love his father had for him and he was grateful that he kept these painful partings casual.

They said little more until the earl stopped the car near the platform at Wendover station and they shook hands firmly.

'Cheerio. Good hunting,' the earl said.

'Cheerio, Father.' Colin leapt quickly from the car and went on to the platform without glancing back.

The earl drove quickly away, carrying the picture of his son standing on the platform in the glow of the warm June sunlight. Suddenly in his mind he saw Raif, smiling his bold carefree smile as he waved at them from the train window the day they saw him off – before Dunkirk.

Like a beast, vicious in its death agony, Germany lashed out at London. The sirens wailed continuously. Buildings that had stood for centuries crumbled into heaps of rubble, burying men, women and children as the weird robot planes plunged from the sky. Londoners went their way quietly, carrying on their business as usual, but on buses and in stores and on the underground the latest phase in the savage attacks they had endured for years was on every lip, and rumours flew of other deadly secret weapons to come. Germany, it was said, was about to launch V2 and then V3.

Speculation was rife. It would be poison gas – deadly disease germs. Newpapers with grim humour printed, 'Famous last saying: There she goes!'

The V-bombs fell all around Sussex Square but 43 Company, Canadian Women's Army Corps, escaped untouched. The V-bomb that fell when Marjorie and Jessy were having their talk landed a street away from Molly's pub. Marjorie had laughed as Jessy remarked dryly, 'They'll never beat Britain, you know, as long as they can't knock out her pubs. Britain's wars haven't really been won on the playing fields of Eton as that poet wrote; they've been won in front of the dartboard in the pubs.'

There seemed to be truth in Jessy's words. In the midst of the devastation raining down on their city the old London pub-goers continued to sit with pipe and pint, discussing politics and enjoying the nightly game of darts with old cronies, never troubling to go to the air raid shelters.

But others, less indifferent to danger, took shelter deep down in the underground stations. Every night as dusk fell old men, women and children spread blankets out on grimy platforms and slept with their heads to the wall and the trains rattling past, only a short distance from their feet.

Marjorie was glad she was a soldier under orders living in barracks. She felt she would rather take any chance above ground than sleep in those gloomy cavernous underground stations with the smell of trains and the heavy air in her nostrils.

While the V-bomb war against London took its savage toll, across the Channel the Germans had thrown everything into a bloody, all-out struggle to halt the relentless allied advance. In her vivid imagination Marjorie felt she could smell the blood and sweat in the air and hear the sounds of the conflict.

News of the fighting filled the papers and the wireless. She was out in the country a great deal, driving Major Middleton to the various Canadian units scattered throughout southern England. The June weather was glorious. She wondered how the blossoming countryside could look so fair when a short distance away the blood of its sons was watering the fields of France. It seemed that even the flowers of the field should be hanging their heads and weeping for the brave men suffering and dying over there so that they could bloom on free soil.

She drove down narrow lanes and roads where Roman legions had trod, choked now with long convoys of trucks and Jeeps and bren-gun carriers, tanks and tank carriers. All moving down to the coast.

Overhead night and day droned the bombers, and with them, she knew, went their fighter escorts. Each time she heard them Marjorie wondered if Colin was up there with them.

She pictured him in helmet and goggles with eyes steel hard behind his death-dealing guns, but she could not keep the picture firm in her mind. She could not picture Colin except with gentle, smiling, love-filled eyes.

She thanked God for Major Middleton.

It was almost impossible for dark, gloom-laced thoughts to take possession of her mind with him beside her in the car, scattering ashes from his old pipe, his eyes twinkling kindly and his face full of cheerful optimism. He treated her as if she were a favourite daughter and not a CWAC driver. She got the feeling from him that he had not the slightest doubt that he would be there at Enderby on Saturday helping her to celebrate her wedding to his godchild.

She scarcely saw Jessy as the wounded poured in from the battlefields and Jessy worked long hours driving her ambulance. Elsie and Bonny were busy also, and they went out every night as soon as they had finished supper.

Bonny was on the ball diamond at Marble Arch every free moment until it grew too dark, practising for the big game against the ATS. And Elsie had taken to mysteriously disappearing every night and not returning until the small hours. She had a kind of bounce to her step these days.

Marjorie hardly recognized her as the same girl who had cowered on her bed each night, eating steadily from her store

175

of goodies. In fact she had recklessly shared her hoard with her roommates and no fresh supply had as yet arrived. Consequently, her figure was a good deal trimmer and her face prettier, and she had lost some of her look of a plump little silver fox.

On Friday morning Bonny and the air raid siren woke the occupants of room 217. 'Hey, you guys, you're all coming to my ball game tonight, aren't you?' Bonny said loudly, leaping out of bed. 'Hey, you shut up! I want to talk,' she yelled up towards the roof as the rumble of a doodle bug cut into her words.

The other girls sat up in their beds. Today was the day of the long-awaited big ball game between the 43 Company CWAC and the ATS to decide the London championship.

'You gotta come and watch us kick the shit out of those Limeys.'

'Who's umpiring?' Jessy asked.

'Moose,' Bonny answered shortly.

Jessy laughed. 'You should have gone out on to Sussex Square with him.'

Bonny snorted. 'If that big lug sides with those Limeys I'll kick the shit out of his shins.'

Helen giggled. 'I'm coming,' she said. 'I don't want to miss a sight like that.'

Marjorie joined in the laughter, but her mind was seething with just one thought. *This is his last day to fly combat missions over there.*

Elsie stopped in her automatic dive for safety under the bed and pulled herself up on top of it. 'I'm coming,' she said. 'Major Ellis said I could get off early for the game. He's coming, too.' Her cheeks flushed up.

Jessy shot her a keen glance. 'I think I'm going to be able to make it. What about you, Marjorie?'

'I'm going to ask Major Middleton – ' Marjorie held her breath as a V-bomb's engine stopped overhead.

They heard it land and the building shivered.

'That was too far away for Molly's,' Jessy said with satisfaction.

On the tail of her words they heard another one approaching. They jumped from their beds and joined the scramble for the bathroom, giggling as they all tried to wedge in at the same time as the girls from 218.

'I say, how jolly,' Major Middleton said. 'You can count me in. I shan't know who to cheer for, though, having a CWAC driver and being liaison officer with the Canadians.'

Marjorie laughed. 'You'll have to cheer for both sides.'

'You'll be in the same boat soon, you know. After tomorrow you'll be an Englishwoman.'

Marjorie caught her breath as a sharp thrill of joy and fear shot through her.

Major Middleton saw her face flush, then pale. He leaned over and patted her hand and smiled reassuringly. They were in the staff car ready to pull away for a short trip around London.

'I shall have to watch out for myself when I'm cheering for the British girls. Your friend Bonny sounds as if she may be inclined to bung a bat at me or something.'

Marjorie laughed, but her mind was not easy. It was nine o'clock in the morning. The day ahead loomed as a large uncharted wilderness. Five o'clock seemed for ever away. After the game she would catch the eight o'clock train for Wendover. When morning dawned Colin's tour of ops would be over. But there was still all of today and tonight . . .

Major Middleton said, 'Brigadier Raham is laying on another driver to take me down to my place this evening. You know I'm only a couple of miles from Enderby, would you like me to drop you off?'

Marjorie accepted gladly. She had been dreading taking the train by herself so late at night and having them come from Enderby to pick her up at the station. But she did not want to disappoint Bonny who was so eager to have all her friends at the big game. They would all be catching the train for Enderby in the morning in time for her wedding.

Five o'clock came at last. Hyde Park was washed in warm sunlight. The ball diamond was lined with spectators in uni-form, the British on one side and the Canadians on the other. A sprinkling of the ancient soap-box men and other civilians were watching the antics of these strangers in their domain with amused tolerance.

Marjorie envied Bonny. She was standing by home plate, sturdy body planted firmly on chubby legs and fresh complexion glowing in the sunlight, facing the ruddy-cheeked, ginger-haired ATS captain. Her eyes snapped as she waited for the umpire to toss the coin to decide who won the choice of fielding or batting first. It was clear to see she was not disturbed by any invading thoughts. She had only one thing on her mind – to take the London district trophy back with her to CMHQ at the end of this game.

Standing between the two girl captains was a burly-shouldered giant with sergeant's stripes on the arm of his fatigue uniform. Brick-red hair clustered in curls above his broad, florid, wide-mouthed face. His bright blue eyes glinted with life as he looked from one girl to the other, holding the coin in his fingers ready to toss it in the air.

'That has to be Moose Morrison,' Marjorie said to Jessy.

Bonny won the toss. 'We'll take the field.'

'Good move,' Helen said. 'That gives them last bat. That Bonny knows all the angles, I think.'

Bonny took her place on the pitcher's mound with Moose behind her. 'Play ball,' he bellowed.

Bonny sent the ball sizzling across the plate, somewhere near the shoulder of the tiny, dark-haired ATS girl at the bat. She let it go by. The catcher caught it and deftly pulled it down fast.

'Ball one,' Moose roared.

Bonny turned and gave him a dirty look and the watching Canadians all shouted at him: 'Get your eyes examined, Ump –' 'That was a strike . . .'

The British looked slightly bewildered at this display as they watched quietly.

'Do you see the way that Moose looks at Bonny?' Jessy said to Marjorie and Helen, her lips curling in a smile. 'His eyes glow like a tomcat's every time they light on her.'

'He doesn't seem to be letting it influence his decisions, though,' Marjorie said, looking closely at the big sergeant.

Bonny calmed down and pitched a scorching inning – two ATS struck out, the third caught on a fly ball.

The Canadian girls also failed to bring in any runs at the end of the first inning . . . there was no score in the ball game.

178

The ATS team got first blood in the fifth inning when one of their runners got home on a long ball that sizzled down the third base-line. Bonny, backed up by the rest of the team, protested volubly that it was a foul ball, but Moose ruled it fair.

She stood with her chin jutting out and her eyes snapping, arguing with him, while all the Canadians on the sidelines screamed for his blood.

The English clapped genteelly for their girl who had come in with the run and said, 'Well played. Well played.'

Major Middleton came up to Marjorie, chuckling delightedly. 'I say, I wouldn't have missed this for anything. Do Canadians always threaten to murder their referees? I wonder you have any left over there, after seeing this display. Really, I wouldn't dare cheer for the British, standing here among you Canadians, you know.'

Marjorie laughed and introduced him to Helen and Jessy. 'This is mild,' Helen told him. 'You should see Bonny when she's really riled up.'

'I wouldn't be surprised if that happens before the end of this game,' Jessy predicted.

Order was finally restored and after scowling savagely at Moose Morrison, Bonny settled down, grimly, to pitching. She fanned the next three ATS girls one after the other, and then the CWACs brought in two runs and the Canadians cheered wildly. Bonny's face flushed with triumph.

The score see-sawed, standing at four to three for the CWAC team at the end of the seventh inning.

Bedlam broke out in the eighth. Bonny put out one ATS batter, but the three following players took short hits. The bases were loaded, and the three runners ready to tear for home plate as soon as the ball was hit. The air raid warning, sounding just as the ATS star batswoman Bruiser Brewster took her stance, was ignored.

Bonny wound up and sent a vicious curve towards the plate.

Brewster swung her bat. It cracked against the ball, sending it sizzling towards left field, between Bonny and first base.

Bonny sprang sideways, bringing it down, but not enough – it slipped over her head. The girl on first base dived to scoop it up and Bonny shot across to cover first base. In her frantic haste to get it there in time the girl threw it too high. A groan went up from the Canadians.

But Bonny, with a superhuman effort, sprang high, stretched to her utmost, and caught the ball in one hand, just as Bruiser Brewster slid into the base.

A mighty shout went up from the Canadians.

Grinning like a Cheshire cat, Bonny started to walk in, as the last of the three ATS runners flew in to home plate.

'Safe on first!' Moose roared.

Pandemonium broke loose. Bonny rushed at Moose. 'She was out – OUT!' she yelled. 'I caught that ball before she got in.'

'But you were still up in the air, not touching the base when her toe touched it,' Moose said.

'Like shit I was,' Bonny raged. 'I was back on base before she touched it. She was out, I tell you.'

Moose shook his head. 'The tip of her toe touched the base before your foot came back down on it. She was safe,' he said decisively. 'Get back in the pitcher's box and play ball.'

Bonny flew at him. 'You big carrot-headed Limey lover,' she screamed. 'Just because you got the same-coloured hair as their captain! You don't need to think you can pull one on us!' She started kicking at his shins.

Moose stretched out one giant hand, caught her by the front of her sweatshirt and held her, kicking and yelling and thrashing her legs. He shook her, while the Canadians swarmed around him like angry hornets, shouting protests and demanding his blood. Even Helen joined in, her eyes flashing. 'She was out,' she shouted.

'GET back in there and play ball,' Moose bellowed, shaking Bonny up and down. 'ALL of you settle down, or I'll call this game and give it to the ATS by default. Now SIMMER down.'

Bonny was too furious to listen. She kept squealing and trying to kick his shins.

'ALL RIGHT,' Moose bellowed, 'that's IT!'

Before he could say anything else the loud sound of a buzz bomb cut into his words. They all fell instantly silent and looked skywards to see it approaching low over Marble Arch. Then abruptly the noise stopped.

Horrified, Marjorie watched the long, ghostly silver plane

gliding towards the ball diamond, drifting slowly out of the clear blue sky, as if savouring the destruction it would wreck on its enemies below. She flung herself down into a crouch with the others, with her head down and her hands over her ears.

'Not now,' she prayed. 'Oh, please, not now. Colin – oh Colin!' Through her mind flashed the thought: I'm glad I had those moments with him out there under the bushes. *I'm glad I'm not a virgin.*

Bonny's voice cut into the terrified silence: 'Listen, you guys, we're going to settle down and play ball and beat those Limeys. We're not going to knuckle down just because they got a few runs on us. We've still got another inning left. We'll show 'em!'

Marjorie looked up and gasped. Bonny was standing upright, looking down at her team, her face flushed and her eyes blazing, ignoring the impending doom coming at them from the sky. Jess, too, was standing, smiling as she watched the scene.

God, Marjorie thought, how brave! *But we're all going to die!*

At that moment the buzz bomb, caught by some changing current of wind, no doubt, but as if halted by Bonny's defiance, stood straight up in the sky, flipped over and sailed off in the other direction, skimming the rooftops. They heard it land somewhere in the distance as they scrambled to their feet.

'Okay,' Bonny said. 'Now, let's show those Limeys how to play ball!'

'By Jove,' said Major Middleton, who had been standing quietly throughout everything, 'if we had that little scrapper on the front line, the Germans would be laying down their arms and fleeing for dear life.'

'She doesn't seem to scare Moose,' Jessy said with a laugh.

Moose called, 'Play ball!' and the players resumed their positions on the ball diamond.

Bonny's jaw was set and her eyes glittered with determination as she concentrated on retiring the side. 'Come on, gang, we gotta get some runs this time,' she urged.

The Canadians went into their last inning trailing four to six. They managed three hits and loaded the bases with

181

runners – but then two players struck out. The whole match depended on the next batter.

The next batter up was Bonny.

Feet spread wide apart and jaw jutting, she stood up to the plate and faced the little ATS captain.

The ATS girl pitched the ball.

Bonny threw her whole body into her swing and the bat cracked against the ball like the sound of a shot.

Brigadier Raham was approaching the ball diamond from the direction of Marble Arch in company of Brigadier Sutherland of the British Staff, each with an aide in attendance, the British aide carrying the coveted cup to be presented to the winners of the ball game. Bonny's ball struck Brigadier Raham right in the middle of the row of ribbons across his chest. He pulled up with a snort.

Brushing aside the attentions of his aide he barked, 'Find out who hit that ball!'

No one had noticed the approach of the red-tabbed staff officers. The Canadians were shouting and wildly mobbing Bonny. Even the British were cheering and calling, 'Well played,' for Bonny's magnificent hit.

Brigadier Raham's aide finally managed to extricate Bonny and lead her over to face the brigadier.

Red-faced, with perspiration running down her forehead and her breath coming in great heaves, Bonny stood stiffly at attention and met his frosty stare.

'I understand you are the one who hit the ball that struck me on the chest,' he said sternly.

Bonny gulped. 'Sorry, sir,' she stammered. 'I didn't know you were there.'

'Of course you wouldn't have hit the winning home run if you'd known it would hit me,' he said, a smile crinkling up his eyes. 'At ease.' He held out his hand. 'Congratulations, Captain. Even Babe Ruth never hit a more important home run than yours.'

The all clear sounded as he finished speaking.

Flushed, Bonny stood among her teammates holding the London district cup aloft in triumph while army photographers took pictures.

'Look at that Moose,' Jessy said. 'He's as proud of her as a tomcat.'

182

Marjorie turned to see Moose's great red face beaming as he looked at Bonny.

The girls from 43 Company, with Bonny in their midst, carrying the cup, marched back to Sussex Square, singing lustily: 'Roll out the barrel' – then 'The Quartermaster's Song' – and finishing with the CWAC marching song, 'Here Come the Khaki Skirts', sung to the tune of 'Colonel Bogey'.

Marjorie, Jessy and Helen were laughing breathlessly when they went into 43 Company barracks with arms linked.

At the foot of the stairs the girl on orderly duty stopped them. 'Hey Hatfield, you're wanted on the phone,' she called from the sitting-room door.

Marjorie felt her heart do a dizzy leap. Who could it be? She had no friends in London who might be phoning her. A shiver of fear turned her face to ashes. She crept across the twenty miles of tilting floor to where the receiver hung from the hook. Clinging to the mouthpiece, she put the receiver to her ear.

'Hello,' she whispered.

Chapter 21

'Hello, soldier girl.' The room faded and returned as the familiar drawly English voice, warm with excitement, came into her ear. Marjorie clung to the phone, swaying, unable to say a word, the tears trickling down her cheeks.

'Marjorie, dearest, are you there?' Colin's voice became tinged with anxiety. 'I say, what's wrong?'

'Colin,' Marjorie whispered at last. 'Oh Colin. Yes, yes, I'm here. I'm here.' Her voice broke on a sob.

'I say old girl, are you crying? What sort of a way is that to greet your liege lord, back from the wars to claim his bride?'

'Oh, Colin,' Marjorie said again.

'I say, I hope you haven't changed your mind, have you?' his voice teased.

'Colin,' Marjorie said brokenly, 'oh, Colin, I'm sorry. It's just that I – I didn't know – the phone . . . When they said it was for me I thought it might be . . . I didn't know who it could be.'

'Well, it's your young lord coming out of the west to claim his fair bride.'

'Where – where are you, Colin?'

'Well, I'm phoning from a place we call the officers' mess, and it certainly warrants the name.'

'Have you – ' she broke off, unable to finish.

'I've finished my last tour of ops,' he said quietly. 'We tally-ho'd over there and I just dropped back down here a few minutes ago. I rushed to phone you. The girl who answered said you were out, then she heard you come in and I could hear a dickens of a row in the background. What's going on there?'

'Oh, Colin, it's Bonny and the team. We – they won the London district championship. Remember I told you about

Bonny's big game that was coming up?'

She heard him laugh. 'You mean, they beat the British? How dreadful. Who did you cheer for?'

'I – I,' Marjorie stammered. 'Oh, Colin, I just had to cheer for the Canadians, because of Bonny, you know. And – and Major Middleton was there and he said I would have to cheer for both sides.'

In her relief to know that Colin was safely out of combat, she found herself babbling, scarcely knowing what she was saying. Her heart was saying just one thing: Safe, safe, safe. Colin was safe. 'Oh, thank you, God,' she whispered under her breath.

'That will have to change you know, as soon as you become Lady Enderby, which will be at eleven o'clock tomorrow morning – if I survive my bachelor party. A few of the chaps are putting on a bit of a binge for me. I hope you don't mind, darling.'

'Oh no,' Marjorie said. 'But when are you coming to Enderby?'

'Early in the morning, darling. I'm coming with the best man, and the CO is sending down a small guard of honour. You're going to Enderby tonight, of course?'

'Yes. Yes, Major Middleton is going to take me in his staff car. He's waiting for me now.'

'Good. You'll be there soon, then. Tell Mother I phoned. I bet you have a bit of a party at Enderby, too, if I know Father.'

There was a brief pause in which neither of them could find words, but each could feel the heart of the other, then Colin said softly, 'From tomorrow, my little wife, we'll be together for the rest of our lives.'

'Tomorrow, Colin – tomorrow,' Marjorie whispered. 'Oh, I'm so glad – so glad you're back from – from over there.'

'So am I. Things were sticky for a bit. Much nicer at Enderby with all the ghosts and ancestors. I do hope you're not getting the wind up about the lot of them. You sound awfully solemn, you know. I'd love to hear your pretty laugh. If it gets too rough on you being Lady Enderby, I shall arrange to have some sandwiches frozen for you.'

Marjorie laughed, feeling the world suddenly spin joyously into place.

185

'That's better,' Colin said. 'I was beginning to think you were becoming as stern as the Gurkha. Now, my darling, these fellows are waiting to carry me off. It's my last night to be one of the lads, you know, and they aren't going to let me get away from them. Dream of me tonight, my darling. Goodbye until tomorrow.'

'Until tomorrow, Colin, dearest, until tomorrow,' Marjorie answered joyfully.

Darkness had fallen on the English countryside by the time the staff car carrying Marjorie and Major Middleton turned through the lodge gates at Enderby. The driver threaded his way cautiously between the tall shadowy trees. The tiny slits of light from his black-hooded headlamps shone faintly on the dark drive.

Now that she was finally arriving at Colin's ancestral home, Marjorie felt the elation, which had soared inside of her all through the drive from London, become tinged with nervousness. This couldn't really be Marjorie Hatfield approaching this castle of an earl, to marry an English lord she had known for only two weeks.

They came out of the dark drive and Enderby Hall loomed, a huge shadow in the night. The full moon struggling to push through the dark, low-hanging clouds gave a faint glow of silver to their tumbling, restless mass. A beam forcing its way between their shifting, changing shapes cast weird shadows on the ancient turrets, walls and windows of Enderby Hall, creating the strange illusion that the vast, castle-like building was not solid stone and mortar, but a misty, ghostlike, changing substance that might at any moment vanish into the night.

Marjorie reached out impulsively and put her hand on Major Middleton's arm. He patted it comfortingly and chuckled.

'Quite the old spot, isn't it?' he said cheerfully.

He had insisted that Marjorie ride with him in the back seat, instead of up front with the driver as Other Ranks were supposed to do. On the trip to Wendover he had regaled her with stories of life among the landed gentry of Wendover, including the legend of the great black stag that was supposed to haunt the Enderby woods.

186

'Lot of poppycock, of course,' he said, puffing on his pipe. 'Just some great hulking deer with the moon shining on its antlers. But of course, we English have to have our family ghosts, you know. Only the Enderbys had to go one better and have a stag, instead of some clanking old chap in bloody armour. Then there's old Tea Kettle. Lives just down the road from Enderby. Been friends with Teddy all his life. He has some beastly ghost of a Cavalier who prowls around the halls, dripping blood, with his long blond curls hanging down on his shoulders, all dressed in white. Scared the dickens out of a Yankee liaison captain old Kettle had up from London for a weekend.

'Saw it bobbing about in the corner of his room; he'd got to bed late, after having one over the eight with old Kettle. Jumped up and ran downstairs and phoned for his driver to come from London and take him back, right in the middle of the night. Almost got killed by one of those flying things after he was back in his own bed. Blew part of the roof in on him. Put him in the hospital for a week. Ghost he saw turned out to be a dustmop with a housemaid's white uniform hanging on it, which she'd left in the corner.'

Marjorie had laughed at Major Middleton's droll stories, but now as they arrived at Enderby Hall and she and the major mounted the steps to the great oak door, cloaked in mysterious shifting shadows, she could imagine any kind of phantom prowling in the night.

The door was opened by the elderly butler, Giles. He greeted Marjorie correctly, with a politely expressionless face. Then his eyes lit up as he spoke to Major Middleton. 'How very good to see you, sir,' he said as he took the major's cap and stick.

'Good to see you, Giles,' Major Middleton said, returning his warm smile. 'By Jove, how do you manage to stay so young? Upon my word, you haven't changed since the earl and I were boys running around this place, plaguing you.'

While they were exchanging pleasantries, Marjorie looked around the great hall, dimly lit and cold to conserve fuel and electricity for the war effort. The dogs rose from their place on the rug in front of the unlit fireplace and ran up to greet them. They recognized Marjorie and nuzzled up to have their heads

187

patted, wagging their tails delightedly. In the dim light the suits of armour on the stairs looked like the shadowy figures of ancient knights, standing guard over the hall of the Enderbys.

As the heavy door shut behind them, Marjorie had a sudden sense of being cut off from the world she knew. After tomorrow she would belong to the life of this great history-steeped castle – an Enderby woman; part for all time of their tradition. All at once overawed, she clung to Major Middleton's arm as they followed Giles across the hall to the small sitting room. Only her love for Colin kept her feet moving.

Giles opened the door of the sitting room and announced them. Lady Ashley was with the earl and countess. The two ladies were in long evening dresses and the earl in a dinner jacket. He sat at one of the small tables with his pictures of the Grand National winners spread out before him. The countess was in her favourite chair in front of a low coffee table, with Lady Ashley sitting across from her on a small green velvet chair.

The earl and Lady Ashley stood quickly and crossed the room to greet her.

'You've come,' he said delightedly, kissing her cheek.

'We've been waiting for you to phone us from Wendover to pick you up.' Lady Ashley embraced her affectionately.

'Major Middleton was kind enough to let me come with him in the staff car.'

'Oh, splendid. Jolly good of you to bring our bride to us, Roger,' the earl said, shaking the old friend's hand.

'You're a jolly lucky fellow to be getting a daughter-in-law like Marjorie,' Major Middleton said.

'You're absolutely right,' the earl agreed, putting his arm across Marjorie's shoulders and taking her across the room to where the countess sat very straight in her chair with a gracious frozen smile of welcome.

Marjorie didn't know what to do. She wanted to stoop and kiss the countess's cheek, but she felt, as she had the first time they met, that she was in the presence of a queen, and she ought really to curtsey. Instead, she took the countess's gracefully extended hand in hers for a brief moment before the countess withdrew it to her lap.

'Welcome to Enderby Hall, my dear,' she said in her beautifully modulated voice. Then her eyes lit up with warmth as they met Major Middleton's. He came to her and kissed her on the cheek.

'Honora, you grow lovelier every day. But you're so regal tonight, I couldn't imagine you keeping up with Teddy and me climbing apple trees.'

The countess gave a low amused laugh, her eyes twinkling up into his. 'I think, Roger, keeping up to you two today would be a good deal easier than it was forty years ago.'

The earl joined his wife and Major Middleton laughing at their shared memories, and Marjorie felt herself to be standing outside their familiar, intimate circle. But nothing could chill the bubbling happiness in her heart to know that Colin was safely back in England, not to fly combat again.

'Colin phoned,' she said.

They turned their eyes towards her flushed, excited face.

'He's back. He's safe. He's finished his last tour of ops,' she said jerkily.

For a moment, a look of intense joy flashed in the earl's eyes. Then he said matter of factly, 'Oh, jolly good show. I hope he gave those blighters what for on his last trip over there.'

Ashley's face lit up and she came across to Marjorie and threw her arms around her and kissed her cheek. Only the countess's expression did not change.

'How very fortunate he was able to get through to you with the news,' she said. 'Sometimes the beastly telephone lines are tied up for hours, you know.'

Marjorie wondered if the countess was thinking that her son's phone call should have been to his parents.

The earl said, 'They'll be giving him a bachelor send-off party down there, I'll be bound. Well, we'll have a bit of a party ourselves. I've been saving something for just this occasion for years. You'll stay of course, Roger? I'm going down to the wine cellar. I'll be back in a tick.'

Major Middleton readily agreed to stay, saying he would dismiss his driver.

'Good, good,' the earl said. 'Old Kettle and his wife are coming over for a bit, too.' He turned to Marjorie. 'I'm sorry there aren't more young people here for you, but I'm afraid they're all away, not like before the war.'

After the earl and Major Middleton had left the room, Marjorie stood uncertainly, not knowing what to say next.

'Please do sit down,' the countess said, indicating a stiff-backed green velvet chair. 'Or, perhaps, you would like to go upstairs to your room and freshen up?'

Marjorie shook her head. 'No thank you.' She felt she could not face that cavernous upstairs at the moment.

Now that she was really here at Enderby on the eve of her wedding, she was suddenly possessed by a feeling akin to panic.

Joy and fear were racing inside of her. She felt her legs trembling as she slid down on to a chair and sat very still with her back pressed against it. Only the warmth in Ashley's face kept her panic at bay. I shall never fit in here, she thought, looking at the calm, still, regally aloof face of the countess. Everything has happened too fast. What do I really know about this country, or these people? What do I really know about Colin?

Swift on the heels of this treacherous thought came the picture of Colin's smiling, kindly eyes, the memory of his lips on her lips, his body pressed against her body. I know that I love him with every bit of me, she thought, feeling a flush rise to her cheeks, and tomorrow at this time I will belong to him for ever. But where would she be with him? There had been no mention of a honeymoon somewhere. Where would they spend their first night together?

As if she read her future daughter-in-law's mind, the countess said, 'I have had the dust covers removed from the bridal rooms and they are ready for you and Colin tomorrow night. I've even managed to find a bit of wood for the fireplace. Giles had some trouble getting the chimney to draw. It's been so long since it's been lit. However, I think you'll find the room quite comfortable considering the wartime restrictions. Only, I'm afraid you won't have a maid to wait on you.' She paused, looking steadily at Marjorie.

'The Enderby heir and his bride always spend the first night of their honeymoon in the ancestral home, before going away,' she explained, as Marjorie stared at her in bewilderment. 'Of course you and Colin have only four days before he rejoins his squadron in his new post, not like it would have been in peacetime . . . ' She broke off abruptly.

Ashley laughed gently. 'I'm sure, Aunt Honora, Marjorie and Colin's honeymoon would be gloriously happy even if they were forced to spend it at the Boarshead Inn.'

With a flash of inner amusement, Marjorie wondered what the countess would say if she calmly announced that she intended to spend *all* her honeymoon at the Boarshead Inn. Where, she wondered, did the Enderby brides live for the rest of their lives when the honeymoon was over? Did they share the castle with the Countess and Earl of Rivermere, or did they have homes of their own? She realized, all at once, that she had given very little thought to anything beyond lying close and warm in Colin's arms, his liege lady for life.

She began to see dimly what the countess had meant when she told her there was far more to marriage than she understood.

The earl returned in triumph, carrying two dusty bottles of champagne. He patted them with a smile lighting up his eyes. 'These have been saved from the day I married my own dear lady, for the happy day when our son and heir takes a bride,' he said happily. 'There's a case of it for the wedding tomorrow, but these two bottles can be spared for us, tonight. I'm afraid we don't have any ice, but fortunately the wine cellar is absolutely icy.'

Marjorie felt that it would be cruel not to share in drinking the champagne the earl had so carefully hoarded all these years. In any case, she thought with a quick twist of wry humour, I've already done that 'dreadful thing' my mother hinted women do when they drink, and I didn't even have anything to drink.

Only, now that she was on the eve of marrying Colin and she knew he was safely home in England, what she had done didn't seem so very dreadful. After eleven o'clock tomorrow morning the 'dreadful thing' would be acceptable.

She watched fascinated, waiting for the cork to pop, as the earl pushed it out with his thumbs. She felt almost as if she were in a play. She had read so many stories about the opening of a bottle of champagne among the rich and titled.

When it did pop she jumped. It sounded like the bang of a gun.

191

The earl handed her the first glass of champagne and she watched with fascination the little bubbles floating up to break at the top of the shimmering liquid.

When they each had a glass the earl proposed a toast to the beautiful young lady from Canada who tomorrow would make them all happy by becoming the bride of their dear son and heir, Colin.

Marjorie noticed that the countess barely touched her glass to her lips.

After Marjorie had thanked them, they all settled down to enjoy their evening. Conversation flowed as easily between them as the champagne in their glasses. Marjorie could scarcely believe it was really alcoholic. It tasted like some lovely, refreshing soft drink. The bubbles caressed her tongue like nothing she had ever tasted. Certainly, she thought, this can't be very intoxicating.

The bubbles tickled her nose delightfully, and by the time her glass was half empty she had an airy, light-hearted, happy feeling, coupled with an acute longing for Colin that tingled all through her being. She glowed with the memory of her ecstasy as he had entered her body. The feel of his lips, and his arms pressing her to him, was hot in her blood and she throbbed with desire.

This is what my mother meant, she thought. Drinking makes you want someone even more, but I know I could never want anyone but Colin, no matter how much I drank. Secure in the knowledge that Colin was safely out of the skies she began to enjoy the evening.

The conversation was lively and stimulating. It flitted lightly from subject to subject, the theatre, books – and horses. As Marjorie was well read and knowledgeable about most subjects she had no trouble keeping up with everything under discussion and, relaxing under the influence of the champagne, she joined in animatedly, laughing merrily at the amusing little incidents, related for her benefit, which had taken place among their set in the country.

All her life she had been intrigued by stories of the English aristocracy. They're exactly the way I imagined them, she thought, as someone mentioned Peter Pan and the Christmas pantomime in London.

She thought happily, Colin has promised to take me this Christmas. And now I'm not afraid to look forward to it. Of course a doodle bug could get me.

But that has to be impossible. Nothing bad could happen now. Colin and I will grow old together. She giggled, thinking of Colin white-haired and with glasses and a walking stick, tottering around the estate with her hanging frailly to his arm.

Only the countess remained quiet and graciously aloof from the rest of the glowing party, still sipping her first glass of champagne very slowly, with a sombre light in her deep-set grey eyes. She is thinking of Raif, Marjorie realized.

Once Marjorie caught the countess looking wistfully at Ashley, and knew that with all her heart the countess was wishing that it was this dear godchild who was marrying her son tomorrow, not this unknown Canadian who had stolen into their lives.

I can understand how she feels, Marjorie thought with a rush of sympathy. Her son, the only child she has left, must be infinitely precious to her. She wished she could go and put her arms around the countess's stiff figure and kiss her cheek and reassure her that she would always do everything in her power to make her son happy. But she knew it would be an unheard of liberty, like touching the person of a queen.

Marjorie liked old Kettle. He was just as she had imagined him, a bluff, red-faced, stocky English squire. He looks as if he might whinny at any moment, she thought. Whatever direction the conversation went, he always pulled it back to horses. His wife was a tiny, quiet woman with a humorous face who listened to her husband's long horsy stories with the tolerant affection one accords to a precious child.

Marjorie wondered why Major Middleton had never married. She asked Ashley about it when the two girls were alone for a moment in a corner of the room.

'Don't you know?' Ashley said. 'He's always loved Aunt Honora, but she preferred his best friend. He was best man at their wedding and he's still their best friend.'

How awful, Marjorie thought, and shivered. *Never to marry because you could not have your one true love.* Would this be Ashley's fate – to live the rest of her life with just the memory of Raif? Tears stung her eyes at the thought.

Ashley laughed, seeing the look on her face, and squeezed her arm affectionately. 'It's all right, Marjorie. Don't be sorry for dear Major Middleton. He really is cut out to be a bachelor, you know. The role of uncle-brother suits him to a T.'

It was amost midnight when the countess announced that Marjorie must be growing very tired. Ashley was to spend the night at Enderby so as to be there early in the morning to assist the bride with her wedding preparations. She volunteered now to show Marjorie up to her room. Her parents had asked to be excused from coming to the celebration tonight as they had a long-standing engagement in Aylesbury. Marjorie wondered if that had only been a pretext on their part to avoid having to spend this evening with the interloper they believed was robbing them of their hearts' desire, to see their only child marry Colin Enderby.

However she was feeling too light-hearted and bubbly to let the thought trouble her. When she stood up she felt as if she could float upstairs. Ashley slipped her arm through hers, smiling. 'Hang on,' she whispered. 'You've never had champagne before and I think you're a little tiddly.'

'Oh, is that what it is?' Marjorie said with a giggle. 'I just feel as if I love the whole world. I don't even hate Lord Haw Haw, and I'm not afraid of anything, but my feet do feel a little as if they don't belong to me.' She said good night to everyone and floated out of the room on Ashley's arm.

She stopped in front of a suit of armour on the stairs and saluted. 'Private Hatfield reporting for duty as an Enderby woman, sir,' she said and giggled. When they reached the dimly lit gallery she said, 'Oh Ashley, do you think we could just walk around and take one look at the ancestors before we go to bed? I do think I should say good night to them, since tomorrow I'll be a part of the Enderby tradition, too.'

Ashley smiled and squeezed her arm and led her around the gallery. The faces in the portraits were shadowy in the subdued light. Marjorie imagined that their eyes looked down at her as if she were on trial and they would withhold their approval until they found how she measured up as an Enderby. Only Raif's eyes seemed to smile at her with warm acceptance.

But it was the black-sheep Enderby who arrested her attention. His portrait was under a light and his eyes looked boldly

194

down into hers and she imagined a mocking smile on his lips, just as she had seen him in her dream. For some reason a little shiver ran down her spine.

They quitted the gallery and Ashley led her to her room. Marjorie gasped when they entered the huge bedroom with its ancient heavy furniture and great window facing on to a balcony.

'Oh,' she said, 'this is the room where Queen Elizabeth slept. Colin showed it to me when he took me on a tour of the house.'

'Don't let it overawe you,' Ashley said comfortingly. 'My room is right beside yours, though we're some distance from the rooms of the others. It's been all dusted out for you, even though it is a bit chilly.'

They sat on the great fourposter bed.

'Do you want me to draw the curtains for you?' Ashley asked.

Marjorie shook her head. 'No. Please, I like to be able to look out.'

'You won't see much tonight, I'm afraid. The clouds are so heavy. Happily, they've updated things a little since the days when Queen Elizabeth honoured this room. There's now a quite up-to-date bathroom adjoining. This room is used only for very special guests. It was last used when the King and Queen stayed here. Now would you like me to stay and be your personal maid and help you unpack and get to bed?'

Marjorie laughed. 'No, thank you. I think I can manage to get my toothbrush and clean shirt and khaki underthings out of my haversack, and my flannelette pyjamas.'

Then, she said, blushing, 'I did manage to scrounge up enough clothing coupons to buy myself one set of elegant underthings and a nightgown for tomorrow night, though.'

Ashley squeezed her arm.

Marjorie caught her hand. 'You're so kind Ashley,' she said earnestly. 'I'm so thankful you're here with me tonight. I should feel so strange away off here in this big room, so far from everyone, if I didn't know that you're right next door. I think I'm a bit like that Yankee officer Major Middleton was telling me about on the way down here, who was scared out of his wits by a white thing on a broomstick.'

Ashley laughed. 'I've heard about him. These great old

houses of ours can make almost anyone imagine they see ghosts, if you're not used to them.'

She spoke lightly, but for a moment Marjorie saw a strange far-away look come into her eyes. It was gone so quickly she could not be sure she had really seen it. Ashley smiled tenderly at her.

'Now we'd better pop off to sleep. That champagne should send you right off. Tomorrow will be the happiest day of your life. Why the wistful look?'

'It – it's the countess,' Marjorie said hesitantly. 'She's so – so aloof. I'm afraid she'll never take me in, as you say.'

'She will. She will. I know that in her heart she's already drawn to you. Only she hasn't yet let down her barrier. It's a sort of – sort of, well a waiting for you to prove yourself that we English have. Once you've crossed that barrier, you'll see a different Countess of Rivermere. Good night now. God bless.'

After she had gone Marjorie got into her army-issue striped pyjamas and into bed. She was glad of their warmth, as the sheets felt damp and cold. But the feather comforter was warm and gradually she stopped shivering. *Tomorrow night I'll be sleeping in Colin's arms*, she thought as she drifted off.

She woke with a start, icy cold, the moonlight shining with unearthly brilliance across the bed on to her face. She sat up, her heart pounding with a nameless, unreasoning terror. Then she heard a wild, trumpeting call out in the night.

Chapter 22

As if a power outside her own will drew her, she went, on trembling legs, to the window. The disc of the full moon filled the sky and in its ghostly radiance, standing at the top of the hill against shadowy trees, its huge antlers glowing white in the moonlight, *was a great black stag.* It raised its head towards the full moon as she looked and vanished into the trees.

Reeling, Marjorie clutched the window ledge. 'Athelstane,' she whispered. She drew the heavy velvet curtains across the window to shut out the night, stumbled back to bed in the stifling darkness and cowered down under the covers, listening to the pounding of her own heart. What did it mean? Had it been a dream, or was the creature she had seen really the ghostly stag that appeared at Enderby whenever an Enderby died in battle for his king?

But the earl and Colin were the last of the Enderbys and Colin was safe in England. It was the champagne on an empty stomach, and sleeping in this room. She fumbled for the bedside lamp, switched it on and looked at her watch. It was three o'clock. In the lamplight the room looked very normal. Resolutely, Marjorie went again to the window, pulled the heavy curtains and looked out.

Everything looked beautiful and peaceful in the moonlight and there was nothing out there at the top of the hill but the dim shadow of the great oak trees.

She pulled the curtains again and returned to her bed. This is nonsense, she told herself as she pulled the covers tight around her. If I can sleep through those V-bomb raids, I can certainly sleep here where it's peaceful and safe. After a while she fell back into sleep.

It was a restless sleep, laced with taunting dreams. She was looking up a long green lane between towering rhododendrons. At the other end stood Colin, smiling and holding out his arms to her. She was in her white wedding dress and the long veil of lace trailed out behind her like a cloud as she rushed joyfully towards him, her feet floating soundlessly across the velvet grass.

With a glad cry she was about to throw herself into his outstretched arms, when a great curtain of flame swept between them, carrying Colin back, away from her. Through the red, shimmering, dancing wall, she could see his face, twisted with pain. His lips were moving as if he were trying to tell her something and his eyes beseeched her. She tried to plunge into the flames to reach him, but her feet would not move, and his face and beseeching eyes faded away from her.

Then, in the heart of the flame she saw the mocking face of the disinherited Enderby. His black eyes laughed wickedly at her and his lips curled in a taunting smile.

She woke up shivering and sobbing, 'Colin, Colin.' She sat up, dazed and gasping. At last her mind started to function again. 'Thank God, it was a dream,' she whispered.

She went to the window and pulled the curtains. The bright morning sunlight was dancing on the hillside and the leaves of the oaks fluttered in a light summer breeze. I dreamed the whole thing, she thought. That champagne. But she could not quite shake the turmoil from her mind.

A tap sounded at her door and Lady Ashley entered. Her face was pale. She came to Marjorie and kissed her cheek, watching her face intently. 'How pale you are, dear,' she said. 'Did you have a troublesome night?' Her eyes had a strange look of masked anxiety.

'I had such awful dreams, Ashley.'

'Too much champagne and Queen Elizabeth,' Ashley said lightly. 'Put those nightmares out of your mind. This is your wedding day!'

Her wedding day! Today was her wedding day!

'Oh,' Marjorie said, 'I have to bathe and wash my hair. Do you think there's any hot water?'

'Yes,' Ashley said. 'I'll come back for you. How long will it take you?'

'Not more than ten minutes. We have to move fast in the army, you know.'

Marjorie towelled her hair and her body vigorously and looked at herself in the mirror. Her short blonde hair was gleaming, her big blue eyes were shining and her body was pink and glowing and delicately curved. She wondered if Colin would be pleased with her tonight, and blushed to the top of her head. This was the day she had dreamed of since feelings for the other sex first stirred in her – *but she was not a virgin.*

I'm supposed to feel soiled, she thought. But I don't. Perhaps it's all that hot water and that nice soap from Canada. She giggled.

Actually, she had never felt so alive as she had since she and Colin made love. It was as if something inside of her were singing a wonderful new song. She was, all at once, intensely aware of the soft sounds and the smells and the beauties of nature all around her. I feel as if I am more a person, she thought.

The water seemed to have washed away all her gloom-laced thoughts. Her spirits rose and she was smiling cheerfully when Ashley came to take her down to breakfast.

The countess was already seated at the head of the table behind a silver tea service in the small breakfast room. She greeted Ashley with warmth in her eyes and Marjorie with gracious old-world courtesy. Marjorie was in her khaki skirt and shirt with the neck open, and her blonde hair clung in damp gleaming curls to her dainty head. A flicker of admiration touched the countess's eyes.

She looks a bit white and strained, Marjorie thought, and I suppose I'm the cause. How happy she would be today if it were Ashley her son was marrying.

'The earl has had his breakfast already and gone out to see to the horses,' the countess said. 'Will you have tea or coffee, my dear?' she asked Marjorie.

Remembering the quality of English coffee, Marjorie said that she would have tea. The countess smiled faintly.

'No doubt you share the opinion of the rest of North America about our English coffee.'

Marjorie said politely, 'I find your tea so very delicious, Lady Rivermere.'

For a moment the countess's eyes twinkled approval of her polite, noncommittal answer.

Marjorie wondered as she ate her toast and raspberry jam what she would call her father and mother-in-law after she was married: shall I always address them as Lord and Lady Rivermere? I certainly can't imagine calling them Teddy and Honora, or Mom and Pop. She smiled to herself and her dimples showed.

The countess looked at her keenly and a faint twinkle came into her shrewd eyes.

They were finishing breakfast when a visitor was shown into the breakfast room. He entered with his hat in his hand and Marjorie gave a glad cry as she recognized Blaine. He greeted the countess and Lady Ashley with respectful affection.

'Blaine,' the countess exclaimed. 'I'm delighted that you could come. Is Mrs Blaine with you?'

Blaine shook his head. 'She couldn't get away, my Lady. There was quite a do in London last night. One of those nasty flying things landed near St Paul's. Didn't 'alf mess the street up. Coming down like bees all over the city, they were. My missus is doing double time in the canteen.'

Marjorie paled, wondering about her friends at 43 Company. Seeming to read her thoughts, Blaine turned towards her with a wide smile. 'Nothing landed around Sussex Square,' he said. 'I guess even old 'Erman Göring knows as 'ow you Canadians owns the 'ole street.'

Ashley started a bit at his seemingly rude remark, but Marjorie laughed and came and took his hand. 'After today, they tell me, I shall only own half of it. And they tell me I shall have to cheer for both sides when the Canadians and the English play a game against each other. I'm so glad you've come to my wedding, Blaine. After all, if it hadn't been for you I never would have gone to the George and Horses that night.'

'Nearly got you blown up, I did,' he said, 'but it turned out all right, didn't it now? I knew right off when I saw you and 'is Lordship sitting together in the George and 'Orses that you was meant for each other.'

Ashley said with a smile, 'How clever you are, Blaine. I knew the same thing before I even saw Marjorie.'

200

The countess said briskly, 'Come and sit down and have some breakfast, Blaine. I'm sure you can't have eaten so early.'

'Thank you, my Lady. As a matter of fact I am a mite 'ungry. Left London bright and early this morning. I brought my cab. Thought as 'ow there might be something I could do to 'elp out like.'

'How very kind of you, Blaine,' the countess said. 'I'm afraid there won't be a very big celebration, though. This beastly rationing, you know. If it weren't for that we should have had everyone on the estate for a big party on the lawn with a big cake and all that sort of thing. But as it is, we're just going to be able to have our family and a few very close friends, like yourself, Blaine, and, of course, the guard of honour. I did manage to buy a small wedding cake in Wendover.'

The earl came striding into the room with a look of pleased excitement. 'Honora, come outside. I have something to show you.' He caught sight of Blaine. 'Blaine, old chap, how fine that you are here. Come on, all of you.'

Curiously they followed him outside. They stopped in amazement on the wide steps. The broad expanse of green lawn was swarming with people, putting up tables and spreading them with white tablecloths and setting out chairs.

One of the group detached himself from the others and approached the countess with his hat in his hand.

The countess was smiling. 'Whatever are you up to, Martin?'

'Beggin' your pardon, my Lady, but when we was all invited to the church to see our young Lord Enderby married and 'im such a 'ero and all, and knowing 'ow things are with those ration coupons, we felt as if we couldn't let 'is Lordship get married without 'is tenants 'ere to elp 'im celebrate like they always 'as done when the Enderbys gets married. So by your leave, my lady, we've put our ration coupons together and the women 'as done a bit of baking and we've got a bit of a feed like. My missus 'as made a cake,' he said proudly, indicating with a nod of his head a table close to the steps where a plump red-faced little woman was placing a big cake decorated with white and pink icing and with a little bride and groom on top.

'With your Ladyship's permission we'll just set things up 'ere so 'is Lordship can 'ave the proper kind of wedding party

201

'e should when 'e gets back from the church.' He faltered to a stop, red in the face and turning his hat round in his big hands.

For a moment Marjorie imagined she saw something like a tear in the countess's eye. 'How very kind you are, Martin,' she said. 'Please thank the others for us. We are indeed honoured to have you help us celebrate the marriage of our dear son. Without you all here it would not have been the same. When this beastly war is over we'll have a proper party here at the hall and you shall all be our guests. Colin will be delighted to see you all here today.'

Martin's face wreathed in smiles. He went off to continue supervising the setting of tables and arranging of chairs.

'How really jolly decent they all are,' the earl said, tears gleaming unashamedly in his eyes.

Marjorie said mischievously, 'Especially since you're always bashing them about with your riding crop and evicting them.'

The earl chuckled and they all went inside. They had hardly re-entered the house when Giles, wearing a bewildered expression announced, 'There are some – er – ladies in uniform here who say they have been invited to the wedding, your Ladyship.'

Before he had finished announcing them, Marjorie's roommates marched in, led by Bonny. Marjorie's heart leapt up with joy at the sight of the dear kahki uniforms and the smiling faces of her comrades. Now everything was perfect. She was not alone among strangers.

She rushed forward to greet them. 'These are my roommates,' she said. 'Lady Rivermere, may I present my friends, Bonny and Helen and Jessy and Elsie.' In her excitement she gabbled off all the names together. To her friends she said, 'This is – this is . . . ' She wanted to say my future mother-in-law, but she didn't dare. 'This is the Countess of Rivermere,' she finished.

'Welcome to Enderby,' the countess said, smiling graciously at the four girls.

Bonny rushed forward and stuck out her hand. 'Pleased to meet you, Countess, ma'am,' she said. 'I never met a real English countess before. This is sure some place you got here. Marjorie told us how Queen Elizabeth slept here. Gosh, I've been in so many places, driving around the country, where

202

they told me Queen Elizabeth slept I think that babe really got around.'

The countess accepted her outstretched hand and Bonny shook her hand vigorously. 'I hope you don't mind us coming down before the ceremony like this. We were going to go straight to the church, then I says to the gang here, our Marjorie is there all alone without any of her pals to help her out on her big day. We were sure surprised when she told us she was going to marry a real English lord and be a lady.'

She looked aggressively into the countess's eyes and said belligerently, 'But I said to the gang here, our Marjorie doesn't need anyone to make her into a lady. She's the best darn lady there is already. You know, Countess, she's so darn refined she wouldn't say anything dirty if she had a mouth full of it.'

Marjorie felt her breath come up into her throat, but instead of the icy hauteur she expected, the countess's eyes lit up with a warm twinkle.

'That is as high a recommendation as anyone could wish for,' she said. 'You are all most welcome to stay and help Marjorie to dress. This is Lady Ashley Medhurst, her bridesmaid. Will you show them where to go, Ashley dear?'

'Gee, Marj, you're so damn beautiful it's scary.' Bonny looked in open-mouthed awe at Marjorie, standing in their midst in her bridal dress and veil. They were in the room where she had spent such a restless night.

Jessy felt a strange little shiver run down her spine at Bonny's words. She's almost *too* beautiful a bride, she thought. And it's not that soft, delicately coloured skin, or those exquisitely moulded features, or that shimmering blonde hair, or even those great blue eyes of hers. It's that look, as if she had a light inside of her.

With Ashley assisting, they had gone through the ritual of making their buddy ready for her wedding, helping her into her dress and putting the veil in place, talking and laughing excitedly.

'You got to have something old and something new, something borrowed and something blue,' Bonny said.

Jessy had brought a blue garter she had worn in one of her acts at the Glen Club. 'I wowed them with that, in my tight red

203

dress with the slit right up to my thigh,' she said, smiling wickedly, as Marjorie slipped it on to her leg. Elsie took the gold wrist watch off her own wrist and loaned it to her, and Helen insisted on giving her the pair of new silk stockings she had just received in a parcel from Canada.

'I'll be going back to Canada soon,' she said. 'Anyway, Carl likes me just as well in my khaki issue.'

'I think he likes you in nothing,' Jessy said, laughing.

Ashley had supplied Marjorie with a pair of white satin pumps. 'Luckily our feet are almost the same size,' she said. 'They're a tiny bit big for you, but not enough to notice.'

'Oh, you're all so kind,' Marjorie said. 'Do I really look all right?'

'Just look at yourself in the mirror here,' Ashley answered her.

Marjorie caught her breath as she stared at herself in the full-length mirror. 'Is that really me?' she said in wonder. Her eyes caught Ashley's, smiling at her in the glass. She turned quickly to the other girl. 'Oh, but you look lovely, Ashley.'

Ashley's dress was a floating blue chiffon, with a wide-brimmed matching hat and a single string of pearls.

'She sure does,' Bonny said. 'But if that old Queen Elizabeth had looked like you do, Marj, she wouldn't have spent all her time running around, sleeping in those old castles.'

Just then the countess came into the room. She looked completely regal in a dress of heavy, pale green silk with an elegant off-the-face matching hat sitting like a crown on her white, proud head. Around her neck she wore a heavy gold chain and locket. Marjorie knew that in it was Raif's picture. Looking at her, with the dignity and pride of race in every line, Marjorie thought in awe: I'm just pretend. She's the real thing. Even Colin's great-great-grandmother's dress can't make me into an aristocrat. She and Ashley are different from the rest of us. If they were wearing sacks they'd still belong. I'm just a little Canadian farm girl.

Ashley spoke quickly, smiling at the countess. 'Isn't she lovely, Aunt Honora?'

The countess's eyes widened in admiration as she looked at Marjorie's ethereal loveliness. Then she said, 'You are indeed lovely, my dear. Now, I think we should go downstairs. Major

204

Middleton and my husband are waiting in the morning room. We did not have time for a proper rehearsal in the church, of course. But we'll go through things a bit so you can have an idea of how it will go when you arrive at the church and you won't be so nervous.'

She glanced at her watch. 'It's almost ten o'clock. Colin should be arriving at any moment.'

Ashley said, 'Yes, we have to get you downstairs and safely hidden away before he arrives. We can't have him seeing his bride on his wedding day, until she comes up the aisle to him in church.'

With her heart pounding, treading carefully, Marjorie followed the countess down the great stairway, with Ashley beside her and her friends bringing up the rear, holding up her trailing veil.

Colin will be here soon. The words sang inside of her. In just over an hour, I'll be his wife. *I'll really be his wife.* She shivered a little as she passed the grim suit of armour, standing on the stairs like a brooding reminder of bloodletting and ancient wars and Enderbys dead in battle for their king.

Major Middleton and the earl were waiting for them in the morning room, which had been rearranged so that the furniture made an aisle down its length. They stood up as the countess led the little group into the room, and their eyes sparkled with admiration as they fastened on Marjorie.

'By Jove,' Major Middleton said, coming forward. 'I swear, Honora, she's the most beautiful Enderby bride that ever graced these halls – except for one,' he added, looking meaningfully at her.

'My nose was always too long,' the countess answered with a slight smile.

The earl was beaming at Marjorie with open pride. 'Lucky young bounder, that son of mine.'

Marjorie met the look of joy in the earl's face and smiled at him. Her dimples flashed as their eyes met in mutual affection.

'We must start,' the countess said briskly. 'We will imagine this is the aisle of the church. Colin and his best man will be standing there at the other end with the minister . . . '

'We can take that part,' Bonny broke in enthusiastically. 'I'll be the best man and Jess can be Colin, and Helen can be the

205

padre – she's so darn religious she's always counting her beads and praying for all of us.'

Before anyone could say another word, she raced to the other end of the room and stood smiling at them down the length of their improvised aisle.

The countess nodded at Jessy and Helen, with an amused smile touching her lips, and they took up their positions with Bonny.

Elsie stood pouting.

'Very good,' the countess said. 'Now, Marjorie, you take Major Middleton's arm. Ashley will precede you up the aisle. When the strains of the wedding march start, Ashley will move very slowly a few paces ahead of you. You will each be carrying your bouquets – roses and flowers from our garden. Giles is making them up now.' She turned to Elsie. 'Perhaps you could hum a little of the wedding march and we will start?'

'Jeepers,' Bonny said softly to Jessy, 'when he says with all my worldly goods I thee endow, she's sure going to get a load.'

Marjorie took Major Middleton's arm with trembling fingers and he smiled reassuringly down into her face. The countess nodded at Elsie and she started to hum 'Here Comes the Bride'.

They were interrupted by Giles. 'You wanted me to inform you, my Lady, when Lord Enderby arrived. His Lordship is at the front steps now. I just saw the air force car drive up.'

'Good,' the countess said. 'Go to the door, Giles, and see to it that they stay in the hall and do not come in here. I will come out directly. Come along, Teddy. Just hold your positions. We'll be back in a moment, as soon as I greet my son and his friends and send them off to his room, out of the way.'

She and the earl left, closing the door quickly behind them.

Marjorie's face suffused with excitement. 'Oh,' she said, 'he's here! Do you think I could just open the door a tiny crack and peek through just to see him? He doesn't have to see me.'

'I think it would be a jolly good idea,' the major said.

Holding Marjorie by the hand, he slipped across to the door and opened it a tiny crack and she peeked out into the hall.

Giles was preceding two young British Air Force officers across the great hall to where the earl and countess stood just outside the door in front of Marjorie. Marjorie thought: Colin must still be out in the car.

Suddenly a stillness seemed to fall upon the hall of the Enderbys. The faces of the two airmen were pale and drawn in the morning light. They stopped in front of the earl and countess with their hats in their hands. Marjorie felt a cold hand clamping itself on her heart.

A remembered line of poetry came searing into her mind: '*They knew so sad a messenger some ghastly news must bring . . .*'

Chapter 23

'Sir, we are very sorry to bring you bad news.' Marjorie clutched at Major Middleton's arm as the words of one of the young airmen sifted faintly to her ears. She saw the earl shiver and then draw himself up, and the countess grow rigid by his side.

The room was growing hazy around her as through a wild humming in her ears she caught the words '. . . Your son . . . shot down in flames . . . '

For a moment everything went dark around her. She would have fallen except for the major's arm around her. Clinging to him, she fought her way back to consciousness. Gradually the mist cleared. She saw as in a dream the anxious faces of her friends around her. She brushed them all away from her, pulled herself free from the major's arms and walked out into the hall to where the countess and earl stood with the two airmen.

'Tell me,' she said, 'tell me what has happened.' She heard the words drop like stones from her cold lips.

The countess's hand was at her bosom, her slender fingers wrapped around the gold locket so tightly that her knuckles stood out white. Her face was the colour of marble. It was as if a ruthless hand had passed over the earl's face, leaving it lined and old and white. They looked at her without speaking.

She turned back to the airmen. 'Tell me,' she said again, 'tell me what happened.'

The earl found his voice. He put his shaking hand on her arm. 'My dear,' he said, 'my dear, let us take you back into the room there and sit down and we will tell what you must hear.'

She shook off his hand. Her eyes met the troubled gaze of the young airman. 'Tell me.'

'It happened early this morning,' he said. 'We were to take off on a very special secret mission. Our squadron leader doubled up at the controls and had to be carried away, appendictis, I think. Colin volunteered to lead the mission. We told him one of us would take over but he was the senior there and he had been over with us so many times, he said he couldn't let us down. He said he had plenty of time to get over there and back in time for his wedding.' He paused for a moment, a look of pain on his face. Then he went on softly.

'Things got a bit sticky. We'd accomplished our mission and were turning for home. There was rather heavy flak. I was flying just behind Colin on his right. He was caught in the searchlights.' He stopped and looked away for a moment with his hand knotted into a ball, then he said, speaking almost mechanically, 'I saw his plane shudder and explode in flames and spiral down.'

'He volunteered,' Marjorie said slowly.

'Of course. What else could he do?' the countess said flatly.

Marjorie stared at her. She wanted to shout, 'This is your son! And he is dead. And you say, of course, what else could he do!' Then her eyes met those of the countess and she saw a depth of sorrow such as she had never witnessed in any human eye before.

The earl pulled himself up. His face lost its rigid stunned look. 'Thank you so much for coming to tell us, Ian,' he said. 'Awfully hard on you. Would you care for a glass of port, or something?'

The two airmen shook their heads. Ian said, 'Thank you, sir, but no. We have to report back to the squadron at once. Awfully sorry, sir.'

The earl saw them to the door and then returned to his wife's side. Major Middleton and Ashley and the four army girls were gathered around Marjorie and the countess. The earl told them quietly what had happened. A stunned silence fell.

Jessy Cole moved in beside Marjorie and put her hand on her arm.

The countess was very erect, her face pale and calm. She said to her husband, 'Teddy, those people of ours out there have come to celebrate with us and brought their provisions and used up their ration coupons. We must go out and tell them.

And they must not be sent home hungry. There is hardly one of them who has not suffered a loss in this war, as we have. Tell them there will not be a wedding. Our son has given his life for his country, but ask them please to stay and dine with us here at the tables they have so generously prepared. We are proud that our son did not shirk his duty.'

She turned to Marjorie. 'You, my dear, had better stay inside with your friends and Ashley. They will take care of you until we are free. Perhaps you would like to have a little brandy and lie down.'

Marjorie met the countess's eyes. Her head was high and two bright red spots were burning in her white cheeks. 'You forget, Lady Rivermere, that I am a soldier. I will go out there with you. I am the bride they came to see your son marry.'

For a long moment the countess's eyes held hers. Then Marjorie saw a different look come into them – a warmth and acceptance, the look she had seen in her eyes when she looked at Ashley and the earl and Major Middleton, as if an invisible barrier had been lifted and she was one of them. She put her hand on to Marjorie's arm. 'Come then,' she said.

Ashley fell in on her other side and she walked outside with the countess's hand still on her arm, and the earl beside his wife. The four army girls followed.

'Jesus Christ,' Bonny said. 'You mean her airman is dead?'

'Holy Mary, mother of God,' Helen was saying over and over, with her fingers on her rosary.

'Yes,' Jessy said.

The tears coursed down Bonny's cheeks. 'Then, why the hell aren't any of these Limeys crying?' she said hotly. 'Haven't they got any damn feelings at all? How come they're walking out there like nothing had happened and taking our Marjorie with them?'

'It's called noblesse oblige,' Jessy said softly. 'They're dying inside, but they keep a stiff upper lip.'

'Stiff upper lip, my ass!' Bonny said. 'They've got shit for blood. Why the hell did he have to volunteer anyway, on his wedding day?'

'That's part of the noblesse oblige,' Jessy said.

Elsie started to snivel disconsolately. Jessy turned on her and Bonny. 'Cut it, kids. We have to back up Marj. Remember, our boys are over there right now with those Limeys, and we're Canadian Army girls. I always figured our little Marjorie had more spunk than any of us when the chips were down.'

Word of what had happened had already spread among the tenants gathered by the tables on the lawn. Martin came up to them with tears in his eyes. 'I'm right sorry, my Lady,' he said. 'What can we say? You know how we all loved Lord Enderby.'

The countess took his hand. 'Thank you, Martin,' she said quietly. 'You came here to celebrate with us. Now fortune has decreed that this may not be. We know it would be our dear son's wish, if he could tell us, that you should stay now and partake with us this feast that you have so kindly prepared. Will you please ask them all to stay?'

Marjorie felt as if all reality had slipped away. Every emotion she had ever felt was packed in ice. She was looking at the world through a curtain of glass. Her limbs moved mechanically as she walked beside the countess. Her veil lifted in the light breeze. She saw everything very clearly – the sunshine on the grass and the trees and flowers, and the solemn faces of the men and women who had gathered to celebrate her wedding – And they were all in another world. She was utterly alone.

They walked among these devoted tenants of the Enderbys and the countess and earl spoke to all of them in turn. Then Marjorie and the other army girls sat at a long table with the earl and countess, Major Middleton, Ashley, Kettle and his wife, and the family servants and Blaine, and they ate.

Marjorie sat beside the earl, with Ashley on her right. Ashley's face was very pale. Across the table Marjorie saw Major Middleton's eyes on her with such a look of sympathy as she had never seen in a man's face before. For once his cheery optimistic look had vanished.

Subdued conversation broke out at the tables.

Marjorie's eyes wandered up to the hill where last night she had seen the great black stag. She turned her head and met Ashley's eyes, full of deep pain and understanding. 'You saw him, too, didn't you?' Ashley said softly. 'Over there against the hill.'

Marjorie nodded dumbly. It was real, then. Ashley had seen it, too. No dream, but the ghostly stag that prowled the estate when an Enderby died in battle for his sovereign.

'I'll ride over one day this week, Henry, and see that horse you're so anxious to show me,' the earl said to Kettle. 'Though I must say I fancy the Queen's horse to win.'

'I'm sure I have the winner this time,' Kettle said.

The countess spoke to Mrs Kettle. 'Those roses are really lovely at this time of the year, are they not? July is such a marvellous month in England.'

'Oh, shit!' Bonny said under her breath.

The army girls sat, hardly touching their food. Suddenly Jessy stood up from her place, walked to the end of the table and turned to face the assembled guests. All eyes riveted on the tall, dark girl with the magnificent brown eyes and seductive curves which even the khaki army uniform could not hide.

She stood compellingly still, with her eyes on them until complete silence fell, then her head went back and her husky, moving contralto voice reached out to them: 'There'll always be an England ... ' They sat as if stunned while her rich, emotionally loaded voice rolled over them; then they stood and with one accord joined her in the song they all knew so well. Tears rolled down their cheeks.

There was silence for a moment when she had finished. Then quickly Jessy broke into the CWAC marching song: 'Here come the khaki skirts ... '

They listened spellbound as Jessy's full voice carried the stirring notes on the summer air: 'Good girls. We've cut off our curls, and the Nazis, the blighters, will pay Churchill, you say you need the tools ... '

Marjorie and the other CWACs went to stand beside Jessy and joined in. When the song ended a cheer went up from the guests. They looked at the little group of Canadian army girls through a mist of tears.

Blaine came and took Marjorie's hands in his. 'You Canadian girls can 'ave the 'ole street to drive on,' he said huskily. 'You bloody well deserve it.'

Marjorie said, 'Blaine, if you're going back today, could we ride with you back to London?'

'I should just 'ope you can. And it's right proud I am to take you, soldier girl.'

Marjorie looked at the watch Elsie had, giggling merrily, slipped on to her wrist so short a time ago. It was eleven

212

o'clock. The hour when she should have been standing at the altar with Colin. Jessy linked her arm through hers. Her bright smile flashed.

'I think we'd better get you out of that dress and back into uniform, and go back to London.'

'As soon as they've all gone,' Marjorie said. 'I have to go back to the countess and earl and Ashley. I have to see this out with them.'

'What the hell for?' Bonny said. 'You better come back to London with us.'

'I will, Bonny,' Marjorie said. 'I will. But for just a little longer I belong here with Colin's people.'

No one lingered over their meal. Marjorie stood beside the earl and the countess as their tenants filed past in silent sympathy. The earl and countess shook their hands and thanked them. The understanding was strong and unspoken. They, too, had sons, and husbands, and loved ones for ever gone, consumed in the fire of this war.

At last only the empty lawn remained, with the gentle breeze rippling through the grass, playfully lifting Marjorie's white veil in its teasing caress.

Silently they all returned indoors and Ashley and the army girls went with Marjorie, back to the room where she had dressed to go to her wedding. They helped her out of her wedding dress. She put on her khaki skirt and shirt and knotted the brown tie around her throat, and put on her heavy brown oxfords, fastening the laces tightly. Then she slipped into her tunic and buttoned it and donned her peaked hat with the goddess Athene badge on the crown, picked up her shoulder bag and slung it over her shoulder.

She took one look around her at the room, put her hand down and caressed the white wedding dress lying across the bed. Ashley, too, had silently changed into an old tweed suit and heavy shoes. A kind of dumb misery was in her wide hazel eyes. She put her arms around Marjorie and kissed her. They clung together, then Marjorie pulled away and went downstairs with the other army girls.

'I'll see you outside,' she said. 'Leave me for a few minutes.'

Quietly the four CWACs said goodbye to the Earl and Countess of Rivermere, who stood together in the hall to see them off. The earl and countess shook hands with each of them and the countess thanked them graciously for coming. To Jessy she said, 'And thank you, my dear.'

Their eyes met with understanding. Then the girls filed out to where Blaine waited in the car at the front steps.

Marjorie was left alone with the two people who by now should have been her parents-in-law. Carefully she pulled Colin's ring from her finger. A shaft of sunlight set the diamonds blazing and the ruby was a great drop of blood. She held it out to the countess.

'This belongs to the Enderby family,' she said.

The countess took it in her hand and looked at it, then she held it out to Marjorie again. 'No, please keep it Marjorie,' she said. 'There are no more Enderbys left to pass it on to now. You gave my son the greatest happiness he ever knew, just before he was to die. Please keep the ring he gave you. It's what he would wish. I'm sorry you are not my daughter-in-law. My son chose well.'

Silently Marjorie slipped the ring back on her finger.

The earl took her in his arms and kissed her. Tears ran silently down his cheeks. 'My dear,' he said, 'my very dear girl. If ever you need anything. If there is any way we can help you, ever, please come to us.'

Chapter 24

I know now why soldiers don't cry, Marjorie thought. Blaine had brought the silent little group back to 43 Company barracks the night before. The others had all gone to their duties this morning, but Marjorie was still on her four-day wedding pass. She lay on her bed staring at the ceiling. She had feigned sleep when her friends had gone to breakfast and they had not disturbed her. Silence engulfed the block of flats that housed 43 Company.

Soldiers don't cry because they've seen the comrades they love fall around them, and when someone you love dies something in you dies, too. And tears are for the living.

At Enderby the birds would be singing. This was the morning she should have been waking up in Colin's arms. She must get up and dress and do something, but what – and why?

They might come this morning to inspect the barrack rooms. She did not wish to be here if the orderly officer came in. She did not want to see anyone.

She dressed and went downstairs and walked aimlessly out on to the pavement. Automatically her feet led her in the direction of Hyde Park. She went through the wide gates into the park and followed the path to Peter Pan's statue.

The sky was very blue and the grass very green. She saw it all, etched there clearly, but none of it was real. It should all have died with Colin. The whole world should have stopped.

Peter Pan's statue was aloof and removed. She sat on a bench in the warm sunshine. Her body was cold. She felt nothing at all. Perhaps I'll just sit here like this forever, she thought. Perhaps, like Lot's wife when she looked back, I'll turn to salt.

Was this her punishment for the love she had shared with

215

Colin before it was sanctified by the Church? Had Colin died because of her? Colin had told her she was his wife, but was she in fact a fornicator – a woman fit only to be stoned? These thoughts came to her, but they were powerless to torture her as they would have a short time ago.

She had no feeling of reverent fear. With a cold awfulness, she realized why – *She had stopped believing in God.* She was all alone out here in the park, completely, utterly, terribly alone.

Hours passed and still she sat. She was not conscious of the passing hours. Time, too, had ceased to be. She heard the crunch on the path and a voice said, 'Hatfield, is that you?'

She looked up into the face of Captain Burns. She noticed, with detachment, that the officer's face was pale and miserable and her eyes were tormented. Marjorie made no effort to stand and salute, only continued to look up expressionlessly.

Captain Burns sat down beside Marjorie and put her hand on her sleeve. 'I'm sorry, Hatfield,' she said in a choked voice. 'I'm sorry about your fiancé.'

'Thank you, ma'am,' Marjorie said quietly, the words dropping from her lips as if on their own.

The other woman looked away. When she turned back to Marjorie tears were trickling down her face. 'I have lost my love, too,' she said huskily. 'At least yours was an honourable love. For you there will be sympathy. I'm just old Hot Burns, whose big heart-throb has gone back to his wife in Canada. Was my love any less real because it was illicit?' she added bitterly. 'Would anyone choose to love someone they knew they could never have, if the choice were their own? Or does your love go where it's sent?'

Marjorie continued to look at the officer's distraught face for a long moment, then she said tonelessly, 'Does it matter?' and looked away.

Suddenly the other woman became the officer commanding. 'How long have you been sitting here, Hatfield?' she said briskly.

Marjorie continued to stare at her, at them, 'I don't know,' she said in a dead voice.

'When you speak to me you will address me as ma'am,' Captain Burns said. 'I repeat the question. How long have you been sitting here, Hatfield?'

Marjorie looked at her emotionlessly. At last she said mechanically, 'I don't know, ma'am.'

Captain Burns got up. 'You are to return to barracks with me at once,' she said firmly.

Marjorie continued to look at her without expression. 'I'm on a four-day pass, ma'am.'

'Are you questioning my orders, Hatfield?' Captain Burns said sternly. 'Get up at once and come back to barracks with me.'

Automatically Marjorie obeyed and the two women walked silently back to 43 Company, where Captain Burns led the way up to her office and told Marjorie to sit down. She took her own place behind her desk.

'Would you like a few days' sick leave on top of your four-day pass?' she asked abruptly. 'I'm sure the MO will okay it if I explain the circumstances to him.'

'No thank you, ma'am,' Marjorie answered. 'I'm not sick.'

Captain Burns gave her a penetrating look, toyed for a moment with the paperweight on her desk, then said, 'I want you to go back to your quarters now, Hatfield. You are not to leave them until your friends return. We will talk about this later. You may go.' She watched Marjorie leave, with a distressed face. Then, when she was alone, she buried her face on the desk and wept.

Marjorie went slowly up the stairs to her room. She took off her hat, tie, tunic and shoes and lay on her bed, staring up at the ceiling. After a while, her eyes closed and she dropped into sleep. She dreamed that her mother came into the room and told her that she could not go to the Christmas concert because she was too sick.

Jessy came home from duty and found her moaning pitifully in her sleep. She looked at her friend's white tired face, moving restlessly on the pillow, put her hand down tenderly on her forehead, and looked up towards heaven. 'God,' she prayed softly, 'I think we've got a war on our hands.'

She sat down on the bed beside Marjorie and shook her gently into wakefulness.

Slowly Marjorie came back to consciousness and sat up, blinking dazedly into Jessy's warm, smiling eyes.

'Have you had anything to eat today, Marjorie?'

217

Marjorie shook her head and lay back again on the pillow. 'I'm not hungry.'

'It hasn't really stopped, you know,' Jessy said. 'It never stops and we can't get off.' She reached in to her tunic pocket and pulled out a small silver flask. 'Sit up, Marj,' she said. 'And take a little gulp of this.'

Marjorie stared at the flask. Jessy laughed. 'Oh, it won't hurt you. One of the Calgary Highlanders liberated a bottle of extra old cognac from a Heimey major, just before an 88 came along and put him on the road to Twenty-three General. He filled this confiscated flask and gave it to me when I picked him up today.'

Obediently Marjorie took the gulp. She scarcely felt the burning warmth as it trickled down her throat. She took another swallow and then another and another, until Jessy was rewarded by seeing a faint pink glow come into her pallid cheeks.

Gently she took her flask away. Marjorie's hand reached out and caught hers. 'Jessy,' she whispered. 'Jessy, something terrible has happened. I don't believe in God any more.'

Jessy squeezed her cold fingers, looking down at her with a faint, kind smile in her eyes. 'Well,' she said at last, 'I guess if He was smart enough to make this whole wide universe, including Marjorie Hatfield, He's smart enough to know that this could happen, too. That doesn't mean that He has stopped believing in you. Let's just examine this for a minute. You believed in Him yesterday when you thought Colin was safely back, and yet you knew that the doodle bug that passed over our heads when we were watching Bonny's game blew the guts out of a whole bunch of people, some of them little kids. But as long as you thought *your* love was safe, you could believe in God. Now, all of a sudden, because it hits you, He's gone like fairy gold. But He isn't *really* gone, you know. What you have, Marj, is what some of those boys over there get — battle fatigue.'

Marjorie lay back on the pillow. Jessy's words made sense, but they couldn't reach her.

'If you really didn't believe in God, you wouldn't be so worried about not believing,' Jessy said. 'But, you must have something to eat.'

Marjorie shook her head. 'No, Jess, I couldn't. I'm not hungry.'

'Well, I am. I've had one heck of a day today, and I have to go on duty again at midnight. They're really short of ambulance drivers and our wounded boys are pouring in from the front. Sergeant Cook said we have to get hold of some more ambulance drivers quick.'

Marjorie sat up. A faint light came into her eyes. 'Oh, I'll ask if I can go. I don't want to go back to driving Major Middleton. Somehow, I can't face all that. I want to be somewhere where I feel I'm doing something real.'

'Okay, I'll tell Sergeant Cook at the garage. I'm sure he'll take you on. But you know how you get lost. You'll have to come with me first and learn the ropes. Why don't you come with me tonight?'

Marjorie nodded wordlessly.

'But you must eat first. Get dressed and come to the mess hall with me.'

Fog swirled around the station wagon like funeral wreaths as Jessy piloted it through the black gloom of London, on her way to pick up her ambulance. Marjorie sat beside her.

'It will be some kind of a trip down to the coast tonight,' Jessy said, with a note of soft exultation in her voice. 'It's a real pea-souper.'

Silence shrouded the city. Only the vehicles which had to be there were on the London streets tonight. Expertly, as if by a sixth sense, Jessy slipped by the other pinpricks of light that loomed in front of her station wagon from time to time. The thick, choking smell of the fog was in their nostrils. To Marjorie, it seemed a miracle how Jessy kept the station wagon on the black street. Jessy sang softly with a laugh in her voice: 'Roll me over in the clover. Roll me over, lay me down and do it again.'

The silence was shattered by the air raid siren and in a few minutes they heard the approach of a V-bomb. It droned over their heads without hesitating and they saw in the sky the long trail of fire and the silver, bullet-shaped outline against the glow.

Jessy said softly, 'Those bastards will be really pelting the city tonight with their little toy dragons.'

219

Marjorie spoke for the first time since they had left the garage. 'Oh,' she said, concern in her voice, 'I hope they'll all be safe at 43 Company.'

In the darkness, Jessy smiled.

If she lived to be ninety-five, Marjorie knew she would still smell the stench in her nostrils. They had gone, not to the coast, but to the military airport at Farnborough to pick up wounded soldiers flown in directly from the battlefield.

'I'm glad there are two of you,' an attendant said. 'We have no one left to go with the wounded in the ambulance.'

Reeling from the shock of what she was seeing, Marjorie helped to load the wounded soldiers into the amublances.

These were the boys who had waved at her with laughter and mischief brimming in their eyes, on their way to the coast; filthy and reeking with the stench of battle and with bloody bandages hiding gaping holes in their bodies and their heads.

Marjorie climbed into the back to tend the wounded. A boy, so bandaged only his blue eyes looked out at her, clutched her hand. In a feeble whisper he said, 'Hey, I got to have died and gone to heaven and you're a pretty blonde angel.'

Jessy, on her way to the driver's seat, stopped and put her face down near his. 'What about me?' she said, flashing her brilliant smile.

Through the pain in his eyes a faint, naughty twinkle gleamed. 'Honey, you ain't no angel,' he whispered.

Jessy laughed.

The hospital was not far away, but it seemed a million miles. The putty features of one of the men told Marjorie that he was dead. In a few minutes, she heard the rattling death sigh of the man above him. The boy with the blue eyes who had called her an angel was unconscious. The awful stench of blood and dirt and death choked in her throat.

A soldier, so bandaged she could not see his face, called in a sobbing voice for the bedpan. She held it for him, then she went into a corner of the ambulance and quietly vomited. She was ashamed of her weakness, but she could not stop herself.

Feeling came back to her in an agonizing rush. She was praying to herself, Please, oh, please, help them. And please, stop wars. A sudden hate surged up in her. She clenched her small fist and shook it skyward.

'And, please,' she said out loud, 'get those Nazi devils!'

In her cruel, twisting emotions, came a sort of savage pride, that Colin – her man – had given his life to hold back this tide of monstrosity.

With the thought of Colin agony raked her and she doubled up, seeing him going to an agonizing death as his plane spiralled to earth in licking flames. Then she thought, I know now why I hated that story about a Viking's funeral.

The night was peaceful and calm as they drove back to London. The moon had come out and was silvering the hedges and bushes beside the winding country road. Jessy was humming a little tune under her breath. Marjorie sat beside her, drooping like a withered flower on its stalk.

'How can you, Jessy,' she whispered, 'how can you sing when you've just come from seeing what we've seen tonight?'

Jessy deftly wheeled the station wagon round a bend. With the moonlight playing on her rich warm skin and voluptuous features, Marjorie thought she looked like some Greek goddess of old. She turned her head slightly and looked down at Marjorie huddled beside her.

'Because singing and dancing are as old as life, or death,' she said. 'Wasn't it Miriam who danced in front of the Ark of the Covenant when the Israelites were having a rough time of it? Things have never been so hot in this world, you know, since Adam wolfed down that apple. But people have always danced and sung and made love and it's something to think that no matter what happens in this old world they can't knock that out of people. If I cried all the way back to London those boys back there would still be lying in that hospital beat up and dying; so I might as well sing. Besides, when you're a singer, no matter what happens you've just got to sing, and when you're a dancer you've got to dance.' Her quick smile flashed. 'And if you're a lover, you've got to love.'

For the first time since they brought her the news about Colin, Marjorie laughed – a small shaky laugh. 'But what about tears? Aren't they made for something, too?'

'Of course they are. They're darn good for those who need them, but you and I aren't the crying kind, Marj, and tears are not for us.'

221

'Soldiers don't cry,' Marjorie said softly.

Since Major Middleton had specifically asked for her to be his personal driver, Marjorie could only be released from the assignment by him. In any case, she felt after all he had done for her she owed it to him to go and see him. She went to his office the next day.

He dismissed the corporal who showed her in. Then he put his arms around her and kissed her on the cheek and sat her on the chair beside his desk. He lit up his pipe and sat on the edge of his desk, looking down at her with the familiar, good-humoured smile. But there was a sadness lurking in his kindly eyes.

Marjorie told him of the shortage of ambulance drivers and of her trip to fetch the wounded with Jessy and repeated that she wanted to leave him and go to drive an ambulance. Major Middleton nodded, puffing at his pipe.

'I feel I have to do this, sir,' Marjorie said. 'I feel that I – I can't just go on driving around London and to all those lovely places in the country now. I – I want to be where I can feel I'm really doing something for those boys. I feel I'm doing it for Colin. But I don't want to leave London, either. I feel – well, as if I'm just a little in the front line, too, when I'm here.'

'My dear girl,' Major Middleton said emotionally. 'My very dear girl. What an Enderby you would have made. What a mother of sons. You know, you're the first fair lady the Enderbys have ever picked? How jolly it would have been to see some fair hair and blue eyes in those dark Enderbys. But there'll be no more Enderbys now.' He sighed and turned away, wiping a tear from his eye.

Marjorie's heart leaped strangely at his words. He was speaking her dreams, but hearing them spoken was almost more than she could bear. Her face drained of colour and she started to tremble.

Major Middleton was immediately contrite. He put his arms around her shaking shoulders. 'I say, I am sorry, Marjorie. Forgive me. Thoughtless old fool. Never should mention might-have-beens. Always upset you, those might-have-beens.'

222

He looked away and Marjorie wondered if he was thinking of the Countess of Rivermere and his own might-have-been.

He patted her shoulder and went on briskly, 'I'll speak to Brigadier Raham about you. I'm sure he'll see to it that you can stay in London and go down to Farnborough to drive the ambulance.'

That night Marjorie was assigned to her own ambulance. She and Jessy continued driving in the station wagon from London to pick up their ambulances at Farnborough. Wounded were pouring in quicker than they could be handled. Marjorie entered an endless world of wounded and dying men. She worked long hours of overtime, driving countless miles through the blackness with only a thin pencil of light to show her the way, and she never once got lost. She went to Taplow and Horsham and Horley, to 23 General near London, and to Basingstoke.

She was both driver and attendant. The convoy stopped each half hour or so, and she got out and went in with the wounded to give them the bedpan and comfort them as best she could. Endless, agonizing times when her wounded were unloaded at the hospital she saw the perspiring doctors pull the sheet up over many of their faces and go on to tend the others.

The smell of dirt, death and blood never left her nostrils or her battledress. She slept and ate and drove the ambulance without a day off, and that was all. Sometimes she scarcely ate. Her face became white and drawn and her eyes enormous, with dark shadows under them.

Always inside of her she carried the picture of Colin's face. There were times when she almost believed he was riding with her in the blackness of the English night. She could hear his voice, his happy English drawl: 'You're a funny little soldier girl.'

Often she dreamed of trying to go to him through a wall of flames and always his eyes beseeched her, trying to tell her something.

On her third week of driving the ambulance she was shaken by a strange occurrence. She had stopped on the road to give the men the bedpan and comfort them as best she could. A dark-skinned young halfbreed Indian from the Winnipeg

Rifles was among the wounded. He looked up at her with a faint flash in his naughty black eyes. 'Hey, little blonde angel,' he whispered. 'I want to give you a present. You are a little blonde angel, you know.' He tugged weakly until he pulled the ring off his finger, and held it out to Marjorie. 'It's supposed to be worth a pile,' he said with a lopsided attempt at a grin.

Marjorie shook her head. 'You'd better keep it, but thank you just the same.'

'Naw,' he said. 'It don't mean nutting to me. A buddy of mine he give it to me to keep for him when he going out on dirty patrol. He say there no one left but him in family and he want me to keep it if he not come back. He not come back. But I don't want the damn ting. I'll lose her in poker game, or someting. I don't think it worth much. Got some crazy design on it. Come on, you take it. You like blonde angel. If you not want it you hock it on black market in London. Crazy Limeys buy anything. You buy yourself something with dough you get.'

To humour him, Marjorie took the ring and put it in her battledress pocket. Not until she was back in her room in 43 Company did she look at it. It was a heavy gold ring. It looks like a signet ring of some kind, she thought. It does have some kind of a design on it, just like that poor soldier said. She looked at it again. *That design!* It was familiar. Where had she seen it before? She drew in her breath sharply. Above the mantelpiece in the great hall at Enderby – *The Enderby coat of arms!* She sat stunned.

Jessy came in and found her turning the ring over and over in her hand.

'You look as if you'd seen a ghost. What *is* the matter, Marj?'

Marjorie held out the ring and told her how the wounded soldier had given it to her.

'They often want to give you something. They're so grateful when you bring them in. What's to get spooked out about that?'

'It's the Enderby coat of arms,' Marjorie whispered.

Jessy picked up the ring and examined it. She smiled and shook her head. 'You can buy almost any coat of arms in some of those little gyp-joint stores they've got around London.

They just copy them and stick them on a ring or something and the boys who buy them pass themselves off as being related to some big Limey house over here.'

Chapter 25

Helen Huntley sat on her bed with tears running down her cheeks, looking at her roommates. 'Now that I really am going home to Canada tomorrow morning, I can't bear to leave all of you. Just think, this is the last night we'll all be together like this – That is, we'll all be together when Bonny comes in.'

'She should be here any minute. She said she was just going to have a couple at Molly's and be right back,' Jessy said.

Elsie was fishing a parcel out of her barrack box and making little purring sounds. 'When she comes in, I'll open up my parcel from home. You look as if you need something good to eat, Marjorie. Your face is so thin and pale and you have circles under your eyes.'

Helen looked anxiously at Marjorie. 'You do look a bit peaked, Marji. Maybe driving those big ambulances is too much for you. You're so tiny.'

Marjorie smiled and shook her head. 'After six weeks I'm getting used to it. We're all going to miss you, Helen. Things won't be the same around here without you.'

'I wish I could be here with you kids to help finish it off,' Helen said, 'except, of course, I want to be with Carl.'

'When we all get back home we'll have a big reunion,' Elsie said.

Yes, Jessy thought, but it will be like when a play closes and the cast disperse and you never catch quite that same feeling again. She said, 'Speaking of us all getting together, this is the first time we've seen you around for a while, Elsie. Do you have some big secret you're keeping from us?'

Elsie blushed to the roots of her hair. Before she could answer, they heard footsteps pounding up the stairs and Bonny flung herself into the room.

'That damn rotten skunk. I fixed him this time,' she said furiously.

Her tie was hanging sideways, the top button of her tunic was undone, her hat was perched crookedly on the back of her head and her eyes were darting fire.

'Fixed who?' Helen said.

'Moose Morrison. Who else? He said he just wanted to take a little stroll through the square and kiss me good night for good luck. Then when he got me out there he said I was just playing hard to get and he tried to pull me down on the grass. I showed him whether I was playing hard to get or not. I kicked him on the shins and then I punched him in the eye and on his big ugly nose and I pulled away and ran up here.'

'Good heavens!' Marjorie said.

Jessy was doubled up with laughter.

Elsie said primly, 'I don't know why you even speak to that big brute. He's so uncouth.'

Bonny snorted and shot her a furious glance.

Before anyone else could say anything, there was the sound of a commotion downstairs. They heard the girl on orderly duty yelling: 'Stop. You can't go up there,' then the stamping of feet on the stairs, and Moose Morrison burst into the room, one eye swollen and shut and blood trickling from his nostrils. Helen instinctively jumped off her bed and stood in front of Bonny.

'Where is she?' he roared. 'Where is that girl?'

'Don't you dare touch me, Moose Morrison,' Bonny said, leaping out from behind Helen, 'or I'll smash you to a powder.'

'You're coming with me, you buzz bomb.' Reaching out with one great arm he caught her around the waist, pinning her arms to her sides. Then he waded towards the door carrying her face down like a sack of potatoes, squealing and thrashing her feet.

Helen and Marjorie leapt up to help her, but Jessy called them back. 'Let them go,' she said laughing.

'Oh. Do you think he's going to rape her?' Elsie said, licking her lips.

'Not a chance,' Jessy answered. 'He wants to see the war out.'

'Well, I can't wait for her to get back. I'm hungry.' Elsie

227

started bringing her goodies out and spreading them on her bed. 'Moose will probably be court martialled,' she said as she spread potted meat on to crackers.

'I wouldn't make a book on it, if I were you,' Jessy warned.

Half an hour later, Bonny walked quietly into the room. They all looked up as she entered. Her eyes were shining and her cheeks were redder than ever. 'Hey, guess what, you kids? Moose asked me to marry him.'

'Of course, you refused,' Elsie said, pursing her lips.

'Like fun, she did,' Jessy said, flashing her wide smile. 'When's the big day?'

'Moose wants us to get married as soon as we can get permission,' Bonny answered, blushing. 'He says he's waited long enough to get his hands on me. Hey, Elsie, did you save me any of that good grub?'

'There's plenty,' Elsie answered. 'Marjorie didn't even touch any.'

'Oh, I had a little piece of cheese,' Marjorie said.

The searing emotions of the last six weeks, since she started driving the ambulance, coupled with her own agonizing thoughts of Colin, had drained her strength and dried up her appetite, until she felt constantly nauseated; and yet, through it all, she felt, strangely, as if some inner thing was keeping her going.

The next morning they all went to breakfast at their favourite table in the mess hall. Immediately after breakfast, Helen was to leave to join Carl on the hospital ship bound for Canada and civilian life.

Elsie's old animosity and jealousy towards Helen were completely gone. In fact, she found it hard, in the light of the new thing that had come into her life, to imagine how she could ever have been so silly.

Helen looked at her friends sitting with her at the long mess table, and the other army girls grouped with their own buddies, eating their powdered eggs and dark, coarse bread and margarine and felt a wistful pain coupled with her joy at the thought of going home with Carl.

She knew that this closeness to these girls with whom she had shared a portion of her life – which she would never be able to explain to anybody, unless they had been there too –

228

was passing swiftly from her, never to be recaptured. True, as Elsie had said, they would meet for reunions, but they would be civilians then, with their own separate lives, and this feeling would be a memory that could not be pinned down; and yet it would bind them with invisible threads for the rest of their lives.

Immediately after breakfast, Jessy, Marjorie, Bonny and Elsie shook hands with her and said goodbye. Soldiers don't cry, but there was a brightness in their eyes as they spoke their final words of farewell. The all clear was sounding.

Jessy glanced up. 'We've got them on the run now. We'll soon be back over there with you, Helen. This show will be winding down pretty soon.'

'Yes,' Bonny said enthusiastically, 'and we'll sure as heck get together. Moose and I are going to live in Red Deer, Alberta, and so are you, so we can set it up there. But gee, I wish you could be here for my wedding, Helen.'

'So do I,' Helen said, laughing. 'I don't know how you two ever stopped scrapping long enough to get engaged.'

Bonny grinned. 'Well he finally found out I really meant it when I said I wasn't that kind of a girl. He said I was playing so damn hard to get there was only one way he was going to get me and he was going to get me even if he had to marry me.'

'You look after yourself, Marjorie,' Helen said, looking anxiously into Marjorie's pale face and squeezing her hand. 'Take care of her, Jessy.'

Jessy said, 'Marjorie does a pretty good job of taking care of herself and all those boys we bring in on our ambulances, too. But I'll try to teach her a few bad ways.' She laughed softly.

Jessy and Marjorie did not have to go on duty until the evening. Marjorie looked at Helen's empty bed, neatly made up with the blankets folded in an envelope at the foot, and felt a lump come up in her throat. 'We're going to miss Helen so much,' she said to Jessy, walking across to sit down on her own bed. Before she reached it the room began to swim around her. Jessy's face advanced and receded before her. She put out her hand as a black curtain descended on her and she felt herself slipping down into its folds.

The next thing she knew she was lying on her bed. Her collar and tie had been loosened and Jessy was bending over her, rubbing her wrists and gently slapping her cheeks. Gradually Jessy's face became clear. Marjorie blinked.

'Whatever happened to me?' she whispered. 'Everything just went blank. Did I faint?'

Jessy nodded. She was smiling quizzically down into Marjorie's face.

Marjorie passed a hand across her forehead. 'I've never fainted before,' she said, bewildered, 'or even come close to it. I suppose it's because I haven't been eating enough, but it seems like everything I eat makes me feel sick, especially breakfast.'

Jessy continued to look at her with a faint warm smile in her eyes. She said gently, 'Marjorie, without three wise men suddenly appearing in the east, is there any way you could be pregnant?'

Marjorie felt a tremor through her whole body. She stared back into Jessy's face, her mind for a moment unable to digest what her friend was suggesting. Then, all at once, she remembered. She had been too busy and too lost in her emotions to give any thought to when her last period had been, but she realized now she had not had it since before the day she and Colin had made love. Those moments with him under the rhododendrons blazed back into her mind.

At once she was certain that what Jessy suggested was so. Colin's baby was in her womb. Joy, so intense it was almost agony, pulsed through her. All of him was not gone for ever from the earth. Something of their love would live on. She sat up, feeling the colour rush up into her cheeks. Clutching Jessy's hand tight, she told her in quick bursts what had happened between herself and Colin.

'I've been so sick after breakfast, but I never thought about being pregnant,' she said, blushing.

'Did you think that people just did that for fun and there was some other way of getting babies?' Jessy said with a twinkle. 'What do you propose to do now?'

Marjorie's chin came up. As if she had come out of an endless, dark tunnel she felt suddenly resolute and strong. There was a light and a reason for being.

'I don't want anyone to know I'm pregnant,' she said. 'They'll send me back to Canada if they find out. I want my baby to be born here in England. I want to carry on like I've been doing. Will you help me, Jessy?'

'Not letting anyone know you're pregnant can be a bit of a tricky secret to keep, unless you can convince everyone you've suddenly developed a passion for potatoes and that glue they call macaroni cheese in the mess hall, but I'll see if I can stage it. What about seeing a doctor?'

'Oh, I'm young and strong and healthy. I don't need a doctor. Women never used to go to doctors when they were pregnant.'

Jessy looked into Marjorie's enormous blue eyes into which a new light had come. Yes, you'll make it, little Marjorie, she thought. I always knew you've got more guts than any of us, when it comes time to show your cards, because you have more goodness in you. Out loud she said, 'Well, anyway, if you told that MO we've got that you're pregnant, he'd likely say you were just swinging the lead and give you a laxative. I remember a girl in the club in Montreal got pregnant and she insisted on dancing right up to the time the kid was born. She said exercise was good for you. We rigged it so she always had to have some baggy costume that hid her figure. Her baby was born in the dressing room right after the last act. She weighed eight pounds, and we named her Pavlova.'

Marjorie smiled. 'I think, Jessy, you just make up some of those stories to make me laugh.'

She went to the bathroom. She was suddenly intensely aware of her own body and the new life she was sure it carried. The simple function of urinating became significant. As she pulled up her khaki bloomers, she passed her hands lingeringly over her stomach and navel. Did Colin's baby really nestle there, sheltered inside her? Those moments of perfect love in the secret glade at Enderby — were they even now blossoming in the secret place inside of her to bring forth the fruit of their love?

A verse from the Bible came into her mind: 'Be fruitful and multiply and replenish the earth.' Swiftly on top of the thought came the vision of her father's face as he had read passages from the Bible. Fear shot through her like an arrow. Her parents and her brother and his family would never understand. In their eyes she would be a sinner. A girl who had let her family down and got into trouble with some man over here in England.

She pulled up her pants, straightened her skirt and went to look at herself in the mirror. Her eyes, large and luminous with fear and wonder, looked back at her.

Jessy shot her a quick look as she returned to the room. She said nonchalantly, 'Come on, Marj, let's take little Lord Fauntleroy for a walk in the park. You can't dance, you know.'

Marjorie felt the world steady around her again. 'Jessy,' she said fondly, 'you could make escaping from the Gestapo look like a piece of cake.'

Chapter 26

'I hope Moose isn't umpiring the game tonight,' Jessy said to Marjorie as they left St Martin's-in-the-Field, 'or the groom will be too badly beaten up to enjoy his honeymoon.'

Marjorie laughed. 'No. I understand they've detailed someone else for the job tonight. Imagine Bonny refusing to go on her three-day honeymoon pass until after the ball game.'

'Well, it's against the air force girls and you know how Bonny feels about beating them,' Jessy said, laughing.

'I know how she feels about beating everyone,' Marjorie said.

Everyone had been in uniform for Bonny's wedding to Moose Morrison at eleven a.m. Bonny had insisted that Marjorie, Jessy and Elsie all be bridesmaids.

'Did you notice Elsie and her Major Ellis when they left the church?' Marjorie said. 'She went out with him and I saw them squeezing hands.'

'I've noticed our Lovey arching her back and purring for weeks,' Jessy said. 'I suspected that was the reason. Did you see old Moose's eyes glowing when he watched Bonny come up the aisle?'

Marjorie thought with swift pain of the last time she was to have been at a wedding and of a white dress lying forlornly across a great fourposter bed.

A month had passed since the day Helen had left. She was sure now of her condition. She could feel subtle changes in her body. Her early feelings of nausea had passed. In fact, she felt almost buoyant. Colour had returned to her cheeks and her great blue eyes had taken on a new depth and radiance. She could feel her breasts, tender and sensitive, beginning to thrust against her tunic. The slight thickening of her body was noticeable only to herself.

233

A strange inner calm, almost elation, had come over her, coupled with an intense longing for Colin that at times was almost unbearable. Sometimes in the darkness and fog of the English countryside she felt, as she drove along, almost as if he were sitting beside her in the ambulance. She felt his presence as strongly as if he were trying desperately to tell her something.

Meanwhile the V-bombs fell relentlessly on London as Hitler made his last desperate attempt to stem the tide of war that had turned against him. In August the allies had invaded southern France from Italy and North Africa. The cost of allied victories was high and the wounded continued to pour into England. The V-bombs fell all around Sussex Square, but 43 Company and Molly's pub escaped.

The day Moose and Bonny returned from their three-day honeymoon, Jessy and Marjorie met Toothy Stevens coming out of the door of 43 Company with a worried look.

'Hey,' she said anxiously, showing her buck teeth, 'do you kids know what's wrong with Bonny? I went in to call on her to go to the practice with me – you know we're playing a return match next week against those Limey air force girls who beat us. She was lying on the bed bawling her eyes out. She told me to go away – she wasn't coming to practice. What the heck do you suppose is wrong? You know, we can't win without her, and we were going to plot our strategy tonight.'

Marjorie and Jessy raced up to room 217. They found Bonny lying face downward on her bed sobbing and pounding her fists into the pillow. She heard them come in and sat up gulping and hiccuping, with tears running down her cheeks. 'I'm sorry kids,' she gulped.

Marjorie flew to her and put her arms around her. 'Oh, Bonny, what's wrong?'

'That big lug,' she sobbed. 'He never told me he went for another re-board – though he always said he was trying to get away from all those chickenshit people at HQ before they drove him nuts. His re-board came through while we were away and they shipped him out an hour ago. He's on his way to join the Canadians in France.'

'Oh Bonny, dear,' Marjorie said, distressed. 'I'm so sorry. I

234

thought he was out of it on account of his category.'

'Big stupid lug,' Bonny sobbed. 'Why did he have to go and get a re-board?'

Jessy crossed over to her own bed, kicked off her shoes and lit a cigarette as she flopped down. 'Guess who I bumped into today?' she said.

Bonny stopped sobbing and she and Marjorie both looked at her.

Jessy went on, 'The Captain of that Limey air force team who beat you the day you got married. We had coffee together at Horsham. She said her air force team are going to jolly well knock spots off your CWAC team. She said the CWAC team's big reputation is just a lot of bally wind, really.'

'She did!' Bonny shouted, dashing the tears from her cheeks and jumping to her feet, her eyes blazing. 'Why that little Limey turd. I'll show her. Just because we had an off day last time.' She headed for the bathroom, still muttering.

'Where are you going?' Jessy asked innocently.

'To wash my face and go down to the ball practice,' Bonny called back. 'We'll show those Limeys. And I bet Moose kicks the shit out of those damn Germans, too.'

After she had gone stamping out, Marjorie said to Jessy, 'I was with you all day and I don't remember seeing you having coffee with any Limey air force girls.'

Jessy laughed. 'I'm going to Molly's,' she said. 'David is up on leave.'

In October Marjorie felt her baby move inside of her.

She was sitting beside Jessy, driving back to London through the clear night when she felt the stirring. She started and put her hands on her stomach.

'He moved,' she said with awe in her voice.

'He'll really be kicking up a storm before he makes his grand entry,' Jessy said with a laugh.

Marjorie looked out of the window of the station wagon at the star-filled heavens and thought, since the beginning of the world those same stars have shone down on the earth.

'It is going on, Colin,' she whispered. 'It isn't the end. You are going on. The Enderbys are going on.'

Hard on her whispered words came the chilling thought: *He*

won't really be an Enderby. He'll just be Marjorie Hatfield's bastard son she brought back from England.

Fiercely she fought down the cold thought: He will be part of me and part of Colin. Our lives will go on in him and in his children and in his children's children. In spite of all this bloodshed and destruction our love will live on. She wondered why she felt so sure the child she carried would be a son.

Fog and rain descended thickly on London in November, but the V-bomb attacks lessened. Londoners went about their daily business with less tension and there was less talk on buses and on the underground of where bombs had fallen; but rumours persisted of a second deadly secret weapon soon to swoop from the skies on the ancient city – V2.

'It's getting so peaceful around here, we're going to have to go somewhere else to find a war,' Jessy quipped as she and Marjorie turned in their duty sheets at the garage on Dilke Street, near the Chelsea Embankment.

Almost before the words were out of her mouth, they heard a tremendous explosion in the distance, followed in a moment by a rumble like thunder. Instantly they snapped alert.

'V2,' Jessy said softly, a glow of excitement coming into her eyes. 'I wonder where it landed. Let's go down to the Thames and see if we can see anything.'

With several of the other drivers they ran down to the dark embankment but they could see no fires burning.

'It must have landed a long way off,' Marjorie said.

'And it must have been one powerful toy,' Jessy said softly. 'Old Herman still has some tricks up his sleeve. Let's get the wagon back to Moon's. I think I can still make it to Molly's before closing time.'

In the paper the next day they saw a report of a gas main blowing up in Chiswick.

'A gas main with wings,' Jessy said dryly.

The next day more mysterious explosions, followed by the long ominous roll, like heavy thunder, continued to disturb the peace of London. On the third day the news was released in the papers. The government announced officially that a German V2 rocket attack had been launched against London. This powerful new weapon approached its target without warning,

236

travelling faster than the speed of sound and carrying enough explosives to wipe out a whole block of buildings. Unlike the V1, there was no means of defence against it. The rumble that followed the explosion was the sound of the V2's arrival – it travelled faster than sound.

Jessy told Marjorie, 'We'll be able to tell our kids, we were among the first people to hear the sound barrier broken.'

On buses and the tube the Londoners talked about this eerie new weapon. Outside 43 Company, the paper boy, selling his daily paper, looked at Marjorie with his head cocked on one side and said cheerfully in his rich cockney accent, 'We ain't 'alf goin' to cop it one of these days, miss. That 'Itler bloke is workin' 'is 'ead off on V3 right now, I betcha.'

But the war went on, and no V3 came, and the allies continued their relentless advance, driving the Germans back mile by bloody mile.

On December the twelfth Red Army stormtroopers entered the eastern suburbs of Budapest and, as if this was a signal for a last desperate stand, on the sixteenth the Germans opened a major offensive against the US 1st Army, driving into Belgium and Luxembourg. The war news became alarming as a huge bulge appeared in the allied lines.

The Christmas pantomimes were on in London and Marjorie went and sat alone one night to watch Peter Pan fly across the stage, and she thought of Colin and felt his baby stirring.

On the twentieth of December, when the Germans were only ten miles from the French border, Field Marshal Montgomery was called on to assume command of US 1st and 9th armies in addition to his own command of British 2nd and Canadian 1st armies, and the tide turned back.

Marjorie and Jessy hardly saw their room at 43 Company, so busy were they picking up the Canadian young men who were paying the bitter price of victory in Europe with their battered, bloody bodies.

Marjorie was feeling the weight of her pregnancy now. But so far only Jessy knew of her condition. She wore her loose-fitting trench coat over her battledress, and when she was resting in her room she concealed her body under the bed-clothes.

But one evening Bonny came home unexpectedly when her

ball practice was cancelled, just as Marjorie was starting to put on her trench coat. She stared at her.

'My gosh, Marj, you're sure getting fat,' she blurted.

Unnoticed, Elsie had come into the room behind her. Her eyes flew wide as she looked at Marjorie, and her mouth dropped open. 'Marj, you – you're pregnant!'

Bonny turned on her, raging. 'Of course she's not.' Then she looked at Marjorie again and her jaw dropped and she flushed scarlet. 'Are you, Marj?' she whispered.

Jessy was right behind Marjorie with her hat and coat on, ready to go on duty with her. 'Do you think she's been eating too much macaroni cheese?' she drawled lightly.

'Oh gosh, Marj. I am sure as shit sorry,' Bonny stammered. 'I never thought – Darn it – I wish it was me. When that big lug gets back we're going to have six kids.'

Marjorie smiled at her distressed face. 'It's all right, Bonny,' she said gently, putting her arm around the other girl. 'Don't look like that. It's Colin's baby and I want it.'

'Damn those dirty rotten Germans,' Bonny said, clenching her fists. 'Wouldn't I like to get my hands on them. If it hadn't been for them, you'd be married to Colin now, and you wouldn't have to worry.'

Jessy said, 'Well, Bonny, you have to look at it like this, if it wasn't for them none of us would be here in the first place and Marjorie wouldn't have ever met Colin, and you wouldn't be married to Moose. Don't look so pale, Elsie. It isn't catching, you know.'

The others turned to look at Elsie. She had, indeed, turned white as she stared at Marjorie.

'I have to go,' she said and almost ran from the room.

Jessy raised her eyebrows and whistled.

Chapter 27

Elsie bolted from 43 Company barracks to Lancaster Gate tube station on Bayswater Road, just around the corner from Sussex Square. Fear propelled her. She thought through her panic as she descended the escalators to the train platform: At least I'm safe from those horrible V2's down here.

Others had the same idea. The platform was crowded with women, children and old men, settling down on their blankets for yet another night. The train rumbled swiftly into the station as she reached the platform and she jumped aboard. The door slid swiftly shut and she sank down on to a seat. Her heart was pounding in her ears like a gong. Seeing Marjorie's condition had awakened her with a shock to the realization that she was more than two weeks past time for her period.

All those ecstatic evenings she had been spending secretly with Major Ellis became suddenly as menacing, almost, as the buzz bomb raids.

'Pregnant, pregnant, pregnant,' the train wheels seemed to clang out derisively at her. She felt suddenly as if she had ballooned out and everyone on the coach was eyeing her and saying to themselves, 'Look at that pregnant CWAC.'

All at once, her breasts felt tender and her back was aching. The very thought of having a baby, even if she were married, had always thrown Elsie into a complete state of panic – The swelling of her body – the dreadful time of delivery. And then having to feed it while it spat its food all over – and its whining and clinging to her – robbing her of her freedom . . . She shuddered. Then the thought came to her: That's what my mother felt like. I'm just like her.

By the time she reached Baker Street station the perspiration was running from under her hat and her soft pink and white complexion had faded to a pasty white.

A mocking little verse of Jessy Cole's kept running in her brain: 'I didn't mean to do it, Lord. 'Twas that last drink that threw me. Oh, please, dear Lord, unscrew me.'

She writhed in her seat.

It had all started that night after she had driven Helen down to the hospital to see Carl. They were almost at his apartment in Seymour Mews, after letting Jessy out at CMHQ garage, when he reached over and put his hand on her knee. A new sensation ran through her body. She twitched. Expertly his hand crept up until it found a spot between her legs. She gave a squeal and almost lost control of the car.

She had never felt anything like this before in her life. When he started moving his fingers tantalizingly to and fro, she thought she would choke with delight at the delicious sensations that went quivering through her body. She managed to pull the staff car up in front of the building where he lived and realized with dismay, as he removed his hand, that her pants were soaking.

It was three nights later, after returning from a trip out into the country, that he sneaked her quietly up to his quarters. He had been very quiet on the trip and to her intense disappointment had only rested his hand lightly on her knee once or twice. When she was about to let him out of the car, he reached across and squeezed her knee and said in a silky tone, 'Come up to my flat for a few minutes.'

With her heart pounding wildly, Elsie followed him up the back stairs to his secluded little flat, looking down on the mews. It had a small kitchenette and living room, and through a door she saw a huge old-fashioned bed.

He sat her down on the settee in the living room and, excusing himself, disappeared into this bedroom for a few minutes.

He reappeared wearing a gold dressing gown tied about him with a cord. His pale blue eyes were sparkling and his moustache was quivering. He produced a bottle of good French champagne — which had been presented to him by one of his staff, wanting an extra weekend pass — filled two glasses with the sparkling fluid and gave one to Elsie.

'A little reward for being such a good driver,' he said in a purring voice.

It was her first taste of champagne and it went to her head immediately. She began to feel light, and carefree and tingling all over, and wishing he would touch her again. But he merely let his hand rest for a moment caressingly on her shoulder and poured her another glass of champagne. She gulped it down greedily and held out her glass for more. But he took it away from her and set it down on the end table. Elsie pouted.

He pulled her up from the settee into his arms and kissed her, biting her gently on her full lips and running his fingers up into the back of her hair. His moustache tickled her delightfully and she felt, through his thin robe, the hardness of a rod pressed against her body.

He led her off to the big bedroom and laid her down on the big featherbed, with his body ecstatically close to hers. Then, to her intense delight, he ran his hand slowly up her leg and inside the top of her khaki bloomers and slipped them down, undid her garter belt and stripped off stockings and bloomers and belt. His hands caressed her buttocks and he ran them up and down her bare legs until she almost screamed, wanting him to touch her in between them.

At last his tantalizing fingers found the warm soft, throbbing secret spot and she almost sobbed for joy. At the same time his other hand expertly unbuttoned her shirt and pulled down her brassiere. His lips fastened on her plump, thrusting nipples.

Elsie was writhing with desire by now. Just before her sensations reached a height, he stopped and removed the rest of her clothing.

His eyes were gleaming, his moustache was quivering and his breath came in little short puffs as he looked down at Elsie's soft, round pink and white body spread out on the bed.

'Oh, my,' he drooled, as if viewing a delicious concoction. Then he stood up and undid his sash and let his dressing gown fall open.

Major Ellis was a very small man, but there was nothing small about the part that mattered. He had always been the amazement and envy of the other men in the latrine.

Elsie's eyes flew open as through the haze of champagne she

241

saw his penis standing on end, with the heavy balls hanging below. The thought flashed into her mind of Bonny's baseball bat.

He stood looking down at her for a moment with a little proud smile on his lips; then he whipped a French letter from the pocket of his dressing gown and expertly pulled it over the throbbing knob of his penis.

Major Ellis had barely made it through OTC and he had been dismal in battle drill. He had almost broken his neck jumping from a moving truck when they were doing debussing on the run; but he would have taken top marks for the thing he liked to do best. Tonight he got an extra bonus. He had suspected Elsie was a virgin, but he hadn't been sure, and he had been fooled so many times before.

Cleverly and with great patience he parted the maidenhead. Elsie's squeals of delight were music to his ears as he went on to the climax, pushing and thrusting deep inside of her soft, warm eager body. He thought: She's the best piece I've ever had.

Once aroused, Elsie's appetite was insatiable. Fortunately for her, Major Ellis was almost a match for her, and his powers of recovery were amazing. Elsie never knew how she got the staff car back to Moon's Garage that night and then found her way back to Sussex Square in the darkness.

They had finished the bottle of champagne before she left and Major Ellis joyfully mounted her five more times before, looking a little pale, he sent her reluctantly home. Her body was still throbbing ecstatically when she finally climbed into her own bed and lay pouting in the dark, wishing she could have had yet more.

That was the start. But there were no delicious memories or delightful anticipation milling around in her head tonight as she rushed down Baker Street towards Seymour Mews. As she turned on to the street leading to it, in the gathering twilight she saw with terror that the whole street was cordoned off, and the air was heavy with the smell of dust and rubble.

She gave a choking cry. Where Seymour Mews had stood there was nothing but a flattened mass of rubble, with the smell of dust and destruction still rising from the tangle of bricks and mortar. The whole row was flattened.

242

A crowd had gathered and the wardens were busy, searching among the ruins for survivors. Elsie stood looking at the scene of destruction, her breath heaving in terrible sobs.

'Oh,' she moaned. 'Oh, oh! What shall I do now?' Her mind went completely blank with terror. Someone in the crowd said with that matter-of-factness that had always irritated her about the British, 'One of them damn flying things took the 'ole street out. Never 'eard a bloomin' sound until it landed a few minutes ago. Looks fair like 'e's going to knock this 'ole city out before 'e's done with it.'

Another voice cut in, 'No, 'e bloody well won't. Them Canadians is right up there with our lads. They'll knock 'is bloody bombsites out before long, you just wait and see. Even the Yanks are doing a bit over there.'

Elsie put her face against the wall and covered her ears with her hands. She was a quivering mass of panic, unable to think.

A tremulous voice at her elbow said, 'Elsie – Elsie – Is that you?'

She turned to find Major Ellis standing beside her, his face so pasty that even his moustache looked white. His pale eyes goggled at her like a fish out of its tank. 'Look. Look!' he said, pointing a shaking finger towards the rubble. 'That is – that is my quarters in there. Think what would have happened to *me* if I had been inside. Just lucky I had to go somewhere.'

Elsie grabbed his quivering arm. 'Let's get away from here,' she quavered. 'I want to talk to you, and another one of those horrible things might come down.'

He convulsed into action at her mention of 'those horrible things'. They rushed away and found a quiet little pub some distance away and he ordered a gin and bitters for them and Elsie told him of her fears.

If possible, he turned even paler than before. 'Pregnant,' he quavered, 'But – but – You can't be. What will my colonel say? You – you know we aren't supposed to mix with Other Ranks. And you're my driver. They – they might cashier me. I'll be in dreadful trouble.'

Elsie stiffened and looked at him speculatively and then she said in her most purring voice, 'Yes, and you'll be in worse trouble when Mother and Father find out. Isn't Daddy holding your job open for you until you get back?'

243

He goggled at her.

Elsie went on demurely. 'You know, I'm their only child and whoever marries me will get a big position in Daddy's company, and of course, one day I'll inherit the business.'

Major Ellis stopped goggling and a calculating gleam came into his eye. Elsie would probably make quite an attractive wife, now that she had thinned down a bit, and her father was *very* rich. He did have a reason for hanging back from marrying her, though. Not only had he been revelling in those stolen hours with her, he had been keeping a little actress at the Haymarket satisfied.

She had beautiful legs and a trick of flipping her body that almost sent him wild. Still, he had been feeling a little tired lately and maybe, just maybe . . . He would do almost anything to get out of London right now. It wouldn't be as if he were marrying just any little CWAC driver. Not, of course, what he had pictured. He had always imagined himself marrying into some titled family.

'Well,' he said, 'I suppose if I'm going to be a father I might get back to Canada on compassionate grounds.'

Elsie stared at him. 'I don't think I ever heard of them giving compassionate leave to fathers,' she said doubtfully.

A week later they were married quietly at Windsor. But Elsie's anticipation of a night of joy was spoilt by the fact, as she was taking off her clothes to put on the frilly nightgown she had bought on the black market, her period came gushing like an oil well blowing in. Relief and disappointment fought it out inside of her. It could have happened three days later. She consoled herself by eating a whole jar of the artichoke hearts her mother had sent her.

Major Ellis sulked on his side of the bed all night and dreamed of doing things to the little actress at the Haymarket, until he came on his own.

Chapter 28

The months wore on and the tide of war moved ever faster against the Germans. And Marjorie kept her condition secret from all but her friends in room 217.

Late in March Moose's regiment, the First Canadian, Highland Light Infantry of the 1st Army, crossed the Rhine.

'He'll sure fix those big shits,' Bonny gloated.

That was the day on which, calculating that some time during the next two weeks her baby would be born, Marjorie had arranged to take her leave. When she went to the CWAC orderly room to pick up her pass, Captain Burns called her in to her office. Marjorie stood in front of her CO's desk, in her loose-fitting trench coat, and saluted.

Major Burns looked hard at her, then she got up from her desk and came around and held out her hand. 'I just wanted to say goodbye, Hatfield,' she said quietly. 'I'm going across to the continent with the detachment of CWAC they're sending over . . . ' She hesitated. Then she squeezed Marjorie's fingers. 'Good luck, Marjorie,' she said huskily. 'You'll find Captain King, your new commanding officer, very sympathetic if you have anything you need to discuss with her.'

'And good luck to you, ma'am,' Marjorie said feelingly, returning the handclasp.

Captain Burns started to turn away, then she turned back and said, 'This war is hell, isn't it?'

Except for the cramps that troubled her legs occasionally, and the general heaviness of her body, Marjorie felt amazingly well. She knew she would soon have to tell the army authorities about her condition so they could arrange for her to have her baby in one of the military hospitals. It did not matter if they knew now. It was too late for them to return her to

Canada before the birth of her child.

She pushed thoughts of the future from her mind. Only yesterday, in a letter from home her mother had told her that her father was not feeling too well, the children were growing, they were all looking forward to her coming home. They thought the war must soon be over now.

They would never understand or accept it when she turned up in that quiet little Bible belt with her illegitimate child in her arms. She was not really trained to make a living for herself, let alone a child. But she would manage, somehow. She spoke her concern to Jessy.

'Well,' Jessy said, 'things are going to be a lot different for women after the war, you know. All sorts of jobs that were closed to them before will be opening up, and single parents are not going to be looked on as something to heave rocks at.

'Women are not going to be satisfied, after playing such a big part in the war, to be just "the little woman" again. Even married women are going to insist on being *persons* in their own right.'

Bonny said, 'They say they're going to be giving vets free training in university, or whatever you want. You'll be able to be a schoolteacher, Marj.'

Elsie said primly, 'But will they want an unmarried woman with a child teaching their children?'

Bonny shot her a dark look. Then she said, 'You know it's the shits. Here's Elsie and me both married and neither of us is pregnant and you're pregnant and you're not married and you're the best damn girl of the lot of us.'

After her friends had all gone off to their duties, Marjorie felt a strange restlessness and, after breakfast, she had a twinge of indigestion. She was seized, all at once, with an overwhelming desire to see Enderby again – the place where her child had been conceived and where she had spent those happy hours with Colin.

She thought constantly of him now. It was almost as if in some mysterious way he was with her.

Also the old earl and countess had been much in her thoughts of late. The earl had told her to come to him if ever she needed anything. Certainly she did not want anything from them, but she was beginning to wonder if it was quite fair to keep from them the knowledge that she was to bear their son's child. Did she owe it to them to tell them? Impulsively she packed her haversack towards the end of the day and caught the five o'clock train to Wendover.

She was the only passenger to leave the train at Wendover station. She found the familiar, winding country road and set off towards Enderby Hall, with the March breeze blowing in her face carrying the scent of spring and growing things. She walked slowly. All of a sudden she was very weary and twinges of indigestion continued to plague her.

Although it was only three miles, the road seemed to stretch endlessly before her, but at last she reached the lodge gates and turned in.

Her feet dragged as she walked up the winding drive between the gently rustling trees. Her back ached intolerably and little drops of moisture prickled under the brim of her hat. At last she broke out of the trees and saw Enderby Hall, serene and stately at the top of the sweeping slope of green lawn.

Marjorie caught her breath. A flood of memories overwhelmed her and she sank down on the cool grass. The tears ran down her cheeks. 'Oh Colin, Colin,' she whispered. 'Why aren't you here? It's so beautiful. So beautiful. Why isn't this the most joyful time of my life? Why, oh why, did that squadron leader get appendicitis?'

She struggled to her feet and wiped the perspiration from her forehead. Setting her army hat more firmly, she squared her shoulders. 'Soldiers don't cry,' she whispered and walked on up the slope towards Enderby Hall.

Her stomach knotted as she pictured the look on the Countess of Rivermere's face when she saw her condition. No doubt she would politely hide her scorn for this Canadian soldier girl turning up pregnant at her door. Well, she would soon make it very clear that she expected nothing from them.

In front of the great oak doors, she stood trembling. At last she reached out and pulled the cord. She heard the bell gong inside, but no answering footsteps came in answer to the summons. She waited and then pulled the cord again, but still there was no answer.

Acting impulsively, she tried the doorknob and the heavy door swung open to her touch. She hesitated, then walked into

247

the great hall. She caught her breath. It was just as she remembered it the day she had first arrived with Colin, except that the dogs were not in front of the fireplace. She stood uncertain for a moment and then crossed the dark, gleaming floor to the door of the countess's private sitting room and tapped gently.

A voice inside called, 'Yes. Come in.'

With her heart pounding alarmingly, Marjorie entered the room. The countess was sitting in her usual chair by the French doors leading to the garden. She was dressed in a heavy, grey silk dress and her gold locket. She was gazing out the window towards the hill beyond the garden.

She turned her head and Marjorie almost cried out at the change in her.

Her face was a tired grey mask with the deep eyes veiled and withdrawn. Her still-erect body seemed to have shrunk. Her blue-veined hands, with the rings gleaming on her tapered fingers, rested on her lap.

Her eyes lit up with surprise as she saw Marjorie standing in the doorway. 'My dear,' she said. 'Do come in. How very kind of you to come. I'm sorry there was no one to let you in. Giles is out in the garden cutting fresh flowers for the table and Meadows has gone to Wendover to buy supplies. I expect Mrs Anderson is napping in her room.'

Her voice sounded thinner than Marjorie remembered.

Hesitantly Marjorie crossed to where the countess sat.

As the light from the French windows shone fully on her, the countess started and sat up with a jerk. All the remoteness left her face and her magnificent grey eyes blazed with life. Colour stained her cheeks and she drew a deep breath. She stood quickly.

'My dear,' she said. The deep timbre was back in her voice. 'Come here.'

Marjorie went to her and held out her hand. The countess put her arms around her and embraced and kissed her. Then she held her back at arm's length and looked at her and their eyes met and locked with understanding.

'Yes,' Marjorie whispered. 'I'm pregnant.'

The countess said, 'I knew something had happened that day when Colin left us for the last time. I saw it in your faces when you returned from your walk. Why did you not come to us before?'

Marjorie said, 'I didn't intend to come, but then I felt somehow that you had a right to know, before I return to Canada, that I'm going to have Colin's baby. You mustn't think that I want anything.'

All signs of weariness dropped from the countess. She seemed to grow suddenly to her old stature. Her face was glowing as if a light had come on inside of her. She led Marjorie over to one of the deep chairs.

'Sit down, sit down, child,' she commanded. 'You did right to come to us. How frightened you look. Did you walk all the way from Wendover?' She gave Marjorie another keen look. 'Your baby is due very soon is he not?'

Marjorie nodded. She felt suddenly almost too weary for words. 'I'm on my two-week furlough,' she said faintly. 'I think he'll be born during that time, if I've figured it rightly.'

'You haven't been to a doctor?'

Marjorie shook her head. 'I've been driving an ambulance, picking up our wounded boys as they come back from the battlefield.'

The countess said, 'Major Middleton told us you had left him to go and drive the ambulance. We've thought of you often, but we did not hope ever to see you again.' She bent down suddenly and kissed Marjorie on the forehead.

'You're a brave girl,' she said. 'Stay there and don't move. I'll bring you some tea. The earl will be here soon. He's out walking the dogs. He'll be delighted.' She swept from the room.

Marjorie lay back and closed her eyes, too weary to think, or move, even if she had wanted to.

After a short interval the countess returned with the tea.

'I sent Giles to fetch Teddy,' she said as she set the tray down on the small table, and a moment later the earl came in, closely followed by Giles.

'What's up, Honora?'

Marjorie was shocked to see how he had aged in the last nine months. It was as if a giant hand had squeezed all the life out of him. He walked slowly, like an old man.

249

'Look who's come to see us,' the countess said, crossing the room and taking him by the arm.

His eyes lit on Marjorie sitting in the chair across the room and a smile came into them. Marjorie drew a quick breath. How like Colin's they were.

'Marjorie,' he said. 'By Jove, by Jove. It is good to see you.' He walked slowly across to her with his hand outstretched. He stopped suddenly as his eyes took in her condition. Colour flooded his cheeks and his hand trembled. He stood staring at her, then, trying to pull himself together, he stammered, 'Oh – Ah – How frightfully good to see you, Marjorie.'

The countess said, 'Oh, do stop stammering about like that, Teddy. Marjorie is going to have our grandson.'

The earl stooped down and took both of Marjorie's hands in his and kissed her cheek. 'Oh, my dear,' he said. 'My dear child. Why didn't you come to us before? I say, are you all right?'

Marjorie laughed shakily. 'Perfectly all right. But I don't think I'd like to try to jump Minnette over Beecher's Brook. I've been driving an ambulance. I don't mean to trouble you. I – I just – as I told the countess, it suddenly came over me that you had a right to know about – about Colin's child.'

'Trouble us!' the earl said. 'My dear girl. My dear, dear girl.'

Like the countess, the years seemed to drop from him. As if he had been given a transfusion, life and vigour flowed back into him. His body straightened and a glow came into his brown eyes.

Lady Rivermere turned to Giles, who was standing, quite expressionless, behind the earl. 'Do go and fetch his Lordship a glass of brandy please, Giles.'

'Yes, my Lady.' Giles glided silently from the room.

The countess sat down and poured the tea.

Suddenly Marjorie giggled. They stared at her. 'I'm sorry, I wasn't laughing at you. It's just the way everyone over here always has tea whenever anything out of the way happens.'

'The empire was absolutely built on it,' the earl said. Then suddenly he and the countess were both smiling at Marjorie, warm tender smiles that drew her inside their jealously guarded circle and the three of them, all at once, were very close. For the first time since she had come here, Enderby Hall

250

lost its aloof watchfulness, and Marjorie felt it was welcoming her home. The great house seemed to wrap itself around her, warm and protective.

She buttered one of the scones and covered it with raspberry jam from the little dish on the tea table.

'I hope,' she said, 'Lord Rivermere was not stung again.'

'Managed to sneak the berries away from right under their noses,' the earl answered. 'Did a recce first.'

'How is Minnette?' Marjorie asked.

'Oh, top form,' the earl answered. 'But she doesn't get much riding these days. Hasn't jumped Beecher's Brook since you took her over.'

'Since she took me over, you mean,' Marjorie said, and they both fell silent remembering that happy day.

The countess broke in. 'Tell Marjorie about Kettle's horse.'

The earl's face brightened. 'Oh, rather. Most extraordinary thing, you know. I was wrong about that. Old Kettle's horse beat the Queen's. Old Kettle was beside himself.'

After tea the countess said to Marjorie, 'Now you must go upstairs and lie down and rest until dinner. Of course, you'll be staying with us for a time.'

Marjorie shook her head, coming back to reality with a jolt. 'Oh, no. I can't. I have to go back to London. There are – I have arrangements to make. I – I haven't told the army that – that I'm pregnant. Perhaps, if it isn't too much trouble, someone could drive me to the station. If there's any petrol?'

'Rubbish,' the countess said briskly. 'You're tired out. You must stay tonight at least.'

Marjorie felt, all at once, that the journey back to London tonight was more than she could take. Her body felt leaden and everything ached. She said weakly, 'Thank you. You're very kind and I am tired. But I must return to London first thing in the morning.'

'We'll talk about it in the morning,' the countess said. She took Marjorie upstairs to an airy bedroom beside her own, overlooking the walled rose garden, with the grassy hill beyond, and brought her a silk nightgown and dressing gown.

'I wore them when I was pregnant with Raif and Colin,' she said, smiling protectively at Marjorie.

After she had gone, Marjorie fell back on the bed and was

251

almost instantly asleep. She dreamed that she was in the garden with Colin and he was holding her in his arms and kissing her.

It was so real that she could feel the warm tenderness of his lips on hers. She came reluctantly to reality when the countess knocked on the door.

So real was her dream, Colin seemed with her as she went down to dinner with the countess. Another twinge of pain caught her body on the stairs and she paused and drew a sharp breath.

The countess gave her a sharp look, but said nothing.

Mrs Meadows had outdone herself preparing a tasty meal, but Marjorie could scarcely force herself to eat any of it. The heaviness in her body had increased and she felt faintly nauseated. She managed to converse with the earl and countess through the meal, but when she was nibbling into the raspberry tart at the end of it, a sudden sharp pain made her gasp. She stopped eating. 'I am sorry,' she told them. 'I'm afraid I'm more tired than I thought. Will you forgive me, please, if I go back to bed? I must go back to London quite early in the morning.'

The countess stood up instantly. 'My dear child, of course. You must go to bed at once. I'll take you upstairs.'

The earl pulled Marjorie's chair back for her and helped her to her feet. 'I do hope,' he said, looking down at her tenderly, 'that you won't rush off to London and leave us like that. We'd be so jolly happy to have you stay here with us for a time, wouldn't we Honora?'

'Very happy indeed,' the countess said, taking Marjorie firmly by the arm and smiling down into her face.

At the top of the stairs Marjorie paused with her hand on the countess's arm. 'Please,' she said, 'Lady Rivermere, do you mind, I – I want to look at the pictures before I go to my room.'

Wordlessly, the countess turned her steps and led Marjorie around the long gallery of Enderbys looking down on her from their heavy frames. She passed them quickly until she came to Raif's portrait where they both paused. His fine eyes, so like those of the countess, smiled down at them.

Then they turned to the picture that had been added to the gallery since Marjorie last looked at them, hanging beside his

252

brother. Marjorie caught her lip in her teeth to keep from crying out. Colin was smiling down at her, just as she remembered him in his air force uniform, looking so lifelike she felt that, if she reached out her hand to him, he would speak. She could almost hear him saying, 'You are a funny little soldier girl.'

She stood trembling.

'Come, my dear,' the countess said in a low voice. 'Come away to bed now.'

Marjorie let herself be led away, but before she left the gallery, drawn by the strange fascination it always held for her, she turned to look at the portrait of the black sheep. His smile still seemed to mock her, as if he knew an amusing secret.

She started in sudden fascination. On the second finger of his right hand was a heavy gold ring with the family crest on it, exactly like the one the soldier had given her in the ambulance.

'What is it?' the countess said.

I'm being foolish, Marjorie thought. Of course it would look the same if they copied it. 'Nothing,' she answered.

After the countess had settled her in her room and gone away, Marjorie undressed and put on the silk nightgown the countess had provided. Her heavy dog tags felt out of place against its smooth elegance. She untied Colin's ring from among them and put in on the third finger of her left hand. The ruby picked up fire in the glow of the lamplight and the diamonds were winking pools, as they had been that first day when Colin slipped the ring on her finger in the little teahouse in Windsor.

Marjorie whispered, 'From now on, no matter what the army rules say, I'll keep your ring on my finger, Colin.'

She removed the ring the soldier had given her from her purse and turned it over in her fingers. It did look exactly like the one in the portrait. Perhaps, tomorrow, she would show it to the countess and ask her about it. For now she wanted only to sleep and rest. She put out the light and sank back on the pillow in the soothing darkness.

As she did, another twinge of pain shot through her abdomen. It was yet another, she supposed, of the small pains that had beset her in the last few months of her pregnancy. I suppose, she thought, if I was driving the ambulance, looking after those poor boys, I wouldn't have time to notice it. And of course the trip out here to Enderby had been an ordeal.

She had not realized how much she had dreaded meeting the earl and countess in her condition, until she had experienced her overwhelming relief at their reaction. Her reception had been so totally different from what she had expected. Instead of the scorn and disgust she had anticipated, she had been welcomed like a heroine bearing glad tidings.

I shall never understand these English, she thought as she drifted off to sleep.

She dreamed Colin was standing beside her bed looking down at her with tenderness flowing from him to her. She was not aware of his clothes, except that they were open at the throat and she could see the curly brown hair on his chest. He was telling her something, but she could not hear any words. It was as if he spoke to her from a great distance.

She sat up, reaching out her arms to him, and he faded away from her. As he disappeared into a mist his eyes smiled into hers and held up his two fingers in the V for Victory sign.

All at once Marjorie was wide awake, sitting up with outstretched arms in a world of bewildering pain. Her hair was matted with perspiration and tears were running down her cheeks. She was wet between her legs and she seemed to be sitting in a pool of water. 'My God!' she whispered. 'Those pains I've been having all day . . . The water has broken. *I'm having my baby!*'

The pain passed from her. She sank back on her pillow. The world had gone strange around her. She tried to think what she must do, but her thoughts came in a jumble.

Then another pain engulfed her. *Help! She must get help. If her baby came and there was no one to help he might die!* She moaned. Then the light went on. The countess stood in the doorway in her nightgown.

She crossed swiftly to the bed and took Marjorie's hand in hers. Marjorie clutched convulsively and her whole body heaved and strained. Then the pain subsided and the countess smiled reassuringly into her eyes.

'Don't be afraid my dear,' she said calmly. 'You're in labour. It's perfectly normal. I'll send Teddy for Dr Brownly.' She called for her husband and almost at once the earl appeared at the doorway.

'Teddy, go at once for the doctor, Marjorie is in labour. And please, wake up Giles and have him send Meadows and Nanny to me.'

Without a word the earl hurried from the room.

Marjorie bit back a scream as a wave of excrutiating pain rolled over her again. The countess held her hands firmly. When it was over she glanced at her watch. 'Your pains are coming very close now,' she said quietly. She wiped the sweat from Marjorie's face with the edge of the sheet. 'Draw deep breaths and relax.'

Marjorie whispered, 'The doctor won't arrive in time. My baby is coming.'

The countess smiled back at her. 'There's really nothing to having a baby, you know. You don't need the doctor. Lie still and draw deep breaths. I'm just going to wash my hands.'

Marjorie drew in great deep breaths and in a moment the countess returned, carrying a bundle of clean sheets and towels. She raised Marjorie's legs and placed a thick bath towel under them.

Marjorie pressed her arms down on the bed and clenched her fists as pain gripped her body again, until she seemed to be swimming in a sea of agony. And through it all Colin's face seemed to be everywhere.

The countess was at the foot of the bed. Her calm, firm voice came steadily to Marjorie, 'Breathe deep, push – breathe deep – push.'

She felt as if her whole inside were being stretched like an elastic band. Then it was tearing apart. I'm dying, she thought. And it doesn't matter. The pain will stop then. But, my baby – I can't die. She pushed with all her strength. Miraculously, the pain receded, and then she heard a lusty cry. A thrill shot through her.

The countess said with a note of triumph, 'You have borne a son.'

Lying back exhausted Marjorie said weakly, raising her arms, 'Put him in my arms. Let me see my son.'

'Yes. Yes, my dear. In just a minute. First we have to deal with the afterbirth and clean both of you a little,' the countess said with a note of exultation in her voice. 'What a fine big Enderby boy he is.'

After what seemed an endless length of time the countess placed the baby, wrapped snugly in a towel, in Marjorie's eager arms. She looked down into his little red face and saw a shock of dark brown hair. She unwrapped him and examined him from head to toe. His little body was perfectly formed.

She looked at his firm little chin and high cheekbones. A wave of joy shot through her. 'You look just like your daddy,' she whispered as she held him to her.

The countess said proudly, 'No mistaking, he is an Enderby. He looks exactly like Colin did when he was born.'

Mrs Meadows the elderly housekeeper, came into the room. Her eyes widened. She said, 'Yes, my Lady, you sent for me?'

'Get Giles to help you bring the cradle that was Master Colin's from the nursery and put it in here, and ask Mrs Anderson to please come here.'

Marjorie only half heard the countess's words. The love she had felt for Colin seemed suddenly to have grown to an almost agonizing ecstasy that was wrapped tightly around the tiny boy child she held in her arms.

Giles and Meadows returned carrying the cradle between them, closely followed by a thin, elderly woman. Her bright blue eyes lit up joyfully at the sight of the baby in Marjorie's arms.

The countess pulled the covers back so they could see the baby. 'This is Master Colin's son,' she told them. 'Nanny, do you think you can help to care for yet another Enderby?'

The elderly nanny lifted her head proudly. 'Ay, that I can, my Lady,' she said in her broad Scottish accent. 'Praise the Lord. This has been a lonely house, until this happy day.'

Reluctantly, Marjorie gave her son over to the kindly old nurse. The countess soothed her. 'You must rest now. Your son will soon be demanding to be fed.'

'Put the cradle right beside my bed, so I can reach out and touch it,' Marjorie said.

Marjorie was still sleeping peacefully when the earl returned with the doctor, her hand still touching the cradle. The earl gazed down at Marjorie's sweet, fair face on the pillow, a gentle smile curving her lips as she slept, and at his tiny sleeping grandchild in the cradle that had held his own two sons, and tears ran down his cheeks.

'Honora,' he said in a choked voice, 'he looks so like Colin did when he was born.' He sighed and wiped the tears from his eyes. 'If only . . . ' he whispered.

The countess said, 'I know what you're thinking, Teddy, but he *is* an Enderby. I remember when Raif was born, you and Kettle got absolutely squiffy and talked incessantly about all his mares who had ever foaled. Go down to the cellar and bring us a bottle of champagne. You will join us in the library, Dr Brownly, to drink a toast to the new Lord Enderby?'

When the doctor had departed, the countess told her husband, 'In the morning, Teddy, I want you to ask all the servants and tenants to assemble in the hall.'

The earl looked at her questioningly. 'Whatever you have in mind, Honora, I think you should consult Marjorie first, and I also think you should go and rest now.'

The countess smiled at him and patted his arm. 'Don't worry, Teddy. I have to make a list of things we'll need from Wendover. Our grandson cannot continue to wear swaddling clothes made from towels.'

Marjorie woke to the sun shining playfully on to her face. She turned at once to the cradle and started up in alarm. Mrs Anderson came swiftly to her with the baby in her arms.

'Dinna fret, lassie,' she said soothingly, placing Marjorie's son in her arms. 'The wee one is here and a right fine lad he is.'

Marjorie knew there were things she must do and plans she must make, but the only reality now was her small son nuzzling into her breast. 'He's beautiful isn't he?' she said, looking up into Mrs Anderson's kindly face.

'That he is, lassie,' Mrs Anderson answered. 'Nine pounds he weighed and a handsome one he'll be, like all the Enderbys.'

But he won't be an Enderby, really. He'll be a Hatfield, Marjorie thought, with a little wrench.

She looked about her at the big airy room, with its priceless antique furniture and wide windows, with the scent from the garden wafting in, and she thought of the lake with the rhododendrons blossoming around it, and the fish ponds, and the hills and streams of the magnificent estate, and the ancient title that should have been her child's.

She held him tighter to her breast and whispered, 'Your father called me his wife and your blood is the same. But I'll make it up to you. I'll stand between you and the world, my little Canadian.'

The countess came into the room, regal and unruffled as usual. Her eyes were smiling at Marjorie who felt the strength of her presence as the countess crossed over to the bed and stood looking down at them.

'My dear, how well you look. And my grandson, also. I've sent Giles and Meadows into Wendover to find him something more appropriate to wear than a towel. Later on someone will come to the house to register his birth. Have you decided on a name?'

'Colin,' Marjorie answered. 'He must be named Colin.'

'Colin Dudley Percival,' the countess said softly.

The day became more and more bewildering to Marjorie as it went on. At ten-thirty the countess came and told her, 'I want Nanny to bring baby Colin to the hall for a short time. Some of our people want to see him.'

While Marjorie had been asleep Mrs Anderson had dressed her baby in his new clothes, including a gown of heavy gold silk with the Enderby coat of arms embroidered richly on the front. Marjorie watched, bewildered, as they left the room, with Mrs Anderson carrying young Colin, following the countess.

The countess stopped on the stairs and took the baby from the nurse's arms.

The servants from the household and the tenants from the estate, crowding the great hall, all looked up curiously at the Countess of Rivermere, standing proudly on the steps. A little gasp went up as they saw the bundle she held in her arms. They each held a glass of wine, poured by Giles and Meadows.

The countess held the baby up in her arms so everyone could see him and said in a loud, clear voice, 'This is Master Colin's son, born here in Enderby Hall last night to the lady who was to have been his wife, whom you will all remember meeting here in her wedding dress, on the day he was killed defending his country. As has always been our custom when a new Enderby heir is born, I have called you all together here in Enderby Hall to drink the health of the new Lord Enderby.'

The Earl of Rivermere had been standing talking to his foreman. He came quickly to his wife's side. 'I say Honora . . .' he began.

'A drink, Teddy,' she cut him off sharply. 'Let us join in the toast to our grandson. And one for Nanny.'

The earl took three glasses of champagne from the tray Giles held out to them and gave them wordlessly to his wife and the nurse, with one for himself.

'To the new Lord Enderby,' the countess called out in a ringing voice.

'To the new Lord Enderby. God bless him,' came back in a shout from the assemblage.

Putting her glass down on the tray, with her face flushed and her eyes gleaming, the countess slowly descended the stairs with the sleeping baby in her arms and carried him about the great hall, pausing to chat to the tenants as they admired him.

Upstairs in her room, an inexplicable panic swept over Marjorie. She was unreasonably relieved when Mrs Anderson brought her son back. She gathered him protectively against her breast, then she looked curiously at the gown he was wearing. 'What in the world is that?'

The countess smiled at her. 'It has been in the Enderby family for generations. The heir to Enderby always wears it when he is presented to the servants and tenants in Enderby Hall.'

Marjorie looked at her with increasing bewilderment and an incomprehensible uneasiness. The gown looked so heavy on the tiny sleeping boy, as if the weight of all those centuries were embroidered into the heavy crest.

'Would you please take it off him now?' she said. 'He looks too small to carry it.'

'Of course,' the countess said. 'He only wears it for the ceremony.' She added with a twinkle in her eyes, 'Wait until you see the christening gown.'

Late in the afternoon the registrar came with the papers to register the birth. Marjorie sat up in bed as the countess brought him in. He spread his papers on the small table beside the bed. When he asked her what she wished to name the baby, Marjorie said slowly, 'Colin Dudley Percival . . .'

'Enderby,' the countess broke in before she could finish.

Marjorie shook her head vigorously. 'No, Lady Rivermere. He has to be called Hatfield. You've been most kind, but Colin and I were not legally married. He must take my name.'

'Is there any reason, William, why the child may not be registered in his father's name?' the countess said, fixing her eyes on him.

The registrar shook his head. 'No, your Ladyship. If no one objects there is no reason he cannot have his natural father's name.'

Marjorie continued to shake her head. 'My son must be called Hatfield,' she insisted, feeling her voice crack.

The countess took her hand and looked imploringly into her eyes. 'Marjorie,' she said, 'Colin loved you dearly. He would have been so proud. Will you not let his son bear his father's name?'

Marjorie looked into the deep, steady grey eyes. She felt suddenly very weary. Her baby stirred and whimpered. As if he were in the room with them, she felt Colin's presence. Overcome with her own longing to have her baby bear his father's name, Marjorie smiled weakly. 'Colin Dudley Percival does fit better with Enderby.'

Chapter 29

'Jessy, you have a beautiful body,' David Carlton said, smiling down at Jessy Cole, who was lying naked, propped up on her elbows on the deep persian rug, looking through the pages of a manuscript spread out before her. He was standing in front of a long wall mirror knotting his uniform tie.

Jessy tilted her head to look up at him, her brown eyes glinting mischievously. 'Even in Montreal they won't let me show it off. When I danced Salome, I had to wear tights and when that last veil came off they dimmed the lights. I bet things will be different after this war. They'll be prancing around the stage without a stitch on.'

David smiled at her. 'Maybe that's what you should have written about in your play.'

'I wrote this before I joined the army,' Jessy answered. 'It's been kicking around in the bottom of my kitbag everywhere I went. Do you think your friend will like it?' She glanced around the elegantly furnished sitting room. 'If his flat reflects his personality I think my play might suit him.'

'Knowing Jasper, I'm sure he'll like it.'

She gave a low laugh. 'I'd say if he would lend his airman friend his flat to seduce a CWAC he'd appreciate my play.'

David finished knotting his tie and put on his hat. He came and looked down at her with a smile. 'Did I seduce you, Jessy?'

Jessy laughed again. 'Seduction is a romantic word, but it doesn't fit us. You've been married and I've been bedded before.' She stretched herself languidly. 'And last night was very pleasant – for both of us, I hope. It was something we both needed.'

David looked down at her steadily, his eyes very gentle.

'Jessy, if I come through this thing, would you consider marrying me?'

Jessy slowly shook her head. 'You're being gallant. You're such a nice man, David. But it wouldn't work for either of us. You'd be thinking of that lady you liked to have around and I . . .' She shrugged.

He finished for her, speaking softly. 'You'd be thinking of that Yankee major.'

Jessy said, 'In time we will really get over it and be able to find someone else – if there is anyone else left for us when this is over – but now it's too soon.' With a quick movement she gathered up the pages of her manuscript. 'I hope your influential friend can get me into the theatre.'

'I've arranged for you to meet him for lunch at the Savoy. I'm sure with your talent and looks it will be no problem. Probably you wouldn't even need him, but he does pour rather a lot of money into backing plays, and they'll be anxious to do what they can for anyone he wants to promote.'

'Just get me in to see them and I'll do the rest,' Jessy said, smiling.

'I have to leave now, but there's no need for you to hurry,' he said. 'Sorry I can't see you home, but it's not far from Mayfair to Sussex Square.'

'I'm going to shower and dress and get back to barracks at once. I have to find out how Marjorie is. She's disappeared on us.'

'She must be almost ready to have her baby,' David said seriously.

'Who told you about that?' Jessy said.

He smiled. 'You forget you're talking to an ex-married man. It wasn't hard to notice what was underneath that trench coat. You see, when I came home from that flight and found our little house buried under tons of rubble and Sheila killed . . .' He stopped for a moment, then said softly, 'That was the weekend I was rather hoping to become a father.'

Jessy drew in her breath sharply and jumped to her feet and kissed him. 'There ought to be some way of getting rid of people who think up wars.'

In the afternoon Marjorie began to recover her strength. It was

262

just as well, because a stream of visitors came to the room to admire little Colin. They all had the same look of wonder and excitement she had seen in the faces of the earl and countess. Among them was old Kettle, huffing and puffing and red in the face.

'Just like the Enderbys,' he said, looking down at the sleeping baby. 'Good blood line. I remember when his father was born – same day Dolly foaled.'

Marjorie hid a smile.

A little later, Major Middleton came into the room. He stood beside the bed holding Marjorie's hand. 'By Jove,' he said, looking from her to little Colin, 'good girl,' as if she had performed some miracle. She saw the glint of tears in his eyes. 'You don't know what this means to Teddy and Honora – to all of us. But I wish I'd known. Might have been able to make things easier for you. But still, this is the way you wanted it.'

Ashley, too, came. She kissed Marjorie affectionately, but her eyes were all for the sleeping baby in the great old cradle. 'He looks so much like Colin,' she whispered, 'but I can see – Raif in him, too.'

Marjorie felt a little sigh escape her.

Ashley was instantly contrite. 'How foolish we all are to come and bother you like this. But you've given us a miracle. You can't know what it means to us to see another Enderby born, when all our hopes for the future had died with Colin.'

Marjorie smiled weakly up into Ashley's face. 'I'm glad you're all so happy, but he's really a Hatfield, you know. He's *my* son.'

The other girl's eyes clouded over, then she stooped and kissed Marjorie on the forehead. 'Of course. We're all being very foolish. Please forgive us. It's this beastly war.'

After she had gone, an aching wave of loneliness surged over Marjorie. How different everything would have been if Colin were here and she were Lady Enderby. She had received nothing but kindness from them all, but she felt – strangely – as if she were watching a play in which she had no part. It was only the baby in the cradle who mattered.

If only someone would really look at me. If only someone would say, 'Marjorie *you* have a beautiful baby boy.' She laid her head back on the pillow and two tears ran down her cheeks. She closed her eyes.

A knock sounded on the door and Nanny got up from her chair to answer it. 'Oh please,' Marjorie whispered to herself, 'no more visitors. I can't bear to see any more of them just now.'

Gratefully she heard Mrs Anderson say, 'I think the young lady is too tired to see anyone else today.'

Then her heart leaped as she heard Bonny's voice. 'I bet she'll see *us*, all right.'

She sat up and called out, 'Mrs Anderson, let them in. Let them in!'

Bonny burst into the room, closely followed by Jessy and Elsie. She crossed the room in a rush, with the others on her heels, and grabbed Marjorie's hand. 'You little shit,' she said excitedly. 'You went and had him without us. Hey, he sure is a cute little turd.'

Jessy laughed softly, looking at Marjorie with warm affection. 'The bard himself couldn't have put it better,' she said. 'We brought you a present. When you were still gone this morning I phoned Lady Rivermere.'

'She's a pretty good old donkey, at that,' Bonny said. 'As soon as we got here she told us to come right up. She said you'd be happy to see us.'

'Happy!' Marjorie said. 'More than you will ever know.'

Elsie said, 'I brought you something, too, Marjorie.'

Bonny chimed in, 'You know she's getting to be a pretty good shit. She got a parcel from home and she brought you the whole darn thing. Never pigged down a crumb herself.'

Marjorie laughed delightedly when she opened her present from Bonny and Jessy. 'Blue Grass,' she said. 'Now I'll smell so different from all the other CWACs.'

It was a standing joke. Blue Grass was the only perfume sent to the canteen from Canada and after a shipment came in every girl in barracks smelt of it.

'A fresh lot just came in,' Jessy said with a laugh.

Eagerly, Marjorie dabbed it on. The sweet, familiar scent was the Canadian Women's Army Corps and barracks and her pals. 'I'd sooner have it than all the rare scents of the Indies,' she said shakily. 'It's a wonder you didn't bring me a tin of Spam.'

'Elsie has lots better things than Spam in her parcel from

home, I bet,' Jessy answered.

At the army girls' insistence, Mrs Anderson joined them in their feast. Marjorie felt all her loneliness melt away as they ate and chatted. She laughed heartily at Bonny's play-by-play description of how they had 'kicked the shit out of the opposing team' in her latest ball game. She refused the chocolate. 'Nanny says it will give my baby a tummy ache.'

When they had eaten, they took turns holding little Colin.

'Jeepers, what a big little guy,' Bonny said admiringly. 'He'll make the defence line on the Maple Leafs when he grows up. I can just see him knocking them on their asses.'

Marjorie thrilled at Bonny's words.

After they had all gone, she whispered to her little son, holding him close, 'You little Canadian, you'll want the 'ole street, and by gum, Mommy is going to get it for you, somehow.'

Marjorie decided not to tell her parents of the birth of her baby until she arrived in Canada. In the back of her mind was the hope that when they saw him, they might be so captivated with him that they would forgive her and take him to their hearts. But in the depth of her being she had little hope of this.

At the end of the week she brought up the subject of returning to London. She was sitting having tea with the countess and earl in the library. Little Colin, wrapped snugly in his blankets, was sleeping peacefully on a heavy leather chair.

'You've both been so very kind and hospitable, but I must go back to London now and take Colin with me. The army will have a place for me to stay until they can send us back to Canada.'

The countess passed her a buttered scone. 'Do have some of that jam Teddy risked his life for,' she said, smiling at Marjorie.

After Marjorie had obediently helped herself, the countess said, 'Marjorie, why don't you stay here with us for a few weeks and get your strength back? Teddy will speak to the brigadier and arrange it. I know he can. Then, why not go back to your duties and leave Colin here with us until the war is over?'

Marjorie gasped and put her tea cup down with a rattle on

the saucer. 'I – I don't know,' she floundered, bewildered.

The earl spoke, leaning forward in his chair. 'Dear girl, we should so much love to have him with us just a bit longer. The war cannot go on so much longer now. We've got Jerry on the run. And little Colin will be so much stronger for travel when he's a little older, don't you think?'

As Marjorie sat looking at the wistful pleading face of the earl and the quiet face of the countess, conflicting thoughts tore at her. The prospect of three more peaceful weeks here in Colin's home with her baby enticed her, and she hated the thought of leaving Jessy and Bonny and Elsie and all her other comrades at 43 Company until they had seen the war out together. But she wondered on the other hand if it was fair to these two grandparents to allow them to become too attached to this tiny boy child of hers who was the last of the Enderbys.

The countess said, smiling, 'Teddy may even be able to teach you to ride English style before you go.'

The day she had raced down the hill and fallen off Minnette jumping Beecher's Brook flashed back to her. Such a happy day. All at once she felt Colin's presence as if he were in the room with them. She heard her own voice as if a force outside herself directed the words, as she agreed to the countess's proposal. She felt strangely light-hearted after she had made the decision and joy leapt up in the faces of the earl and countess.

The three of them were suddenly very cosy as they sat sipping their tea in front of the small fire burning in the grate.

The day before Marjorie left to go back to London, the tenants and servants gathered at the little chapel in a wing of the great house to christen little Colin. Lady Ashley and her parents were there and Major Middleton and old Kettle.

Little Colin, dressed in an elaborate christening robe with the Enderby coat of arms embroidered on it in gold, cried lustily as the minister dabbed the water on his forehead and made the sign of the cross.

Lady Ashley was his godmother and Major Middleton and Kettle were his godfathers.

Marjorie was overjoyed to see Blaine among the guests as she was leaving the chapel with Colin in her arms. She handed Colin over to him to hold for a few minutes. Blaine was beside himself with delight.

'What a proper young gentleman 'e is,' he said looking proudly down at the baby in his arms, who looked back up at him with wide, dark eyes. ' 'E is Lord Enderby all over again. A proper little lord, if I ever saw one.' Tears shone in his eyes.

'Don't forget he's a little Canadian,' Marjorie teased him.

'Only 'arf,' Blaine said, 'only 'arf.'

If it had not been that she was a soldier under orders Marjorie would have found it impossible to tear herself away from her son when the day came when she must return to London. She had been gradually weaning him, giving him his bottle as well as breast feeding him, so the process would be less painful for him. He cried as she was saying goodbye to him.

She whispered as she kissed him, 'This war must soon be over now. Then Mommy will take you home to Canada and we'll never be parted again, my darling.'

The next day, when she reported back on duty, on the twenty-second day of April, the Red Army were fighting in the heart of Berlin, and no more V-bombs fell on London.

At his request she was once more assigned to drive Major Middleton. There was no longer a shortage of ambulance drivers and she did not feel guilty about her jammy assignment. She spent every spare moment at Enderby.

In the month she had stayed with them after Colin was born she had come to feel a closeness to the earl and countess. The countess had shown her a side of her character that made Marjorie wonder how she could ever have thought her cold and aloof. She had had Giles bring out the pram that had been both Colin's and Raif's and which, like everything else, had been in the Enderby family for generations, it seemed. It stood high and proud with the Enderby coat of arms in gold on the side.

Marjorie thought it like a chariot of old as she and the countess pushed it around the walks and gardens, with little Colin riding in state like a prince. Marjorie discovered on these walks that the countess was a woman of fascinating conversation and possessed of a dry sense of humour. She was delighted to learn that they had many similar tastes in literature, and she spent many happy times discussing books they had both read.

But still there was something in the countess's manner that

made her feel vaguely uneasy. Something she could not explain – which she felt rather than saw.

Little Colin was thriving and growing rapidly. Each time she saw him, she noticed some change in him. He had a fresh English complexion, dark curly brown hair, and big deep-set eyes like Colin's.

Her love for him grew until it was like an ache. She had not believed she could love anyone as much as she had loved Colin, but this tiny boy child had wrapped himself around her heart as tightly as had his father.

Once, when she was looking down at him with the blazing love she felt for him in her face and eyes, she had glanced up to see the countess looking at her with a pitying expression.

She was frightened and held Colin tighter to her. But the look was gone in a moment and she wondered if she had imagined it.

On the first of May the Hamburg radio announced the death of Hitler and the succession of Admiral Doenitz as commander of the German nation. News came that Himmler and Goebbels had committed suicide and Hermann Göring had been captured.

On the second day of May, Berlin fell to the Russians, after twelve days of street fighting.

The war in Italy, the Austrian Tyrol and Salzburg ended at noon the same day, with the surrender of nearly one million German troops.

On the fourth, General Eisenhower announced that all German forces in Holland, north-west Germany and nearby islands had surrendered to Field Marshall Montgomery, ceasefire effective at 2 a.m. on May fifth. On the seventh of May the allies won complete victory in Europe with the unconditional surrender of Germany. It was the end of the war in the European theatres – the long-dreamed-of VE-Day had finally arrived.

Marjorie, Jessy, Elsie and Bonny joined the London crowds packing the streets. They stood looking up at Big Ben and heard Winston Churchill's victory speech come to them on loudspeakers.

The London crowd was strangely silent.

Bonny was disgusted. 'Did you ever see anything like these Limeys? They haven't even broken a window or anything. Gosh, back home we have more excitement when we win a ball game. Haven't they got any red blood in them?'

Jessy said softly, 'They've got red blood, all right. But so much of it has been shed in the last six years, they can't let go too far.'

Two days later, Bonny got word that Moose was coming back from the continent on leave.

She was wildly excited. But after he had left to go back to his unit she came charging into the room, swearing ferociously and dashing angry tears from her eyes.

'That damn Moose. He's gone and volunteered for Japan. They've been asking everyone to sign on to fight those stinking Japs.'

'Well, *I'm* certainly not,' Elsie said.

Marjorie said, 'I'm afraid I won't be able to, either, though I suppose if it weren't for my baby I would. After all, it's our duty to help.'

'Oh, I suppose I'd better go over there, too. I hope we can get a ball team together. What about you, Jess?' Bonny said.

Jessy laughed softly. 'I once played the part of a Geisha girl. I signed on. Perhaps I can get some first-hand experience. Though I'm doubtful any of us will ever get into that war.'

The withdrawal of the Canadian forces from England after VE-Day went on slowly. No one seemed in a hurry to repatriate the CWAC. To Bonny's intense disgust, Moose was sent home to Canada in July to train for the Pacific war theatre, while she remained in England.

'He'll be gone over there to fight those damn Japs before I can even get home,' she said. 'Then, I suppose they won't send me.'

Marjorie had the strange feeling that they were all marking time, waiting for something to happen.

On the sixth day of August it happened.

In the early morning as she, Jessy, Bonny and Elsie were crossing the street to go to breakfast they heard the paper boy bawling: 'Atomic bomb on Hiroshima!'

They rushed to buy the paper. Looking over each other's shoulders they read of a terrible bomb that in one explosion had practically wiped out Hiroshima. The end of the war within hours was predicted.

Bonny cheered. 'Hurrah! Now those slant-eyed bastards will give up and our boys can get out of their stinking, rotten prison camps.'

Marjorie said quietly, 'Well, thank God, the war will be over and, maybe, now we can have peace ever after in our world.'

They all looked at Jessy. Her face had gone so white that the bones stood out. Tears coursed down her cheeks. She whispered in a strangled voice, 'Father forgive us, for we know not what we do.'

Three days later, on the ninth, they dropped another atomic bomb on Nagasaki. On the fourteenth Japan surrendered and the war was all over.

The next week Bonny and Elsie were both put on draft for Canada. Bonny's order came through on the day she returned from the continent with her ball team after a successful game against the servicewomen over there. 'We beat the shit out of them,' she exulted.

She yelled with delight when she learned she was on draft for Canada. 'Now Moose and I can go on that farm at Red Deer and start raising a family.'

Elsie pursed her lips. 'Father is buying Ellie and me a big house in Toronto.' She turned and said warmly to Marjorie, 'And, Marjorie, when you come home you can come and stay with us. I know Daddy can find you a job. People won't have to know – I mean – You can say you're a war widow, or something.'

Bonny said, 'Aw, she can come and stay with Moose and me as long as she wants.'

Chapter 30

Bonny was laughing and crying all at once when Marjorie and Jessy said goodbye to her and Elsie as she prepared to board the train to Southampton with the little group of CWACs on their way home to Canada.

'Darn, I wish you two shits were on draft with me,' she said. 'I'm so damn glad to be going back to Canada and yet I'm so damn sorry to be leaving 43 Company and room 217 and all the things we've done together. I'm going to miss those damn doodle bugs.'

Jessy laughed softly. 'What you mean really, Bonny, is that you're going to miss the comradeship of soldiers.'

'Well, anyway,' Bonny said, 'I'll be seeing Helen, and when you guys get back we're all going to get together in Red Deer. Because we're always going to be buddies. Come on, Elsie, let's get on that damn little Limey train. Imagine me going back with you, and you were always the one I wanted to kick in the ass. But you turned out to be a pretty good little shit, after all, even if you are a bit snobby, like you think yours doesn't stink.'

Elsie glared at her, then she tittered. 'Let's hurry. The train's ready to pull out. We don't want to miss it. Ellie's coming to Southampton to see me off. I hope to goodness he gets back before long.' She ran her pink tongue over her lips like a child anticipating a delectable treat.

After the train had pulled out, Jessy said to Marjorie, 'Let's go and have a cup of coffee, since you don't like anything stronger.'

At Lyon's Corner house the waitress brought them a cracked cup of what passed for coffee in London.

At least it was hot. Marjorie looked around her. She said to Jessy, 'Do you notice how weirdly quiet it is since the war

271

ended? It's as if someone had loosened the string on a balloon and it was slowly going down. I thought when it was over at last, you'd see everyone looking excited and happy, but actually they look sadder than when the war was on.'

Jessy nodded. 'It's like closing night,' she said. 'All through the run, the adrenaline has been pumping and you've been putting your all into it. Then, all of a sudden, the theatre is dark and you're walking away from an empty stage.'

'So what do we do now?'

'We find another play,' Jessy said softly.

Marjorie sighed. 'I've already been assigned my part,' she said wistfully. 'I wonder when we'll get our orders to go on draft back to Canada?'

Jessy drank a little of her coffee before she answered, then she said, 'I'm not going back, Marjorie.'

Marjorie dropped her spoon on the saucer with a clatter. 'You're not going back?'

'I've asked to be discharged here in London. I'm going on the stage. You remember my friend, David Carlton? He knows someone with connections in the theatre world. He introduced me to a producer. You know the play I told you about that I've had kicking around in my kitbag for years? He thinks it's going to be a hit and I'm going to play the lead at the Haymarket. I think this is my big break.'

'You mean,' Marjorie said forlornly, 'you aren't going back to Canada ever?' She added quickly, 'Oh, I'm sorry, Jess. I'm being very selfish. Forgive me, please. I'm very happy for you. I know you'll be a famous actress and playwright one day. It's just that – I was so hoping we'd be put on draft together. How I wish that . . . ' She looked away hastily.

'You wish you weren't leaving England,' Jessy said gently.

Marjorie looked back at Jessy with tears gleaming in her eyes. 'I feel so – so much as if it has become a part of me. My love was here and my baby was born here. When I go back to Canada they won't understand. You see my parents are very strict and very religious and our neighbourhood is – well, I guess you'd call it a Bible belt. They won't approve of my son and me. I'll have to go somewhere else, among strangers, to make a life for him.'

'Then why don't you stay here? You can stay with me. I'm

272

going to get a little flat. I'm sure you could find something to do. No one in my world will care if you were ever married or not.'

Marjorie was silent for a long moment, then she slowly shook her head. 'No. I'm sure the army won't let me. And anyway, it just wouldn't work,' she said regretfully. 'But thank you, Jess.'

The following Tuesday Jessy came in from duty at five o'clock in the afternoon to find Marjorie sitting on her bed, white-faced and trembling.

'Jess,' she whispered, reaching over and catching Jessy's hand, 'I'm on draft and I leave for Southampton on Friday morning. That's just two days away. I've been trying to find Captain King, but she's been out all afternoon. I've got to tell her about Colin.' She jumped off the bed. 'I've got to go down to Wendover right away and bring him back here. Oh Jess, I didn't think everything would happen so suddenly. I should have arranged all this before. I should have told the army I have a baby.'

Jessy sat across from her. 'As Bonny would say, don't get your ass in a knot,' she said soothingly. 'When they find you have a baby they'll take you off that draft. You'll likely have to go home with the Limey war brides.'

'Anyway, I'd better get over to that orderly room and see Captain King right away,' Marjorie said excitedly.

Jessy shook her head. 'I gave her a ride to Horsham on my ambulance. She's staying down there overnight visiting a friend.'

'There must be someone I can see,' Marjorie said frantically.

Jessy looked at her from the corner of her eye and was silent for a moment, then she said quietly, 'Why don't you go to Wendover now and tell them? You still have plenty of time to pick up your son. They won't send you home without him. Didn't you say the earl has spoken to Brigadier Raham about him?'

Marjorie's face brightened. 'Yes, Jess. I'll go to Wendover now, but I'll bring little Colin back with me tomorrow. I don't want to be parted from him any more now.'

Jessy gave her a strange, unreadable look. 'I'll walk with you to Lancaster Gate.'

She went with Marjorie all the way down to the platform. Marjorie found the quiet of the platform almost eerie now that the station was no longer used for an air raid shelter. She missed seeing the rows of women and old men on their blankets, and the children playing in the grime of the platform. It was occupied now only by those Londoners waiting for trains, and the pictures on the cement wall advertising ale and stout and Wild Woodbine cigarettes.

'You should make the six o'clock from Baker Street,' Jessy said as the train thundered up to the platform. 'Good luck.'

She squeezed Marjorie's arm, then suddenly leaned over and kissed her cheek. Marjorie wondered as she entered the train and the door slid shut behind her. She was sure she had seen the glint of tears in Jessy's eyes.

On the short ride to Wendover, as the countryside rolled swiftly past the train window, Marjorie's mind was in a turmoil. For nearly four and a half years she had lived with her comrades in barracks and the army had taken care of all her needs, told her when she could go out and when she could come in, controlled her life and posted her where it would; and always there had been the companionship and the laughter of her buddies, and the sense of dedication to a cause. Now it was over. She was going home.

If she sailed from Southampton on Friday, in less than two weeks she would be back in Calgary. Then the short journey back to her farm home, carrying her baby in her arms. She would be a civilian on her own with a baby to support. Life was suddenly very real and coming towards her with devastating speed.

She gripped the strap of her haversack until her knuckles stood out white. Panic such as she had never felt in the worst of the V-bomb raids shook her. She wished suddenly that she was back in those raids, with the excitement and the fear, the friendship and the laughter of her friends.

Most of all, she wished she was back in the George and Horses that night with Colin. If only time could have stopped then and she could have sat there for ever, looking across the table into his warm brown eyes. A hot blush rushed to her face. No. If time was to stand still, she would rather it was later on – that day in Enderby, lying with Colin in the secret place under the rhododendrons. The wonderful earth smell of the trees and the grass and the flowers was suddenly in her nostrils with remembered sweetness – sweet as the song of the hot warm blood of youth and love in their bodies.

But time had not stood still. All too swiftly it had moved on, its cruel hands wresting from her those moments of joy. But it could not take the memory from her. And waiting at Enderby was the living, breathing essence of their love. No one, she thought fiercely, can make me believe that those moments in heaven were a sin, or that it was wrong that my son should be born of that rapture. My love is gone, but my son is here, and the seed will go on and on, perhaps to the end of time, a divine spark.

Her hand relaxed its grip on the strap and impulsively her dimples flashed. Though, I think, at home they'll look on him more as a bonfire, she thought with a flash of quick humour.

Chapter 31

Marjorie walked slowly, feeling the ancient spirit of the countryside wrapping itself around her in the gathering dusk, from Wendover station to Enderby Hall. Tomorrow she would be leaving these green rolling hills and flowering hedges behind her for ever. She must stretch out time, drink it all in for the last time. Yet it seemed no time until she reached the lodge gates and turned up the long, tree-lined drive.

She came through the trees and saw Enderby Hall, massive in the soft glow of the evening. Her heart came up in her throat. A thousand little voices seemed to whisper in her ear as she walked towards the great oaken doors, 'You belong here – you and your son.' On an impulse, she did not ring the bell, but opened the door and entered. The lights had not yet been turned on and it was almost dark inside the great hall. The dogs leapt up from their place and pushed themselves joyously up to her, wagging their tails.

She patted their heads and they followed her across the hall to the door of the countess's small sitting room, where Colin had gone on that first day he brought her here. He should have taken the Gurkha home, she thought.

She tapped on the door and the countess's voice called, 'Come in.'

Marjorie hesitated, then she pushed the door open and stood on the threshold. The sound of laughter greeted her.

The earl, countess and Mrs Anderson were having tea. Their faces were wreathed in smiles and their eyes were on Colin gurgling in his pram, drawn up close to the tea table where the countess sat. Marjorie was struck by the change in them since that evening when she had dragged herself in here the night before Colin was born.

The years seemed to have rolled away from them. Mrs

Anderson had straightened up from a little stooped shell of a woman to a vigorous, bright-eyed, glowing person. The happiness in the room was flowing like a living stream from little Colin in his pram.

The laughter died from their faces when they saw her and quick alarm leapt into their eyes, as if a sudden chill had entered with her. In a moment the countess was her old poised self.

'My dear, what a surprise,' she said. 'Did you walk from the village? You should have phoned and we would have come for you.'

The earl rose and escorted her to a chair. 'How very good to see you,' he said.

The countess rang the bell for Giles. 'Miss Marjorie is here,' she told him when he entered. 'Bring a tea cup and plate for her, please Giles.'

'Good evening, Giles,' Marjorie said, smiling at him.

For just a moment, Giles's face lost its impassive dignity and she saw the same look she had seen in the eyes of the others flash into his. 'Good evening, miss,' he said, his face settling back into its correct mask.

Marjorie went to her son. His eyes brightened and he gurgled and smiled up at her as she bent over his pram, cooing at him. She lifted him up in her arms and he snuggled against her breast with his little arms clinging around her neck. Joyfully, Marjorie thought: From now on, he'll always be with me. I won't have to snatch moments with him. I'll tuck him into bed at night and he'll be there in the morning when I wake up. She hugged him closer and kissed the soft brown curls on top of his head. Then she put him back in his pram and settled down to have tea with the others.

The earl and countess made her welcome with gracious warmth, but under their impeccable manner, she felt a mighty, controlled emotion and an unspoken question – 'Why have you come here *tonight*?'

Marjorie felt anguish for them in her soul. How am I going to tell them that I'm going to take the light out of their lives? she thought. She could not bring herself to speak of it yet. She made small talk with them all through tea and the earl told her a funny story about one of old Kettle's horses. Once she saw

277

Nurse Anderson reach her hand out and tuck the covers protectively around her little charge, and once she caught the countess's eyes on her face with a depth of expression that she could not fathom.

Colin started to fuss at the end of tea and look towards his mother. Marjorie picked him up again and settled into a deep chair with him on her lap. His big brown eyes shone with delight and he gurgled up at her excitedly. Marjorie thought: How much the little English boy he looks with that warm colour in his cheeks. His thick brown hair curled above his wide forehead, crisp and fresh from the soft English climate. How proud Colin would be of him, she thought, and pain shot through her. How different it would be now if Colin were here. How different for all of them.

She could put it off no longer. She must tell them. I've done what they wished, she thought. I've left my son with them for five months. It will destroy their happiness. But at least they'll know that somewhere, even if it's far away across the sea in Canada, the Enderby line will go on.

Mrs Anderson brought Colin's bottle to Marjorie. Marjorie looked with rapture into his little face as he took it eagerly. She looked up to see the eyes of the earl and countess on her. She drew a deep breath. 'I have my orders to return to Canada.'

The earl nodded and cleared his throat. 'When do you leave, my dear?' he said quietly.

Marjorie was glad suddenly that she was to leave so soon. How could I have thought for a moment that I was afraid to take him home with me? she thought. The only thing that could make me afraid would be the thought of not having him with me.

'I leave for Southampton on Friday.'

The earl's face went ashen. 'So soon,' he whispered. For a moment his lips trembled and he looked away. Then he turned back to her and said gently, 'We'll miss you, my dear. You've been a daughter to us. You must let us know if there is anything we can do to help you.'

The countess leaned forward slightly to pass the earl a glass of sherry from the tray. 'You still do not drink?' she said politely. The golden locket with Raif's picture in it gleamed against the navy silk of her high-necked dress, matching the

278

gold of her tiny earrings. The rings gleamed on her slender, blue-veined fingers. She smiled at Marjorie.

Mrs Anderson said in a thin voice, 'Shall I take Master Colin up to bed now?'

Marjorie felt pity rush up in her. The elderly Scotswoman seemed to have shrunk and aged in the short time since Marjorie had arrived. If I were Hitler, returned from that bunker, I couldn't have brought more devastation with me, she thought sadly. But she could not bring herself to let Colin go from her arms. She smiled at Mrs Anderson. 'No thank you, Mrs Anderson. I'll just finish giving him his bottle. I can take him up, thank you.'

The countess looked meaningly at Mrs Anderson. 'You look very tired tonight, Nanny. Why don't you go up to your room and rest? Marjorie and I will see to Master Colin.'

Beneath the gentleness of her words, Marjorie sensed a command. Mrs Anderson bade them good night and walked slowly from the room.

Marjorie looked at the earl and countess. She realized, all at once, that it was a wrench to leave them. She had a great affection for them. They had become a part of her – like Enderby. She hated to have to hurt them so. She said earnestly, 'I want you both to know how very grateful I am to you for all you've done for me and my son. I'll never forget you, or these days here at Enderby.'

The earl said, 'My dear, it is we who are in your debt.'

The countess's eyes were intense, as if she were gathering some inner forces to her aid. She said, 'Our dear son, Colin, would have been so proud of his son. The one thing he wished for after Raif was killed was that he could leave behind an heir to carry on the name and the blood and the tradition of the Enderbys. Young Colin would be the fifteenth Earl of Rivermere.'

Marjorie smiled understandingly at the countess. 'He'll have opportunities in Canada, too. He could grow up to be prime minister, or better still, a star right-winger for the Maple Leafs – That's our national champion hockey team,' she explained as the countess looked puzzled.

The countess smiled faintly. 'I've no doubt that wherever he is young Colin will make his mark, but is it right that he should be robbed of his birthright?'

Marjorie's cheeks flushed. 'I can only do what I can do,' she said in a low voice.

'But we can do much more,' the countess said gently.

Marjorie stared at her, her heart starting to beat rapidly. The countess went on. 'My dear, when you return to your home you will meet almost overwhelming obstacles. I know you have the courage to face up to them, but is it fair to your son?'

Marjorie felt the colour draining from her cheeks. 'The Enderby blood will overcome them,' she said. Then, stung by the countess's words, she added bitterly, 'He will rise above being a bastard.'

The countess's eyes held hers. 'But he need not be raised a bastard. He is our own grandson. We can adopt him as our heir, Lord Colin Enderby, the station he was born to. He can take his rightful place when the time comes – fifteenth Earl of Rivermere.'

Marjorie felt as if all the blood were draining away from her. Her lips moved but she could not speak. She stared at the countess, horror in her eyes. Then she found her voice. 'You – you want to take *my* son,' she whispered. Suddenly her eyes blazed.

'I see it all now. This is what you've been plotting all these months, while I thought you were being kind and generous, all the time you were planning to steal my son.'

She stood swiftly, clutching Colin tightly to her, and stood panting and glaring at the countess. Her rapid movement startled little Colin, who dropped the bottle from his mouth and cried out in fright. Marjorie whispered, holding him fiercely close to her, 'Hush, my darling, hush.' The blood was pounding in her temples. She was smothering. She must get outside. She must take her son away from Enderby.

'I'm taking my son with me NOW,' she panted. 'Don't try to stop me. If no one will drive me to the station, I'll walk and carry him in my arms.'

The earl was by her side in a moment. He put his hand on her shoulder, his eyes full of concern. Marjorie thought how like Colin he was. 'My dear child,' he said. 'My dear child, please don't be so frightened. Please come and sit down. I assure you no one here will try to steal your son from you. Honora, we should have discussed this before you spoke to her. I only said I wanted Marjorie to know that we are *willing* to adopt her son.'

The countess remained very still, sitting erect, her calm, deep eyes holding Marjorie's. 'There is no need for you to be alarmed. Please sit down. I only want you to listen to what I have to say. The decision must be yours alone.'

Under the quiet compulsion of the other woman's eyes, Marjorie subsided, trembling, into her chair again. Her terror was unreasonable. There was nothing sinister about this old couple. They were merely offering – and yet . . . Why did she feel an awful chasm was opening at her feet and she was powerless to avoid it? After all they were Colin's grandparents. In all decency she must hear them out. They had no intent to hurt her.

Colin dropped off to sleep with his head resting securely in the crook of her arm. How he had grown since that morning the countess had put him in her arms five months ago.

The countess said, 'Marjorie, I only want you to hear what I have to say. I am only asking you to consider carefully the future of your son, and your own as well.'

Marjorie answered quickly, 'Lady Rivermere, I have considered it. There is no sacrifice I would not make for my son.'

The countess said softly, 'No sacrifice, except to let him take his rightful place in life.'

'His place is with me. I conceived him and I carried him for nine long months inside my body. He shared those nights driving those ambulances and the danger of the V-bomb raids. He is part of me. He is my life.'

The countess said steadily, 'But he is separate from you. He has a life of his own. It was his the minute he drew his first breath. What will you tell him as he grows older? Will you keep from him who he is and the heritage that could have been his? Will you keep it from him that he is an Enderby, a member of one of the most honoured houses in England?'

Marjorie felt choking anger rise up in her. 'He is *not* an Enderby. What a fool I was to listen to you. I should have christened him *Hatfield*. When I get back to Canada I'll soon change that. I'll register him again. He shall be *Colin Hatfield*. I do not wish to listen to anything else you have to say. He is my son and I will keep him. I came here with sorrow in my heart because of the pain I must cause you, taking him from you, but now I find you want to steal him from me. What do you think I am – a breeding machine?'

The countess met her eyes. 'I think you are the greatest Enderby lady of them all.'

'I am *not* an Enderby. Your son and I were not married, remember. And I am not an Englishwoman. I'm a Canadian. My son will be brought up a Canadian.'

'When you coupled your body and your soul with my son you became an Enderby, with their heritage and their responsibilities,' the countess said.

She leaned forward in her chair and her delicate, blue-veined fingers gripped the arms. Her eyes were suddenly suffused with an intensity of feeling, as if a mask had been torn away revealing her very soul. Her voice shook with the iron will controlling it. 'My country took my two sons. I would not have lifted a finger to keep them from going to do their duty if it had been in my power. But when Colin died it was the end of all hope for the future for my husband and for me. He was the last of our house on both sides. Then, when you came to us and our grandson was born here in this house, life came back to us. But it was because of who you are that we were glad. Do you think, if he had been born to some chit out of a moment of cheap animal passion we would claim him as our grandson?

'I know you think me heartless and selfish, but I'm an old woman and I've seen a great deal more of life than you have. You think your life is over now and you have only your son to live for. Look at you! You are young and beautiful and filled with life. What are you – twenty-five years old? Some day you will meet another man and have children by him and have a new life. The world is not yet ready to accept a single woman with a child. From what you've told me, it will almost destroy your people if you return with a child born out of wedlock. Even if you marry again, what place will he have? He will always be the bastard son you brought back from England. If you truly loved my son would you want this future for *his* son?'

Marjorie said, trembling, 'If I leave him here will he be less a bastard than if I take him to Canada? I understand your

282

royalty and your great families have had many bastards in their history. What about Monmouth, and William the Conqueror? I understand he carried the bar sinister on his shield.'

The countess said, 'There is a great difference between an acknowledged natural child and a disowned bastard. But, I only said that in Canada he would be *looked on* as a bastard. I know he is a child of love, and if my son had not volunteered and given his life, he would be the legitimate heir to Enderby.

'Do you think my son *wanted* to volunteer, when you were waiting here to be his bride? Can you imagine the courage it took to do his duty then? But he did not falter. I know what it costs you to leave your dear son behind. But what do you think Colin would want for his child? Are you less brave than he? Will you deny his child his heritage?'

The countess's words struck cruelly into Marjorie. She was unable to speak. She stared mute and white at the countess.

The earl's face filled with compassion. He had been listening to the two women silently. Looking at Marjorie's haunted face he spoke up. 'Honora, Marjorie is very tired.'

The countess said quickly, 'Dear Marjorie, please don't answer me now. Think of what I've said to you, and in the morning tell me your decision. I have spoken to those in authority and they have told me that, if you consent, they can have the adoption papers prepared without delay and there will be no legal barrier.'

The earl looked startled. 'Honora,' he said. 'When we discussed this I told you that it would not be fair to ask Marjorie to give her son up, dear as he is to us. I only agreed that we should let her know that we are willing to adopt him, if that is her desire.'

Little Colin stirred in his mother's arms, opened sleepy eyes and smiled at her. Marjorie thought: This is a ridiculous nightmare. How can they imagine even for a moment that I would so much as think of giving up my son? She bent and kissed Colin's forehead, and his tiny hand reached out and tangled itself in her blonde hair. She said, 'I am very tired.'

At once the countess was all consideration. 'Of course,' she said. 'I'll show you up to your room myself.'

The earl said gently, 'Will you not allow me to carry little Colin upstairs for you, my dear?'

Marjorie met his warm kind eyes with her own. She placed her sleeping son in his arms. 'Thank you,' she said.

Holding his small grandson tenderly, the earl followed the two women upstairs to the nursery adjoining the room of himself and the countess. Mrs Anderson, as was her custom when Marjorie visited Enderby, had vacated the bed where she always slept beside Colin's crib, so that Marjorie could stay with her son.

The nursery was done out in bright colours and warmed by a fire burning in the small grate. Toys and stuffed animals were scattered about and a rocking horse with a long mane and tail stood in a corner. There were bookcases full of brightly illustrated books, some old and some new – everything that would delight the heart of a small child as he grew up.

Marjorie sank down into the deep chair and the earl put Colin in her arms. He stood looking down at her uncertainly, then he stooped and kissed the top of her head. 'Do have some rest, my dear.'

The countess said, 'We will be dining at eight, but if you don't feel up to it I'll have a tray sent up.'

Marjorie shook her head. 'I'll not require anything else, Lady Rivermere. We had such a large tea. I just want to sleep, if you don't mind.'

'Of course, my dear.' The countess stood for a moment looking down at Marjorie, tiny and weary in the big chair with her son in her arms. 'Don't be afraid, Marjorie. Whatever you decide we will abide by. The earl will take you into Wendover whenever you wish to go. Mrs Anderson is just down the hall if you should need anything in the night and we are sleeping next door.'

Marjorie wondered if the countess were thinking of that other time when she had slipped away while they all slept. She nodded slowly.

'Good night, my dear,' the countess said and turned and walked from the room.

Marjorie was reminded once more of Queen Mary.

In a short while, Colin woke up and Marjorie played with him for an hour. 'What a handsome little boy you are,' she told him, swinging him up in her arms, while he crowed delighted-ly. 'And look at those shoulders. You'll make a fine right-winger for the Maple Leafs.' She sat him on the rocking horse, with her arm around him. 'That was your daddy's horse,' she whispered in his ear.

She blanked from her mind the countess's words. She blanked everything out, all but these moments in this warm sheltered room with her son.

At last he grew tired and she changed him, put him in his crib and tucked the blankets tightly around him. His long dark lashes dropped down on to his cheeks and she watched the gentle movement of his breathing.

She went to bed herself and lay watching the glowing coals in the fireplace. The countess's words had struck deep. She alone had the right to deny her child his heritage. 'But I am his heritage, too,' she whispered fiercely. 'I am his mother.' A remembered sentence from a book she had read leapt into her mind: 'The motherhood that bears and forsakes is less than animal.' I love my child enough to stand against the whole world for him, she thought. Then again she heard the countess say, 'What do you think Colin would want for his child?'

A cold little voice kept whispering to her: 'The countess is right. Colin's son belongs here – Lord Enderby, heir to Rivermere.' She had not dreamed of such a thing for her son. They have given me too big a choice, she thought.

She pictured the time ahead, saw the shame and heartbreak in the faces of her people when she arrived home with her illegitimate baby, saw herself finding work in some strange city, leaving him in the care of strangers through the day. Her mind leapt ahead and she saw him coming crying from school because other children had taunted him with being a bastard. She could take it for herself, but her son did not have to tread that road. Another sunny path was open to him, here in the home of his ancestors, sheltered, protected, honoured. Her love was all she had to give him. Could it ever be enough? My love for you is enough for me, my little son, but what about you? she thought.

With her mind see-sawing to and fro she fell into a troubled sleep. Colin woke her up, crying, and she rushed to pick him up and held him whimpering against her shoulders, while she patted his back and comforted him, until the gas pain passed and he went back to sleep. She kissed his tear-stained little cheek and lay on her back with him on her shoulder, held tight, with his head against her cheek.

'My darling,' she whispered, 'how could I have been fool enough to think, even for a moment, that I could let you go? What if you woke up crying in the night and I wasn't there to comfort you? Together we'll make it. I'll make it up to you. There'll be no great black stags roaming around in Canada, haunting the night. You'll be far removed from all this war and tradition and dying on the battlefield for some English monarch. You'll be playing hockey and baseball and football with other normal little Canadian boys, and going out on Hallowe'en ducking for apples. And I'll put you through university, too, and you'll grow up to be a fine Canadian, free of all this old-world bondage.'

She smiled down joyfully at her sleeping son. 'We'll be together and we'll win. After all, your mama is a soldier.' She felt very happy. She put him back in his crib, tucking the blankets around him and humming lightly to herself.

After she was back in her own bed, lying in the dark, a terrible thought struck her: *What if something should happen to me? What would happen to him then?*

All her indecision returned. If only she had someone to talk to. If only Jessy or Bonny, or Helen, or even Elsie were here. But there was no one here in the still of the night for her to talk to. She thought suddenly of Mrs Anderson in her room down the corridor. There was a gentle kindness in the old Scotswoman and wisdom, too.

She jumped out of bed and put on a robe. Colin was sleeping soundly now, lying on his stomach with his little arms above his head and his face turned sideways. She slipped softly out into the corridor and went towards Mrs Anderson's room. At least she'll tell me if he's happy here, she thought.

As she flitted past the room of the earl and countess, she heard his voice coming through the slightly ajar door. 'Honora, it is too cruel a thing to take Marjorie's baby from her, even if she consents to it.'

'It's best for the child, Teddy, and best for her in the long run.'

'Honora, are you truly thinking of them, or are you thinking of us?'

286

'Did I think of us when I gave two sons to our country, Teddy? If I thought it would be best for our grandson to go to Canada with his mother, do you think I'd raise a finger to stop them? She's only twenty-five. She should not be burdened because she gave her love to our dear son. She sent him to his death with a happiness such as he had never known and a gift greater than he knew. He left behind an heir.'

'He is her son, too, Honora. Do we have the right to break her heart?'

'Hearts do not break, really, Teddy. They scar but they do not break. We all carry scars. Colin's son belongs here with his own heritage, and Marjorie deserves to be free. In the end it will be better for her.'

'I don't see how you can know that, Honora. And if she should agree to have us adopt Colin, why should she not stay here with us, too?'

'A little shadow, moving about this great house, without any real position? You know what the English gentry are. What would she be if she stayed here? Do you think they would ever accept her? And there will be no men here for her to find a husband among. England will teem with single, heart-broken women. Is that what you would wish on her? She's a beautiful girl. I tell you, in her own country her life will be mended again. She's the sort of girl men marry.'

'Nevertheless, I intend to ask her.'

'Do so, if you wish, but she'll refuse,' the countess answered. 'I know what pride and strength and courage she has. She will never consent to such an arrangement. She would have made a great lady.'

'She's a great lady now.'

Marjorie broke loose from the rigid stillness their words had frozen her into, turned and crept back to her room.

Colin was still sleeping. She flung herself down on her knees beside her bed with her arms spread out and buried her face in the covers. Like blood from a deep, internal wound a terrible conviction was welling up in her.

'Oh, God,' she whispered, 'Oh God. Oh God.' Into her mind flashed a picture from her Bible stories of Jesus kneeling in Gethsemane.

After a while she climbed into bed and pulled the covers up

287

under her chin. Exhaustion took over and she fell asleep.

Towards morning she dreamed that she woke up, took the baby from his crib and crept down the stairs to flee with him from Enderby. She was almost at the bottom when Colin appeared before her. He smiled and shook his head at her, took young Colin from her arms and carried him back to the nursery, with her following him, her heart leaping with joy. 'I thought you were dead,' she said. 'I thought you were dead.'

He shook his head and, still smiling tenderly, put young Colin firmly back in his crib and turned to her with open arms. Marjorie woke up with a jerk. She sat up with the tears running down her cheeks.

Her dream was so real, it took a moment for it to fade. Colin was making little fussing wake-up noises and the sunlight was shining against the curtains. Marjorie swung her legs over and sat on the edge of the bed. There was a coldness like death inside of her, but no longer any indecision. She knew what she must do.

Someone was tapping on her door.

Chapter 32

It was Mrs Anderson, bringing Colin's bottle. She came quickly across to Marjorie, concern leaping in her eyes. 'Are you sick, Miss Marjorie?'

Marjorie shook her head.

Mrs Anderson stared at her dubiously. 'I've brought Master Colin his bottle. Would you like to feed it to him, Miss Marjorie?'

'No. You give it to him, Mrs Anderson, and he'll have to be changed. And don't call me *Miss* Marjorie. Just call me *Marjorie*.'

Mrs Anderson started to say something, stopped, and took Colin from his crib and removed his diaper. He wriggled and cooed, looking at his mother, trying to catch her attention.

Marjorie stared straight ahead, the colour completely gone from her face.

Silently, Mrs Anderson started to give Colin his bottle. He wriggled away and pushed the bottle from his lips, pouting and looking towards his mother.

'I think he wants you to feed him,' Mrs Anderson said, smiling.

'He'll have to get used to someone else feeding him,' Marjorie said shortly. Mrs Anderson looked bewildered, then understanding widened her eyes.

Marjorie said, turning her blue eyes full on the older woman, 'You were Colin's nurse when he was young, were you not, Mrs Anderson? Tell me, was he a happy little boy? Is this a happy place for a boy to grow up in?'

Mrs Anderson's old face lit up. 'That he was. You never saw a happier little boy than Master Colin, unless it was Master Raif. He was a wild lad, though, that Master Raif, always setting everyone by the ear. But Master Colin was always such a kind wee lad – Oh, a real little man, mind you, but gentle – with the little things, I mean – animals and birds and such. I mind the time young Master Raif brought home a frog and Colin let it go.'

There were tears in both women's eyes by the time she had finished telling Marjorie the story of Colin's row with his brother over the poor captive frog.

'And young Master Colin, is he a happy baby here too?'

Mrs Anderson said slowly, looking down at Colin, who had finally consented to taking his bottle, 'Ay, he's a very happy little boy.'

'Mrs Anderson, do you think he knows I'm his mother?'

Mrs Anderson nodded wisely. 'He knows, Miss Marjorie, though he's been more with us than with you. It's an instinct they have. Have ye not seen how his wee face lights up whenever ye come to visit him? And see how fretful he is now because you're not giving him his bottle.'

Marjorie winced. She squeezed the older woman's shoulder. 'You feed him, Mrs Anderson. I'm going to get dressed and go downstairs.' She left the room abruptly and went to the bathroom.

Mrs Anderson stared after her stiff back. 'Poor lass,' she whispered. 'Poor lass.' Then she looked down into Colin's little face and gathered him more tightly to her. 'But I hope she means what I think she means.'

When Marjorie returned to the room she found Mrs Meadows had left cups of tea for her and Mrs Anderson. She drank hers while she dressed, glad of the stimulation. Colin watched her from Mrs Anderson's arms with his lip drooping and wide, bewildered brown eyes.

'Will you care for Colin this morning, Mrs Anderson, please?' Marjorie asked.

She could not bear to have him in the room with her when she told the countess and earl what she must tell them. She left quickly.

They were already in the breakfast room. They greeted her affectionately, only starting slightly to see her dressed to leave with her peaked hat on her head, her bag slung over her shoulder, carrying her haversack.

The countess said, 'I hope you slept well, my dear. Mrs

Meadows will bring breakfast in to us in a few minutes.'
The earl stepped forward to escort her to a chair.

Marjorie stopped him with a gesture, and stood facing them both with her shoulders back and her small chin in the air. 'I've been thinking about what you said last night. I've decided you're right. Colin's son belongs here in his ancestral home. How soon can you arrange for me to sign the adoption papers?'

A light came into their faces, like the light she had seen when they saw she was pregnant. The countess's delicate fingers released their grip on the arm of her chair. The earl came swiftly to Marjorie, concern rising in his eyes, and put his hand on her shoulder.

'My dear girl, will you not allow me to escort you to a chair?' he begged. 'You're so pale.'

Mrs Meadows came in at that moment with the breakfast. The countess stood up and came to Marjorie. 'Do, please, come and have some breakfast, dear child. We can discuss this after you've had something to eat.'

Marjorie shook her head. 'No thank you, I'm not hungry.' She felt, strangely, as if she were looking at them from inside a glass cage.

'Oh, do please, at least, come and have a cup of tea,' the earl pleaded.

Marjorie shook her head. She wanted to laugh wildly. How incomprehensible these English are, she thought. I give away my son and they expect me to sit here quietly drinking tea. The earl will be telling me about the blood line of old Kettle's horses next. She felt a mad urge to scream at the countess, sitting there regally at the head of the table, and throw her haversack in her calm, still face. 'No thank you,' she said. 'Mrs Meadows has already given me tea.'

The countess said, meeting her eyes full on, 'You are a brave soldier, Marjorie. I can offer you no consolation, except to tell you that your son will grow up lacking nothing here in the home of his father and his ancestors.'

Nothing except his mother's love, Marjorie thought. But I suppose he won't miss that. No doubt they'll pack him off to some boarding school when he's scarcely out of diapers to make a man of him in the English tradition.

'If you'll make the arrangements for me to sign the adoption papers, I'd like to return to London as soon as possible,' she said. 'In the meantime, I'd like to go for a walk in the gardens, if you don't mind.'

'I'll phone the office in Wendover immediately after breakfast,' the countess said. 'They won't be open until then. Shall I ask Mrs Anderson to bring Colin down so you can take him in his pram?'

'No thank you, I'm going by myself. Please excuse me.'

'Certainly,' the countess said.

Marjorie turned and marched from the room.

She took the path she had travelled with Colin on that last morning before he left. It had been early summer then, and all nature had been sparkling. Today a tinge of autumn was in the air, but the sun shone from a clear sky and the roses were blooming richly. Their scent was heavy and warm.

Upstairs in the nursery Mrs Anderson would be amusing and caring for Colin. She ground her nails into her palms.

She found the secret path down to Smugglers' Cove. She wriggled under the stone wall and lay on the cool carpet where she had lain with Colin, looking up through the branches of the rhododendron to the patch of blue sky. She felt again the warmth of Colin's lips and her groin ached with the remembered ecstasy of their lovemaking. How short-lived had been her exquisite joy. She turned over and dug her fingers into the earth. 'Remember you are my wife.' How sincerely he had said it.

But not legally, Colin, she thought bitterly. In the eyes of the world our son is a bastard. And I must give him up to make him honoured. Yet, if that German gunner had been a less expert marksman I would be Lady Enderby, honoured and respected, and loved for my son. But I'm the same person. She sat up and looked at her hands. These are the same hands. I haven't grown talons. My feet, my body, everything is the same as if I were a married woman. She buried her face in her hands. 'Oh, Colin, Colin,' she moaned.

She was talking to empty air. Colin's presence, which she had felt so strongly all these months, was gone from her now – ever since he had placed his son back in his crib in her dream last night. *As if he has given me the message he stayed to give and now he's gone*, she thought. 'You knew you could trust me

292

to do what you wished,' she whispered. 'You knew it was safe to leave, now.'

She stood quickly and brushed her uniform and straightened her skirt. A tiny smile touched her lips and for a moment her dimples showed. She had done the same thing that other time. But she hadn't fooled Lady Rivermere. Lady Rivermere had known.

She could not bring herself to return yet to the house. She went, instead, to the stables.

Minnette was in her stall and Marjorie patted her glossy neck. 'We never did get back to Beecher's Brook,' she whispered.

Marjorie left the stables and went to her favourite seat beside the fish pond. She sat on the rustic bench and watched the bright golden fish darting about. This was the spot where she always stopped the pram when she took little Colin for his long walks, and sat down to watch the fish. But she always saw more of his little face than she did of the fish.

She looked around her. This is a truly lovely place for a child to grow up in, she thought. If Colin had come back, I know we would have had many other children. There's no way to explain the joy of holding your child in your arms – a joy that grows daily as you watch them develop. But I won't be here to watch my little boy grow – to see him take his first step. Someone else will hold his hand. She closed her eyes and saw in her mind little Colin running along the garden paths, sniffing the flowers, chasing butterflies, asking a hundred questions. I'm sure he'll be kind, like his daddy. I'm sure he won't hurt the little creatures, she thought.

She jumped up. She must stop thinking. She looked up the path and started. Mrs Anderson was approaching, pushing Colin in his pram. She was tempted to turn and run, but she went to meet them. Colin saw his mother and crowed to attract her attention.

Mrs Anderson said hesitantly, 'Miss Marjorie, the earl and countess asked me to find you. They said – the man has come with the – papers for you to sign.'

Marjorie felt the colour drain from her cheeks. 'Thank you, Mrs Anderson.'

Mrs Anderson said gently, 'Would ye like to wheel wee

Colin back to the house with you?'

'No.' Ignoring Colin's entreating eyes, she fled towards the house. If he were in the room with me I couldn't bear it, she thought.

She slowed in the next few paces and returned to the other woman. 'Mrs Anderson, I know they must have told you I've decided to give up my baby.' She held out her hand imploringly to the old nurse. 'Mrs Anderson,' she whispered, coming close to her, 'will you take good care of my little son?'

Tears were running down the nurse's old face. 'Lassie, lassie, I will. I will. We all will. The wee lad will be happy here. May the good Lord bless ye. A proper lady you are. Would ye no like to wheel him back to the house with you?'

Words choked in Marjorie's throat. She shook her head and turned and walked quickly up the path.

The earl and countess were in the library with the man who had come with the adoption papers. It was the same man who had registered Colin's birth five months ago. He insisted that Colin be in the room when the papers were being signed.

'There must be no doubt as to the identity of the child you are adopting,' he told the earl and countess. 'And I'll need another witness to the signatures.'

Events became an unreal blur to Marjorie, as if nature had mercifully thrown a curtain over her mind. She was conscious of Mrs Anderson coming into the library with little Colin in her arms. But it was as if she were in another, detached world.

'Is this your son?' the registrar asked.

'Yes,' Marjorie said. 'Yes that is my son.' She heard the man's voice, coming to her from a vast distance, explaining the procedure to her.

Then the earl and countess signed the papers and fixed the great seal of Enderby on them. The registrar handed the pen to Marjorie. 'You sign here,' he told her.

Startlingly, Colin wailed loudly. Marjorie froze with the pen poised above the line. The paper was advancing and receding in front of her. I mustn't faint. I mustn't faint, she thought. She remembered what the MO had told them back in basic training when they were being inoculated: 'If you feel you are going to faint, bend over and tie your shoelace.'

'My shoelace,' she whispered and bent over and untied and

294

tied it. The world steadied around her again. She straightened up and, while the earl and countess looked on, white-faced, with a steady hand she signed – Marjorie Hatfield. It stood out accusingly on the white paper.

Colin was sobbing and refusing to be comforted by Mrs Anderson. Marjorie threw down the pen and took him in her arms. He sobbed into her neck, clinging to her with his little arms.

Oh, God, Marjorie thought. It's as if he knows I'm leaving him. She turned her back on the others and crossed to the window, tossing him up playfully in her arms. The tears stopped and he gurgled gleefully at her, his eyes bright on her face. She hugged him close and his little fingers twined in her hair. She kissed the top of his head.

The registrar was putting the copy of the adoption papers in his briefcase. Marjorie said to him, 'Will you give me a ride into Wendover, please?'

'Of course.'

'Marjorie, my dear!' the countess exclaimed. 'Teddy will drive you to Wendover. There's no need for you to catch a ride. You've had nothing at all to eat today. Do please stay and have something with us and let Teddy drive you in afterwards.'

Marjorie shook her head. 'No. I wish to go now – with him.'

The earl's face was distressed. He came quickly to Marjorie and put his arm across her shoulders. 'Marjorie, there's no need for you to go to Canada and leave your son behind. Stay here with us. You can live as our daughter.'

Marjorie looked up into his eyes, so kind, so like Colin's. 'Thank you,' she said gently, 'But I must go back to Canada.'

Gently she disengaged Colin's little fingers from her hair. The countess's embroidery scissors were lying on the small table at her elbow. She picked them up and snipped one of Colin's brown curls. Then she kissed the top of his head and placed him in the earl's arms. 'Please,' she whispered, 'be sure, if he wants to put a frog back in the pond, to let him.'

She turned back to the countess standing motionless beside the desk where they had all signed the adoption papers. She took Colin's ring from her finger and held it out to her. The great ruby flashed in the sunlight between the fire of the diamonds.

The countess drew back slightly, rejecting it with a gesture. 'Marjorie, my dear, keep it, I beg you.'

Marjorie shook her head. 'Thank you. But it must stay with the Enderby heir, to be given to his future bride when he becomes engaged. Please take it and keep it for my son to give to his future wife.'

Wordlessly, the countess let her drop the ring into her hand.

Carefully Marjorie put the lock of Colin's hair inside her shoulder purse. The registrar was waiting for her with his briefcase in his hand. 'I'm ready to go now,' Marjorie told him, turning towards the door.

The countess put out her hand in an almost imploring gesture. 'Marjorie, dear, will you not say goodbye?' Her voice had a tremor in it.

Marjorie looked into her proud, aloof face and saw that her lips were compressed exactly as she had seen them that morning when his friends brought the news that Colin had been shot down in flames. Impulsively she put out her hand to the other woman. The countess took it and then, swiftly, drew Marjorie into her arms and kissed her. 'May God go with you, you noble girl,' she whispered. 'You will always be in our hearts. I'm sorry you are not my daughter-in-law.'

Marjorie could not speak. She left the other woman's embrace and turned towards the door. The earl intercepted her, with Colin in his arms. 'My dear, my dear, will you not reconsider and stay here with us?' he begged. Tears were streaming down his cheeks. Colin was nestled close to his grandfather, smiling contentedly.

Marjorie shook her head. Then swiftly she reached up and kissed his wet cheek. 'I'm sorry I never learned how to jump Beecher's Brook.'

Mrs Anderson was weeping. 'May God bless you, my Lady,' she said brokenly.

Marjorie went to her and kissed her withered cheek. 'Take care of him, Mrs Anderson,' she whispered. 'Thank you for everything.'

She turned and marched from the room. The dogs sprang up as she crossed the great hall and ran to nuzzle against her, with wagging tails. She patted their heads. 'He'll love you as soon as he's a little bigger,' she whispered. 'You take care of the little lord, too.'

The registrar was waiting for her in his car. They did not speak on the journey to the station.

Back in the library at Enderby the earl, holding Colin in his arms, turned to speak to his wife when Marjorie had gone. His eyes widened in astonishment. The countess was in tears. 'So brave,' she whispered. 'So brave and so good. How happy our son would have been with her.'

Colin started to whimper.

'I'll fetch him his bottle,' Mrs Anderson said.

Chapter 33

The journey back to London was a blur. Marjorie felt as if her whole body were being torn apart, like the moment when she gave birth to her son, and she could not breathe. Perspiration ran down from under the brim of her hat. She stared out of the train window. Hills and trees and hedges flashed by like pictures in a dream.

Forty-three Company barracks was deserted. Marjorie packed her kitbag and threw away her letters from home and an old, almost-empty lipstick she had been hoarding. One thing about being in the army, she thought, it doesn't take long to pack all your belongings.

She had been told she would be allowed to keep her water bottle, her tin hat, her kitbag and haversack and one uniform and greatcoat when she was discharged. I wonder what I'll do with them? she thought. If it comes to that, I wonder what I'll do with me?

She looked down at herself. Her eyes fastened on her slender, well-shaped hands. Hands are strange things, she thought. They can hold a steering wheel, or a bedpan for a wounded solider, or they can caress a man, or comfort a baby – *Or with a tiny movement of the fingers they can sign him away from you for ever.* She put her hand to her mouth and sank her teeth into the finger that had held the pen.

Jessy came in at five o'clock and found her sitting on the edge of her bed staring down at her kitbag and her haversack with her tin hat strapped on to it packed and ready to leave. She stood for a moment, taking in her friend with a lightning glance, then crossed from the doorway and stood looking down at Marjorie with a half smile curving her lips.

'What's the matter, Marj?' she said softly. 'You look like

the last act of *Camille*, played in uniform.'

Marjorie looked up at her from cavernous blue eyes. 'I've given away my son.'

Jessy sat down across from her on Helen's vacant bed. She tossed her hat down beside her and lit a cigarette.

'I thought this would happen. Do you want to tell me about it?'

Marjorie felt the kindness coming from Jessy, penetrating the wall of bewildering pain smothering her. With the words rushing out of her in a low, steady torrent, she told Jessy what had happened from the moment she arrived at Enderby to claim her son.

She reached out and caught Jessy's hands. 'Oh, Jess, did I do the right thing?'

Jessy was silent, then she said slowly, 'That's the trouble, you don't know until the final curtain goes down and all the reviews are in if you have a turkey or a hit. But, feeling like you do about your baby, and what it's costing you to give him up, I'd say there's a fair chance you made the right decision. When it gets to the final show, the decisions we make for someone else's benefit and not our own usually turn out to be the right ones.'

She squeezed Marjorie's cold fingers. 'Now I have something to tell you. One of the Army Show girls is sick, and they're putting on a big show for our boys who are still over there across the pond. They're flying me over at six o'clock tonight to fill in for a couple of days.'

Marjorie turned white. 'You mean, you won't be here when I leave in the morning? You mean, this is goodbye?' she whispered. She felt that the last support was being kicked out from under her. In a wave it came over her how much she loved Jessy Cole – not the kind of love they all made fun of and the army frowned on, like Dotty and Mike – but like the sister she had always longed for. The others, too, Bonny and Helen and even Elsie – between them all was a bond holding them closer than sisters. Here was no questioning of ethics. They were just for each other. They were comrades.

One more goodbye. The true story of war – not the bloodshed, but the goodbyes. The first hello to a sweetheart or a friend or a place you loved was the first breath of *goodbye*.

Jessy smiled suddenly, her quick warm smile that could light up a room. 'Remember, Marj, when we first went to take the transport course at Currie Barracks, we'd never seen a men's Nissen hut before and they stuck us in one, and some of the girls thought the latrines were little laundry troughs and started washing out their undies in them?'

Marjorie said, 'Machine-Gun Cassidy almost had a fit.'

'I always thought Sergeant Cassidy was in the wrong army. She would have been great in the Gestapo,' Jessy said. 'Remember how she came in and bellowed at that little mouse Timms for talking in her sleep after lights out?'

'What a bunch of babes-in-the-woods we were.'

Jessy looked mischievously at her. 'Some of us knew a little bit more about the birds and the bees than others. Remember when some humorous male soldier sneaked into the entrance to our hut and left a bunch of blown-up French letters hanging from the ceiling, and you saw them in the morning and came rushing back and said, "There's a whole bunch of little balloons hanging out there"? I thought old McFee would come apart laughing.'

'She wasn't a babe in the woods,' Marjorie said.

'I guess not. She was on her third husband then, and she was having an affair with a major in Ordnance.'

'I remember how shocked Nelson was with her. She thought she was going straight down below.'

'Mrs Nelson thought everyone was going straight down below,' Jessy said with a laugh. 'I think she just joined the army to save souls. We used to call her Old Jimminy Crickets.'

'You know that's nearly four and a half years ago, Jess,' Marjorie said wistfully. 'We aren't the same people we were back at Currie Barracks. I feel as if I'm a shell – as if there's nothing left inside of me.'

Jessy said earnestly, 'But there is, Marj. There is. You think it's all over, but you'll go back to Canada and some day you'll find someone and get married and have children, like the countess told you.'

'I wish you were coming with me to Canada, Jess,' Marjorie said sadly.

Jessy smiled at her. 'And I wish you were staying here in

300

England. But I have to get ready. They'll be coming to pick me up soon.'

Marjorie watched silently as Jessy packed her haversack. When she was finished she produced a little bottle of French liqueur. 'One of our boys liberated it and he gave it to me,' she said with a smile. 'Just enough for one small drink each. Join me this once. Let's drink a toast to us and the years we've spent together – to Bonny and Helen and Elsie and all the rest of the soldier girls.' She tilted the bottle and swallowed, then handed it to Marjorie.

'To us,' Marjorie said and choked down a gulp of the sweet-tasting drink, past the lump in her throat.

The girl on orderly duty downstairs called up, 'Hey, Jess, they're here for you.'

They stood up. Marjorie held out her hand. Jessy took it in hers and then she pulled Marjorie into her arms and kissed her cheek. 'Say hello to Canada for me and write to me when you get back,' she said huskily. 'Just send it care of the Haymarket Theatre.'

'I will, Jess, I will,' Marjorie choked out.

'Break a leg,' Jessy said, smiling at her, and swung out the door.

'Soldiers don't cry,' Marjorie whispered. 'Soldiers don't cry.' She sunk down on the bed. Silence hung like fog in the room. She looked at the empty beds with the blankets neatly folded in little sheaves at the foot. An overwhelming terror of loneliness rolled over her. I was never this scared when the V-bombs were coming over, she thought. We were all together then.

She looked at her watch. It was just past six o'clock. Back at Enderby they would be having late tea in the countess's sitting room. Mrs Anderson would have brought Colin down from the nursery, if indeed he had been up there at all. She suspected he spent very little of the day in his nursery. It would not be surprising if he even had his daytime naps in the big pram pulled up close to the countess wherever she happened to be sitting.

She pictured the warm, intimate scene with the countess pouring tea and them all doting over Colin gurgling in his pram. In no time he'll have completely forgotten me, she thought. Mrs Anderson will finish her tea quickly so she can give Colin his bottle. He's such a good-natured little boy. The earl loves to pick him up. Like me, he loves the affectionate way he puts his little arms up around your neck and hugs you. He was always so glad to see me. I think he really did know that I'm his mother.

She put her hands on her stomach. 'And why wouldn't you, my darling? I carried you here, sheltered and safe all those long months,' she whispered.

She stared again at the empty room. The watch ticked loudly on her wrist. How different from when they had all arrived in London, talking and laughing and Bonny slamming things around and swearing. With a feeling of startled guilt, she thought, I even miss the V-bomb raids.

She whispered Colin's name, trying to recapture the feeling of his presence that had sustained her all through the long months. But now there was only a blank wall of silence. Colin was gone.

She jumped to her feet. She must get out of this empty room. Go somewhere. Anywhere. Run from this searing longing for a little brown-eyed boy she was leaving behind for ever.

She rushed down on to the street outside 43 Company and stood bewildered, looking out at the empty square. Where could she go?

The George and Horses! I must see it once more before I go, she thought.

She had no trouble finding it again. She knew how to find her way around London now. The pub looked the same, but the crowd had changed. The feverish atmosphere was gone and there were only a smattering of uniforms in the crowd. Those servicemen there looked subdued, sitting quietly at their tables with drinks in front of them. Piccadilly Commandos no longer swarmed, hungry-eyed, around the bar. Marjorie's was the lone Canadian uniform in the pub.

She found the table where she had sat with Colin and the same round-cheeked barmaid waited on her. She did not remember Marjorie. Marjorie ordered a brandy. She gulped a little, almost choked and then took a larger gulp and then another. She had had nothing to eat since the previous night and it went to her head almost at once. She could feel the heat

302

of it in her blood. Recklessly, she finished it and ordered another.

She sipped it more slowly. It did not burn so much. The room became a sort of soft blur around her. Her table was a little island. She looked from a great distance at the other patrons on their separate little islands. 'You are a funny little soldier girl.' How his brown eyes had twinkled with humour when he spoke the words, and his voice with its English drawl had sent funny little shivers up her spine. He was so handsome in his airman's uniform with the wings on his chest and the row of ribbons.

That night was as clear in her mind as if it had happened yesterday – the happy feeling that had come over her, banishing all her loneliness, as if she had belonged with him from the beginning of her life.

'Oh, Colin, Colin,' she whispered. 'My love, my life, my true husband, what am I to do?'

She felt as if she couldn't breathe. Her forehead was sweating, the room was spinning and she was seeing two of the barmaid. Oh, God, I'm going to be sick, she thought. She stared down at the table, fighting down the nausea and dizziness, trying to stop shaking.

A voice spoke to her, 'Miss Marjorie, lor' love us, what are you doing 'ere all alone? Are you sick?'

She looked up into the concerned face of Blaine, who was standing beside her table. Relief flooded her. She reached out her hands to him. 'Oh, Blaine, I'm so glad to see you,' she whispered. 'I'm going back to Canada tomorrow. I – I just had to see the George and Horses once more before I left London. I feel so sick. It's the brandy. I'm not used to it, you know, and I haven't had anything to eat all day.'

Blaine sat down across from her. ' 'Eaven 'elp us, Canada,' he said. 'We can't 'ave you doing things like that.' He caught the barmaid's eye. 'Bring us one of those meat pies and a cuppa and some chips, will you ducks?' he said. 'As soon as you get a bit of grub into you, I'll take you 'ome, Miss Marjorie.'

Marjorie thought, Of all the people in the world you're the only one I would have wanted to see here tonight. She knew how deeply he had loved Colin and how he had grieved when he was shot down. 'Oh, Blaine, thank you,' she whispered, reaching across the table to clasp his hands in hers. 'I do want to get back to barracks. But I can't eat anything. I feel so sick.'

'You 'ave to eat, miss,' he said. 'It'll put you right. Can't 'ave young Master Colin's mum making 'erself sick, now can we? I suppose you'll be turning 'im into a real little Canadian when you get 'im 'ome.'

Marjorie stared back at him, her blue eyes huge in her white face. 'Oh, Blaine,' she whispered, 'oh Blaine.' Then she told him what had happened at Enderby. ' . . . So I guess you're going to make a little English lord of him after all,' she finished.

Blaine patted her hand gently. His eyes were full of tears. 'It's a proper little 'eroine you are, Canada. I knew Master Colin had picked 'imself a real lidy, the first time I set eyes on you with 'im. Now eat up that pie and drink your tea and I'll take you 'ome. And don't you worry about the young lord. We'll tike good care of 'im. Only I wish you was staying, too.'

Before Blaine let her out of his taxi outside 43 Company, Marjorie leaned over and kissed him on the cheek. 'Thank you, Blaine. Thank you for everything. Now you can have the 'ole street back to drive on.' She fled upstairs to her room.

Completely exhausted and with her head still spinning a bit from the brandy, she fell asleep at once. She dreamed that she was marrying Colin in the little church in Wendover, dressed in the white wedding dress that had been his great-great-grandmother's. He was handsome beside her at the altar in his morning suit, with a flower in his buttonhole. Ashley was beside her in her bridesmaid's dress. Colin slipped the gold band on to her finger and kissed her lips. But she was distressed and whispered in his ear, 'But Colin, I shouldn't be wearing white, I'm not a virgin.'

He laughed happily at her. 'Of course not, my funny little soldier girl, you're the mother of my son and my wife long since. This is just a ceremony.'

When they turned to go up the aisle, the church was full of tenants, with Blaine and the foreman and Giles and Mrs Meadows and Mrs Anderson all close to the front, beaming at her. And in the very front row were the earl and countess, smiling joyfully, with baby Colin sitting on the countess's lap and gurgling at them.

Marjorie woke up smiling. The dream had been so real that it took her some moments to realize it had been only a dream. She looked down at her bare ring finger. It was morning and she was going back to Canada alone.

Three other CWACs joined the compartment with Marjorie when she boarded the train at Waterloo, but they were from another company and Marjorie did not know them. After saying hello, she turned her face to the window, while they conversed in subdued tones. Marjorie thought: How silent everyone is since the war ended. You'd think we were going into battle, instead of going home.

How excited we all were on our way over here on the ship. They put us on the first-class deck with the officers, because they thought we'd be safer there than below with the enlisted men. The Other Ranks didn't think so. She smiled slightly. We would have been safe anywhere with that gimlet-eyed Captain Hawks watching over us.

It seemed so long ago. So much had happened since then and yet it was all so clear in her mind – the creak of the ship ploughing through the seas on its way to the war zone. The little band of CWACs and officers of the army gathered around the piano singing war songs. Then they all fell silent as Jessy took over, with her throaty contralto and tip-tilted sexy eyes. They didn't want to let her stop. That was the same night they had the submarine scare. Poor Elsie, she almost died of fright. I don't really blame her. That ocean looked so vast and cold, Marjorie thought. And we had no way of knowing whether it was for real or only a drill.

Well, we won't have to worry about subs this trip.

As the train moved slowly out of London, the sun was bathing the city affectionately in its warm soft glow. Marjorie watched it lighting up the flowers blooming in the window boxes and tiny patches of gardens.

It shone peacefully on ancient cobbled streets and church spires, on gaping heaps of rubble and bricks where Hitler's Luftwaffe had dropped their bombs in a vain attempt to conquer this ancient indomitable city that had weathered endless centuries, survived plague and famine, fire and rebellion; and stood immovable, like this British race had stood, saying to the centuries, 'Bring what you will, we will be here still, going about our business as usual.'

She had seen the spirit that moved across this land, that ancient devotion to duty, in the old earl's face, in the indomitable face of the countess; and in the face of Ashley, and in Colin's warm, kind, steady eyes.

They left London behind and were out in the countryside. Marjorie looked with an aching longing on the serenity of villages and patchwork-quilt fields and ancient oaks and thatched cottages and gentle, rolling, green hills. The countess was right, when I coupled my body and soul with Colin's I became an Englishwoman, an Enderby, she thought.

The soldiers going on board the *New Amsterdam*, when she had boarded with the others to come over here, had set up a cheer for the little contingent of CWACs, singing 'Roll Out the Barrel' and the CWAC marching song . . . That first green Christmas in England, they had all cried as they listened to Bing Crosby on the wireless singing 'I'm Dreaming of a White Christmas' – Bonny dashing tears from her eyes, saying, 'I'll be so glad to get away from this shitty Limey fog, when I see snow again I'll roll in it. I'll eat it.' Jessy was always adaptable. No matter where she was she became a part of everything. Helen only wanted to be with Carl. Elsie – she smiled slightly, thinking of Elsie, terrified of the V-bombs, getting treats from home. Oh, and Carl – until Major Ellis came into her life.

I'm glad Bonny and Helen and Elsie came through it with their loves and are home again, she thought. And Jessy – Jessy is a survivor. Only Marjorie knew how deep a wound Jessy carried since Bob Anders was killed. But Jessy wouldn't look back, and her heart was big enough to love many people. She had the gaiety of spirit and the courage to demand that life bring her a fresh rose. Some day, Marjorie thought, I can see Jess's name in letters a foot high – And I'm going home a shell. Mrs Anderson will be giving Colin his bath now. He always looked so darling when I bathed him, with his little body all rosy and glowing and his eyes shining. How proud Colin would have been of him. *Soldiers don't cry.*

But I won't have that to hold on to much longer, she thought. Soon I won't be a soldier; I'll be a civilian. God knows what I'll do with the rest of my life.

The ship waiting at the dock was the *Queen Elizabeth*, the

largest liner afloat, converted to a troopship when the war came.

Marjorie fell in with the CWACs lined up on the dock, loaded down with kitbags and haversacks. The CWAC officer in charge put them at ease and, with that patience they had learned through endless parades, they sat down on their kitbags to wait.

Marjorie watched as rank upon rank of sober-faced men marched silently past and up the gangplank into the great ship that was to carry them home. A soldier in the uniform of the South Saskatchewan Regiment saw her and broke ranks. He came to her, his white teeth flashing in his dark face.

'It's the little angel,' he said, his black eyes gleaming mischievously.

It was the soldier who had given her the ring with the Enderby crest.

'You don' look so good little angel,' he said. 'You look sad. Dem big blue eyes not shining, no more. You lose your man in war, I think. Never mind. You pretty little angel. You find someone else, damn fast.' His white teeth flashed again. 'You come to Saskatchewan, I be glad to be your boyfriend. These Limey girls no damn good. Want to marry you. I'd marry *you*, all right, plenty fast.'

Marjorie smiled back at him, showing her deep dimples for a moment. 'Thank you, I'll remember that.' She caught his hand in hers. 'Tell me, the ring you gave me. The man who gave it to you, your friend – What was his name?'

He laughed. 'Oh, dat heap damn funny friend of mine. He have to volunteer for crazy mission – get himself killed, because he say Enderby always die for king. He say he some kind of damn aristocrat.' He laughed again. 'He just damn big halfbreed Indian like me.'

Marjorie drew in her breath swiftly. 'That day he went on that expedition – the day he was killed – do you remember what day it was?'

'Damn right I do,' he answered. 'That day we lose so damn many men I think maybe none of us be left. July third, she were.'

The sergeant in charge of the platoon bellowed at him, 'Get back in line, LaPlant, or we'll leave you here to be a Limey!'

'Got to go, little angel.' He grinned at her. 'Don't forget, you come to Prince Albert, I marry you – big gopher ranch in bush.' With a flash of white teeth he was gone.

Marjorie sat trembling. So the ring was genuine. He really was an Enderby and the last of his line of the family, too. It really had been the end of the house of Enderby, except for the child in her womb.

The end of the long file of men was passing the contingent of CWACs. The officer in charge called the CWACs to their feet and gave the order to fall in behind the men.

They marched three abreast. Marjorie was on the outside of the column. The smell of the sea was strong as they marched towards the gangplank that led into the ship. She remembered Colin telling her with a smile of fond remembrance how he loved the sea, and the fun he had had as a child when they crossed the Channel for a holiday on the continent with his family. Would baby Colin take those same trips? But the earl and countess were growing older. Who would go with him – Lady Ashley, his godmother? Would he ever wonder about his own mother? What would they tell him about her?

There were no bands playing today as they embarked on their homeward journey, as there had been when they were boarding to come over. Just the thud of marching feet, echoing. There was something so relentless in the thud of marching feet – inevitable, like fate striding forward – left, right. Left. Right. One foot in front of the other – going forward to someone else's command. Swing those arms. Get them Up, UP. Just the length of the dock and she would be off England's shore for ever.

A coldness was spreading inside of her. Icy little beads of moisture were gathering under her hatband. A steel band was tightening slowly around her forehead.

The world was unreal. She was not here. Her feet were moving on their own. Left. Right. Left. Right. The sound was louder. It seemed that a new pair of feet was marching beside her. A voice said, 'You are a funny little soldier girl.'

I've gone mad, she thought. She kept her eyes straight ahead. Left. Right. Left. Right.

'Marjorie, my darling. LOOK AT ME.'

She turned her head. I *have* gone mad. Or I've died walking down this dock. That must be it, she thought.

His face was thinner and older looking and there was a scar running from the corner of his right eye back to his ear, and he walked with a limp. His eyes were full of love and tenderness and brimming with tears, and yet they had a twinkle in them, too. She turned her head away and looked to the front again – Left. Right . . . A firm hand reached out and took her arm and pulled her out of the column of marching girls.

This could not be a dream. That hand was too real and warm. That touch too familiar. She cried out. The arms cradled her against a warm living chest and she smelled the clean masculine scent and the uniform. The lips were on her lips, then they were kissing her face and her eyes and the dimples beside her mouth, burying themselves in her hair. They were murmuring her name over and over, like a prayer.

She closed her eyes and swayed against him. 'Colin. Colin. I'm dreaming. Or have I died, too, and gone to heaven? You can't be real. They saw you shot down in flames. *And I saw Athelstane.*'

'Well, I jolly well *am* real.' There was nothing other-world about that voice. It had the old teasing note in it. 'I'm much too hungry and thirsty – among other things – to be a ghost. Now, darling, for heaven's sake, do let us get off this dock before that fierce-looking lady who's leading you comes back and drags you on to that ship.'

Life surged back into Marjorie. The blood pounded through her veins. It was no dream. It was Colin, her Colin. Alive, real, in the flesh. Now, I know how Saint Thomas felt when he touched the nail marks in Jesus's hands, she thought. Then she said a quick prayer for being so presumptuous as to make the comparison. I who am so undeserving, she thought. 'Thank you, God,' she whispered. 'Oh thank you.' Jessy was right. There is a big Director in the sky.

Colin led her from the dock, with his arm around her, holding her against him, looking down lovingly into her face and smiling. 'I say, what a sombre look. You're supposed to look happy, you know. If you don't cheer up, I shall begin to think you've found another husband.'

His teasing words brought her to the full realization of the miracle that was happening to her. She was so overwhelmed that tears rushed down her cheeks.

'There, you see, you're crying,' he said. 'I suppose I shall have to go away and get myself shot down again.'

Marjorie cried out.

He laughed gently. 'Come now, I want to see that dimple.'

Joy bubbled up in her. She laughed, suddenly, joyously, like a little girl and the dimples came into her face.

Colin stopped and kissed her. He gathered her close in the shelter of his arms and held her and kissed her, as if he would never let her go.

When at last he did let her go, Marjorie said, bewildered, 'I can't understand it. If you were a prisoner, why were we never notified? How could you have escaped and how did you know where to find me today?'

'I'll tell you the whole story when we get off this dock. They flew me into the airport this morning and the first person I bumped into as I was leaving there was Blaine. He brought me here. He's waiting for us at the George and Horses, just around the corner from this dock. There's a George and Horses in every town, you know. I think we rather need a brandy.'

'Oh, dear,' Marjorie said in sudden dismay. 'I'm AWOL.'

Colin laughed. 'And with an officer, too,' he said. 'Never mind, after tomorrow there'll be few ladies in England who outrank you.'

Blaine – he had seen Blaine. Then he must know. 'Blaine must have told you about . . .' Her voice trailed off.

'Our son,' he broke in. His eyes filled with tears. 'My dear, sweet little Marjorie. What hell you must have been through.'

She clutched his arm in sudden panic. 'I hope you know,' she said brokenly, 'it was for his sake I had to leave him, and – and because I thought that was what you wanted.'

'Jolly right, too. I shouldn't want the heir to Enderby growing up on frozen sandwiches.' He kissed her gently on the lips. 'Brave little Marjorie,' he said huskily. 'I know what it must have cost you to leave our son behind. But everything is all right now.'

Blaine grinned at them from behind the wheel of his taxi, parked in front of the George and Horses. From under his shaggy eyebrows his eyes shone with delight as they approached. Tactfully he refused Colin's invitation to join

310

them in the pub for a drink.

'It was the V2s we were after, you know,' Colin told her as they sat in the dimly lit little pub sipping brandy.

'But – I don't understand. Your friend said he saw your plane shot down in flames,' Marjorie said shakily.

'But what he didn't see was that before the flak that blew my plane up hit, another had knocked my engine out and I had already bailed out. I remember hurtling downwards fumbling for my ripcord. And that's the last thing I remember of that night. Until yesterday, I couldn't remember anything – not who I was, or the war. Yesterday it all came back to me. I must have hit my head on something when I landed. Some Danish fishermen found me floating in the Baltic, naked – not a bally stitch on. My dog tags were gone, too.

'They thought I must be an allied airman, so they hid me in their boat and got me back to their fishing hut and got the village doctor to look at me. I had a concussion and a rather nasty wound on my leg and this gash on my face.' He touched the scar.

'He patched me up jolly fine, except, as I said, I couldn't remember anything about myself. Only one thing I could remember – your face. Always in my mind was your face. At night I dreamed of you. But I couldn't remember anything about you. I only knew that somehow I must tell you that I was alive. It was the one strong thought in my mind all those months.'

'And I knew that you were trying to tell me something. Sometimes I felt you very near me, but I thought it was from the other side you were trying to speak to me.' She told him of her dreams. 'You were always near me until I made the decision to leave my son in England, after that dream I had in the night when you put little Colin back in his crib. I thought your spirit had stayed near me to be sure I left your son at Enderby. Then it seemed you left me.'

Colin caught her hands across the table. 'That would be when my memory returned. I was confused at first. I couldn't believe so many months had passed while I lived with those Danish fishermen, helping them to fish. I even learned to speak Danish. I couldn't believe the war was over. My one thought was to get back to you.'

311

Marjorie said, 'And I never thought for a moment you were alive. You see, I saw Athelstane.' She told him of how the great black stag had appeared on the hill the night before she was to have married him. 'Ashley saw him too.'

'There you are. What did I tell you – just some beastly old stag wandering about the place. I told you we English love to imagine we have some sort of ghost prowling about.'

Marjorie shook her head, her eyes were huge and her cheeks lost their colour. 'It was no ordinary stag I saw that night,' she said in a hushed voice.

'Then he jolly well got his message mixed up,' Colin said, squeezing her hand. 'For no Enderby died in battle for his king that night.'

'But Colin, an Enderby did,' Marjorie said earnestly. She opened her shoulder purse and took out the crested ring the halfbreed soldier had given her, and held it out to him.

He looked at it curiously. 'By Jove, the Enderby crest,' he said, amazed. 'And it's in that old-fashioned heavy gold you don't find rings made of nowadays. Where did you get this?'

She told him the story. 'Oh, Colin,' she said, 'he must have been some relation of yours.'

Colin nodded, looking down at the ring in fascination. 'It's the same ring my wicked great-great-uncle has on his finger in the portrait. He's reputed to have become a squaw man out in Canada. That soldier who volunteered and died that night must have been his descendant.'

'So you see an Enderby did die in battle for his king that night,' Marjorie said softly.

Colin was silent for a moment, then he handed the ring back to her. 'Let us hope,' he said solemnly, 'that so distant cousin of mine will be the last Enderby to have to make that sacrifice. Let us hope that men will at last give up this madness of killing their brothers every generation.'

Marjorie knew he was thinking of his own little son waiting for him at Enderby. 'Keep the ring, Colin,' she said. 'It belongs to the Enderbys.'

Colin slipped the heavy gold ring on to the second finger of his right hand. It fitted as if it had been made for him – as if it had come home at last.

'Now, my darling,' Colin said, with a boyish smile lighting

his face, 'my friend who flew me back to London promised me he would tell Mother and Father that I'm alive, but I must phone them now. There's a wedding to be arranged, you know. We can't have the sixteenth Earl of Rivermere wearing the bar sinister on his shield when he comes to his inheritance, now can we? Do you mind, darling, if I leave you sitting here for just a few minutes while I phone Enderby? Now please don't move an inch until I return.'

She felt foolishly bereft when he disappeared behind the bar with the bartender. She could not bear to have him out of her sight for even a moment. Then happiness bubbled up in her. She would be able to watch little Colin scamper along the paths at Enderby and hear his childish, excited laughter over the wonders of the flowers and the butterflies. And there would be other little feet. She could feel a stirring in her blood, as if unborn Enderbys were clamouring to join their brother.

She could picture the intense joy of the earl and countess when they learned that their beloved son was alive. Suddenly she giggled and her dimples showed. I bet the first thing they did was have a cup of tea, and I bet that's the first thing they do when we arrive home.

Colin returned, his face alight. 'What a wonder Mother is,' he said admiringly. 'She's made the arrangements already for our wedding to be held in the church at Wendover at eleven o'clock tomorrow morning. She's had Father riding post haste notifying the tenants. We must hurry home now, my darling. Mother says if we leave at once we'll be in time for tea.'

He wondered why Marjorie laughed, showing her dimples, as she took his outstretched hand, and they left the George and Horses with their arms entwined to where Blaine waited to take them home to Enderby and their son.